COOKiES, CONUNDRUMS, AND CRAFTS

Licensed By:

IDW

@IDWpublishing
IDWpublishing.com

COVER ARTIST:
Sophie Scruggs

SERIES EDITOR:
Riley Farmer

COLLECTION EDITOR:
Alonzo Simon

COLLECTION GROUP EDITOR:
Kris Simon

COLLECTION DESIGNER:
Johanna Nattalie

979-88-87240-58-9   27 26 25 24   1 2 3 4

Originally published as MY LITTLE PONY issues #11–15.

Davidi Jonas, CEO
Amber Huerta, COO
Mark Doyle, Co-Publisher
Tara McCrillis, Co-Publisher
Jamie S. Rich, Editor-In-Chief
Scott Dunbier, VP Special Projects
Sean Brice, Sr. Director Sales & Marketing
Aub Driver, Director of Marketing
Gregg Katzman, Sr. Manager Public Relations
Lauren LePera, Sr. Managing Editor
Shauna Monteforte, Sr. Director of Manufacturing Operations
Jamie Miller, Director Publishing Operations
Greg Foreman, Director DTC Sales & Operations
Nathan Widick, Director of Design
Neil Uyetake, Sr. Art Director, Design & Production

Ted Adams and Robbie Robbins, IDW Founders

Special thanks to Hasbro's Ed Lane, Tayla Reo,
and Michael Kelly for their invaluable assistance

For international rights, contact licensing@idwpublishing.com.

"The Old Nag Challenge"

WRITTEN BY
Casey Gilly

ART BY
Abby Bulmer

"The Case of the Missing Cupcake"

WRITTEN BY
Casey Gilly

ART BY
Amy Mebberson

"Maretime Bay Beachside Bake-Off"

WRITTEN BY
Robin Easter

ART BY
Abby Bulmer

"Violette Rainbow"

WRITTEN BY
Tee Franklin

ART BY
Shauna J. Grant

"Treehouse Trouble"

WRITTEN BY
Andrea Hannah

ART BY
Abigail Starling

Colors by
Heather Breckel

Letters by
Neil Uyetake

"The Old Nag Challenge"

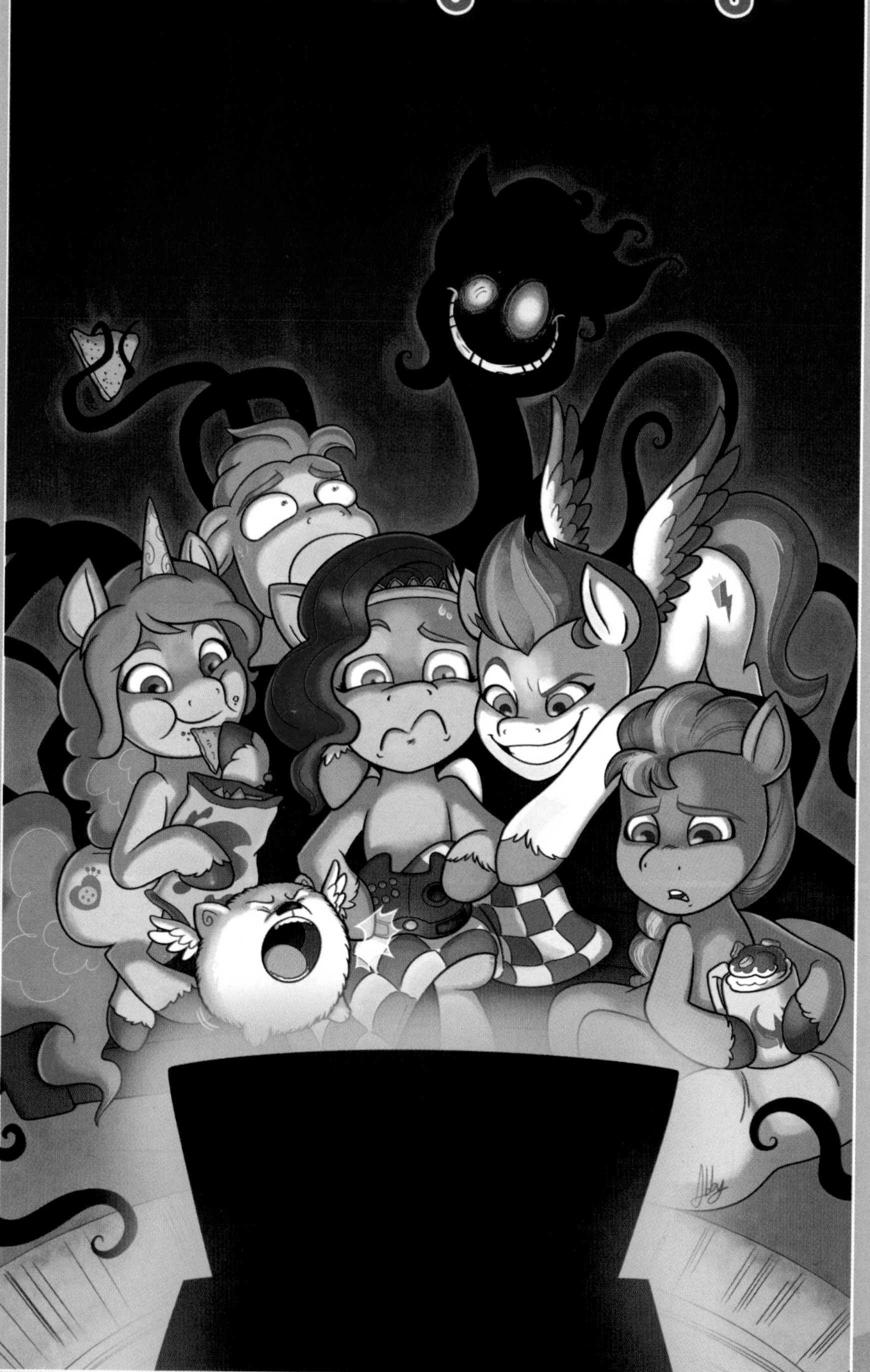

art by **Abby Bulmer**

PIPPPETALS

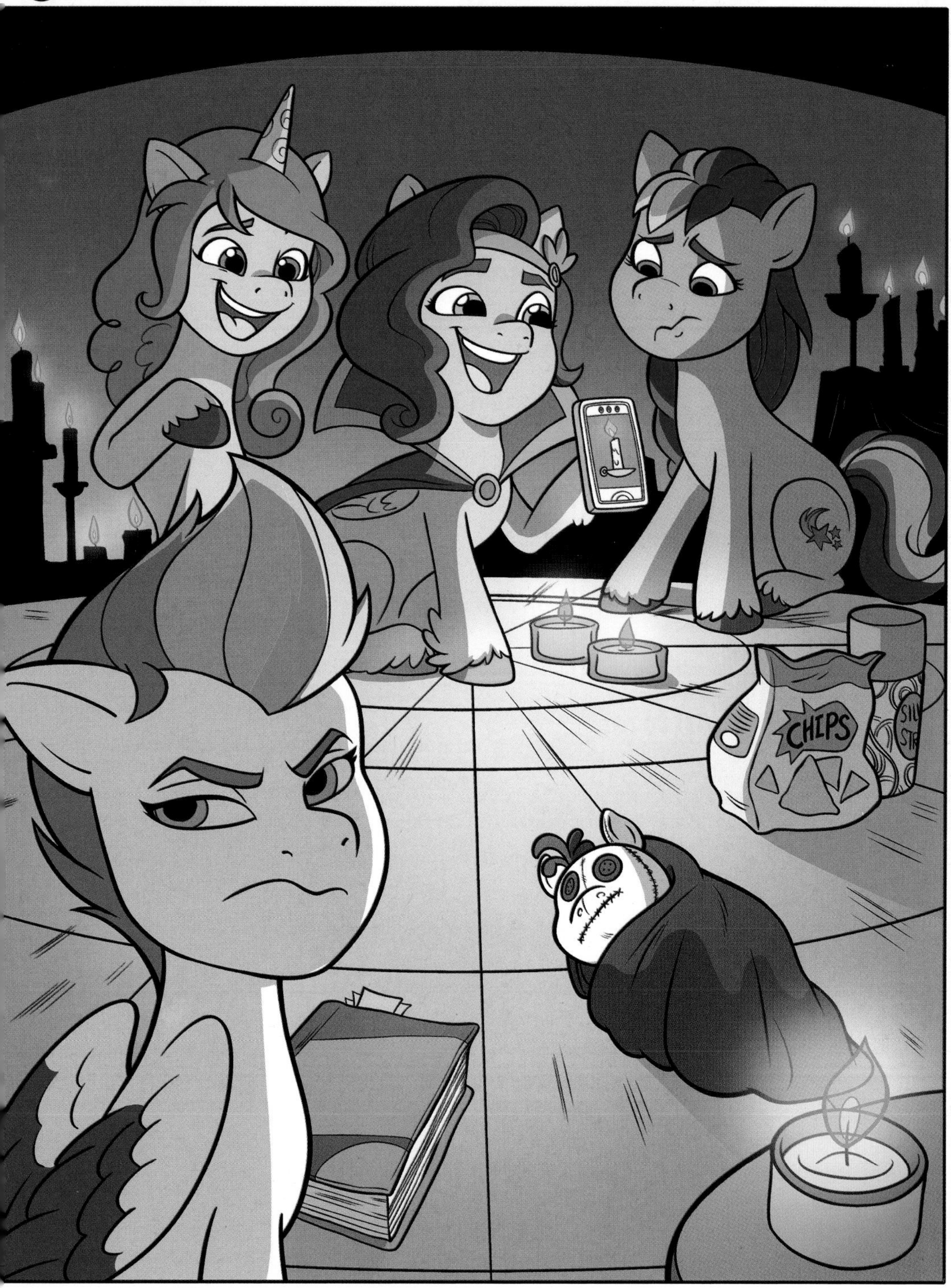
CHIPS

574 102 53

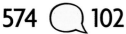

Pippsqueaks, get ready for the conclusion to my adventure into the ~unknown~ as me, @sunnydelight, @moonbro, and @stormyskies complete the final step in the #theOldNagChallenge. If you're just catching up, check my stories from last week...

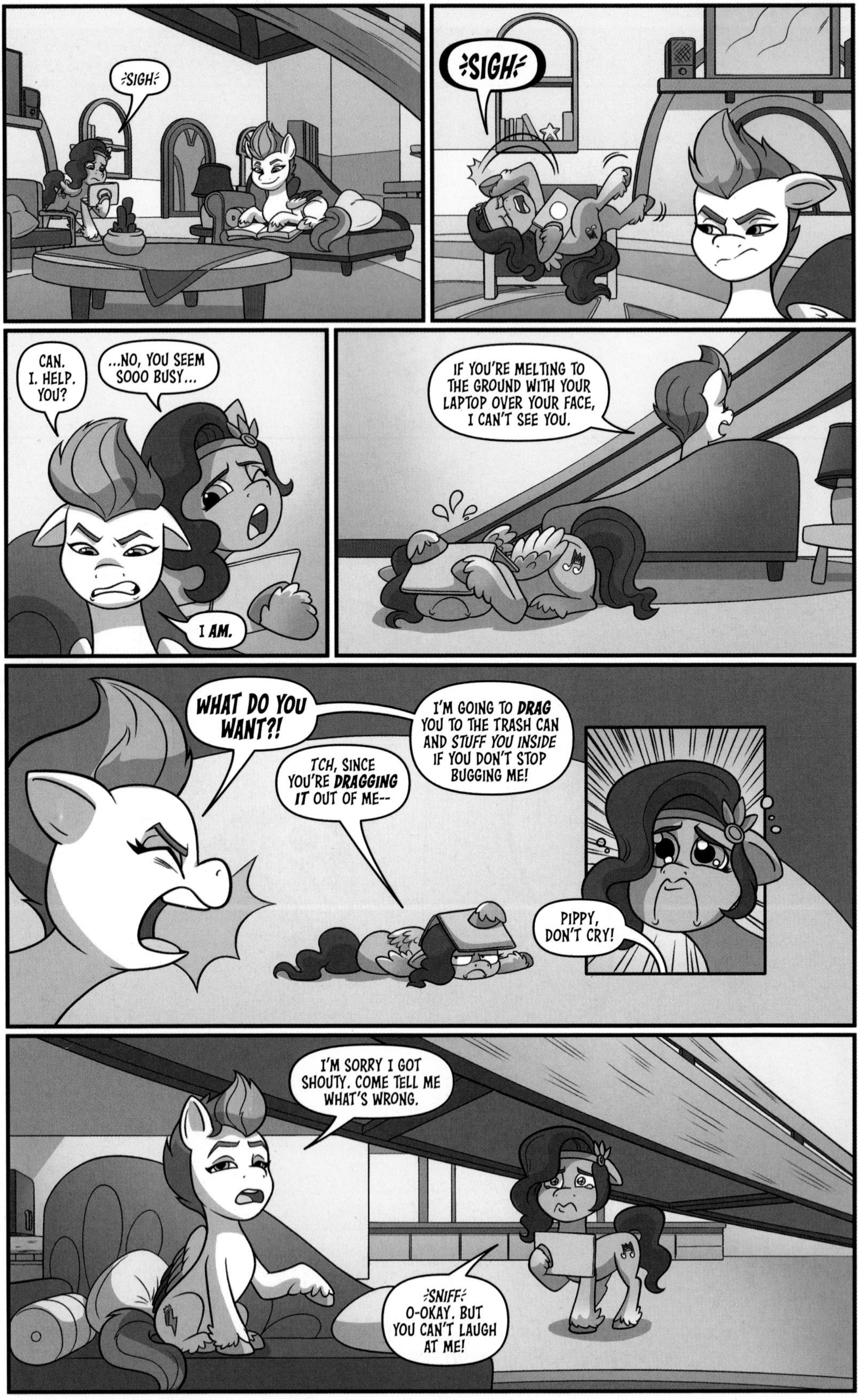

SIGH
SIGH
CAN. I. HELP. YOU?
...NO, YOU SEEM SOOO BUSY...
I AM.
IF YOU'RE MELTING TO THE GROUND WITH YOUR LAPTOP OVER YOUR FACE, I CAN'T SEE YOU.
WHAT DO YOU WANT?!
I'M GOING TO DRAG YOU TO THE TRASH CAN AND STUFF YOU INSIDE IF YOU DON'T STOP BUGGING ME!
TCH, SINCE YOU'RE DRAGGING IT OUT OF ME--
PIPPY, DON'T CRY!
I'M SORRY I GOT SHOUTY. COME TELL ME WHAT'S WRONG.
SNIFF
O-OKAY. BUT YOU CAN'T LAUGH AT ME!

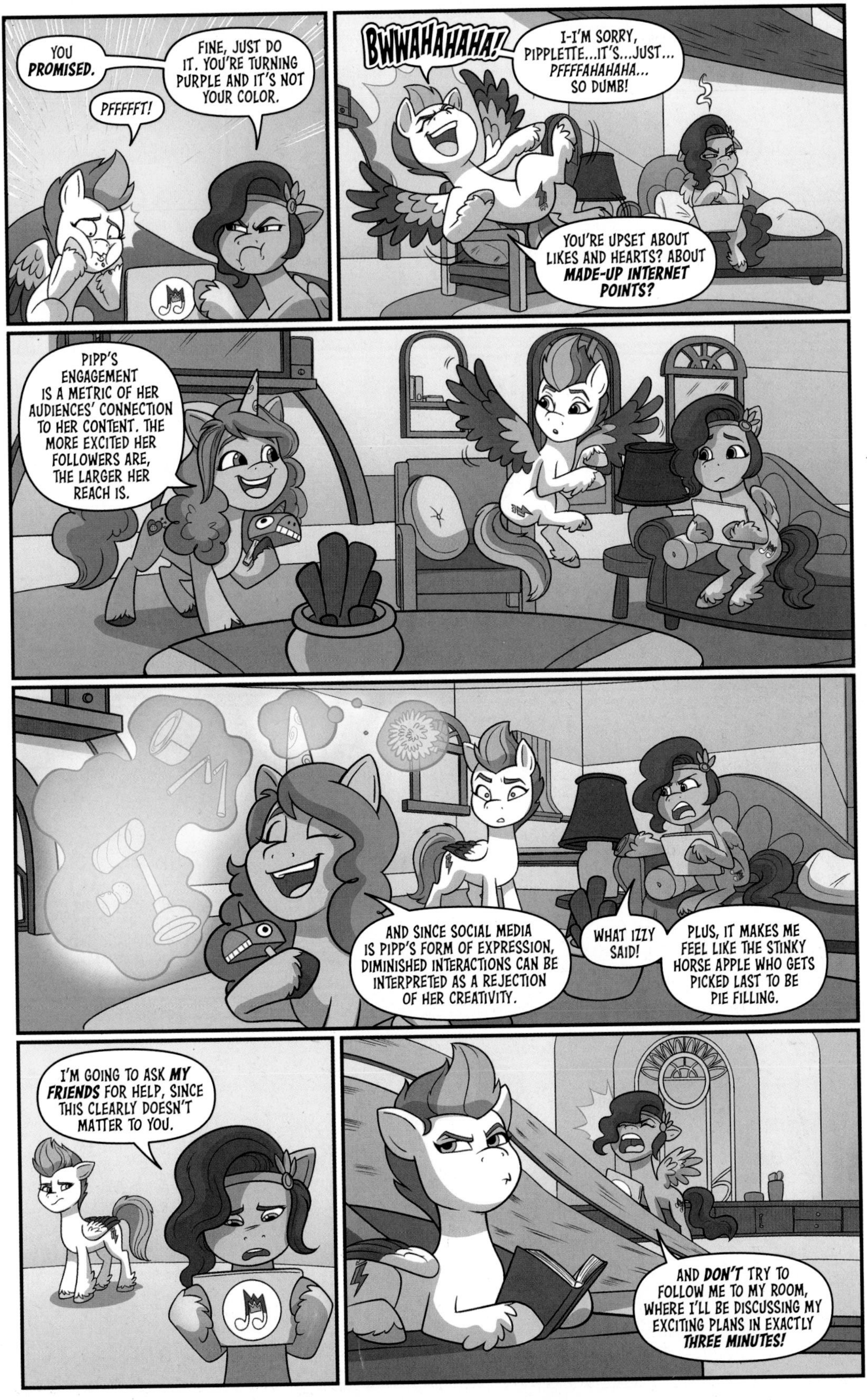
YOU PROMISED.
FINE, JUST DO IT. YOU'RE TURNING PURPLE AND IT'S NOT YOUR COLOR.
PFFFFFT!
BWWAHAHAHA!
I-I'M SORRY, PIPPLETTE...IT'S...JUST... PFFFFAHAHAHA... SO DUMB!
YOU'RE UPSET ABOUT LIKES AND HEARTS? ABOUT MADE-UP INTERNET POINTS?
PIPP'S ENGAGEMENT IS A METRIC OF HER AUDIENCES' CONNECTION TO HER CONTENT. THE MORE EXCITED HER FOLLOWERS ARE, THE LARGER HER REACH IS.
AND SINCE SOCIAL MEDIA IS PIPP'S FORM OF EXPRESSION, DIMINISHED INTERACTIONS CAN BE INTERPRETED AS A REJECTION OF HER CREATIVITY.
WHAT IZZY SAID!
PLUS, IT MAKES ME FEEL LIKE THE STINKY HORSE APPLE WHO GETS PICKED LAST TO BE PIE FILLING.
I'M GOING TO ASK MY FRIENDS FOR HELP, SINCE THIS CLEARLY DOESN'T MATTER TO YOU.
AND DON'T TRY TO FOLLOW ME TO MY ROOM, WHERE I'LL BE DISCUSSING MY EXCITING PLANS IN EXACTLY THREE MINUTES!

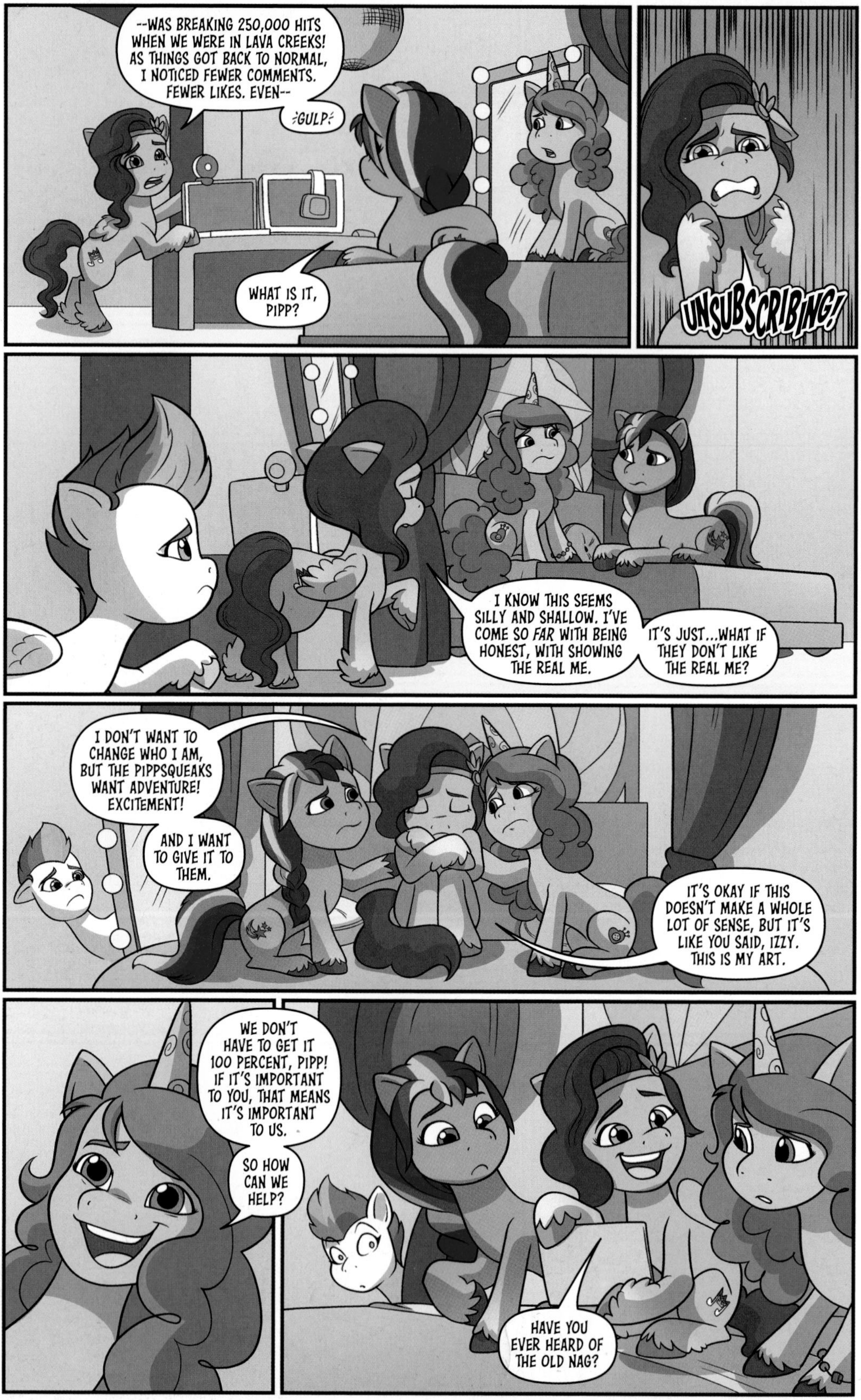
--WAS BREAKING 250,000 HITS WHEN WE WERE IN LAVA CREEKS! AS THINGS GOT BACK TO NORMAL, I NOTICED FEWER COMMENTS. FEWER LIKES. EVEN--
GULP
WHAT IS IT, PIPP?
UNSUBSCRIBING!
I KNOW THIS SEEMS SILLY AND SHALLOW. I'VE COME SO FAR WITH BEING HONEST, WITH SHOWING THE REAL ME.
IT'S JUST...WHAT IF THEY DON'T LIKE THE REAL ME?
I DON'T WANT TO CHANGE WHO I AM, BUT THE PIPPSQUEAKS WANT ADVENTURE! EXCITEMENT!
AND I WANT TO GIVE IT TO THEM.
IT'S OKAY IF THIS DOESN'T MAKE A WHOLE LOT OF SENSE, BUT IT'S LIKE YOU SAID, IZZY. THIS IS MY ART.
WE DON'T HAVE TO GET IT 100 PERCENT, PIPP! IF IT'S IMPORTANT TO YOU, THAT MEANS IT'S IMPORTANT TO US.
SO HOW CAN WE HELP?
HAVE YOU EVER HEARD OF THE OLD NAG?

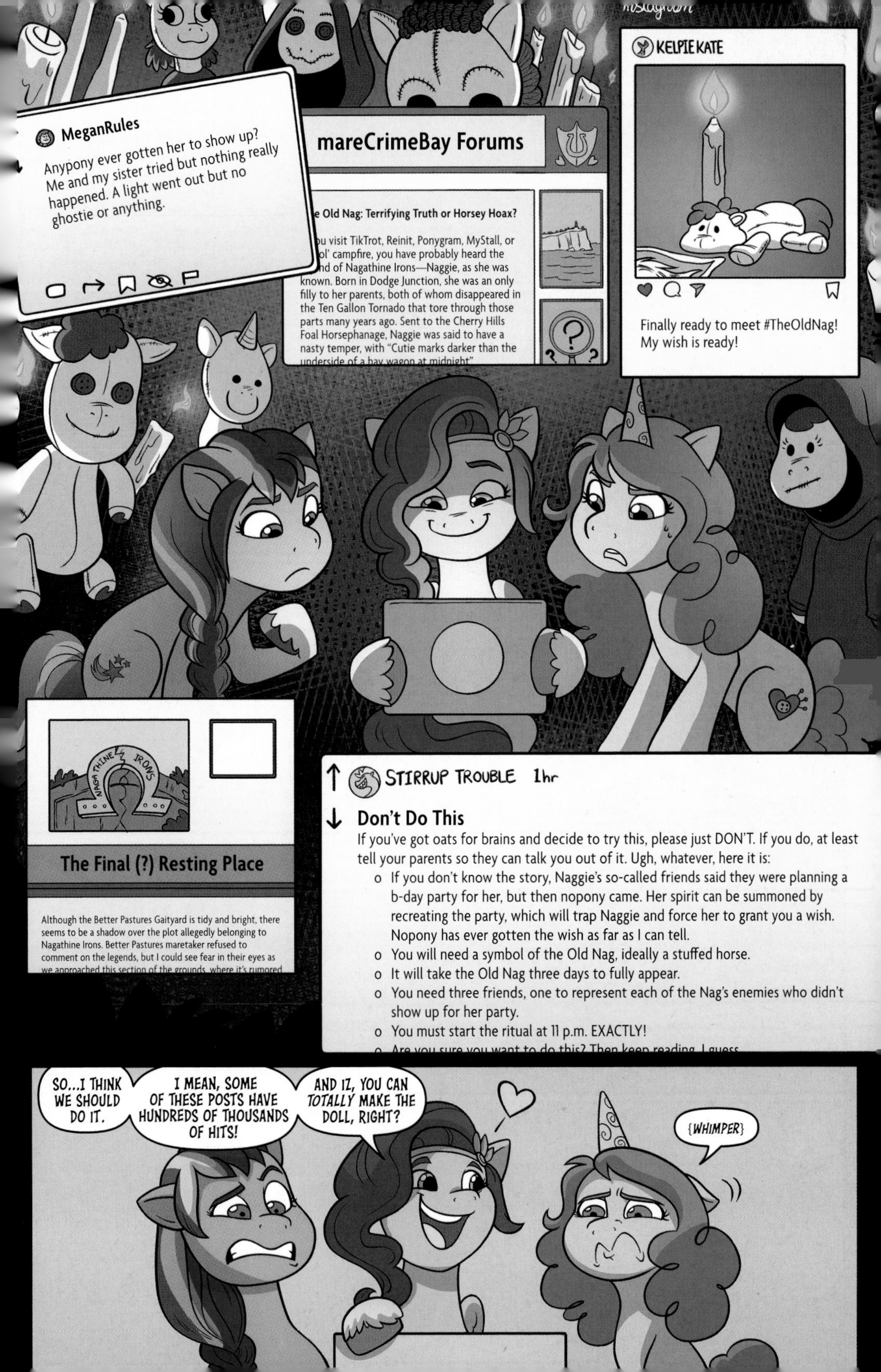

MeganRules
Anypony ever gotten her to show up? Me and my sister tried but nothing really happened. A light went out but no ghostie or anything.
mareCrimeBay Forums
e Old Nag: Terrifying Truth or Horsey Hoax?
u visit TikTrot, Reinit, Ponygram, MyStall, or
ol' campfire, you have probably heard the
nd of Nagathine Irons—Naggie, as she was known. Born in Dodge Junction, she was an only filly to her parents, both of whom disappeared in the Ten Gallon Tornado that tore through those parts many years ago. Sent to the Cherry Hills Foal Horsephanage, Naggie was said to have a nasty temper, with "Cutie marks darker than the underside of a hay wagon at midnight"
KELPIE KATE
Finally ready to meet #TheOldNag! My wish is ready!
NAGATHINE IRONS
The Final (?) Resting Place
Although the Better Pastures Gaityard is tidy and bright, there seems to be a shadow over the plot allegedly belonging to Nagathine Irons. Better Pastures maretaker refused to comment on the legends, but I could see fear in their eyes as we approached this section of the grounds, where it's rumored
STIRRUP TROUBLE 1hr
Don't Do This
If you've got oats for brains and decide to try this, please just DON'T. If you do, at least tell your parents so they can talk you out of it. Ugh, whatever, here it is:
o If you don't know the story, Naggie's so-called friends said they were planning a b-day party for her, but then nopony came. Her spirit can be summoned by recreating the party, which will trap Naggie and force her to grant you a wish. Nopony has ever gotten the wish as far as I can tell.
o You will need a symbol of the Old Nag, ideally a stuffed horse.
o It will take the Old Nag three days to fully appear.
o You need three friends, one to represent each of the Nag's enemies who didn't show up for her party.
o You must start the ritual at 11 p.m. EXACTLY!
SO...I THINK WE SHOULD DO IT.
I MEAN, SOME OF THESE POSTS HAVE HUNDREDS OF THOUSANDS OF HITS!
AND IZ, YOU CAN *TOTALLY* MAKE THE DOLL, RIGHT?
{WHIMPER}

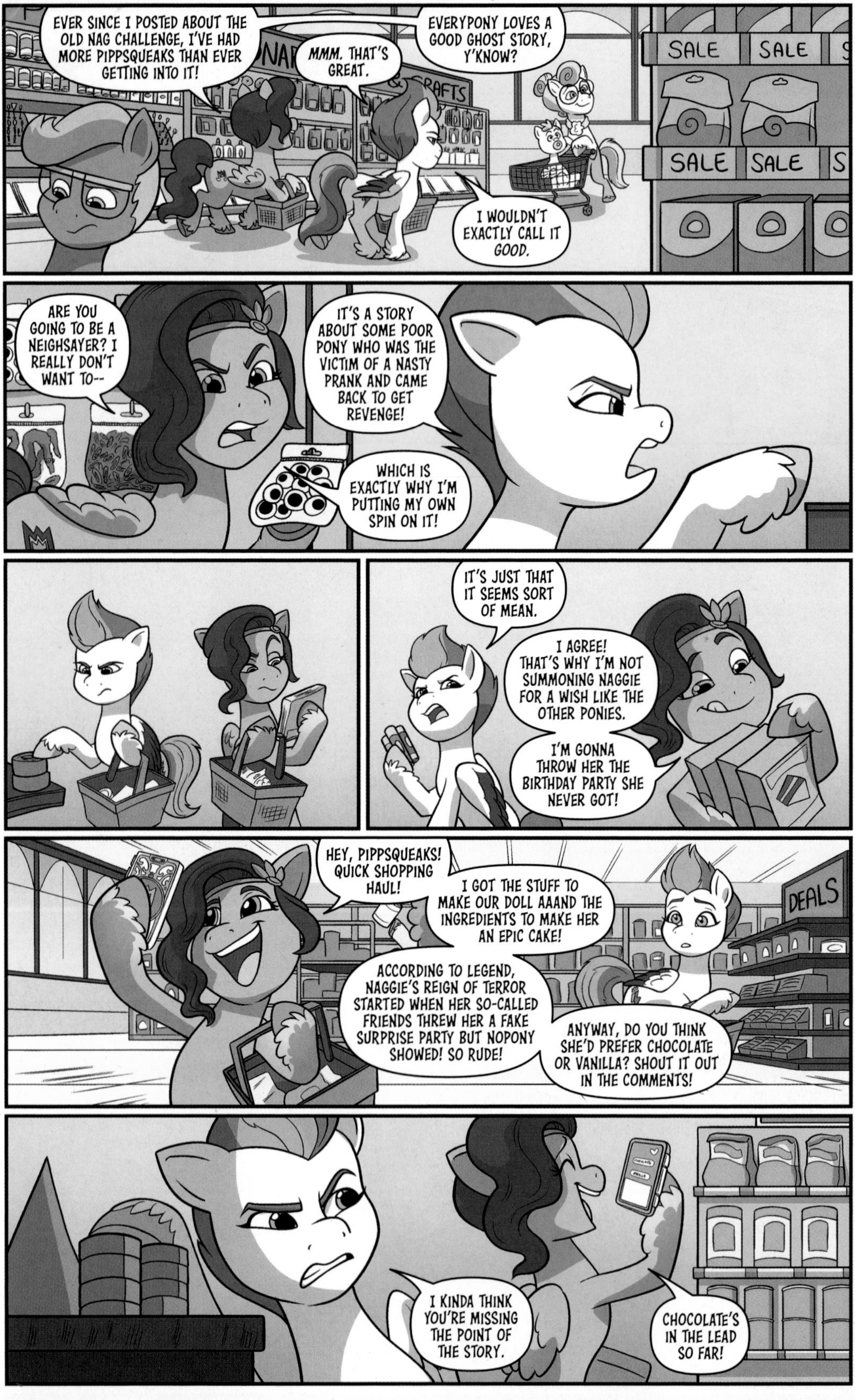

EVER SINCE I POSTED ABOUT THE OLD NAG CHALLENGE, I'VE HAD MORE PIPPSQUEAKS THAN EVER GETTING INTO IT!
MMM. THAT'S GREAT.
EVERYPONY LOVES A GOOD GHOST STORY, Y'KNOW?
I WOULDN'T EXACTLY CALL IT GOOD.
SALE
ARE YOU GOING TO BE A NEIGHSAYER? I REALLY DON'T WANT TO--
IT'S A STORY ABOUT SOME POOR PONY WHO WAS THE VICTIM OF A NASTY PRANK AND CAME BACK TO GET REVENGE!
WHICH IS EXACTLY WHY I'M PUTTING MY OWN SPIN ON IT!
IT'S JUST THAT IT SEEMS SORT OF MEAN.
I AGREE! THAT'S WHY I'M NOT SUMMONING NAGGIE FOR A WISH LIKE THE OTHER PONIES.
I'M GONNA THROW HER THE BIRTHDAY PARTY SHE NEVER GOT!
HEY, PIPPSQUEAKS! QUICK SHOPPING HAUL!
I GOT THE STUFF TO MAKE OUR DOLL AAAND THE INGREDIENTS TO MAKE HER AN EPIC CAKE!
ACCORDING TO LEGEND, NAGGIE'S REIGN OF TERROR STARTED WHEN HER SO-CALLED FRIENDS THREW HER A FAKE SURPRISE PARTY BUT NOPONY SHOWED! SO RUDE!
ANYWAY, DO YOU THINK SHE'D PREFER CHOCOLATE OR VANILLA? SHOUT IT OUT IN THE COMMENTS!
DEALS
I KINDA THINK YOU'RE MISSING THE POINT OF THE STORY.
CHOCOLATE'S IN THE LEAD SO FAR!

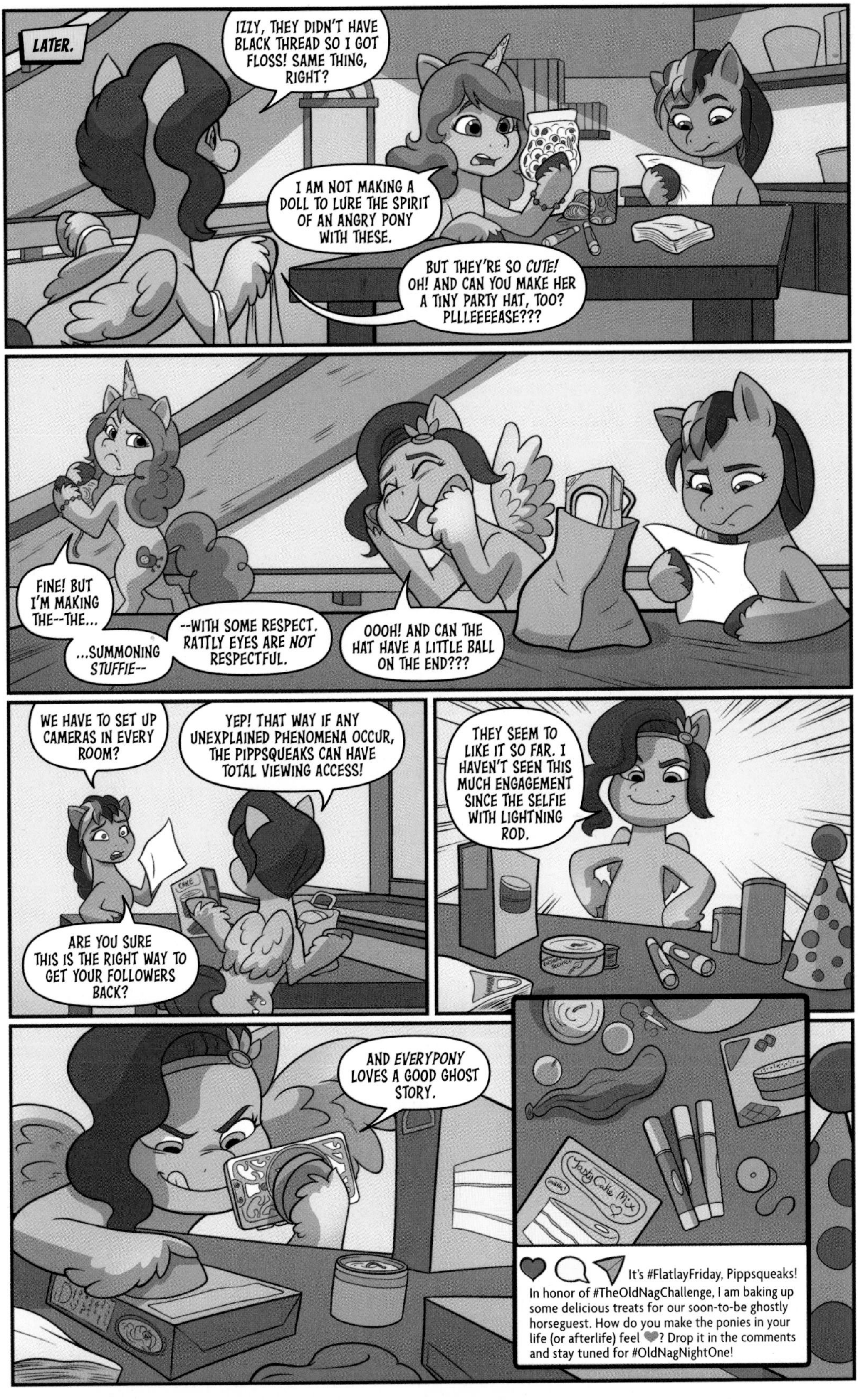
LATER.
IZZY, THEY DIDN'T HAVE BLACK THREAD SO I GOT FLOSS! SAME THING, RIGHT?
I AM NOT MAKING A DOLL TO LURE THE SPIRIT OF AN ANGRY PONY WITH THESE.
BUT THEY'RE SO CUTE! OH! AND CAN YOU MAKE HER A TINY PARTY HAT, TOO? PLLLEEEEASE???
FINE! BUT I'M MAKING THE--THE...
...SUMMONING STUFFIE--
--WITH SOME RESPECT. RATTLY EYES ARE NOT RESPECTFUL.
OOOH! AND CAN THE HAT HAVE A LITTLE BALL ON THE END???
WE HAVE TO SET UP CAMERAS IN EVERY ROOM?
YEP! THAT WAY IF ANY UNEXPLAINED PHENOMENA OCCUR, THE PIPPSQUEAKS CAN HAVE TOTAL VIEWING ACCESS!
ARE YOU SURE THIS IS THE RIGHT WAY TO GET YOUR FOLLOWERS BACK?
THEY SEEM TO LIKE IT SO FAR. I HAVEN'T SEEN THIS MUCH ENGAGEMENT SINCE THE SELFIE WITH LIGHTNING ROD.
AND EVERYPONY LOVES A GOOD GHOST STORY.
Tasty Cake Mix
It's #FlatlayFriday, Pippsqueaks!
In honor of #TheOldNagChallenge, I am baking up some delicious treats for our soon-to-be ghostly horseguest. How do you make the ponies in your life (or afterlife) feel ♥? Drop it in the comments and stay tuned for #OldNagNightOne!

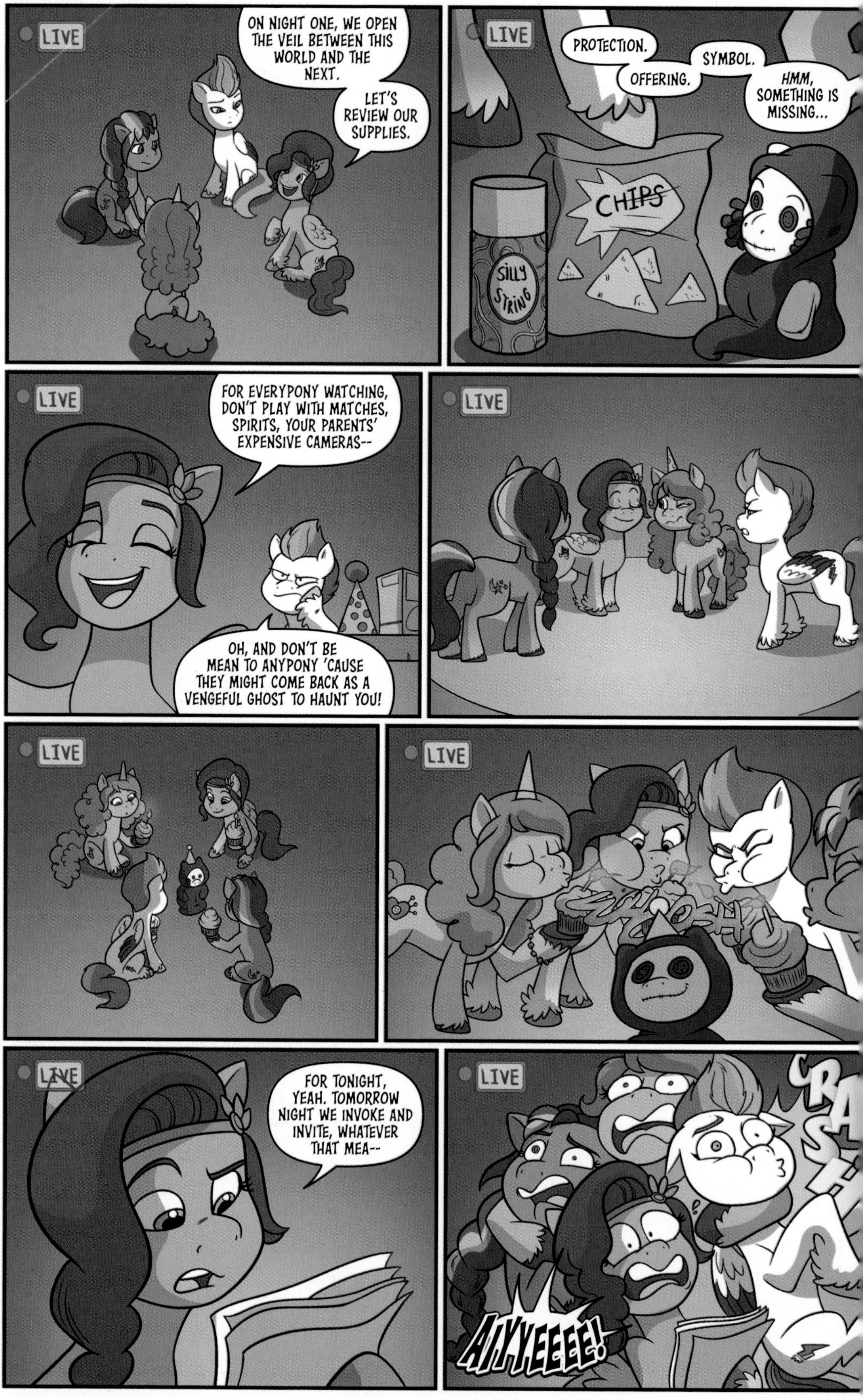
LIVE
ON NIGHT ONE, WE OPEN THE VEIL BETWEEN THIS WORLD AND THE NEXT.
LET'S REVIEW OUR SUPPLIES.
LIVE
PROTECTION.
OFFERING.
SYMBOL.
HMM, SOMETHING IS MISSING...
CHIPS
SILLY STRING
LIVE
FOR EVERYPONY WATCHING, DON'T PLAY WITH MATCHES, SPIRITS, YOUR PARENTS' EXPENSIVE CAMERAS--
OH, AND DON'T BE MEAN TO ANYPONY 'CAUSE THEY MIGHT COME BACK AS A VENGEFUL GHOST TO HAUNT YOU!
LIVE
LIVE
LIVE
LIVE
FOR TONIGHT, YEAH. TOMORROW NIGHT WE INVOKE AND INVITE, WHATEVER THAT MEA--
LIVE
AIYYEEEE!

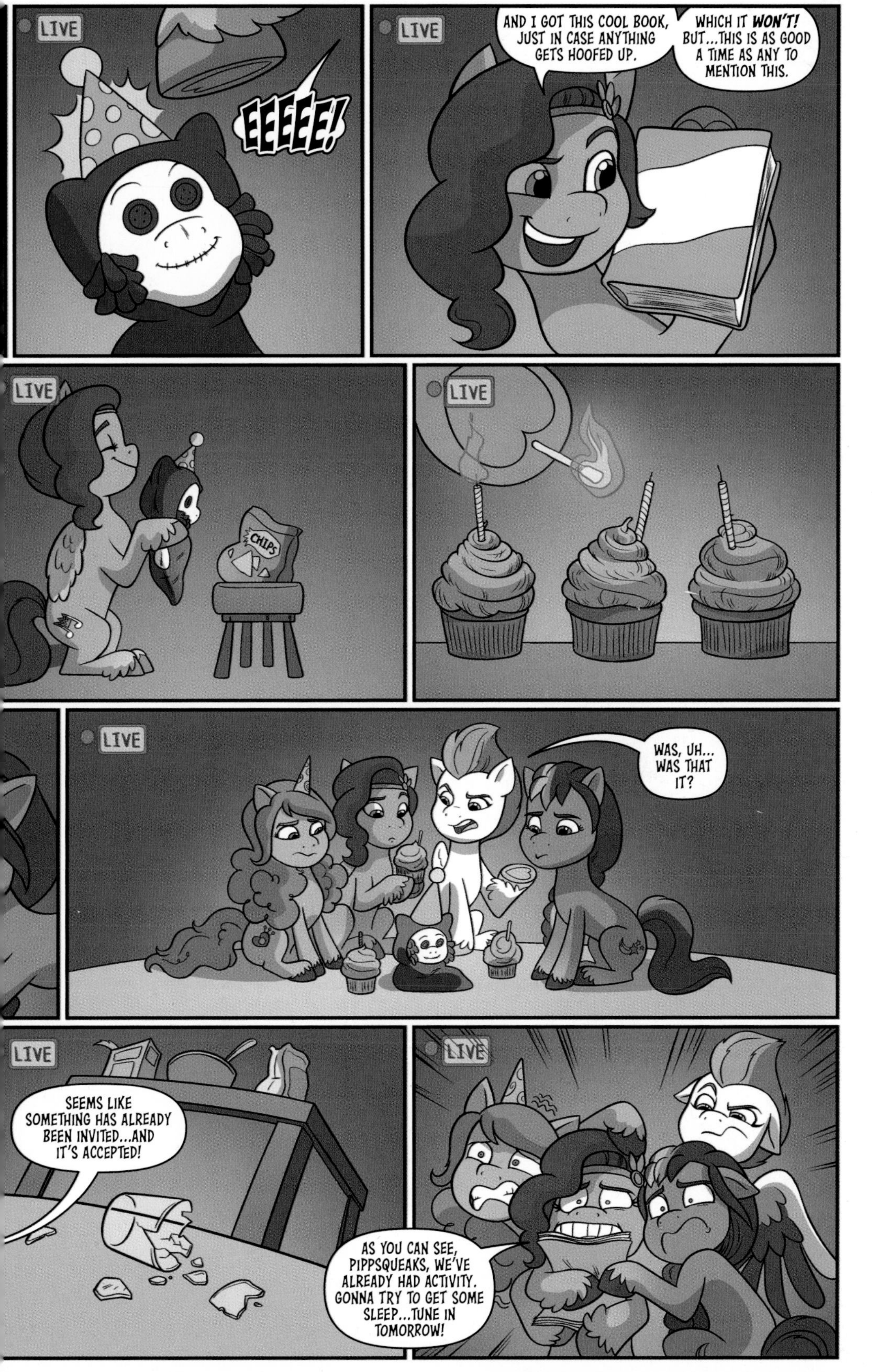
LIVE
EEEEE!
LIVE
AND I GOT THIS COOL BOOK, JUST IN CASE ANYTHING GETS HOOFED UP.
WHICH IT WON'T! BUT...THIS IS AS GOOD A TIME AS ANY TO MENTION THIS.
LIVE
CHIPS
LIVE
LIVE
WAS, UH... WAS THAT IT?
LIVE
SEEMS LIKE SOMETHING HAS ALREADY BEEN INVITED...AND IT'S ACCEPTED!
LIVE
AS YOU CAN SEE, PIPPSQUEAKS, WE'VE ALREADY HAD ACTIVITY. GONNA TRY TO GET SOME SLEEP...TUNE IN TOMORROW!

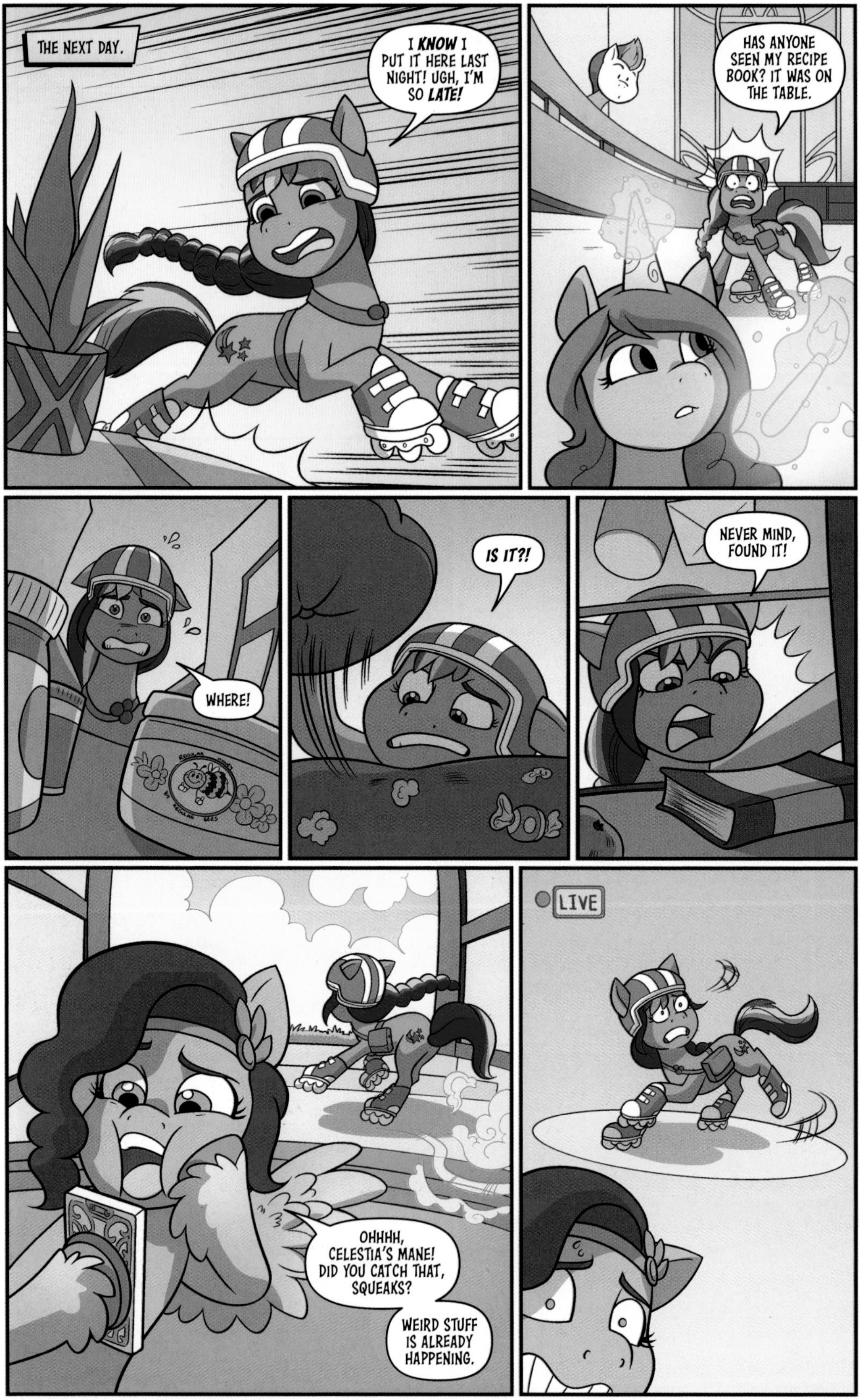
THE NEXT DAY.
I **KNOW** I PUT IT HERE LAST NIGHT! UGH, I'M SO **LATE!**
HAS ANYONE SEEN MY RECIPE BOOK? IT WAS ON THE TABLE.
WHERE!
IS IT?!
NEVER MIND, FOUND IT!
OHHHH, CELESTIA'S MANE! DID YOU CATCH THAT, SQUEAKS?
WEIRD STUFF IS ALREADY HAPPENING.
LIVE

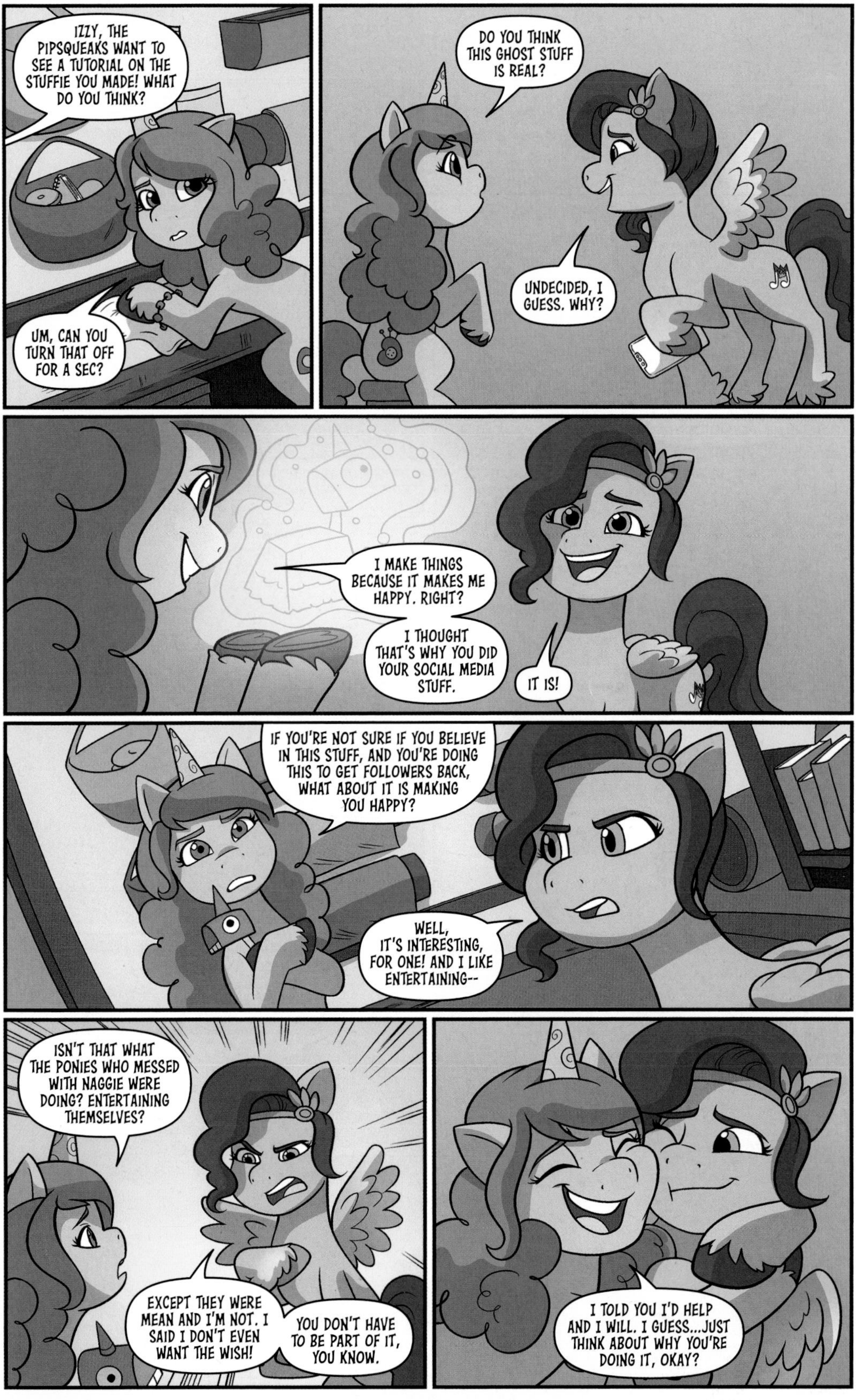
IZZY, THE PIPSQUEAKS WANT TO SEE A TUTORIAL ON THE STUFFIE YOU MADE! WHAT DO YOU THINK?
UM, CAN YOU TURN THAT OFF FOR A SEC?
DO YOU THINK THIS GHOST STUFF IS REAL?
UNDECIDED, I GUESS. WHY?
I MAKE THINGS BECAUSE IT MAKES ME HAPPY. RIGHT?
I THOUGHT THAT'S WHY YOU DID YOUR SOCIAL MEDIA STUFF.
IT IS!
IF YOU'RE NOT SURE IF YOU BELIEVE IN THIS STUFF, AND YOU'RE DOING THIS TO GET FOLLOWERS BACK, WHAT ABOUT IT IS MAKING YOU HAPPY?
WELL, IT'S INTERESTING, FOR ONE! AND I LIKE ENTERTAINING--
ISN'T THAT WHAT THE PONIES WHO MESSED WITH NAGGIE WERE DOING? ENTERTAINING THEMSELVES?
EXCEPT THEY WERE MEAN AND I'M NOT. I SAID I DON'T EVEN WANT THE WISH!
YOU DON'T HAVE TO BE PART OF IT, YOU KNOW.
I TOLD YOU I'D HELP AND I WILL. I GUESS...JUST THINK ABOUT WHY YOU'RE DOING IT, OKAY?

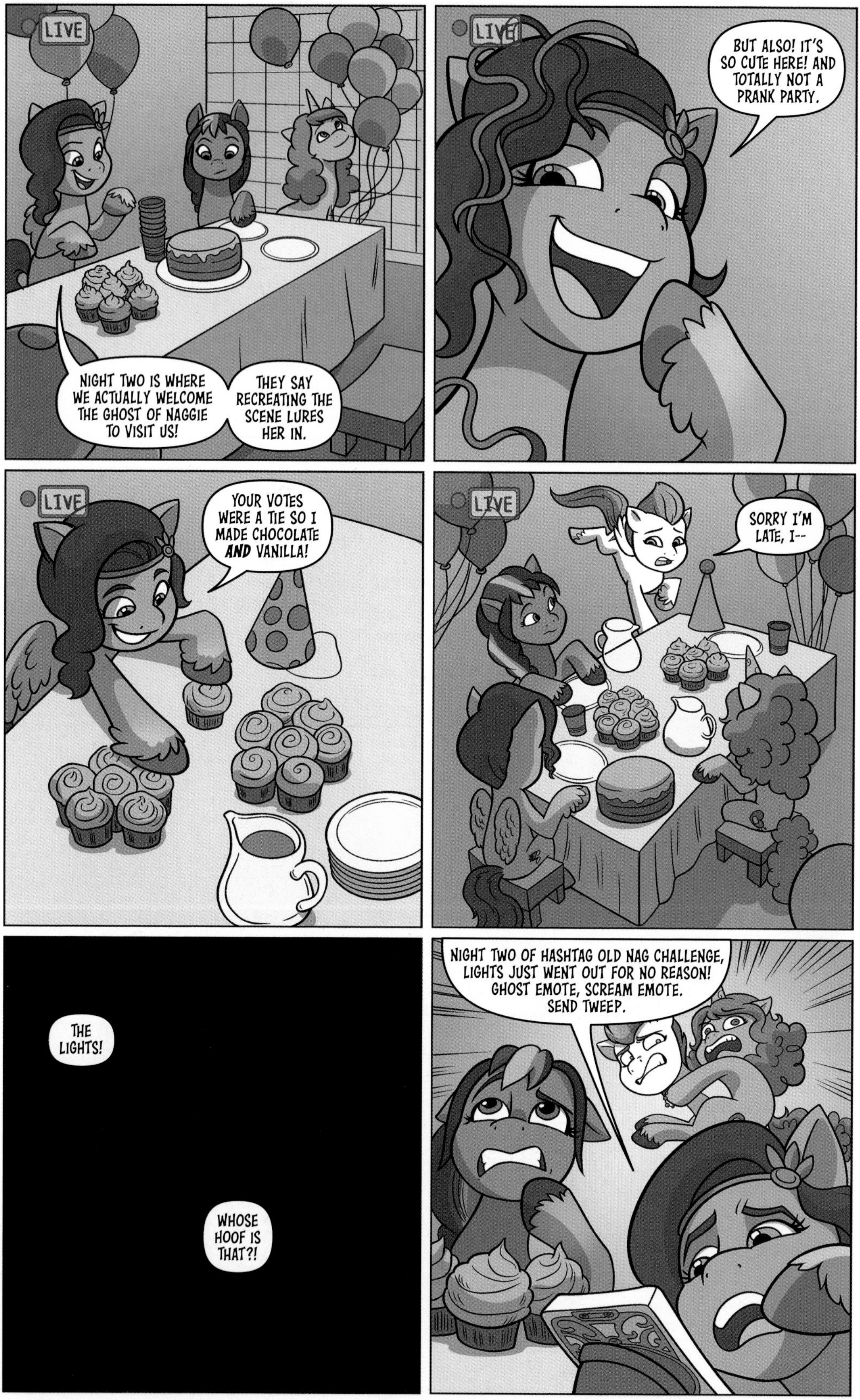
LIVE
NIGHT TWO IS WHERE WE ACTUALLY WELCOME THE GHOST OF NAGGIE TO VISIT US!
THEY SAY RECREATING THE SCENE LURES HER IN.
LIVE
BUT ALSO! IT'S SO CUTE HERE! AND TOTALLY NOT A PRANK PARTY.
LIVE
YOUR VOTES WERE A TIE SO I MADE CHOCOLATE **AND** VANILLA!
LIVE
SORRY I'M LATE, I--
THE LIGHTS!
WHOSE HOOF IS THAT?!
NIGHT TWO OF HASHTAG OLD NAG CHALLENGE, LIGHTS JUST WENT OUT FOR NO REASON! GHOST EMOTE, SCREAM EMOTE. SEND TWEEP.

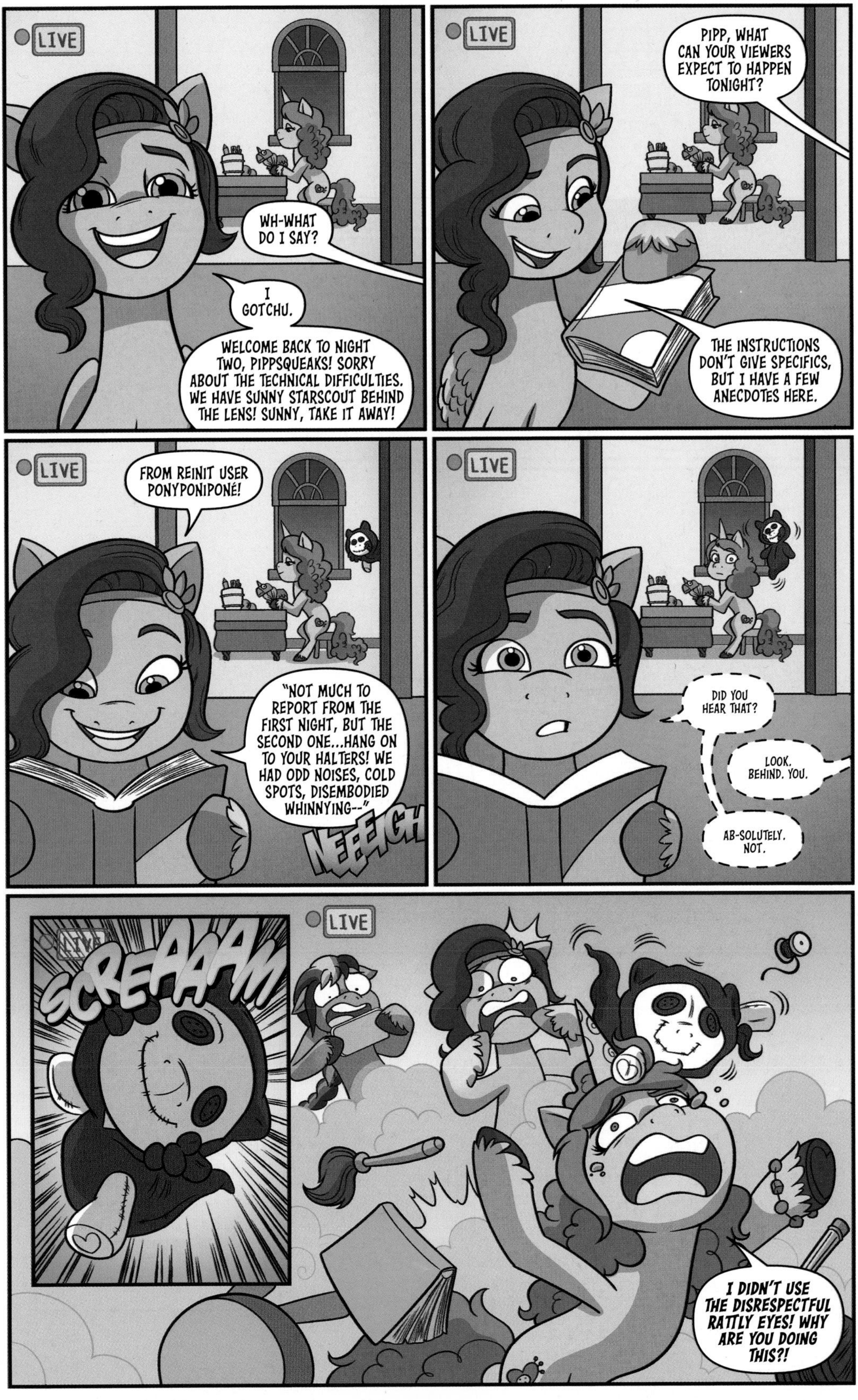
LIVE
WH-WHAT DO I SAY?
I GOTCHU.
WELCOME BACK TO NIGHT TWO, PIPPSQUEAKS! SORRY ABOUT THE TECHNICAL DIFFICULTIES. WE HAVE SUNNY STARSCOUT BEHIND THE LENS! SUNNY, TAKE IT AWAY!
LIVE
PIPP, WHAT CAN YOUR VIEWERS EXPECT TO HAPPEN TONIGHT?
THE INSTRUCTIONS DON'T GIVE SPECIFICS, BUT I HAVE A FEW ANECDOTES HERE.
LIVE
FROM REINIT USER PONYPONIPONÉ!
"NOT MUCH TO REPORT FROM THE FIRST NIGHT, BUT THE SECOND ONE...HANG ON TO YOUR HALTERS! WE HAD ODD NOISES, COLD SPOTS, DISEMBODIED WHINNYING--"
NEEEIGH
LIVE
DID YOU HEAR THAT?
LOOK. BEHIND. YOU.
AB-SOLUTELY. NOT.
LIVE
SCREAAAM
I DIDN'T USE THE DISRESPECTFUL RATTLY EYES! WHY ARE YOU DOING THIS?!

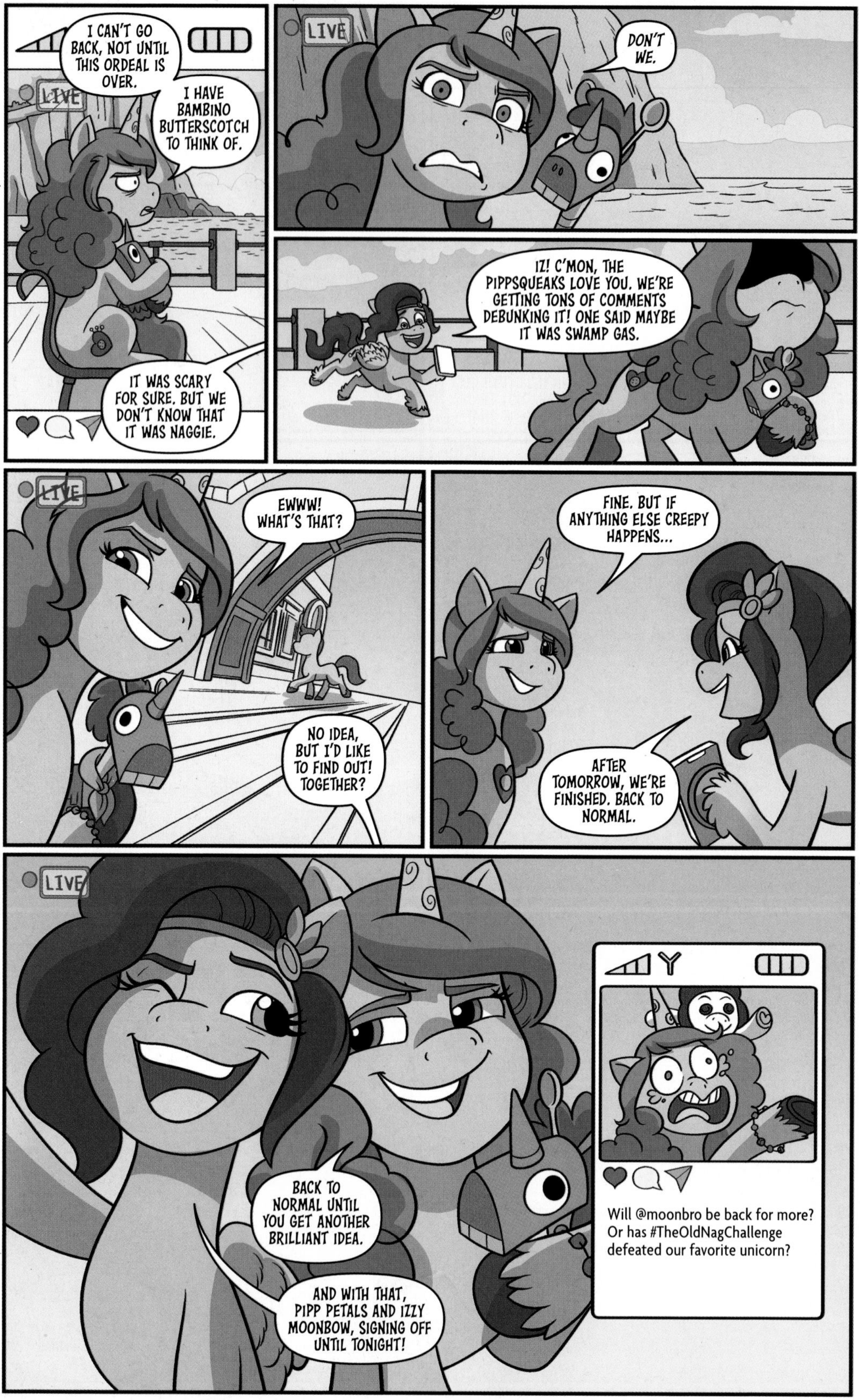
LIVE
I CAN'T GO BACK, NOT UNTIL THIS ORDEAL IS OVER.
I HAVE BAMBINO BUTTERSCOTCH TO THINK OF.
IT WAS SCARY FOR SURE. BUT WE DON'T KNOW THAT IT WAS NAGGIE.
LIVE
DON'T WE.
IZ! C'MON, THE PIPPSQUEAKS LOVE YOU. WE'RE GETTING TONS OF COMMENTS DEBUNKING IT! ONE SAID MAYBE IT WAS SWAMP GAS.
LIVE
EWWW! WHAT'S THAT?
NO IDEA, BUT I'D LIKE TO FIND OUT! TOGETHER?
FINE. BUT IF ANYTHING ELSE CREEPY HAPPENS...
AFTER TOMORROW, WE'RE FINISHED. BACK TO NORMAL.
LIVE
BACK TO NORMAL UNTIL YOU GET ANOTHER BRILLIANT IDEA.
AND WITH THAT, PIPP PETALS AND IZZY MOONBOW, SIGNING OFF UNTIL TONIGHT!
Will @moonbro be back for more? Or has #TheOldNagChallenge defeated our favorite unicorn?

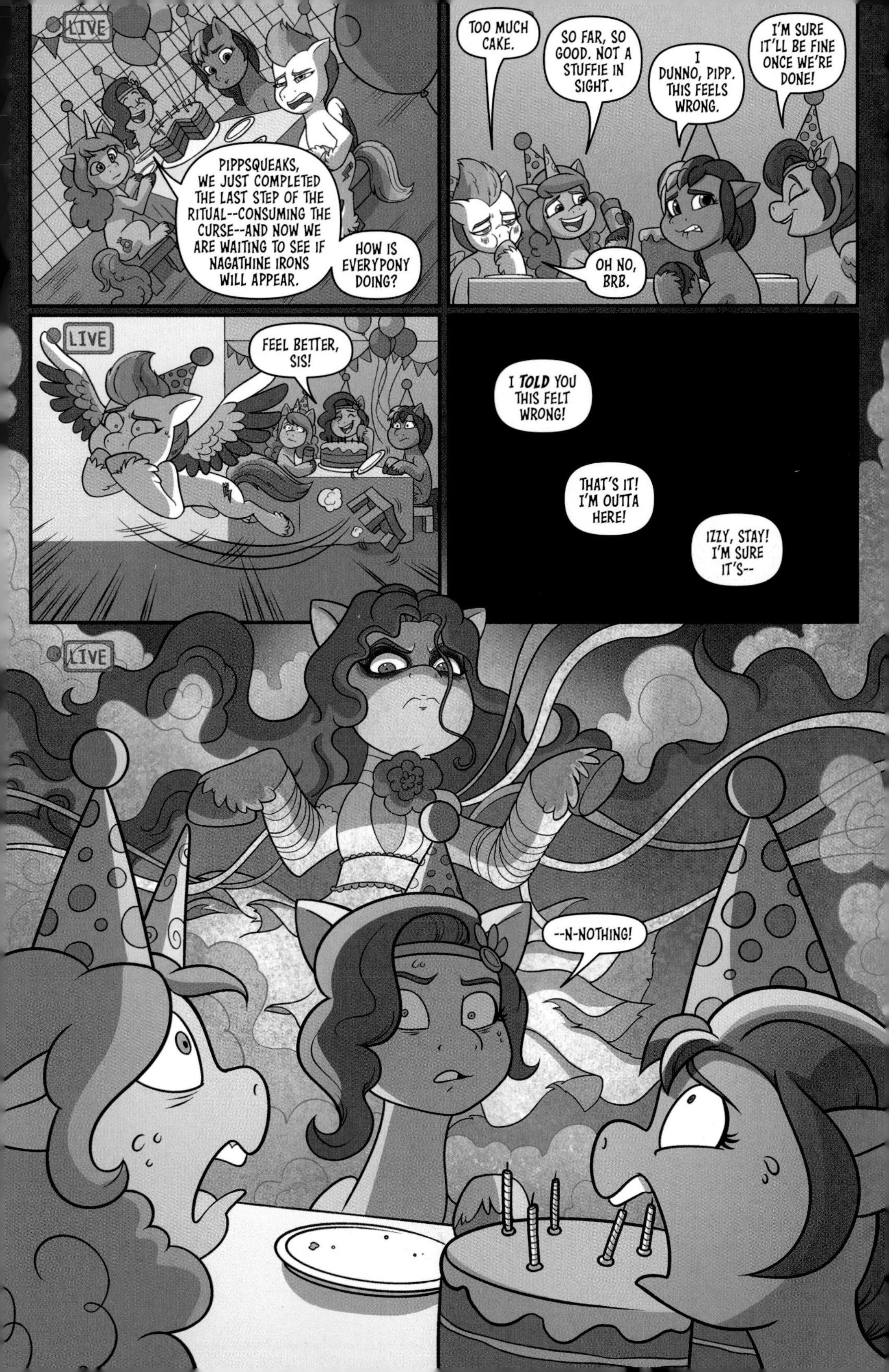
LIVE
PIPPSQUEAKS, WE JUST COMPLETED THE LAST STEP OF THE RITUAL--CONSUMING THE CURSE--AND NOW WE ARE WAITING TO SEE IF NAGATHINE IRONS WILL APPEAR.
HOW IS EVERYPONY DOING?
TOO MUCH CAKE.
SO FAR, SO GOOD. NOT A STUFFIE IN SIGHT.
I DUNNO, PIPP. THIS FEELS WRONG.
I'M SURE IT'LL BE FINE ONCE WE'RE DONE!
OH NO, BRB.
LIVE
FEEL BETTER, SIS!
I TOLD YOU THIS FELT WRONG!
THAT'S IT! I'M OUTTA HERE!
IZZY, STAY! I'M SURE IT'S--
LIVE
--N-NOTHING!

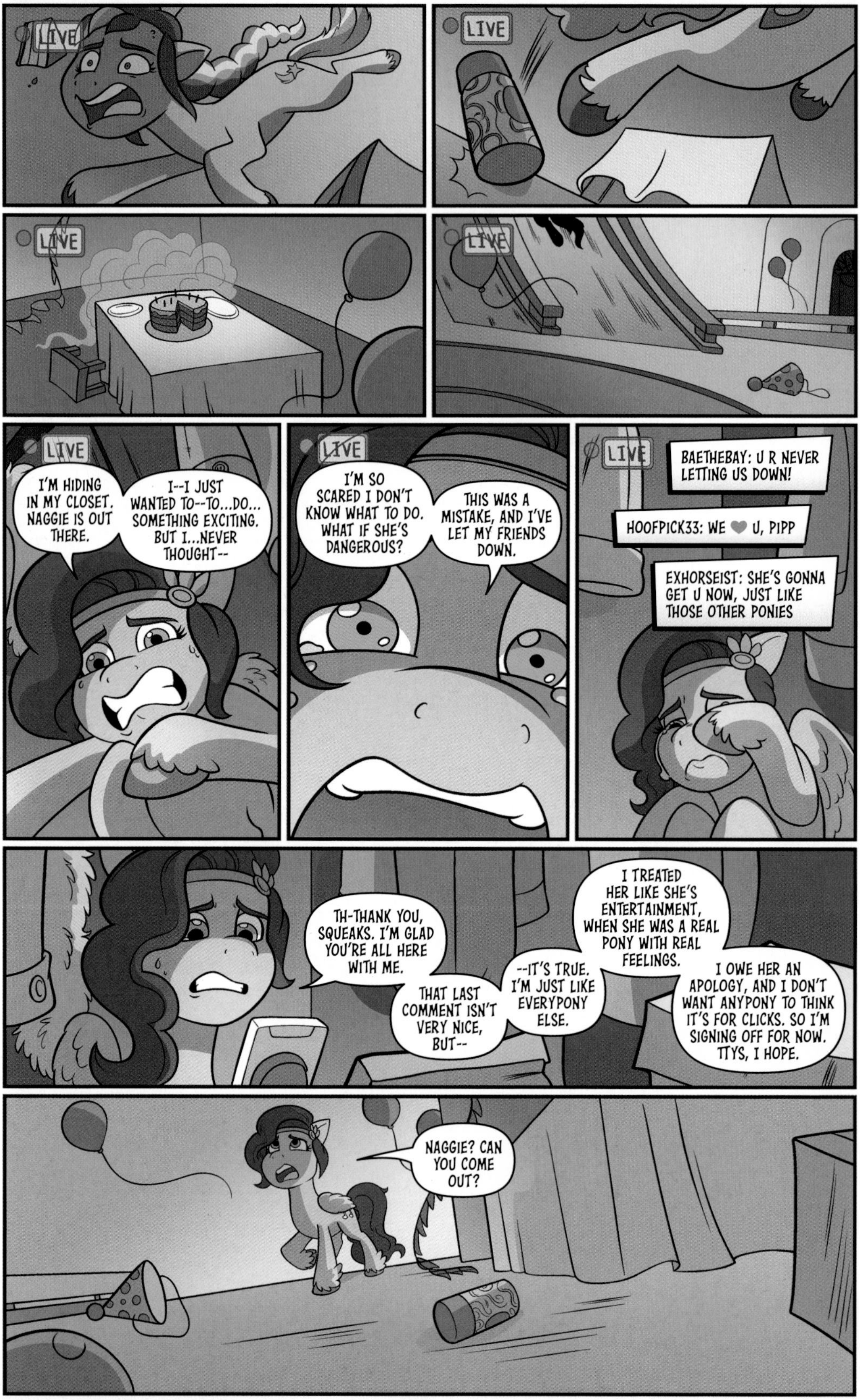
LIVE
LIVE
LIVE
LIVE
LIVE
I'M HIDING IN MY CLOSET. NAGGIE IS OUT THERE.
I--I JUST WANTED TO--TO...DO... SOMETHING EXCITING. BUT I...NEVER THOUGHT--
LIVE
I'M SO SCARED I DON'T KNOW WHAT TO DO. WHAT IF SHE'S DANGEROUS?
THIS WAS A MISTAKE, AND I'VE LET MY FRIENDS DOWN.
LIVE
BAETHEBAY: U R NEVER LETTING US DOWN!
HOOFPICK33: WE ♥ U, PIPP
EXHORSEIST: SHE'S GONNA GET U NOW, JUST LIKE THOSE OTHER PONIES
TH-THANK YOU, SQUEAKS. I'M GLAD YOU'RE ALL HERE WITH ME.
THAT LAST COMMENT ISN'T VERY NICE, BUT--
--IT'S TRUE. I'M JUST LIKE EVERYPONY ELSE.
I TREATED HER LIKE SHE'S ENTERTAINMENT, WHEN SHE WAS A REAL PONY WITH REAL FEELINGS.
I OWE HER AN APOLOGY, AND I DON'T WANT ANYPONY TO THINK IT'S FOR CLICKS. SO I'M SIGNING OFF FOR NOW. TTYS, I HOPE.
NAGGIE? CAN YOU COME OUT?

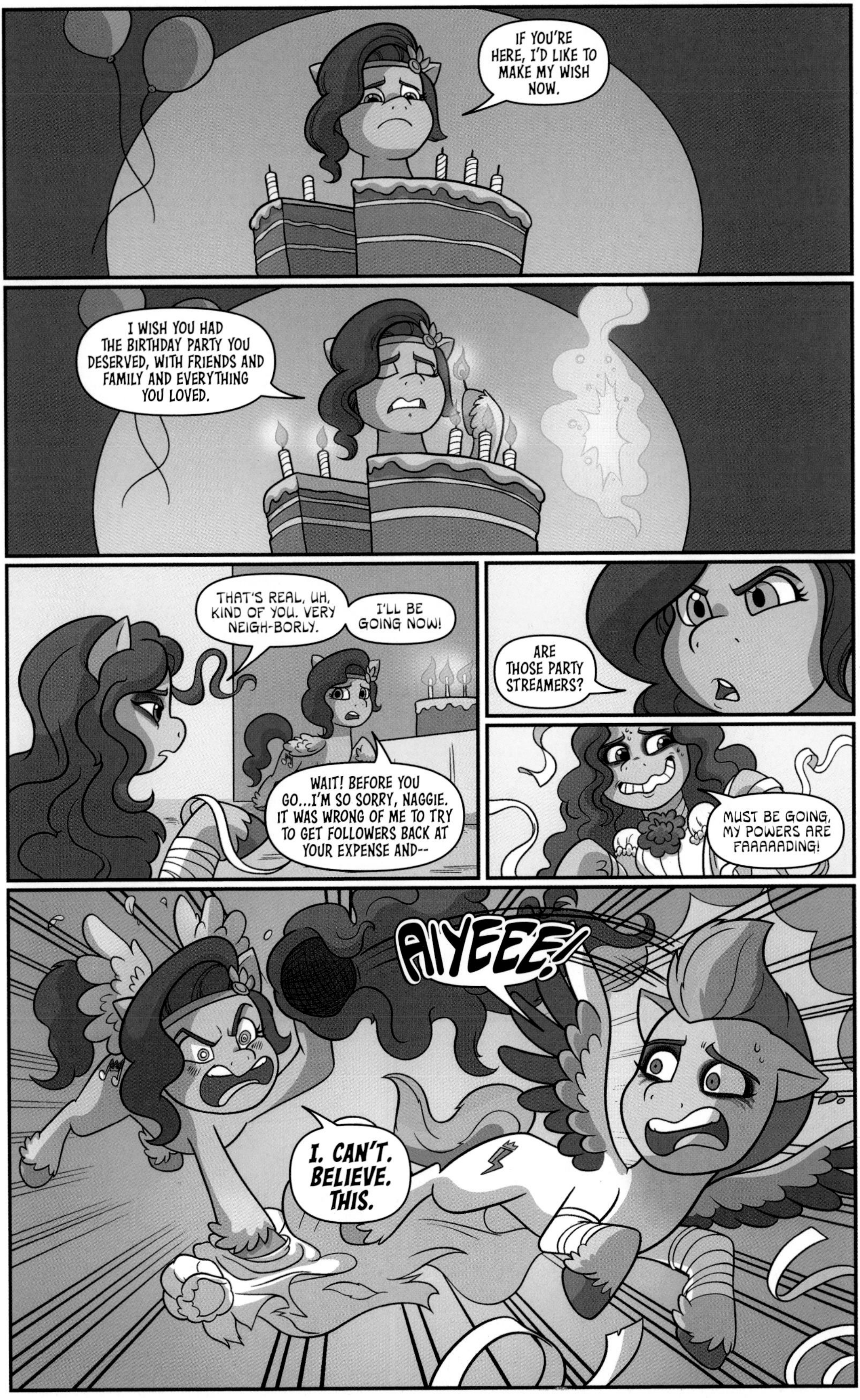
IF YOU'RE HERE, I'D LIKE TO MAKE MY WISH NOW.
I WISH YOU HAD THE BIRTHDAY PARTY YOU DESERVED, WITH FRIENDS AND FAMILY AND EVERYTHING YOU LOVED.
THAT'S REAL, UH, KIND OF YOU. VERY NEIGH-BORLY.
I'LL BE GOING NOW!
WAIT! BEFORE YOU GO...I'M SO SORRY, NAGGIE. IT WAS WRONG OF ME TO TRY TO GET FOLLOWERS BACK AT YOUR EXPENSE AND--
ARE THOSE PARTY STREAMERS?
MUST BE GOING, MY POWERS ARE FAAAAADING!
AIYEEE!
I. CAN'T. BELIEVE. THIS.

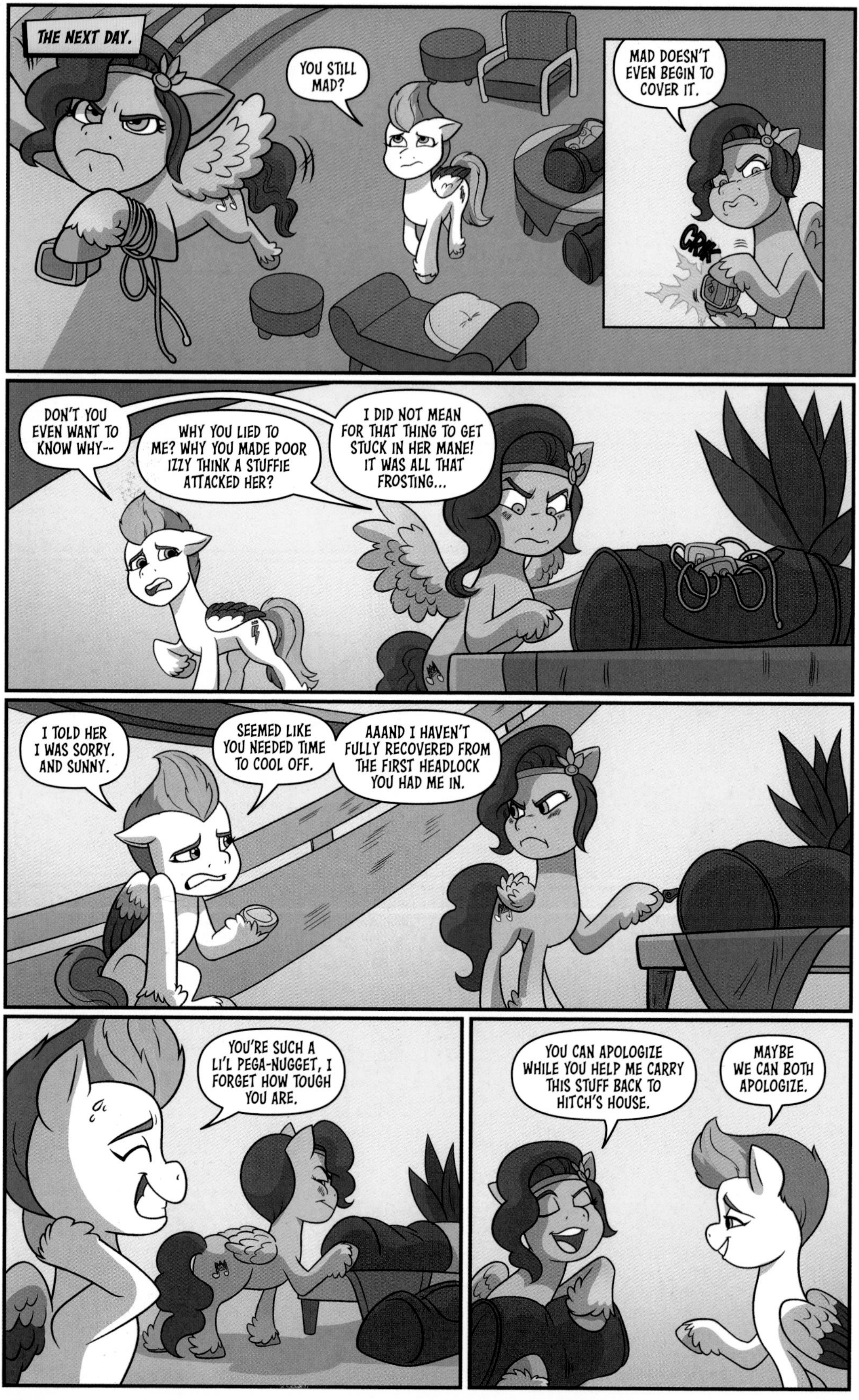
THE NEXT DAY.
YOU STILL MAD?
MAD DOESN'T EVEN BEGIN TO COVER IT.
CRIK
DON'T YOU EVEN WANT TO KNOW WHY--
WHY YOU LIED TO ME? WHY YOU MADE POOR IZZY THINK A STUFFIE ATTACKED HER?
I DID NOT MEAN FOR THAT THING TO GET STUCK IN HER MANE! IT WAS ALL THAT FROSTING...
I TOLD HER I WAS SORRY. AND SUNNY.
SEEMED LIKE YOU NEEDED TIME TO COOL OFF.
AAAND I HAVEN'T FULLY RECOVERED FROM THE FIRST HEADLOCK YOU HAD ME IN.
YOU'RE SUCH A LI'L PEGA-NUGGET, I FORGET HOW TOUGH YOU ARE.
YOU CAN APOLOGIZE WHILE YOU HELP ME CARRY THIS STUFF BACK TO HITCH'S HOUSE.
MAYBE WE CAN BOTH APOLOGIZE.

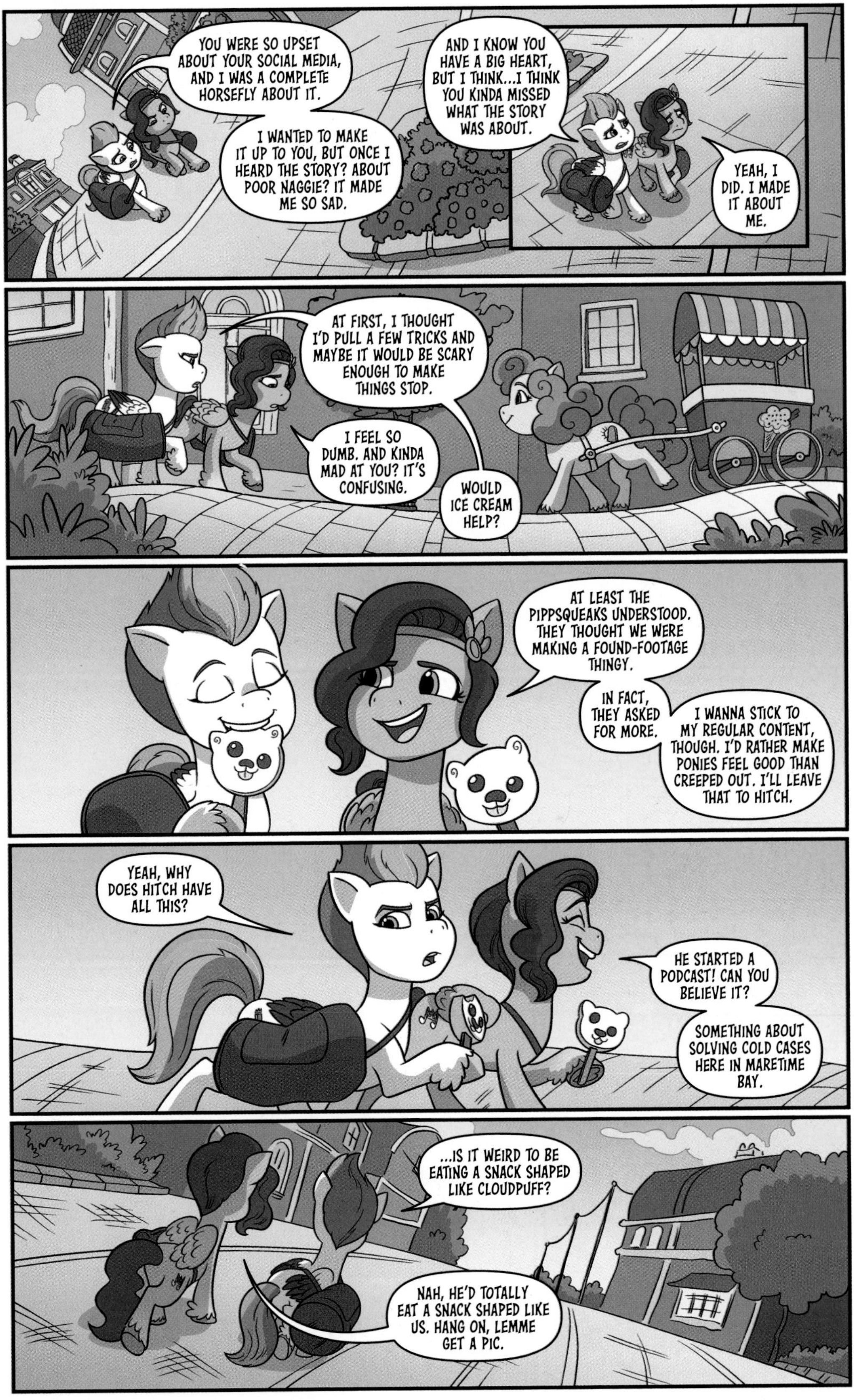
YOU WERE SO UPSET ABOUT YOUR SOCIAL MEDIA, AND I WAS A COMPLETE HORSEFLY ABOUT IT.
I WANTED TO MAKE IT UP TO YOU, BUT ONCE I HEARD THE STORY? ABOUT POOR NAGGIE? IT MADE ME SO SAD.
AND I KNOW YOU HAVE A BIG HEART, BUT I THINK...I THINK YOU KINDA MISSED WHAT THE STORY WAS ABOUT.
YEAH, I DID. I MADE IT ABOUT ME.
AT FIRST, I THOUGHT I'D PULL A FEW TRICKS AND MAYBE IT WOULD BE SCARY ENOUGH TO MAKE THINGS STOP.
I FEEL SO DUMB. AND KINDA MAD AT YOU? IT'S CONFUSING.
WOULD ICE CREAM HELP?
AT LEAST THE PIPPSQUEAKS UNDERSTOOD. THEY THOUGHT WE WERE MAKING A FOUND-FOOTAGE THINGY.
IN FACT, THEY ASKED FOR MORE.
I WANNA STICK TO MY REGULAR CONTENT, THOUGH. I'D RATHER MAKE PONIES FEEL GOOD THAN CREEPED OUT. I'LL LEAVE THAT TO HITCH.
YEAH, WHY DOES HITCH HAVE ALL THIS?
HE STARTED A PODCAST! CAN YOU BELIEVE IT?
SOMETHING ABOUT SOLVING COLD CASES HERE IN MARETIME BAY.
...IS IT WEIRD TO BE EATING A SNACK SHAPED LIKE CLOUDPUFF?
NAH, HE'D TOTALLY EAT A SNACK SHAPED LIKE US. HANG ON, LEMME GET A PIC.

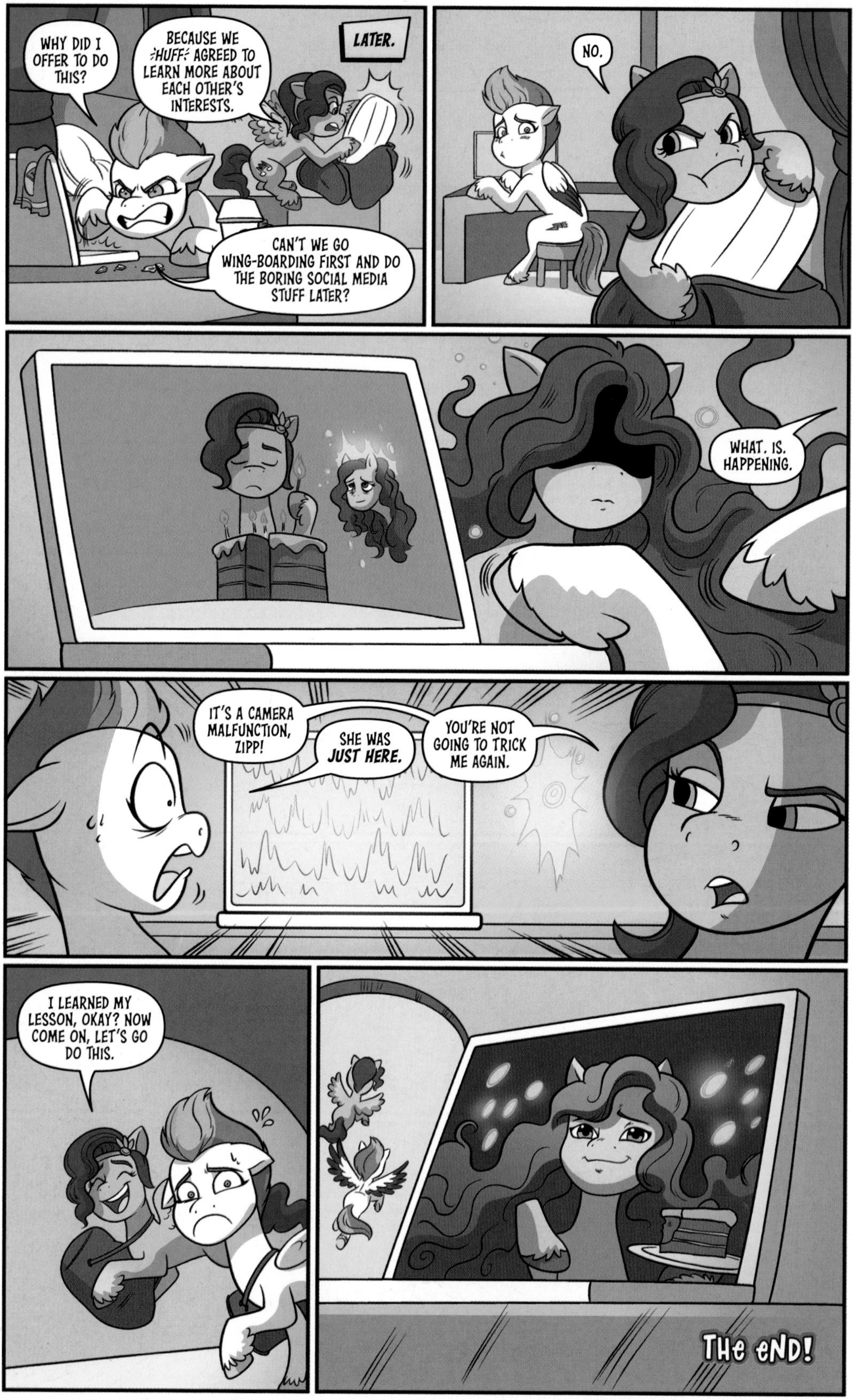
WHY DID I OFFER TO DO THIS?
BECAUSE WE ~HUFF~ AGREED TO LEARN MORE ABOUT EACH OTHER'S INTERESTS.
LATER.
CAN'T WE GO WING-BOARDING FIRST AND DO THE BORING SOCIAL MEDIA STUFF LATER?
NO.
WHAT. IS. HAPPENING.
IT'S A CAMERA MALFUNCTION, ZIPP!
SHE WAS JUST HERE.
YOU'RE NOT GOING TO TRICK ME AGAIN.
I LEARNED MY LESSON, OKAY? NOW COME ON, LET'S GO DO THIS.
THE END!

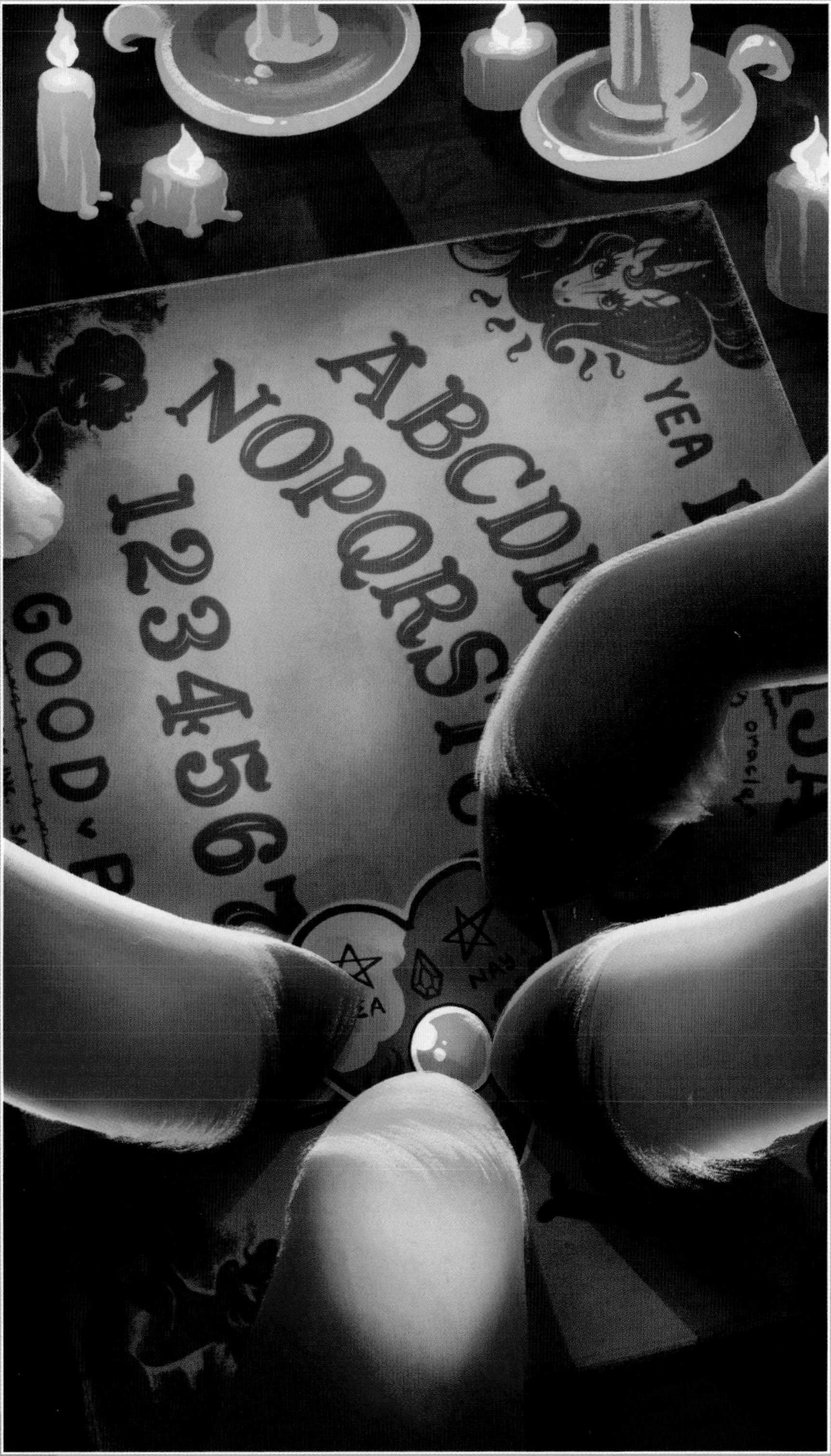
YEA
GOOD

art by JustaSuta

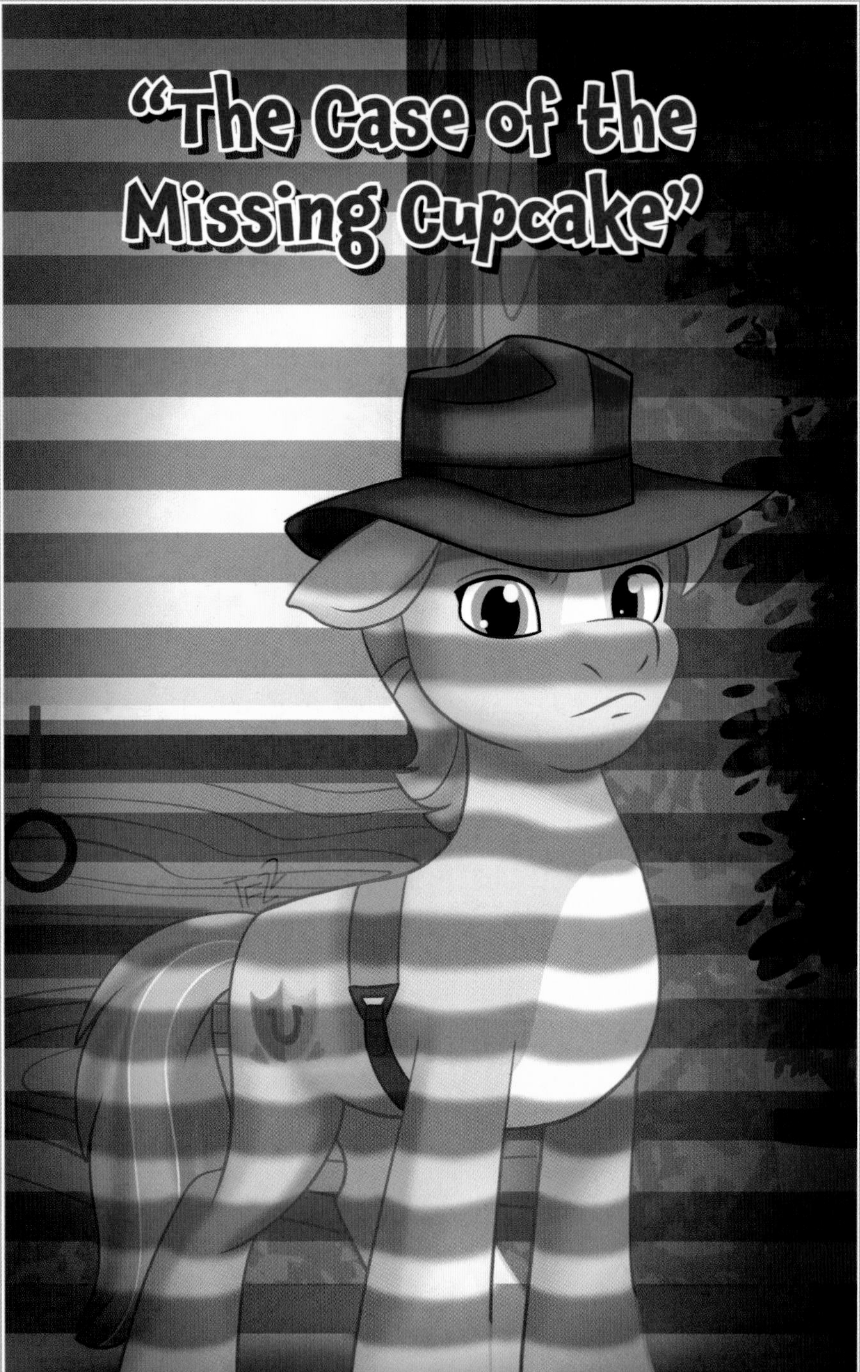
"The Case of the Missing Cupcake"

art by **Trish Forstner**

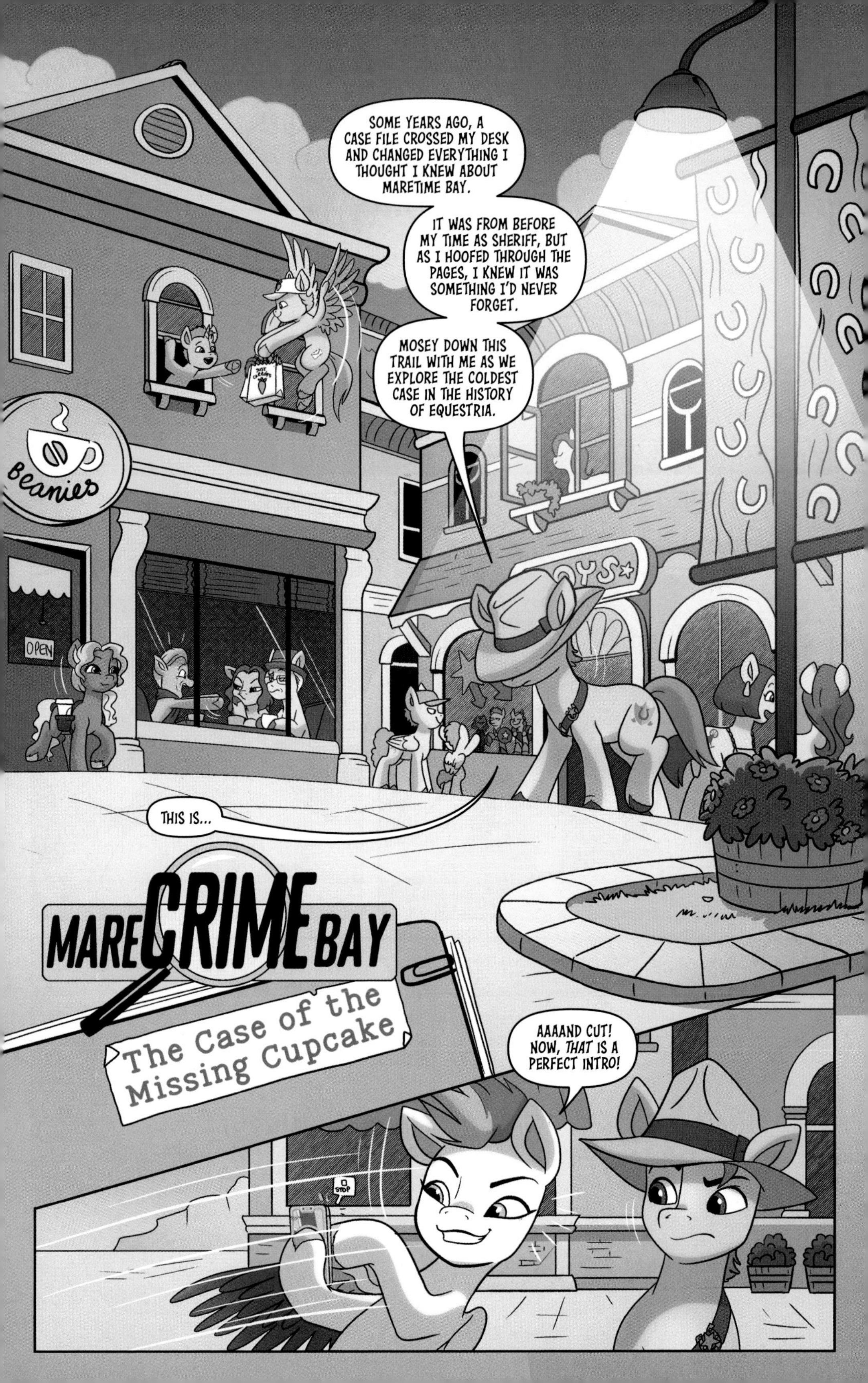
SOME YEARS AGO, A CASE FILE CROSSED MY DESK AND CHANGED EVERYTHING I THOUGHT I KNEW ABOUT MARETIME BAY.
IT WAS FROM BEFORE MY TIME AS SHERIFF, BUT AS I HOOFED THROUGH THE PAGES, I KNEW IT WAS SOMETHING I'D NEVER FORGET.
MOSEY DOWN THIS TRAIL WITH ME AS WE EXPLORE THE COLDEST CASE IN THE HISTORY OF EQUESTRIA.
Beanies
OPEN
THIS IS...
MARE CRIME BAY
The Case of the Missing Cupcake
AAAAND CUT! NOW, *THAT* IS A PERFECT INTRO!
STOP

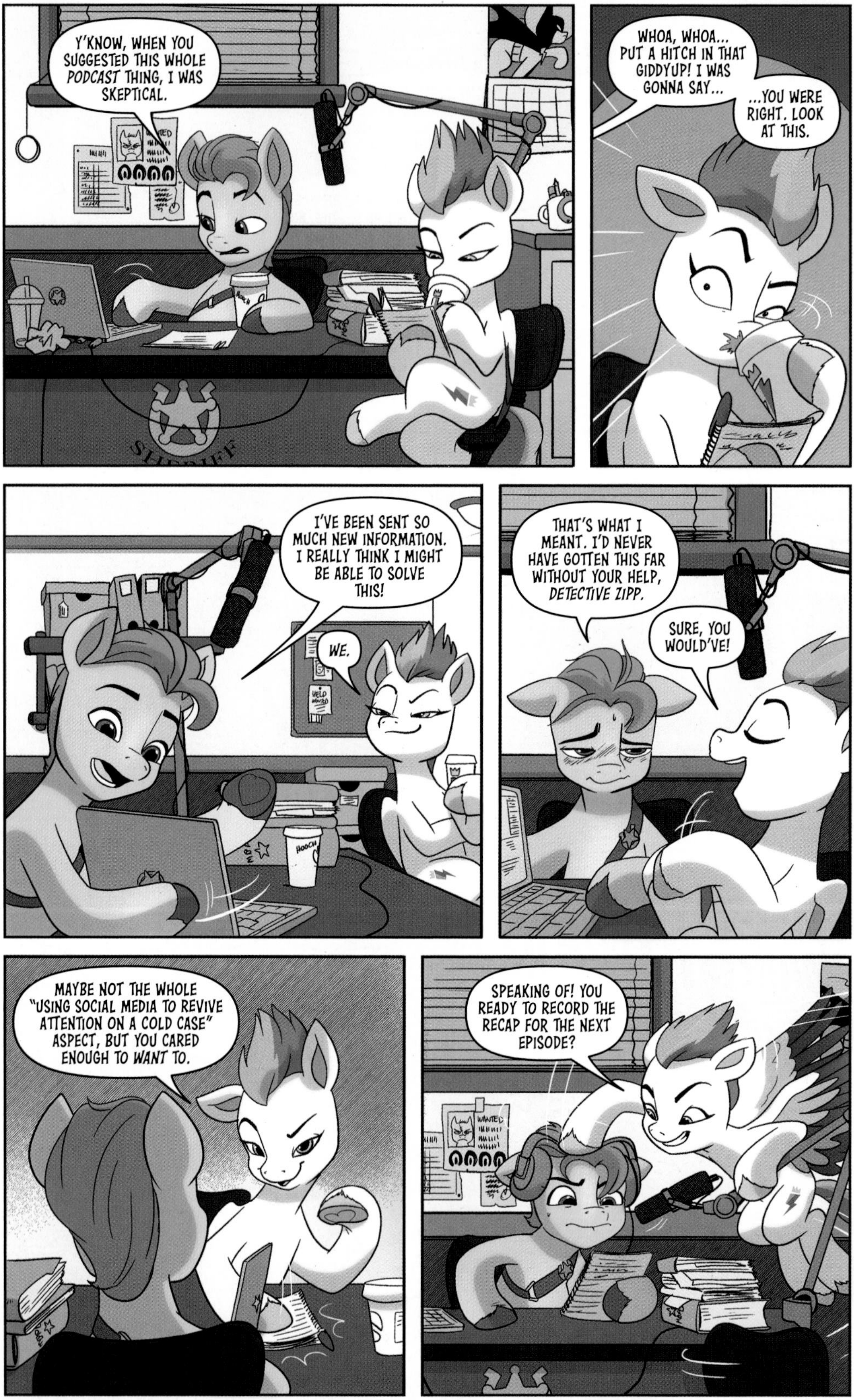
Y'KNOW, WHEN YOU SUGGESTED THIS WHOLE *PODCAST* THING, I WAS SKEPTICAL.
WANTED
HOOCH
SHERIFF
WHOA, WHOA... PUT A HITCH IN THAT GIDDYUP! I WAS GONNA SAY...
...YOU WERE RIGHT. LOOK AT THIS.
I'VE BEEN SENT SO MUCH NEW INFORMATION. I REALLY THINK I MIGHT BE ABLE TO SOLVE THIS!
WE.
HELP WANTED
HOOCH
THAT'S WHAT I MEANT. I'D NEVER HAVE GOTTEN THIS FAR WITHOUT YOUR HELP, *DETECTIVE ZIPP.*
SURE, YOU WOULD'VE!
MAYBE NOT THE WHOLE "USING SOCIAL MEDIA TO REVIVE ATTENTION ON A COLD CASE" ASPECT, BUT YOU CARED ENOUGH TO *WANT* TO.
SPEAKING OF! YOU READY TO RECORD THE RECAP FOR THE NEXT EPISODE?
WANTED

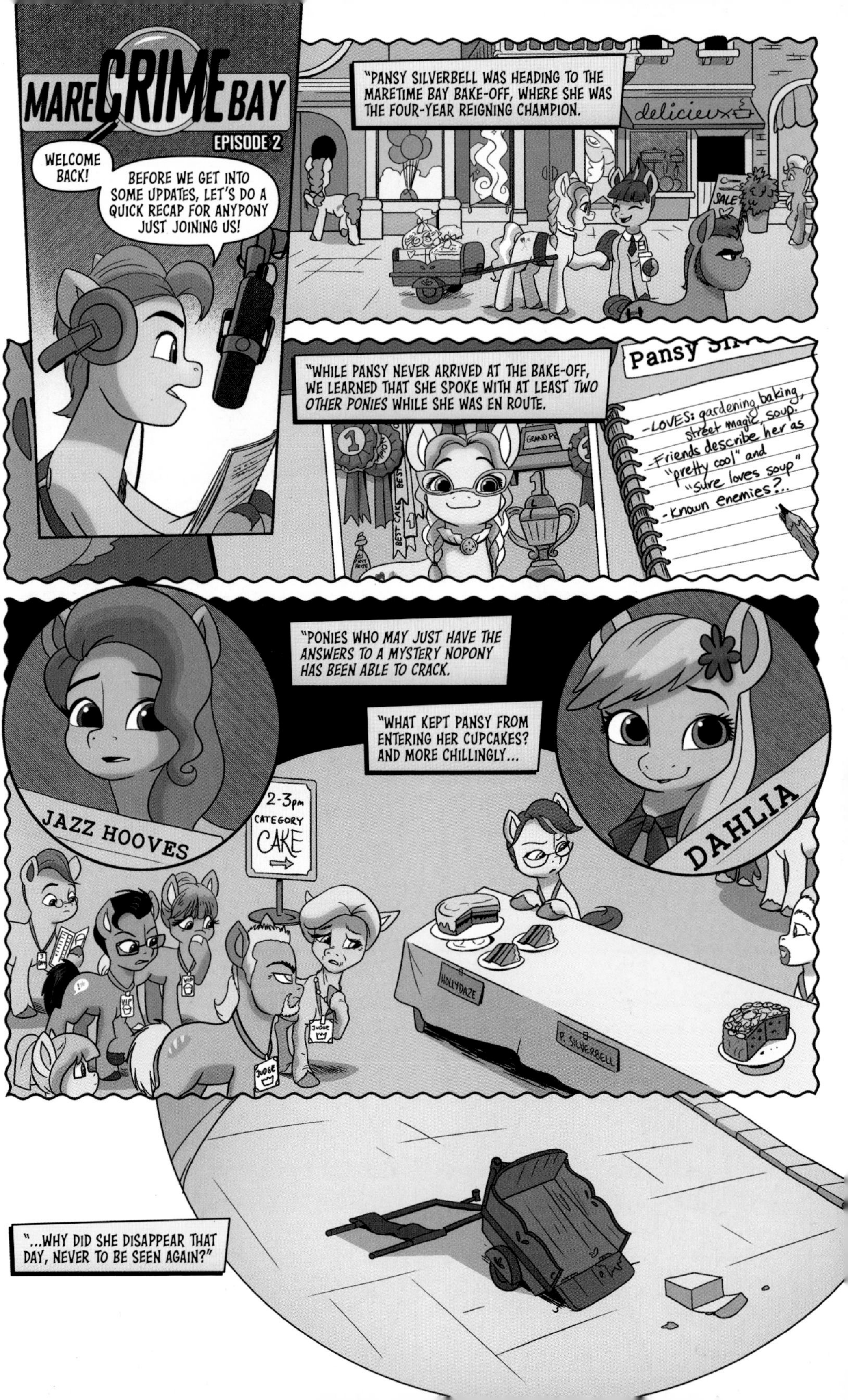
MARE CRIME BAY
EPISODE 2
WELCOME BACK!
BEFORE WE GET INTO SOME UPDATES, LET'S DO A QUICK RECAP FOR ANYPONY JUST JOINING US!
"PANSY SILVERBELL WAS HEADING TO THE MARETIME BAY BAKE-OFF, WHERE SHE WAS THE FOUR-YEAR REIGNING CHAMPION.
delicieux
SALE
"WHILE PANSY NEVER ARRIVED AT THE BAKE-OFF, WE LEARNED THAT SHE SPOKE WITH AT LEAST TWO OTHER PONIES WHILE SHE WAS EN ROUTE.
Pansy Si
-LOVES: gardening, baking, street magic, soup.
-Friends describe her as "pretty cool" and "sure loves soup"
-Known enemies?..
"PONIES WHO MAY JUST HAVE THE ANSWERS TO A MYSTERY NOPONY HAS BEEN ABLE TO CRACK.
"WHAT KEPT PANSY FROM ENTERING HER CUPCAKES? AND MORE CHILLINGLY...
JAZZ HOOVES
DAHLIA
2-3pm CATEGORY CAKE
HOLLYDAZE
P. SILVERBELL
JUDGE
JUDGE
VIP
"...WHY DID SHE DISAPPEAR THAT DAY, NEVER TO BE SEEN AGAIN?"

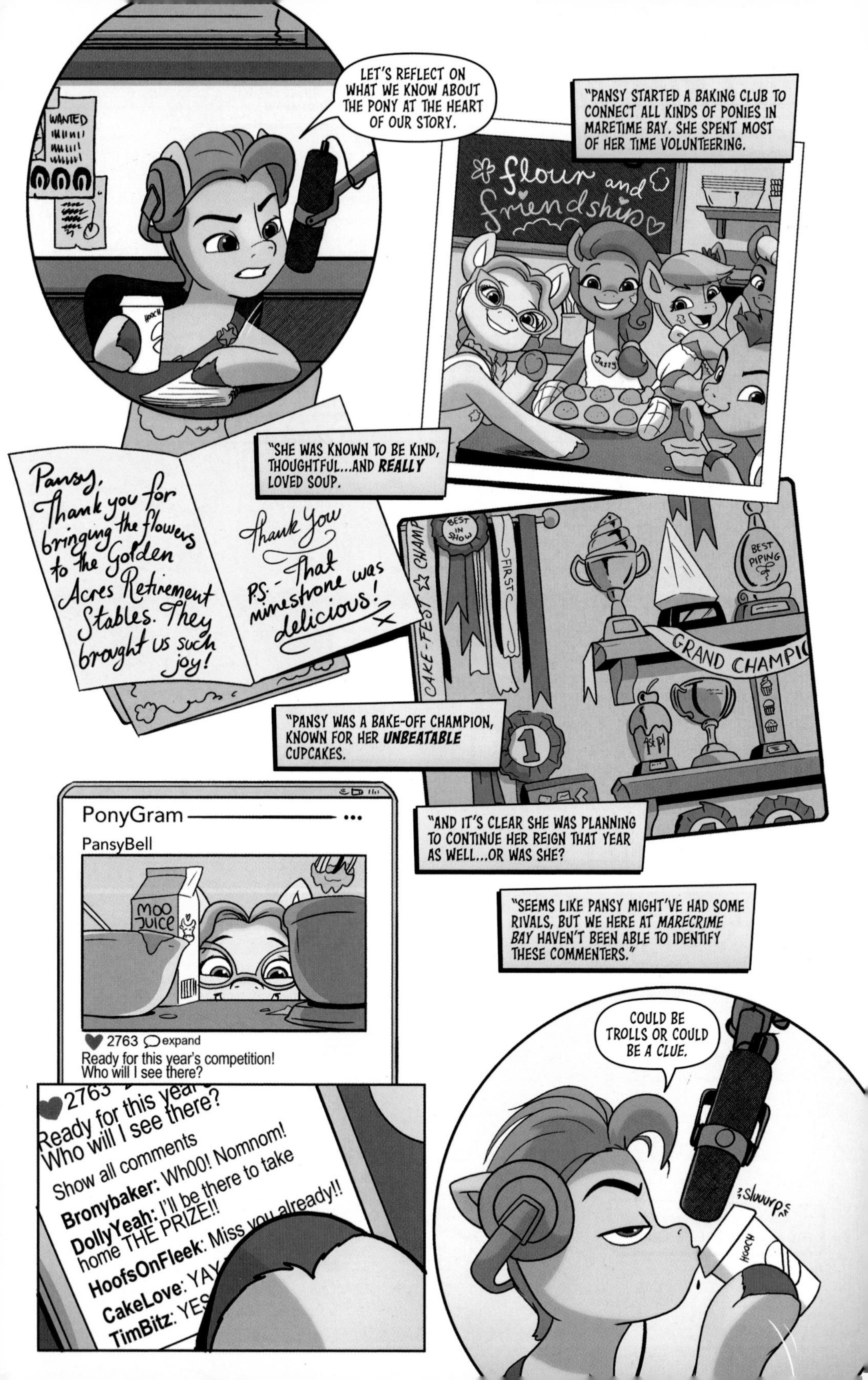

WANTED
LET'S REFLECT ON WHAT WE KNOW ABOUT THE PONY AT THE HEART OF OUR STORY.
"PANSY STARTED A BAKING CLUB TO CONNECT ALL KINDS OF PONIES IN MARETIME BAY. SHE SPENT MOST OF HER TIME VOLUNTEERING.
flour and friendship
Jazzy
"SHE WAS KNOWN TO BE KIND, THOUGHTFUL...AND REALLY LOVED SOUP.
Pansy, Thank you for bringing the flowers to the Golden Acres Retirement Stables. They brought us such joy!
Thank You
P.S. - That minestrone was delicious! x
BEST IN SHOW
FIRST
BEST PIPING
CAKE-FEST ☆ CHAMP
GRAND CHAMPIO
1
1st pl
"PANSY WAS A BAKE-OFF CHAMPION, KNOWN FOR HER UNBEATABLE CUPCAKES.
"AND IT'S CLEAR SHE WAS PLANNING TO CONTINUE HER REIGN THAT YEAR AS WELL...OR WAS SHE?
PonyGram
PansyBell
MOO JUICE
2763 expand
Ready for this year's competition! Who will I see there?
"SEEMS LIKE PANSY MIGHT'VE HAD SOME RIVALS, BUT WE HERE AT MARECRIME BAY HAVEN'T BEEN ABLE TO IDENTIFY THESE COMMENTERS."
2763
Ready for this year's Who will I see there?
Show all comments
Bronybaker: Wh00! Nomnom!
DollyYeah: I'll be there to take home THE PRIZE!!
HoofsOnFleek: Miss you already!!
CakeLove: YAY
TimBitz: YES
COULD BE TROLLS OR COULD BE A CLUE.
sluuurp
HOOCH

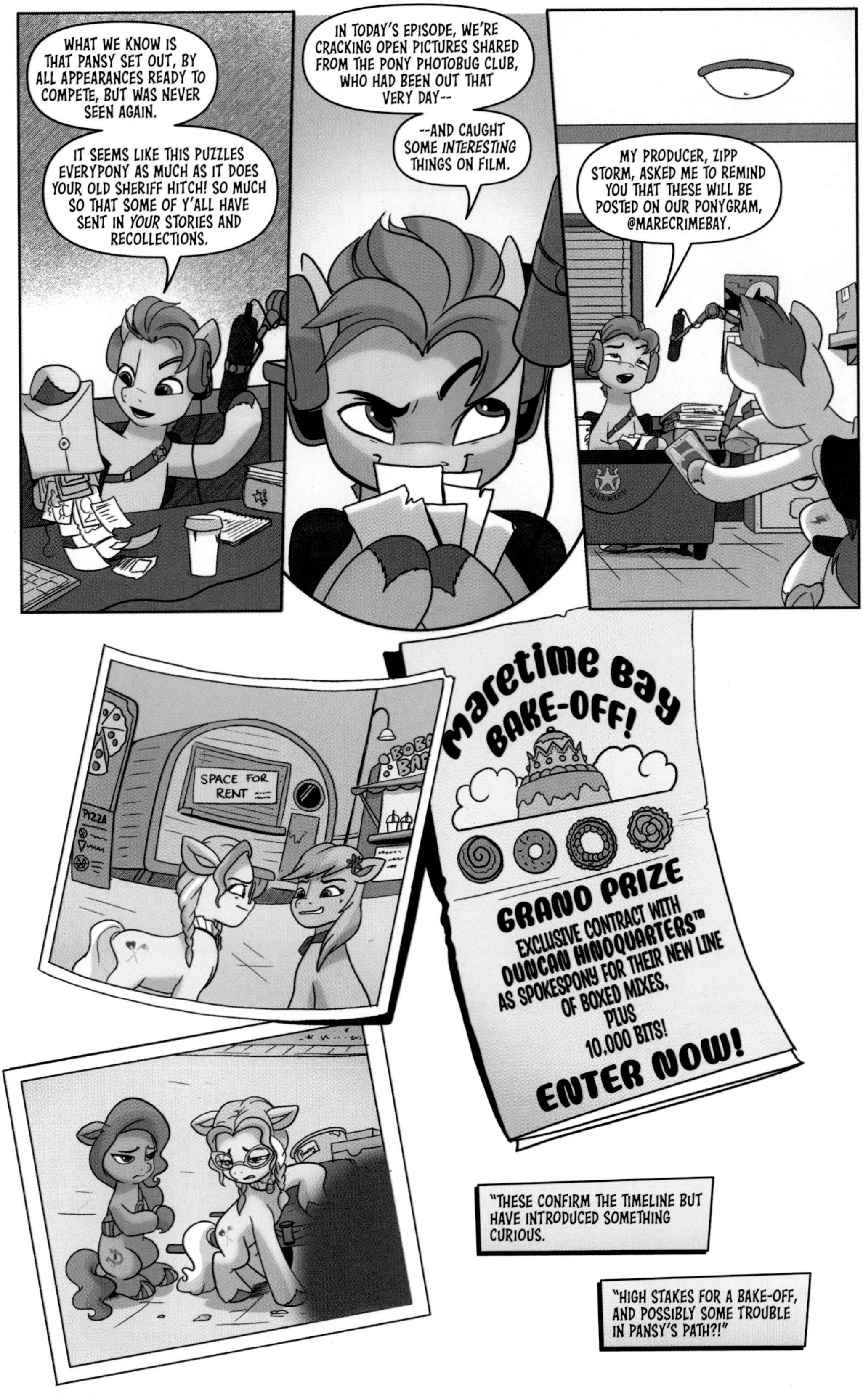
WHAT WE KNOW IS THAT PANSY SET OUT, BY ALL APPEARANCES READY TO COMPETE, BUT WAS NEVER SEEN AGAIN.
IT SEEMS LIKE THIS PUZZLES EVERYPONY AS MUCH AS IT DOES YOUR OLD SHERIFF HITCH! SO MUCH SO THAT SOME OF Y'ALL HAVE SENT IN *YOUR* STORIES AND RECOLLECTIONS.
IN TODAY'S EPISODE, WE'RE CRACKING OPEN PICTURES SHARED FROM THE PONY PHOTOBUG CLUB, WHO HAD BEEN OUT THAT VERY DAY--
--AND CAUGHT SOME *INTERESTING* THINGS ON FILM.
MY PRODUCER, ZIPP STORM, ASKED ME TO REMIND YOU THAT THESE WILL BE POSTED ON OUR PONYGRAM, @MARECRIMEBAY.
SHERIFF
SPACE FOR RENT
PIZZA
Maretime Bay
BAKE-OFF!
GRAND PRIZE
EXCLUSIVE CONTRACT WITH
DUNCAN HINDQUARTERS™
AS SPOKESPONY FOR THEIR NEW LINE
OF BOXED MIXES,
PLUS
10,000 BITS!
ENTER NOW!
"THESE CONFIRM THE TIMELINE BUT HAVE INTRODUCED SOMETHING CURIOUS.
"HIGH STAKES FOR A BAKE-OFF, AND POSSIBLY SOME TROUBLE IN PANSY'S PATH?!"

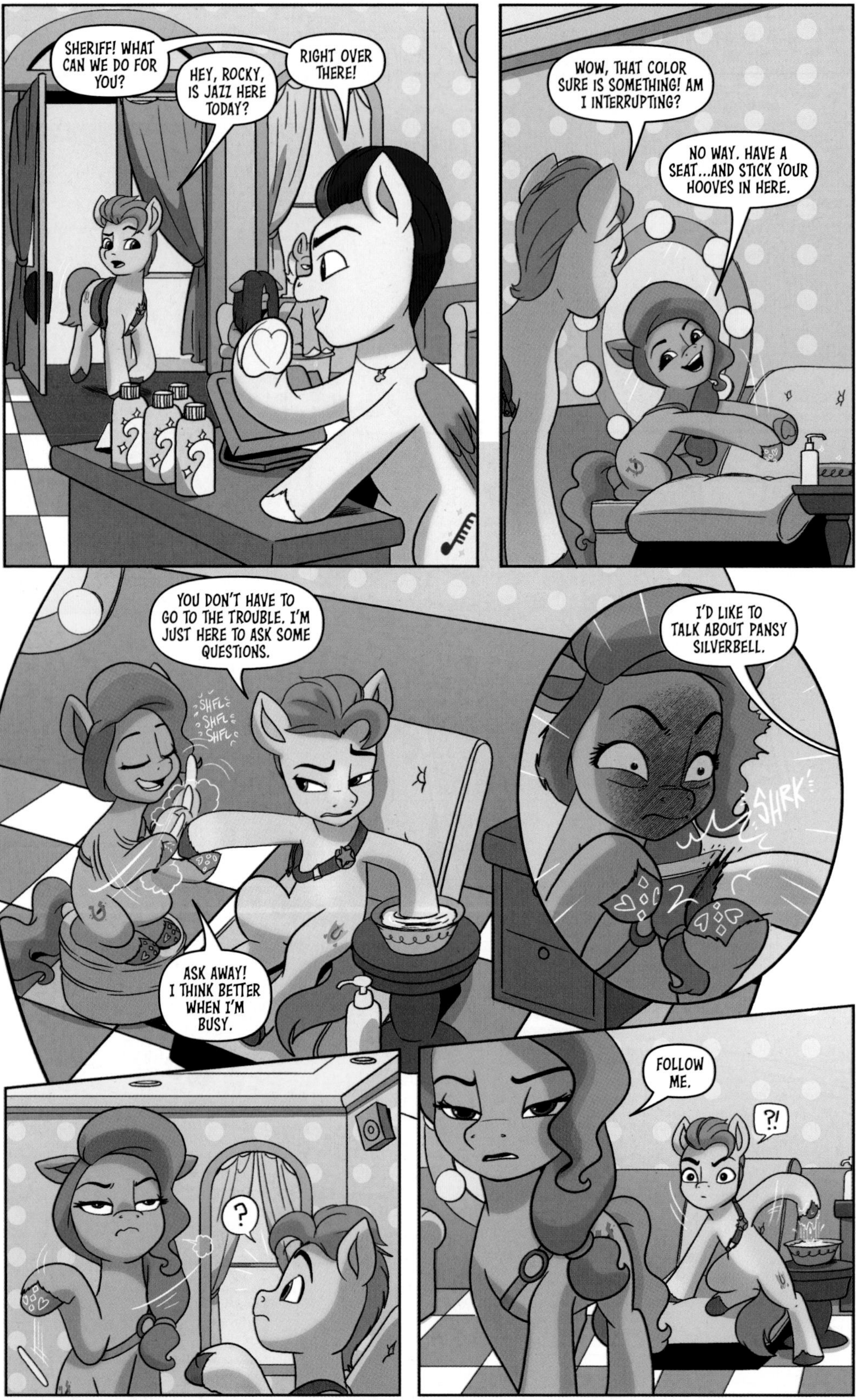
SHERIFF! WHAT CAN WE DO FOR YOU?
HEY, ROCKY, IS JAZZ HERE TODAY?
RIGHT OVER THERE!
WOW, THAT COLOR SURE IS SOMETHING! AM I INTERRUPTING?
NO WAY. HAVE A SEAT...AND STICK YOUR HOOVES IN HERE.
YOU DON'T HAVE TO GO TO THE TROUBLE. I'M JUST HERE TO ASK SOME QUESTIONS.
SHFL SHFL SHFL
ASK AWAY! I THINK BETTER WHEN I'M BUSY.
I'D LIKE TO TALK ABOUT PANSY SILVERBELL.
SHRK
?
FOLLOW ME.
?!

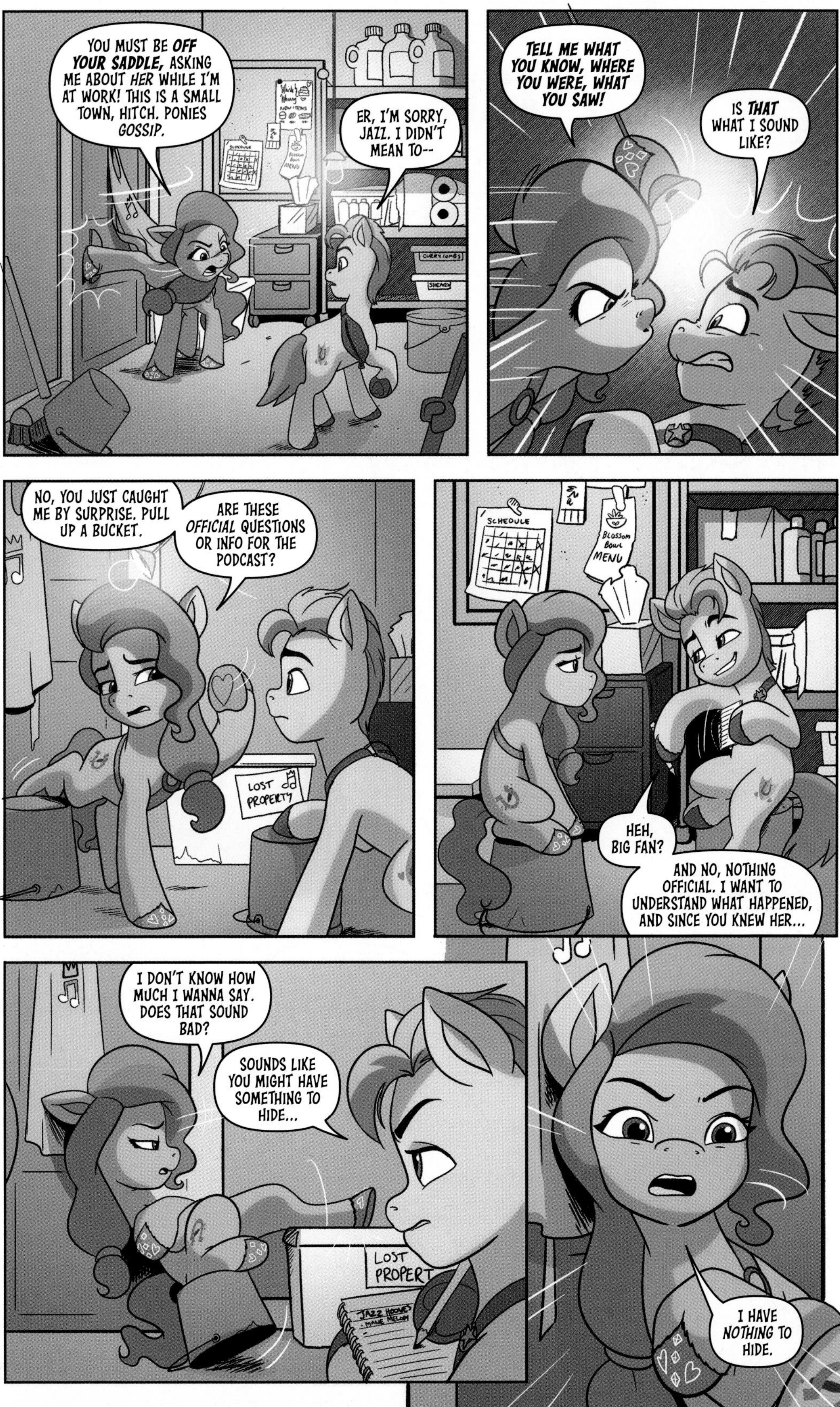

YOU MUST BE OFF YOUR SADDLE, ASKING ME ABOUT HER WHILE I'M AT WORK! THIS IS A SMALL TOWN, HITCH. PONIES GOSSIP.
ER, I'M SORRY, JAZZ. I DIDN'T MEAN TO--
TELL ME WHAT YOU KNOW, WHERE YOU WERE, WHAT YOU SAW!
IS THAT WHAT I SOUND LIKE?
NO, YOU JUST CAUGHT ME BY SURPRISE. PULL UP A BUCKET.
ARE THESE OFFICIAL QUESTIONS OR INFO FOR THE PODCAST?
LOST PROPERTY
SCHEDULE
BLOSSOM BOWL MENU
HEH, BIG FAN?
AND NO, NOTHING OFFICIAL. I WANT TO UNDERSTAND WHAT HAPPENED, AND SINCE YOU KNEW HER...
I DON'T KNOW HOW MUCH I WANNA SAY. DOES THAT SOUND BAD?
SOUNDS LIKE YOU MIGHT HAVE SOMETHING TO HIDE...
LOST PROPERT
JAZZ HOOVES - MANE MELODY
I HAVE NOTHING TO HIDE.

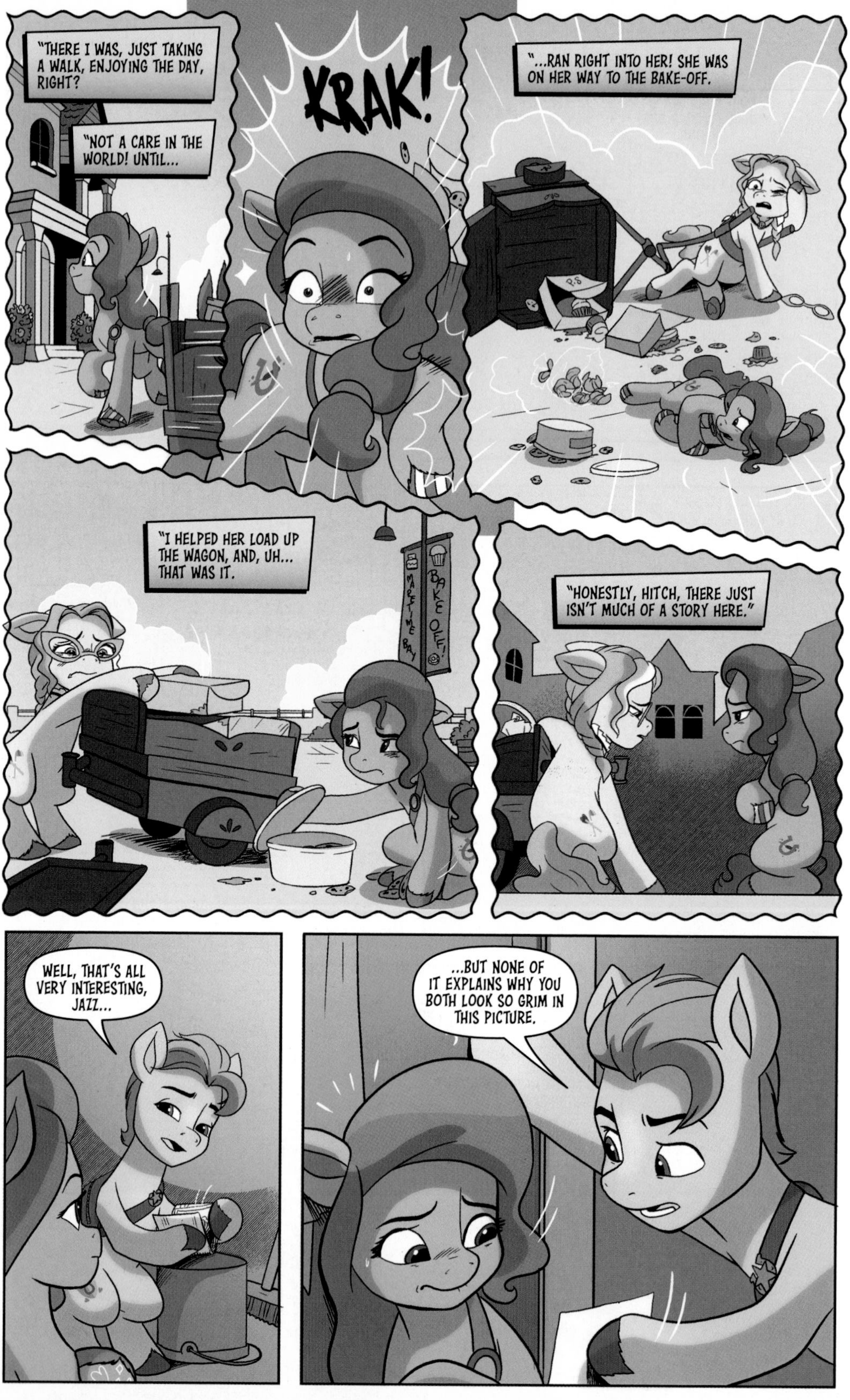
"THERE I WAS, JUST TAKING A WALK, ENJOYING THE DAY, RIGHT?
"NOT A CARE IN THE WORLD! UNTIL...
KRAK!
"...RAN RIGHT INTO HER! SHE WAS ON HER WAY TO THE BAKE-OFF.
"I HELPED HER LOAD UP THE WAGON, AND, UH... THAT WAS IT.
MARETIME BAY
BAKE OFF!
"HONESTLY, HITCH, THERE JUST ISN'T MUCH OF A STORY HERE."
WELL, THAT'S ALL VERY INTERESTING, JAZZ...
...BUT NONE OF IT EXPLAINS WHY YOU BOTH LOOK SO GRIM IN THIS PICTURE.

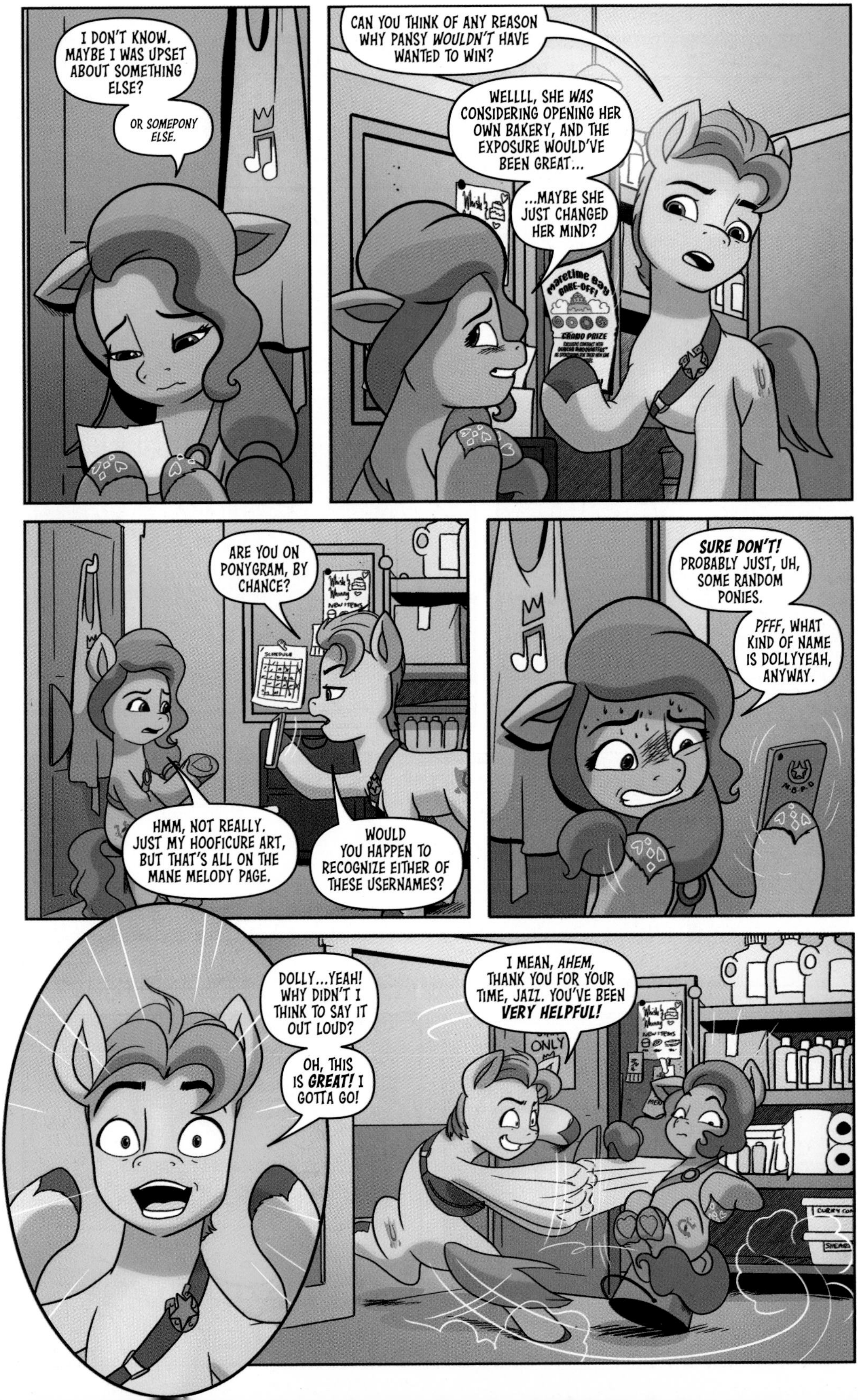
I DON'T KNOW. MAYBE I WAS UPSET ABOUT SOMETHING ELSE?
OR SOMEPONY ELSE.
CAN YOU THINK OF ANY REASON WHY PANSY *WOULDN'T* HAVE WANTED TO WIN?
WELLLL, SHE *WAS* CONSIDERING OPENING HER OWN BAKERY, AND THE EXPOSURE WOULD'VE BEEN GREAT...
...MAYBE SHE JUST CHANGED HER MIND?
Maretime Bay
BAKE-OFF!
GRAND PRIZE
ARE YOU ON PONYGRAM, BY CHANCE?
SCHEDULE
HMM, NOT REALLY. JUST MY HOOFICURE ART, BUT THAT'S ALL ON THE MANE MELODY PAGE.
WOULD YOU HAPPEN TO RECOGNIZE EITHER OF THESE USERNAMES?
SURE DON'T! PROBABLY JUST, UH, SOME RANDOM PONIES.
PFFF, WHAT KIND OF NAME IS DOLLYYEAH, ANYWAY.
M.B.P.D
DOLLY...YEAH! WHY DIDN'T I THINK TO SAY IT OUT LOUD?
OH, THIS IS ***GREAT!*** I GOTTA GO!
I MEAN, *AHEM,* THANK YOU FOR YOUR TIME, JAZZ. YOU'VE BEEN ***VERY HELPFUL!***
ONLY
SHEARS

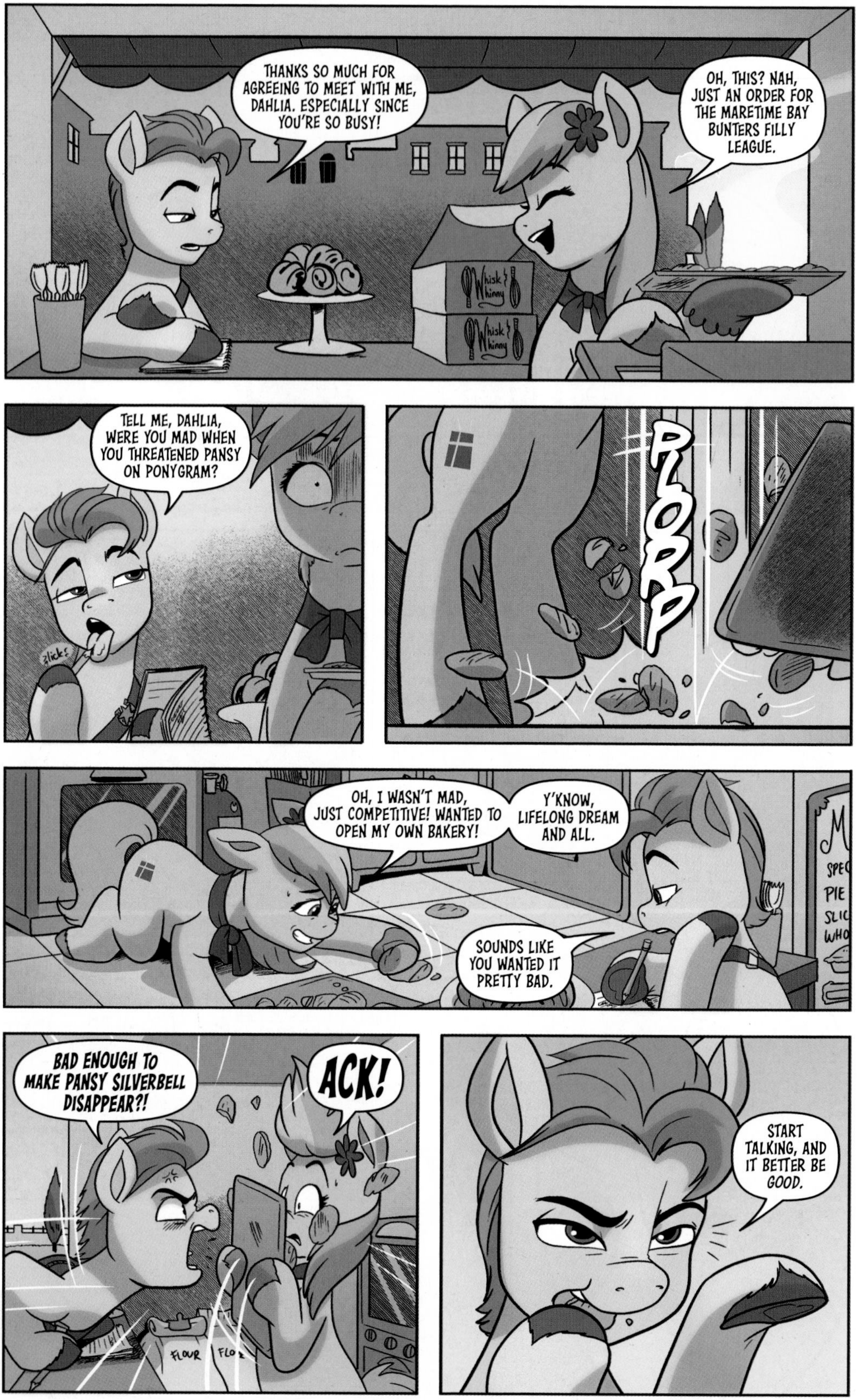
THANKS SO MUCH FOR AGREEING TO MEET WITH ME, DAHLIA. ESPECIALLY SINCE YOU'RE SO BUSY!
OH, THIS? NAH, JUST AN ORDER FOR THE MARETIME BAY BUNTERS FILLY LEAGUE.
Whisk & Whinny
Whisk & Whinny
TELL ME, DAHLIA, WERE YOU MAD WHEN YOU THREATENED PANSY ON PONYGRAM?
PLORP
OH, I WASN'T MAD, JUST COMPETITIVE! WANTED TO OPEN MY OWN BAKERY!
Y'KNOW, LIFELONG DREAM AND ALL.
SOUNDS LIKE YOU WANTED IT PRETTY BAD.
BAD ENOUGH TO MAKE PANSY SILVERBELL DISAPPEAR?!
ACK!
FLOUR
START TALKING, AND IT BETTER BE GOOD.

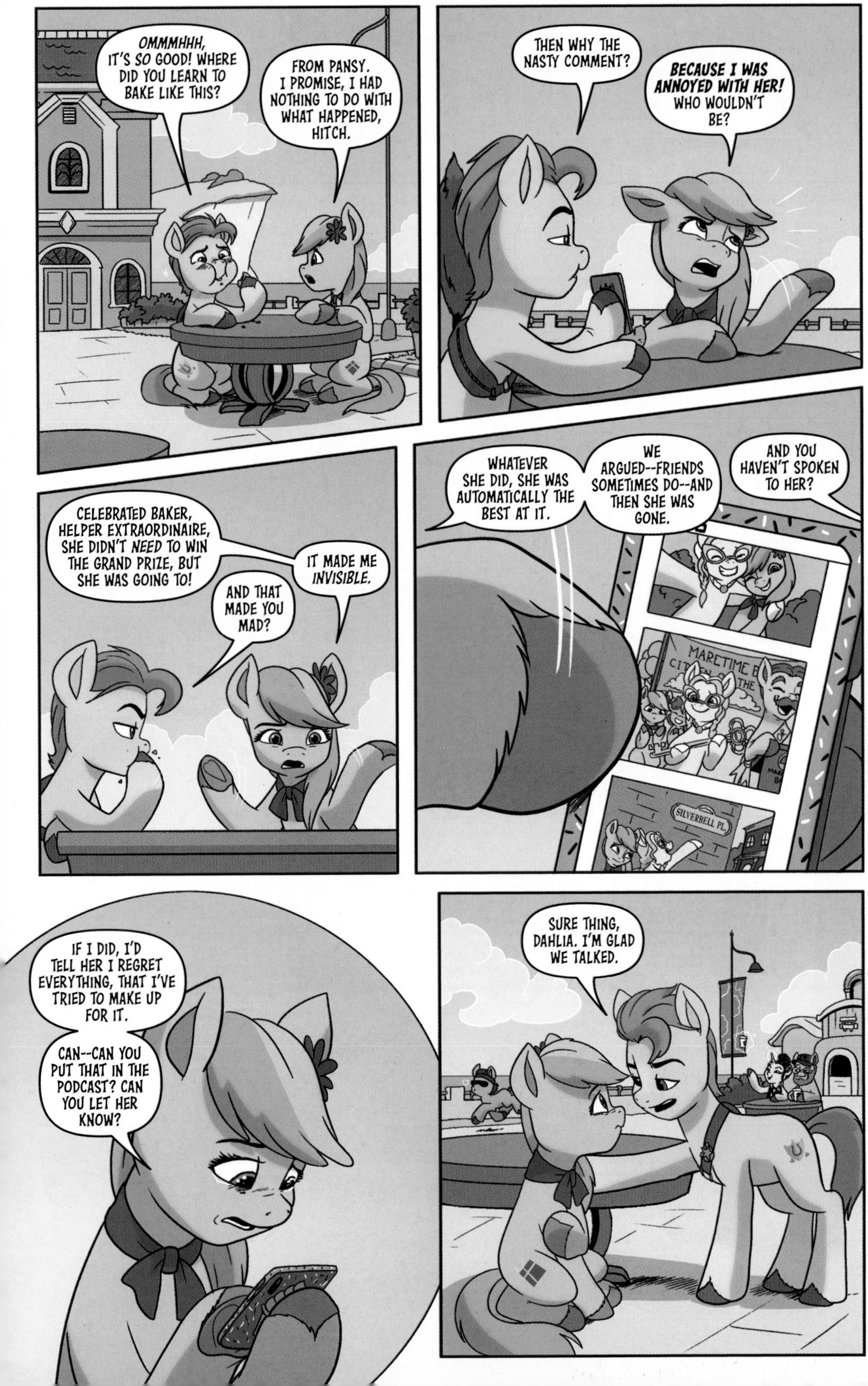
OMMMHHH, IT'S SO GOOD! WHERE DID YOU LEARN TO BAKE LIKE THIS?
FROM PANSY. I PROMISE, I HAD NOTHING TO DO WITH WHAT HAPPENED, HITCH.
THEN WHY THE NASTY COMMENT?
BECAUSE I WAS ANNOYED WITH HER! WHO WOULDN'T BE?
CELEBRATED BAKER, HELPER EXTRAORDINAIRE, SHE DIDN'T NEED TO WIN THE GRAND PRIZE, BUT SHE WAS GOING TO!
IT MADE ME INVISIBLE.
AND THAT MADE YOU MAD?
WHATEVER SHE DID, SHE WAS AUTOMATICALLY THE BEST AT IT.
WE ARGUED--FRIENDS SOMETIMES DO--AND THEN SHE WAS GONE.
AND YOU HAVEN'T SPOKEN TO HER?
MARETIME B
CIT
THE
SILVERBELL PL.
IF I DID, I'D TELL HER I REGRET EVERYTHING, THAT I'VE TRIED TO MAKE UP FOR IT.
CAN--CAN YOU PUT THAT IN THE PODCAST? CAN YOU LET HER KNOW?
SURE THING, DAHLIA. I'M GLAD WE TALKED.

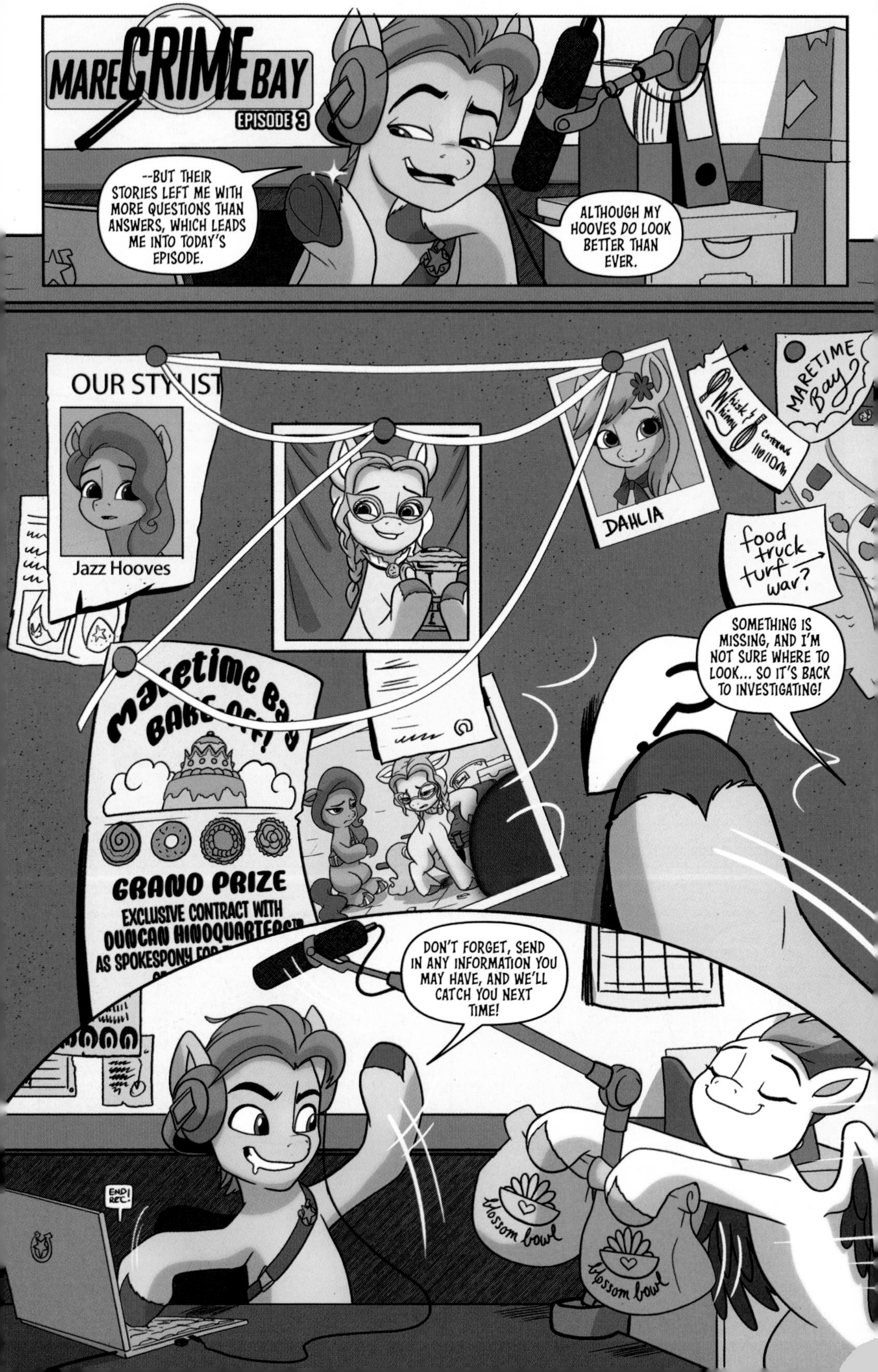

MARE CRIME BAY
EPISODE 3
--BUT THEIR STORIES LEFT ME WITH MORE QUESTIONS THAN ANSWERS, WHICH LEADS ME INTO TODAY'S EPISODE.
ALTHOUGH MY HOOVES *DO* LOOK BETTER THAN EVER.
OUR STYLIST
Jazz Hooves
DAHLIA
MARETIME Bay
food truck turf war?
Maretime Bay BAKE-OFF!
GRAND PRIZE
EXCLUSIVE CONTRACT WITH
DUNCAN HINDQUARTERS™
AS SPOKESPONY FOR
SOMETHING IS MISSING, AND I'M NOT SURE WHERE TO LOOK... SO IT'S BACK TO INVESTIGATING!
DON'T FORGET, SEND IN ANY INFORMATION YOU MAY HAVE, AND WE'LL CATCH YOU NEXT TIME!
END REC!
blossom bowl
blossom bowl

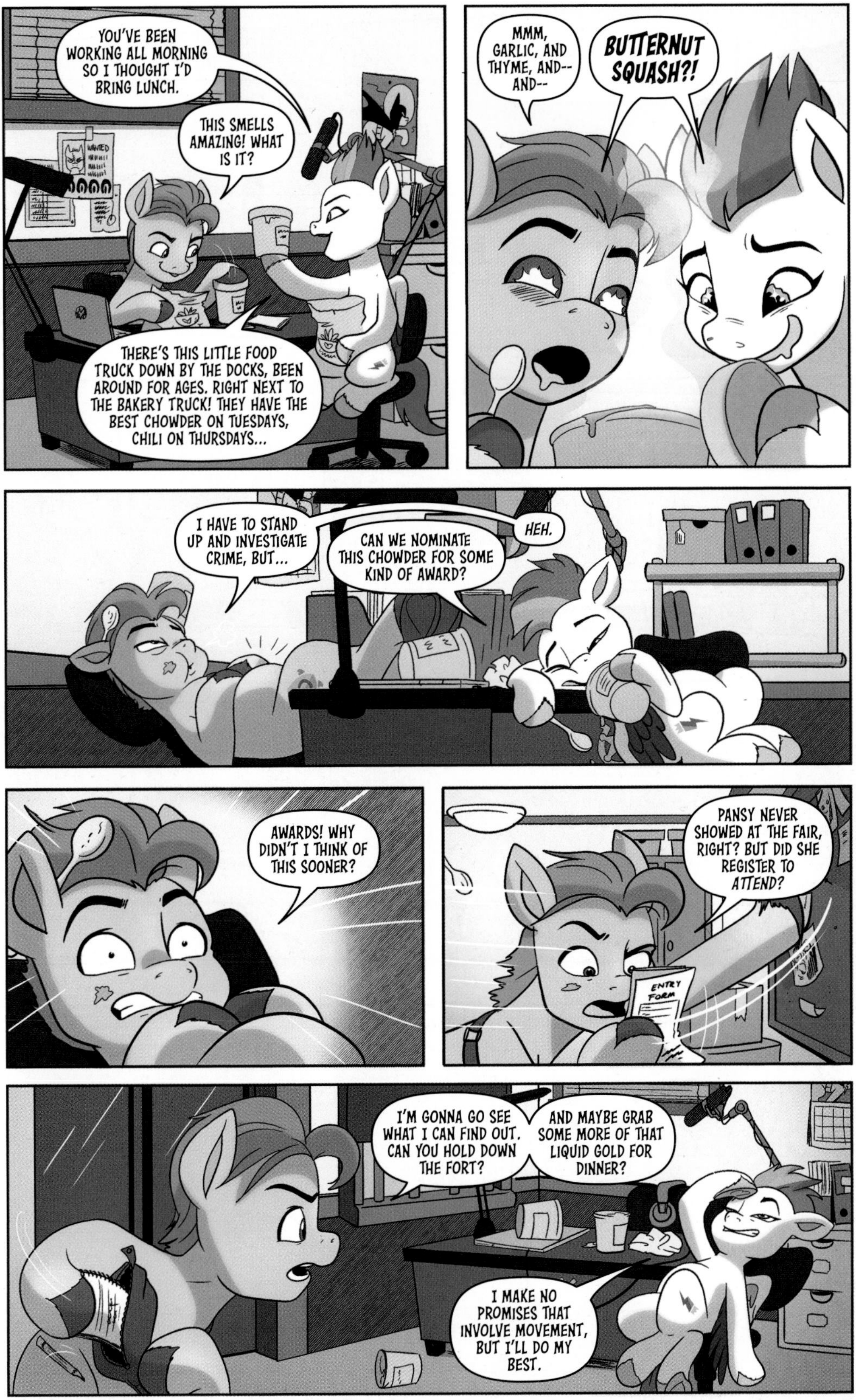

YOU'VE BEEN WORKING ALL MORNING SO I THOUGHT I'D BRING LUNCH.
THIS SMELLS AMAZING! WHAT IS IT?
THERE'S THIS LITTLE FOOD TRUCK DOWN BY THE DOCKS, BEEN AROUND FOR AGES. RIGHT NEXT TO THE BAKERY TRUCK! THEY HAVE THE BEST CHOWDER ON TUESDAYS, CHILI ON THURSDAYS...
MMM, GARLIC, AND THYME, AND-- AND--
BUTTERNUT SQUASH?!
I HAVE TO STAND UP AND INVESTIGATE CRIME, BUT...
CAN WE NOMINATE THIS CHOWDER FOR SOME KIND OF AWARD?
HEH.
AWARDS! WHY DIDN'T I THINK OF THIS SOONER?
PANSY NEVER SHOWED AT THE FAIR, RIGHT? BUT DID SHE REGISTER TO ATTEND?
ENTRY FORM
I'M GONNA GO SEE WHAT I CAN FIND OUT. CAN YOU HOLD DOWN THE FORT?
AND MAYBE GRAB SOME MORE OF THAT LIQUID GOLD FOR DINNER?
I MAKE NO PROMISES THAT INVOLVE MOVEMENT, BUT I'LL DO MY BEST.

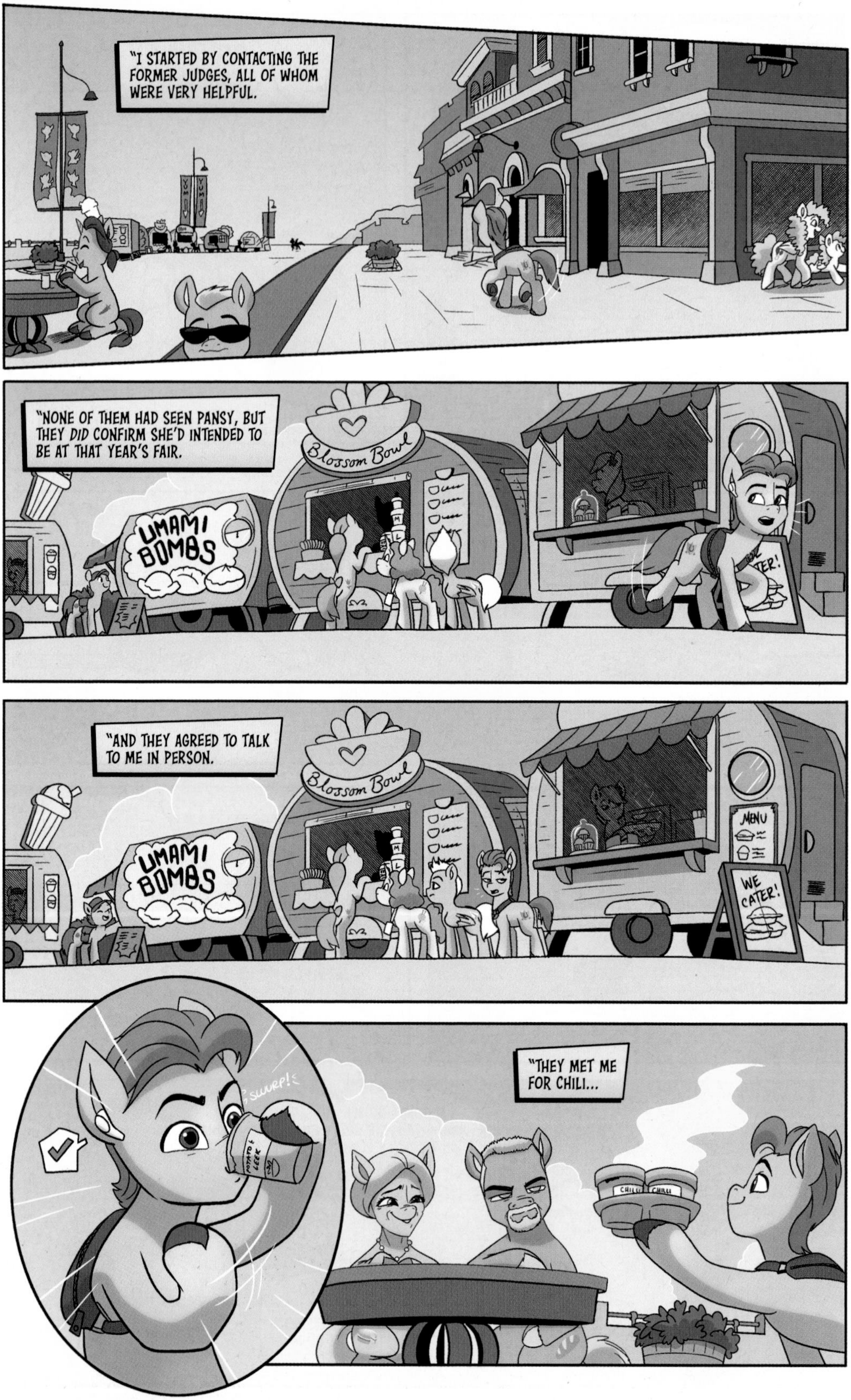
"I STARTED BY CONTACTING THE FORMER JUDGES, ALL OF WHOM WERE VERY HELPFUL.
"NONE OF THEM HAD SEEN PANSY, BUT THEY *DID* CONFIRM SHE'D INTENDED TO BE AT THAT YEAR'S FAIR.
Blossom Bowl
UMAMI BOMBS
"AND THEY AGREED TO TALK TO ME IN PERSON.
Blossom Bowl
UMAMI BOMBS
MENU
WE CATER!
SLUURP!
POTATO & LEEK
"THEY MET ME FOR CHILI...
CHILI
CHILI

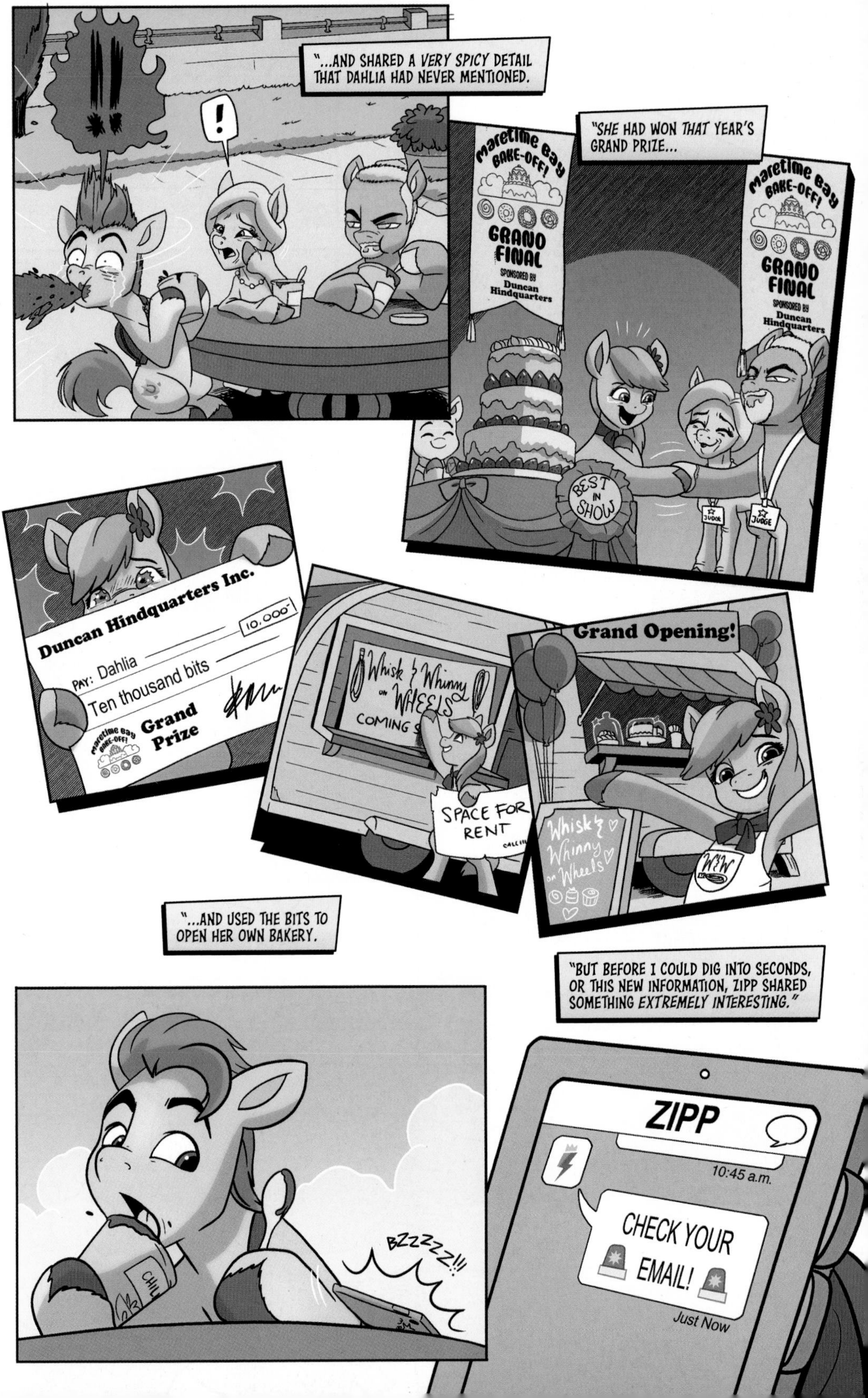
"...AND SHARED A VERY SPICY DETAIL THAT DAHLIA HAD NEVER MENTIONED.
!
"SHE HAD WON THAT YEAR'S GRAND PRIZE...
Maretime Bay BAKE-OFF! GRAND FINAL SPONSORED BY Duncan Hindquarters
Maretime Bay BAKE-OFF! GRAND FINAL SPONSORED BY Duncan Hindquarters
BEST IN SHOW
JUDGE
JUDGE
Duncan Hindquarters Inc.
10,000
PAY: Dahlia
Ten thousand bits
Maretime Bay BAKE-OFF!
Grand Prize
Whisk & Whinny on WHEELS
COMING S
SPACE FOR RENT
Grand Opening!
Whisk & Whinny on Wheels
W&W
"...AND USED THE BITS TO OPEN HER OWN BAKERY.
"BUT BEFORE I COULD DIG INTO SECONDS, OR THIS NEW INFORMATION, ZIPP SHARED SOMETHING EXTREMELY INTERESTING."
BZZZZZ!!!
ZIPP
10:45 a.m.
CHECK YOUR EMAIL!
Just Now

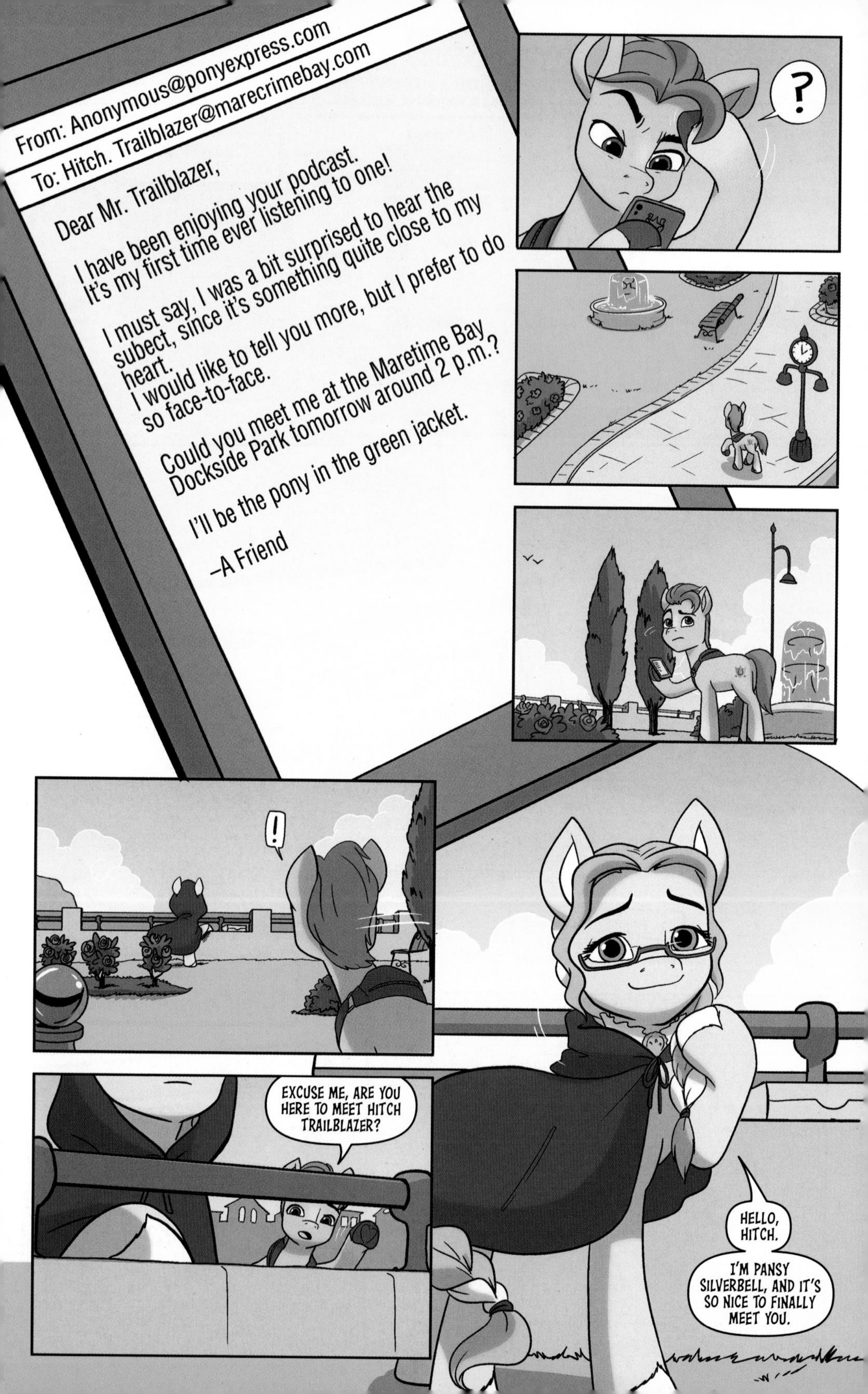

From: Anonymous@ponyexpress.com
To: Hitch. Trailblazer@marecrimebay.com
Dear Mr. Trailblazer,
I have been enjoying your podcast. It's my first time ever listening to one!
I must say, I was a bit surprised to hear the subect, since it's something quite close to my heart.
I would like to tell you more, but I prefer to do so face-to-face.
Could you meet me at the Maretime Bay Dockside Park tomorrow around 2 p.m.?
I'll be the pony in the green jacket.
–A Friend
?
!
EXCUSE ME, ARE YOU HERE TO MEET HITCH TRAILBLAZER?
HELLO, HITCH.
I'M PANSY SILVERBELL, AND IT'S SO NICE TO FINALLY MEET YOU.

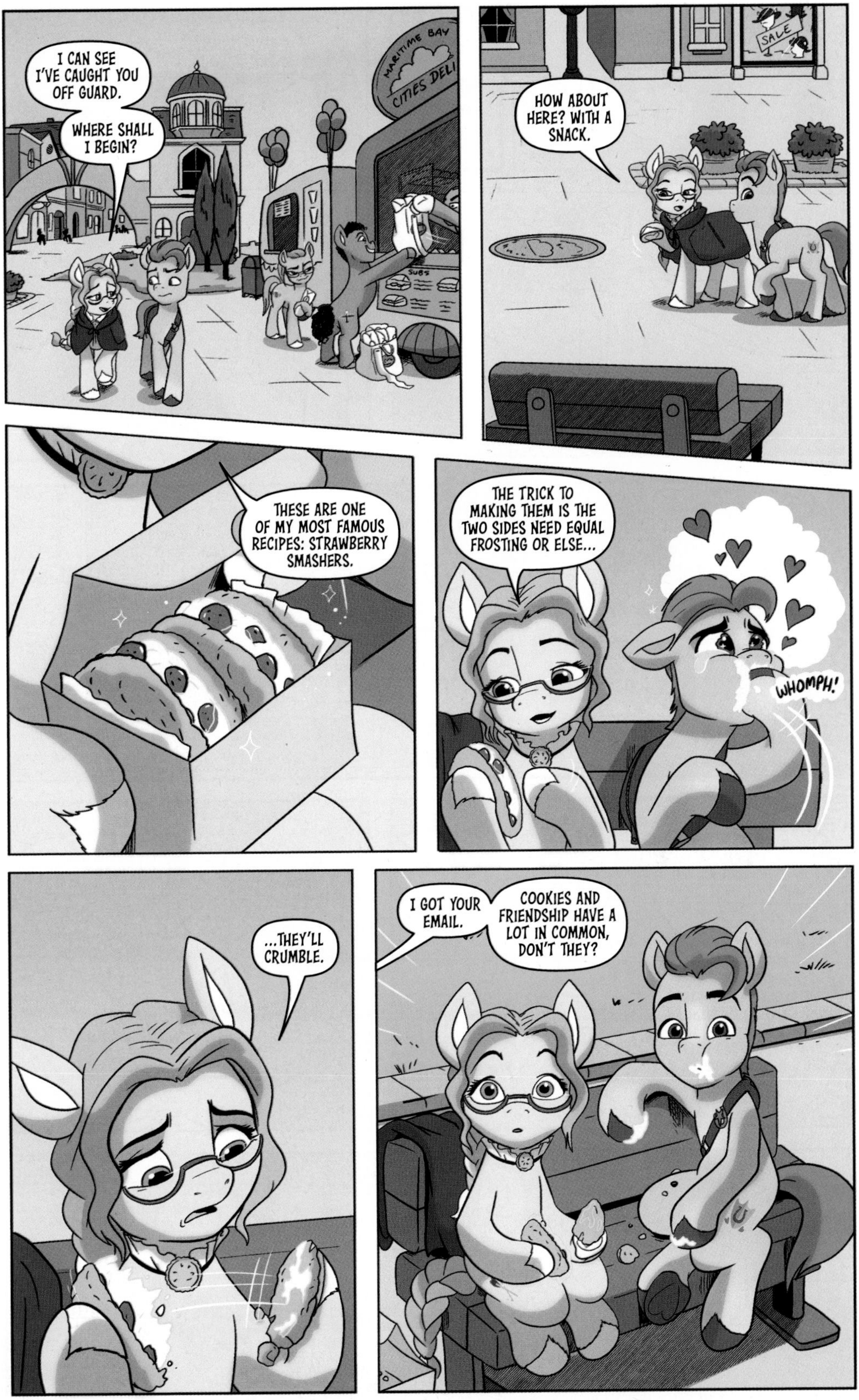
I CAN SEE I'VE CAUGHT YOU OFF GUARD.
WHERE SHALL I BEGIN?
MARITIME BAY CITIES DELI
SUBS
SALE
HOW ABOUT HERE? WITH A SNACK.
THESE ARE ONE OF MY MOST FAMOUS RECIPES: STRAWBERRY SMASHERS.
THE TRICK TO MAKING THEM IS THE TWO SIDES NEED EQUAL FROSTING OR ELSE...
WHOMPH!
...THEY'LL CRUMBLE.
I GOT YOUR EMAIL.
COOKIES AND FRIENDSHIP HAVE A LOT IN COMMON, DON'T THEY?

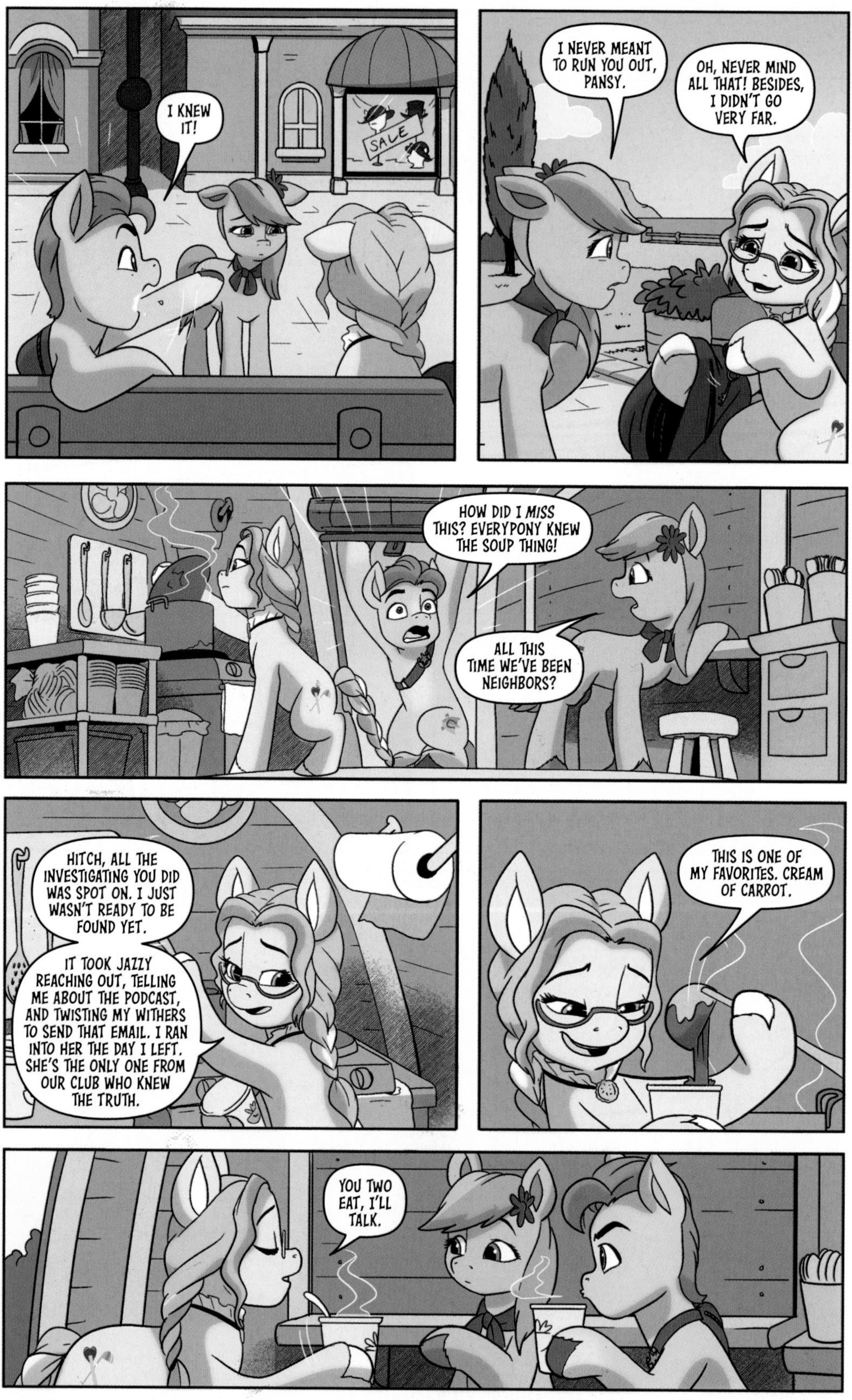

I KNEW IT!
SALE
I NEVER MEANT TO RUN YOU OUT, PANSY.
OH, NEVER MIND ALL THAT! BESIDES, I DIDN'T GO VERY FAR.
HOW DID I *MISS* THIS? EVERYPONY KNEW THE SOUP THING!
ALL THIS TIME WE'VE BEEN NEIGHBORS?
HITCH, ALL THE INVESTIGATING YOU DID WAS SPOT ON. I JUST WASN'T READY TO BE FOUND YET.
IT TOOK JAZZY REACHING OUT, TELLING ME ABOUT THE PODCAST, AND TWISTING MY WITHERS TO SEND THAT EMAIL. I RAN INTO HER THE DAY I LEFT. SHE'S THE ONLY ONE FROM OUR CLUB WHO KNEW THE TRUTH.
THIS IS ONE OF MY FAVORITES. CREAM OF CARROT.
YOU TWO EAT, I'LL TALK.

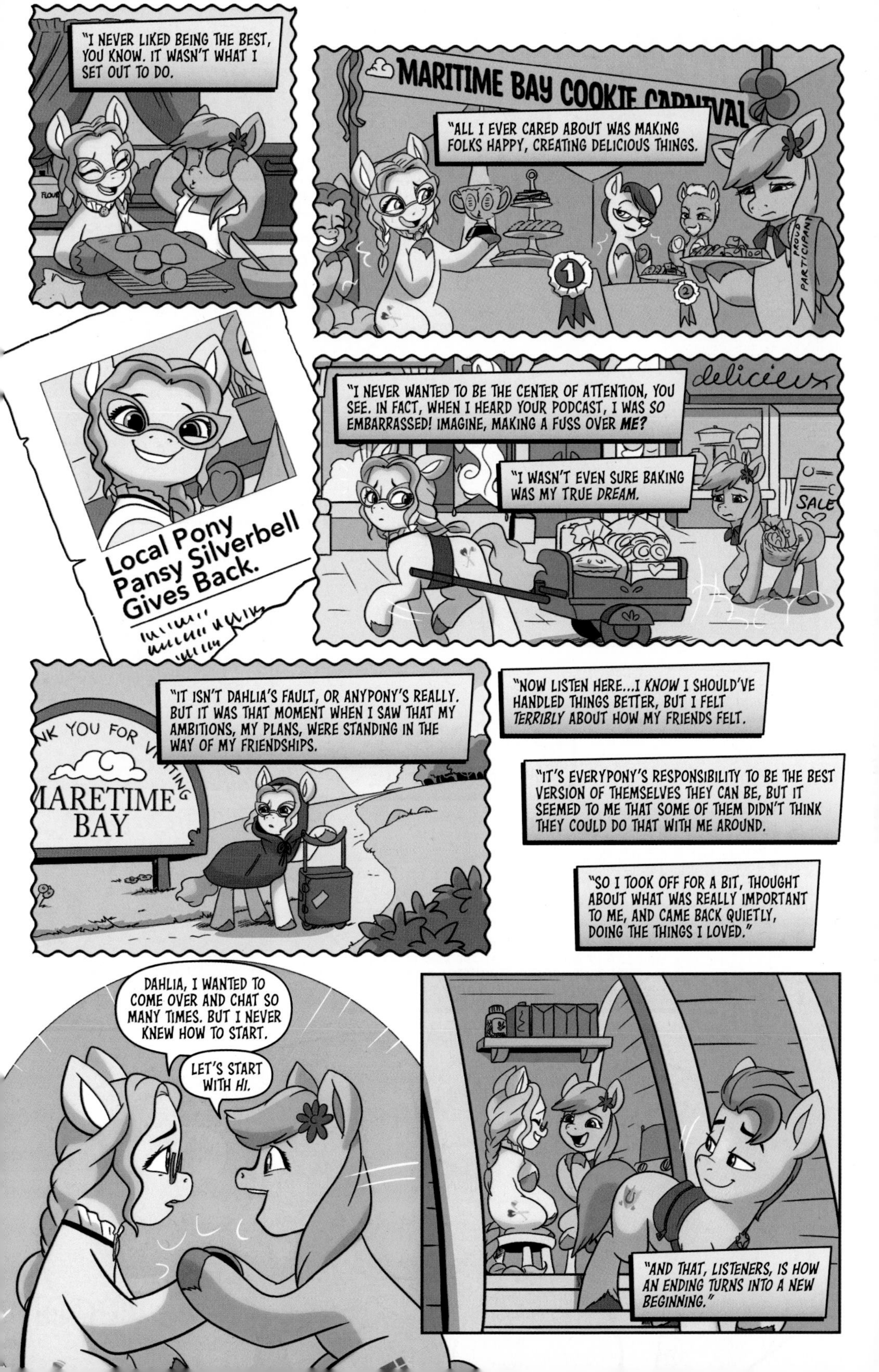
"I NEVER LIKED BEING THE BEST, YOU KNOW. IT WASN'T WHAT I SET OUT TO DO.
FLOUR
MARITIME BAY COOKIE CARNIVAL
"ALL I EVER CARED ABOUT WAS MAKING FOLKS HAPPY, CREATING DELICIOUS THINGS.
1
2
PROUD PARTICIPANT
Local Pony Pansy Silverbell Gives Back.
delicieux
"I NEVER WANTED TO BE THE CENTER OF ATTENTION, YOU SEE. IN FACT, WHEN I HEARD YOUR PODCAST, I WAS *SO* EMBARRASSED! IMAGINE, MAKING A FUSS OVER ***ME?***
"I WASN'T EVEN SURE BAKING WAS MY TRUE *DREAM.*
SALE
"IT ISN'T DAHLIA'S FAULT, OR ANYPONY'S REALLY. BUT IT WAS THAT MOMENT WHEN I SAW THAT MY AMBITIONS, MY PLANS, WERE STANDING IN THE WAY OF MY FRIENDSHIPS.
NK YOU FOR VISITING
MARETIME BAY
"NOW LISTEN HERE...I *KNOW* I SHOULD'VE HANDLED THINGS BETTER, BUT I FELT *TERRIBLY* ABOUT HOW MY FRIENDS FELT.
"IT'S EVERYPONY'S RESPONSIBILITY TO BE THE BEST VERSION OF THEMSELVES THEY CAN BE, BUT IT SEEMED TO ME THAT SOME OF THEM DIDN'T THINK THEY COULD DO THAT WITH ME AROUND.
"SO I TOOK OFF FOR A BIT, THOUGHT ABOUT WHAT WAS REALLY IMPORTANT TO ME, AND CAME BACK QUIETLY, DOING THE THINGS I LOVED."
DAHLIA, I WANTED TO COME OVER AND CHAT SO MANY TIMES. BUT I NEVER KNEW HOW TO START.
LET'S START WITH *HI.*
"AND THAT, LISTENERS, IS HOW AN ENDING TURNS INTO A NEW BEGINNING."

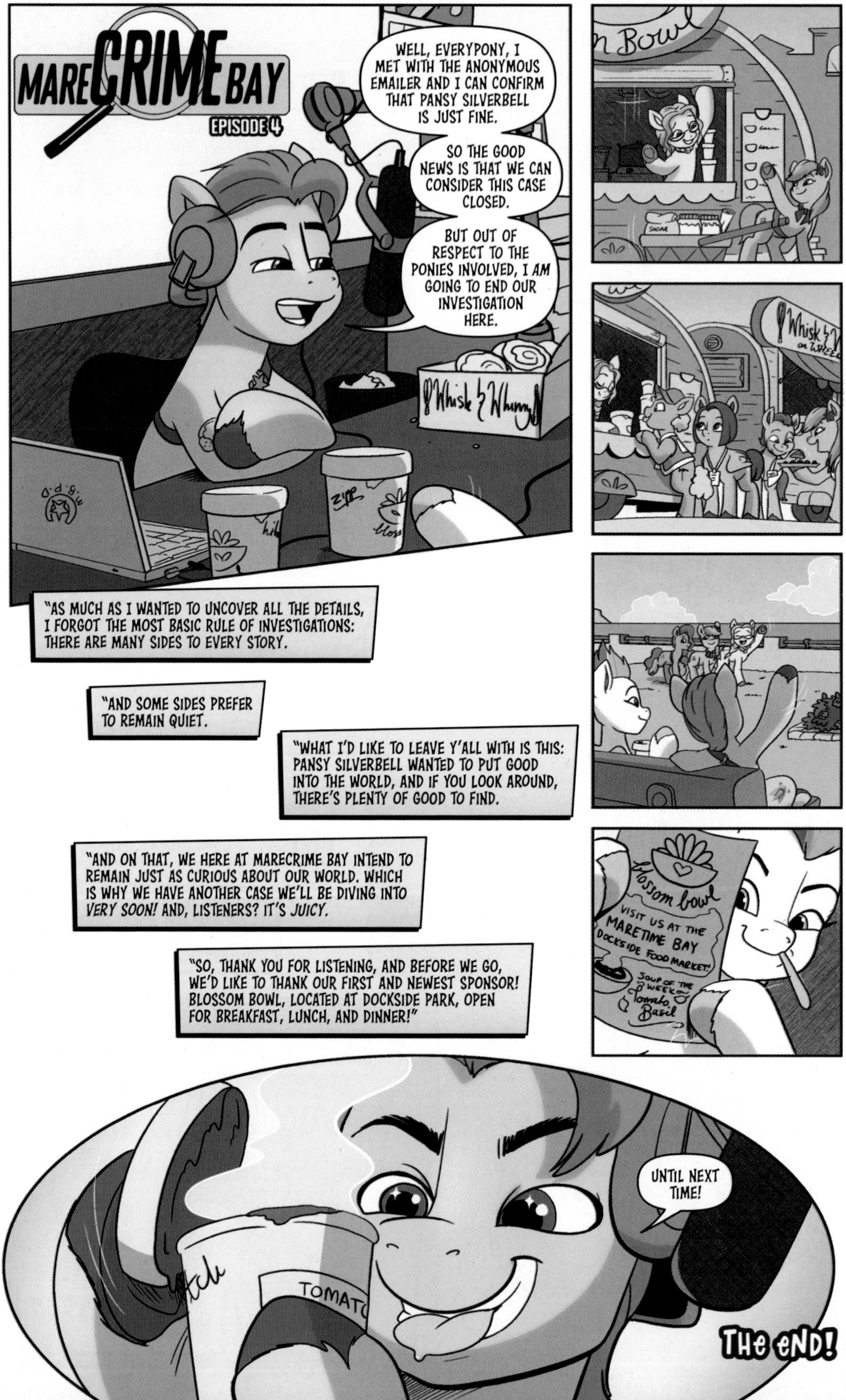
MARECRIME BAY
EPISODE 4
WELL, EVERYPONY, I MET WITH THE ANONYMOUS EMAILER AND I CAN CONFIRM THAT PANSY SILVERBELL IS JUST FINE.
SO THE GOOD NEWS IS THAT WE CAN CONSIDER THIS CASE CLOSED.
BUT OUT OF RESPECT TO THE PONIES INVOLVED, I *AM* GOING TO END OUR INVESTIGATION HERE.
Whisk & Whinny
SUGAR
"AS MUCH AS I WANTED TO UNCOVER ALL THE DETAILS, I FORGOT THE MOST BASIC RULE OF INVESTIGATIONS: THERE ARE MANY SIDES TO EVERY STORY.
"AND SOME SIDES PREFER TO REMAIN QUIET.
"WHAT I'D LIKE TO LEAVE Y'ALL WITH IS THIS: PANSY SILVERBELL WANTED TO PUT GOOD INTO THE WORLD, AND IF YOU LOOK AROUND, THERE'S PLENTY OF GOOD TO FIND.
"AND ON THAT, WE HERE AT MARECRIME BAY INTEND TO REMAIN JUST AS CURIOUS ABOUT OUR WORLD. WHICH IS WHY WE HAVE ANOTHER CASE WE'LL BE DIVING INTO *VERY SOON!* AND, LISTENERS? IT'S *JUICY.*
"SO, THANK YOU FOR LISTENING, AND BEFORE WE GO, WE'D LIKE TO THANK OUR FIRST AND NEWEST SPONSOR! BLOSSOM BOWL, LOCATED AT DOCKSIDE PARK, OPEN FOR BREAKFAST, LUNCH, AND DINNER!"
blossom bowl
VISIT US AT THE MARETIME BAY DOCKSIDE FOOD MARKET!
SOUP OF THE WEEK
Tomato Basil
UNTIL NEXT TIME!
TOMATO
THE END!

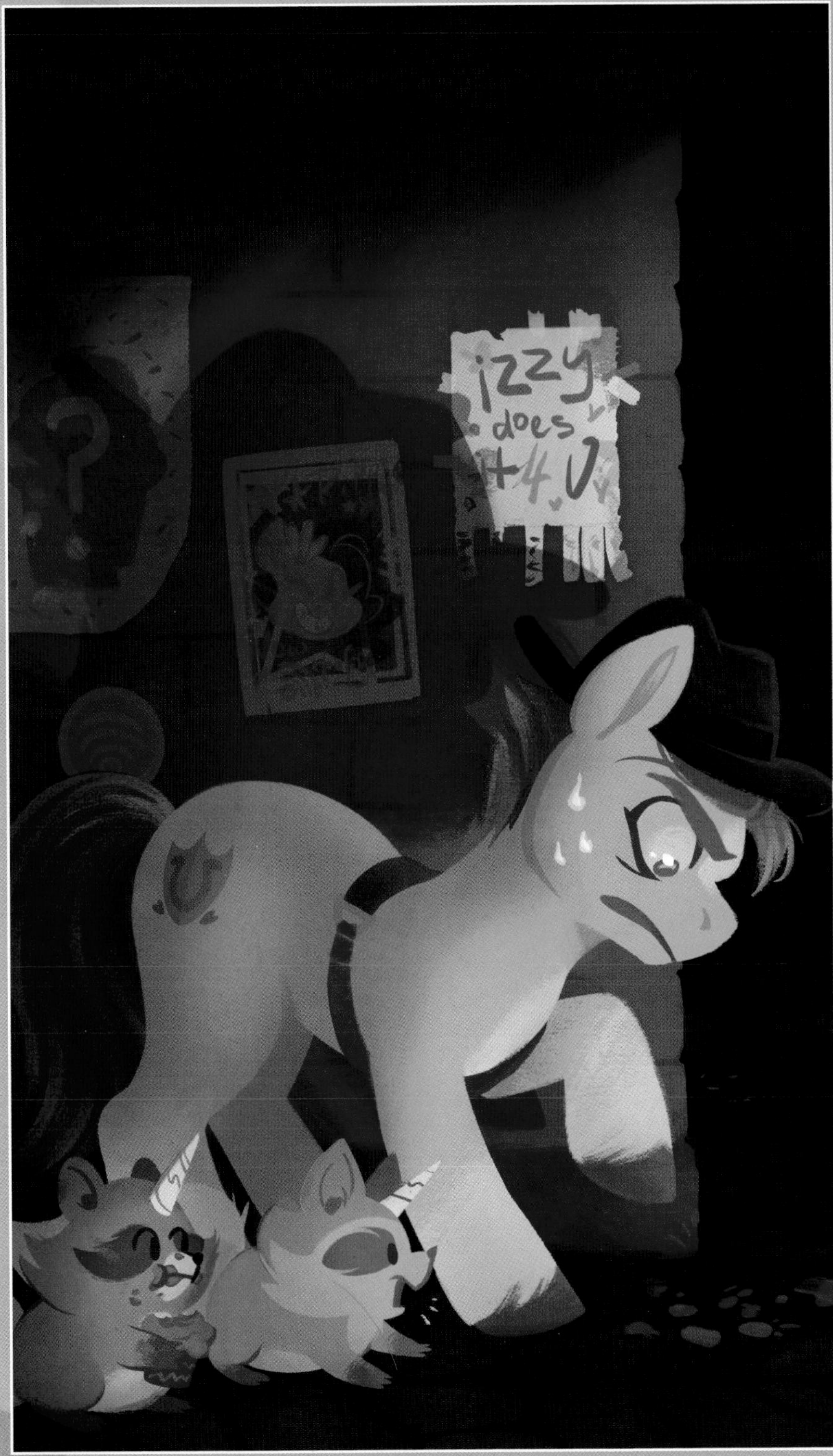
izzy does it 4 U

art by JustaSuta

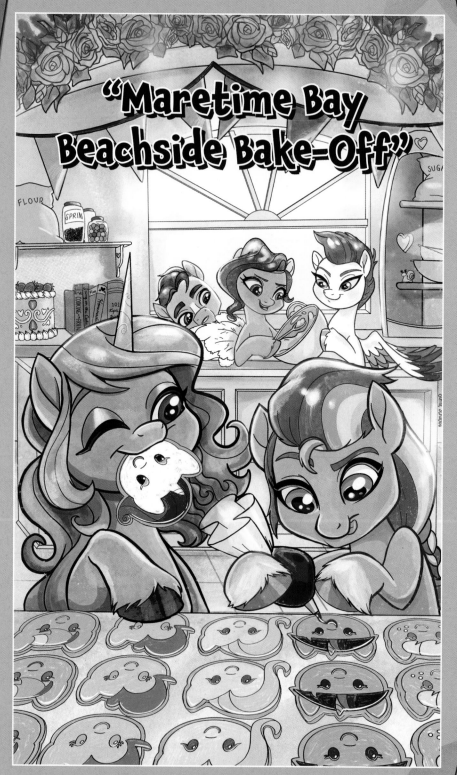

"Maretime Bay Beachside Bake-Off"

art by **Sophie Scruggs**

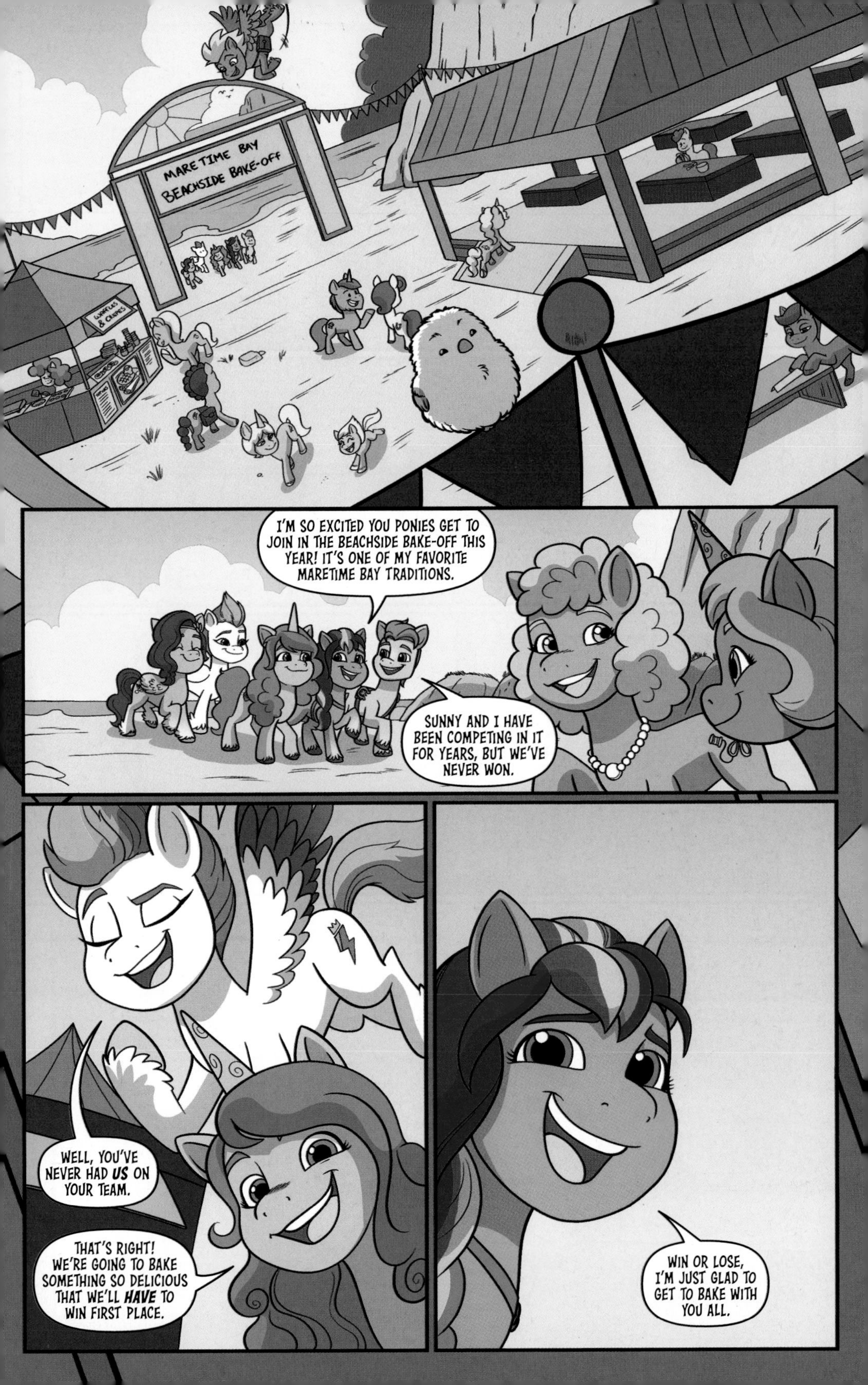
MARE TIME BAY
BEACHSIDE BAKE-OFF
WAFFLES & CREPES
I'M SO EXCITED YOU PONIES GET TO JOIN IN THE BEACHSIDE BAKE-OFF THIS YEAR! IT'S ONE OF MY FAVORITE MARETIME BAY TRADITIONS.
SUNNY AND I HAVE BEEN COMPETING IN IT FOR YEARS, BUT WE'VE NEVER WON.
WELL, YOU'VE NEVER HAD **US** ON YOUR TEAM.
THAT'S RIGHT! WE'RE GOING TO BAKE SOMETHING SO DELICIOUS THAT WE'LL ***HAVE*** TO WIN FIRST PLACE.
WIN OR LOSE, I'M JUST GLAD TO GET TO BAKE WITH YOU ALL.

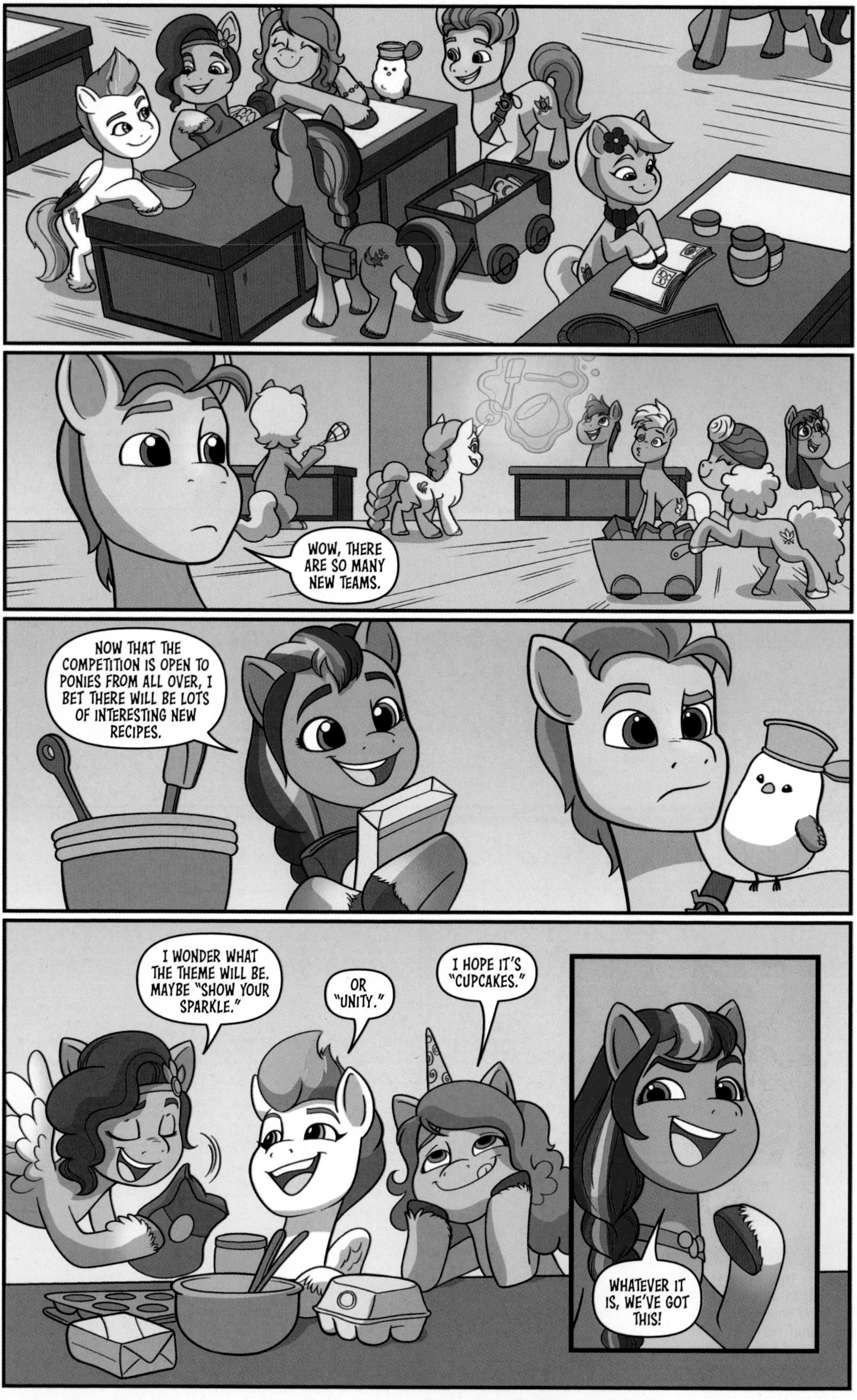
WOW, THERE ARE SO MANY NEW TEAMS.
NOW THAT THE COMPETITION IS OPEN TO PONIES FROM ALL OVER, I BET THERE WILL BE LOTS OF INTERESTING NEW RECIPES.
I WONDER WHAT THE THEME WILL BE. MAYBE "SHOW YOUR SPARKLE."
OR "UNITY."
I HOPE IT'S "CUPCAKES."
WHATEVER IT IS, WE'VE GOT THIS!

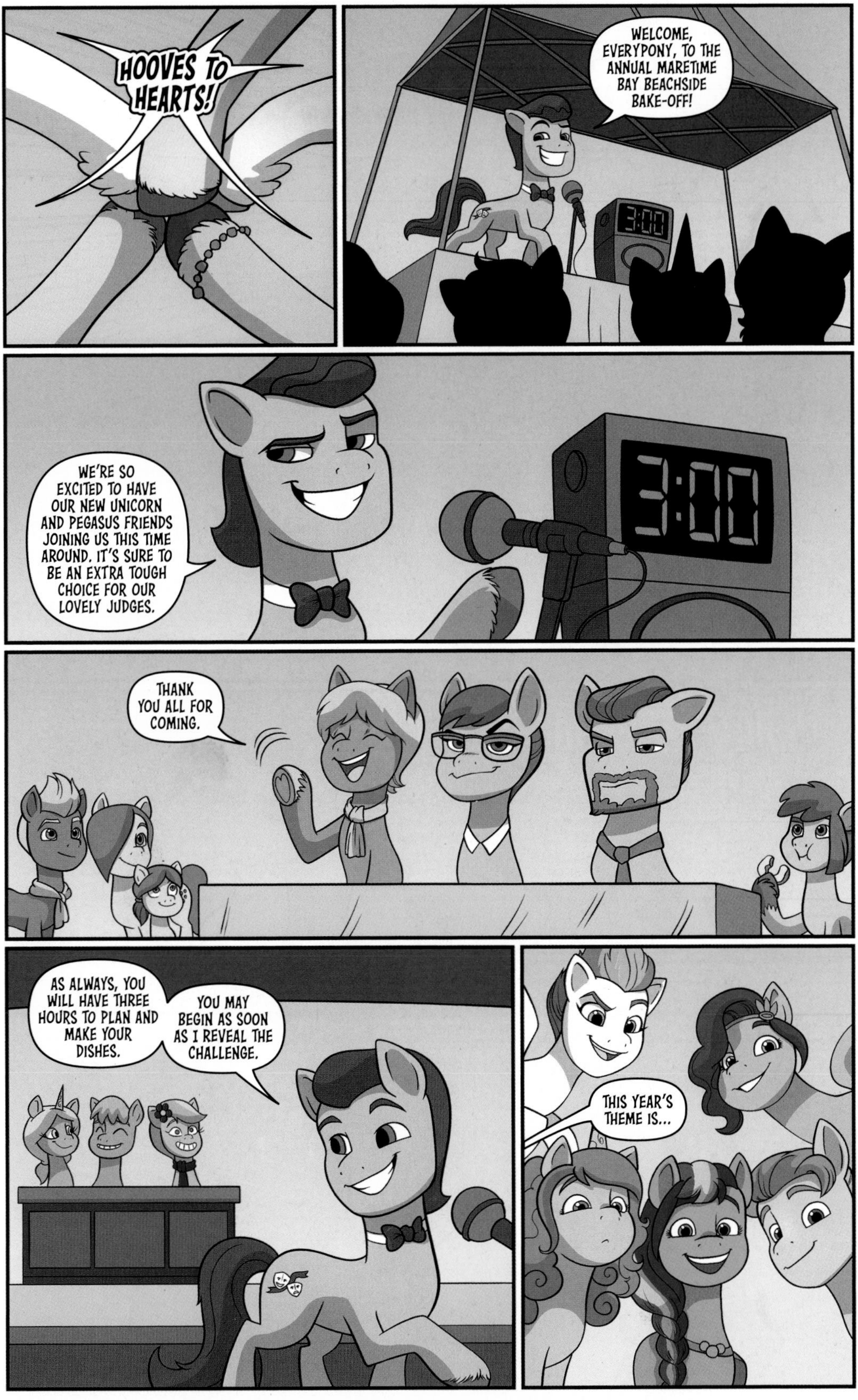
HOOVES TO HEARTS!
WELCOME, EVERYPONY, TO THE ANNUAL MARETIME BAY BEACHSIDE BAKE-OFF!
3:00
WE'RE SO EXCITED TO HAVE OUR NEW UNICORN AND PEGASUS FRIENDS JOINING US THIS TIME AROUND. IT'S SURE TO BE AN EXTRA TOUGH CHOICE FOR OUR LOVELY JUDGES.
3:00
THANK YOU ALL FOR COMING.
AS ALWAYS, YOU WILL HAVE THREE HOURS TO PLAN AND MAKE YOUR DISHES.
YOU MAY BEGIN AS SOON AS I REVEAL THE CHALLENGE.
THIS YEAR'S THEME IS...

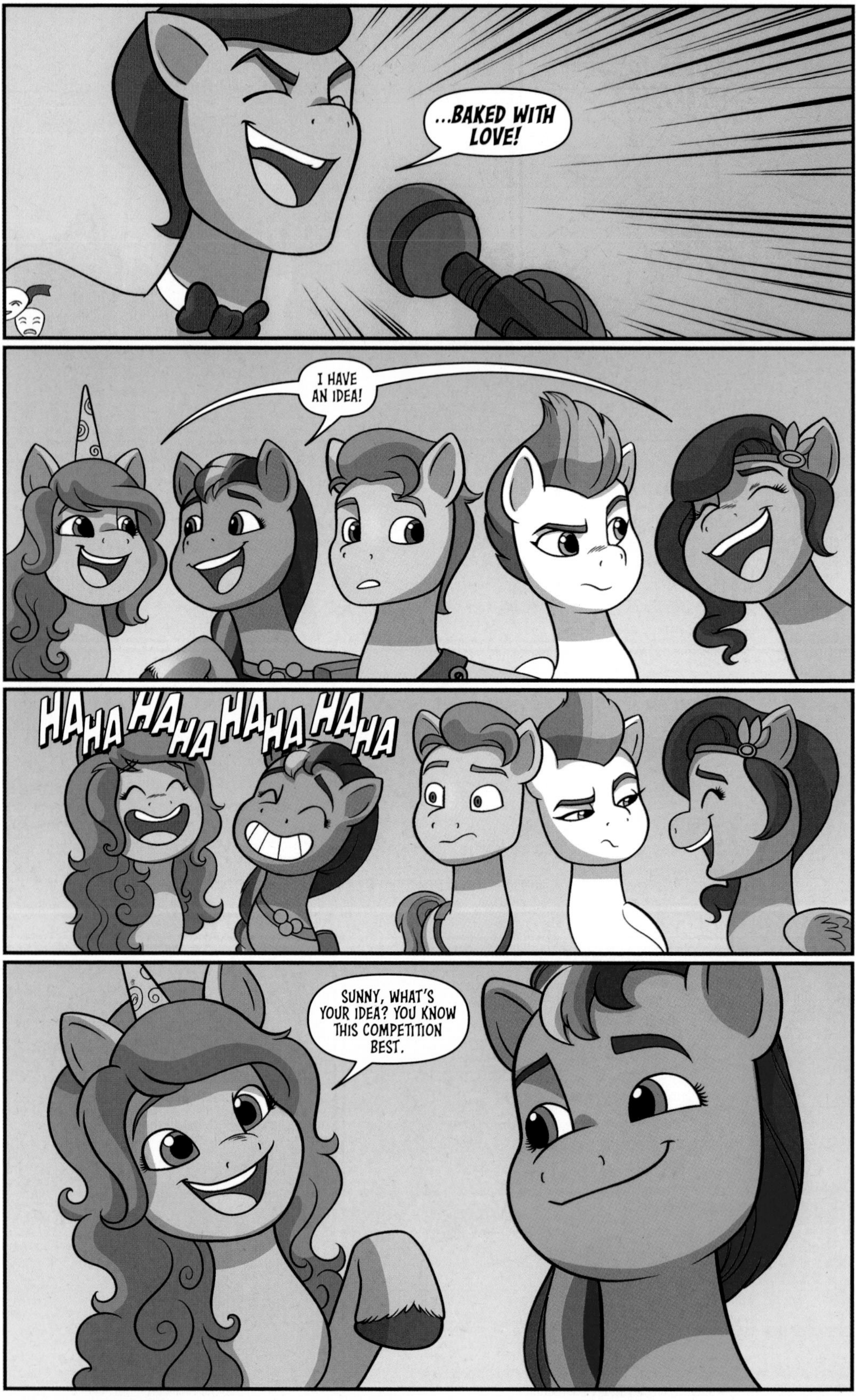
...BAKED WITH LOVE!
I HAVE AN IDEA!
HAHA HAHA HAHA HAHA
SUNNY, WHAT'S YOUR IDEA? YOU KNOW THIS COMPETITION BEST.

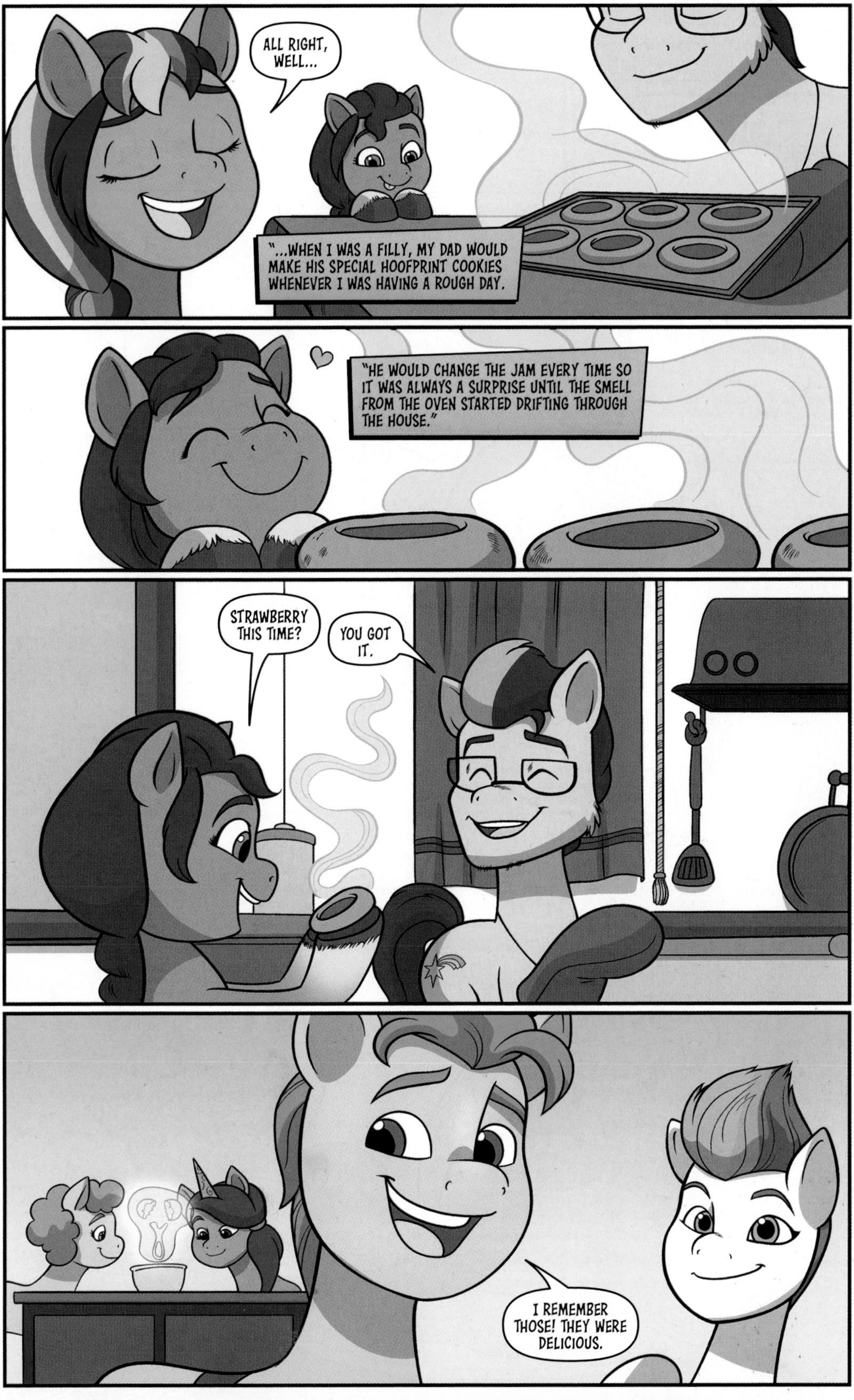
ALL RIGHT, WELL...
"...WHEN I WAS A FILLY, MY DAD WOULD MAKE HIS SPECIAL HOOFPRINT COOKIES WHENEVER I WAS HAVING A ROUGH DAY.
"HE WOULD CHANGE THE JAM EVERY TIME SO IT WAS ALWAYS A SURPRISE UNTIL THE SMELL FROM THE OVEN STARTED DRIFTING THROUGH THE HOUSE."
STRAWBERRY THIS TIME?
YOU GOT IT.
I REMEMBER THOSE! THEY WERE DELICIOUS.

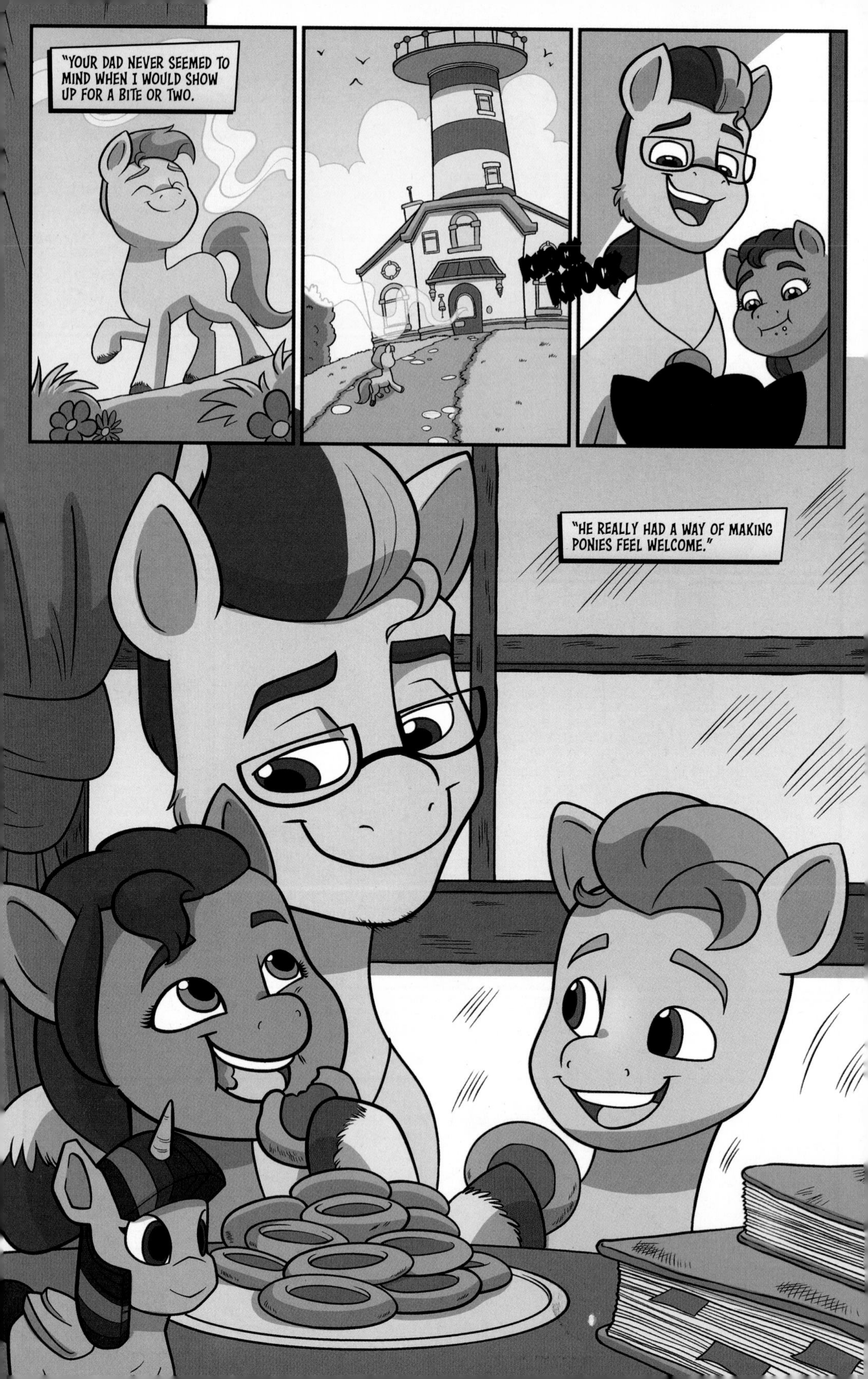
"YOUR DAD NEVER SEEMED TO MIND WHEN I WOULD SHOW UP FOR A BITE OR TWO.
KNOCK KNOCK
"HE REALLY HAD A WAY OF MAKING PONIES FEEL WELCOME."

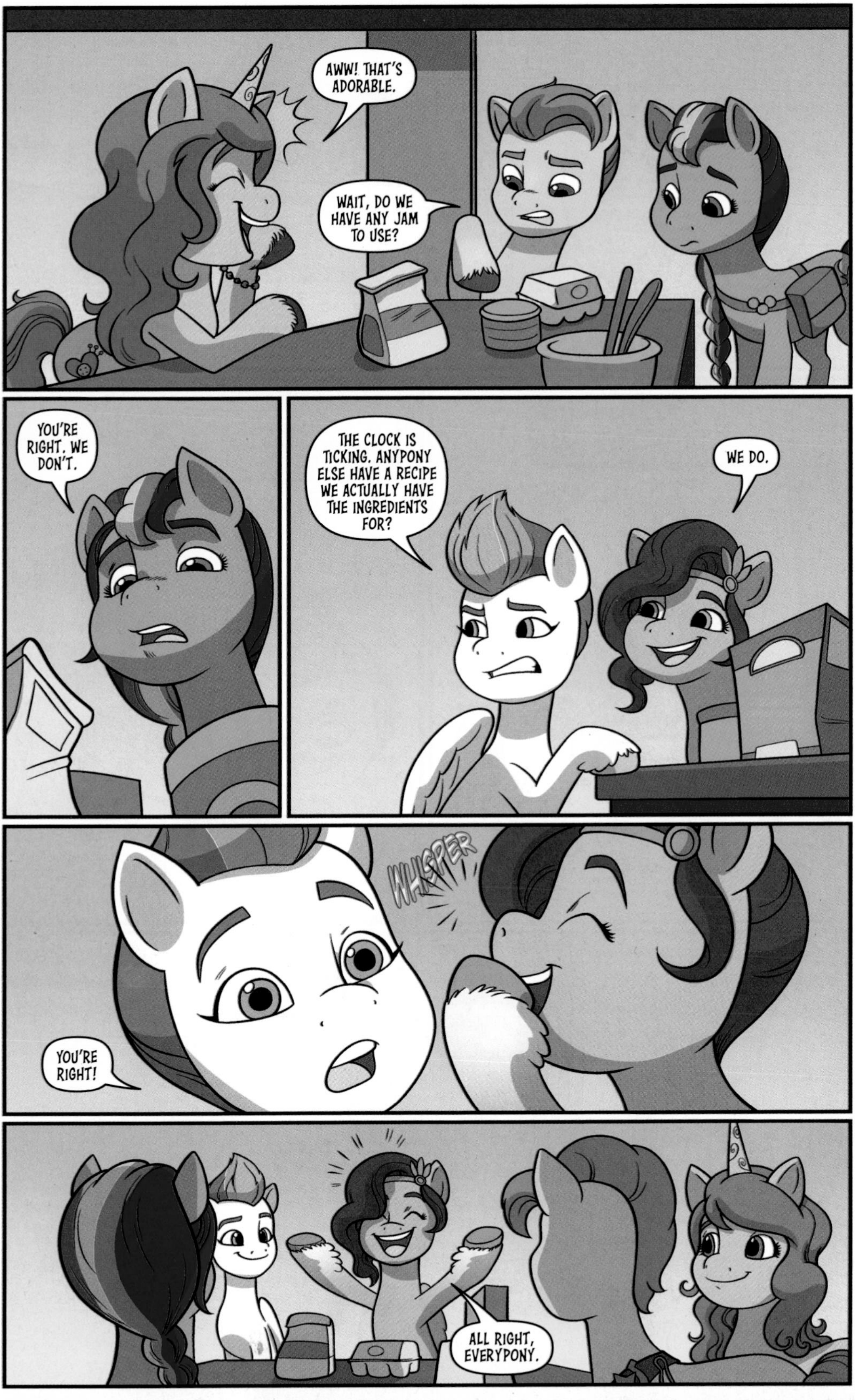
AWW! THAT'S ADORABLE.
WAIT, DO WE HAVE ANY JAM TO USE?
YOU'RE RIGHT. WE DON'T.
THE CLOCK IS TICKING. ANYPONY ELSE HAVE A RECIPE WE ACTUALLY HAVE THE INGREDIENTS FOR?
WE DO.
WHISPER
YOU'RE RIGHT!
ALL RIGHT, EVERYPONY.

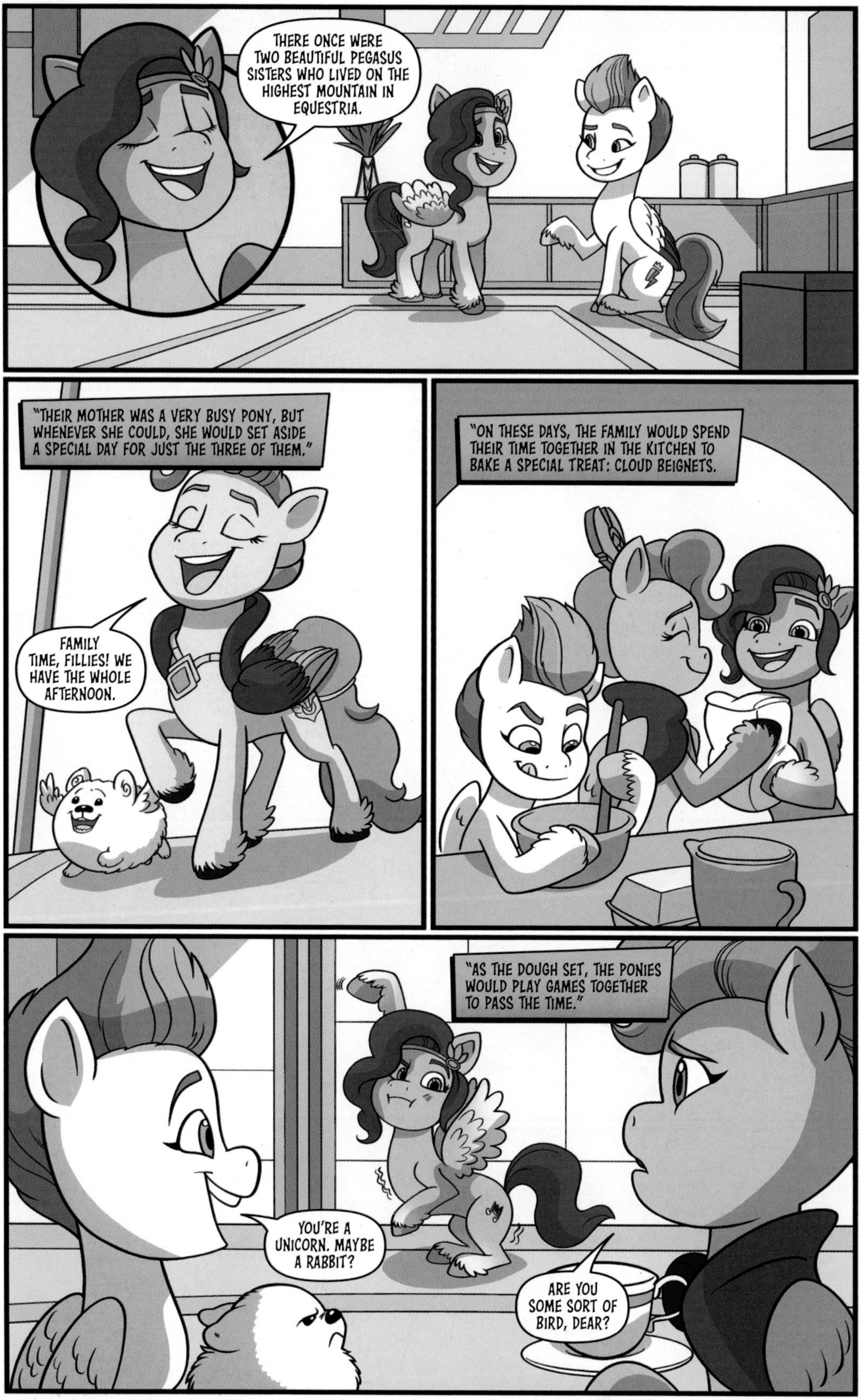
THERE ONCE WERE TWO BEAUTIFUL PEGASUS SISTERS WHO LIVED ON THE HIGHEST MOUNTAIN IN EQUESTRIA.
"THEIR MOTHER WAS A VERY BUSY PONY, BUT WHENEVER SHE COULD, SHE WOULD SET ASIDE A SPECIAL DAY FOR JUST THE THREE OF THEM."
FAMILY TIME, FILLIES! WE HAVE THE WHOLE AFTERNOON.
"ON THESE DAYS, THE FAMILY WOULD SPEND THEIR TIME TOGETHER IN THE KITCHEN TO BAKE A SPECIAL TREAT: CLOUD BEIGNETS.
"AS THE DOUGH SET, THE PONIES WOULD PLAY GAMES TOGETHER TO PASS THE TIME."
YOU'RE A UNICORN. MAYBE A RABBIT?
ARE YOU SOME SORT OF BIRD, DEAR?

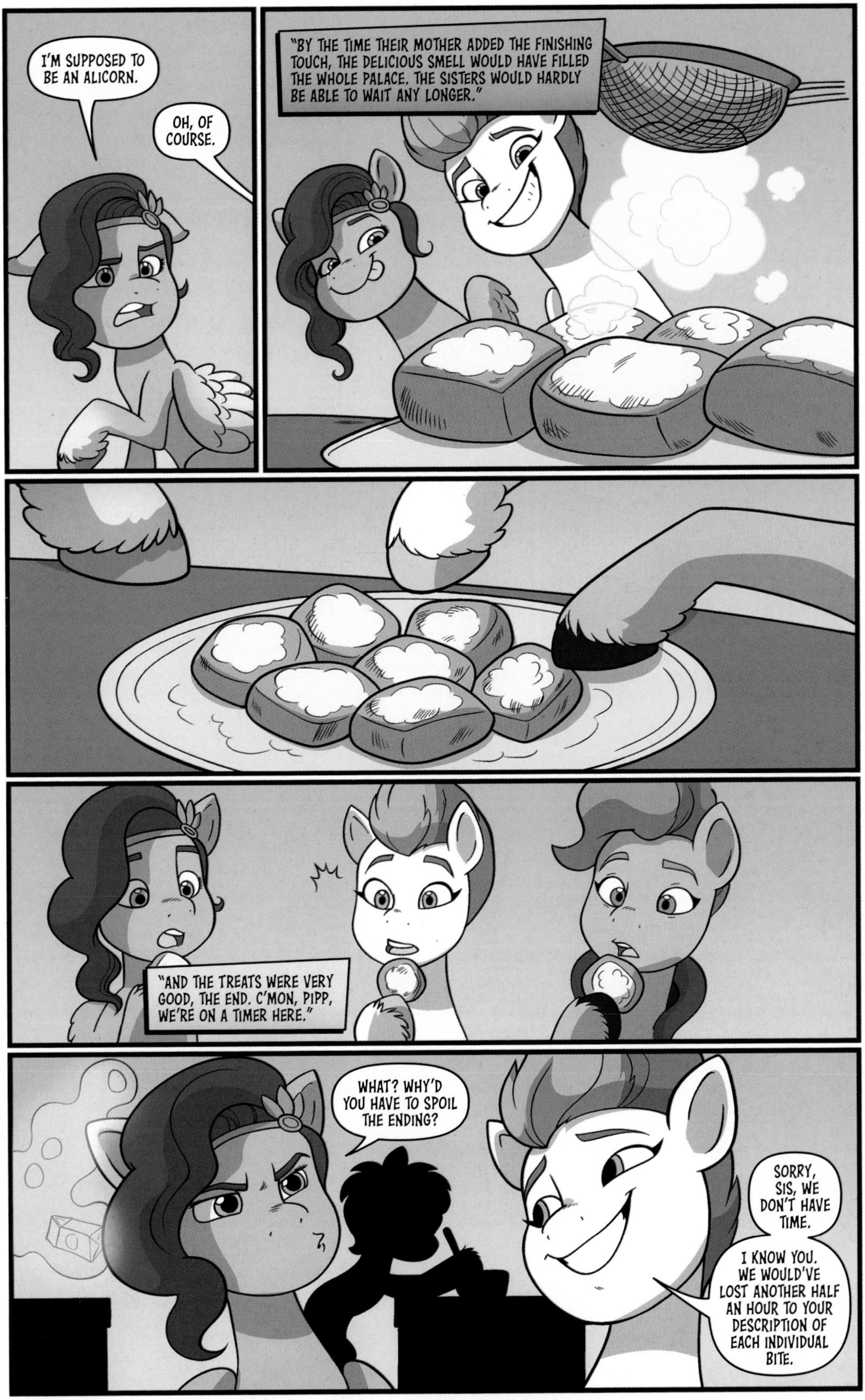
I'M SUPPOSED TO BE AN ALICORN.
OH, OF COURSE.
"BY THE TIME THEIR MOTHER ADDED THE FINISHING TOUCH, THE DELICIOUS SMELL WOULD HAVE FILLED THE WHOLE PALACE. THE SISTERS WOULD HARDLY BE ABLE TO WAIT ANY LONGER."
"AND THE TREATS WERE VERY GOOD, THE END. C'MON, PIPP, WE'RE ON A TIMER HERE."
WHAT? WHY'D YOU HAVE TO SPOIL THE ENDING?
SORRY, SIS, WE DON'T HAVE TIME.
I KNOW YOU. WE WOULD'VE LOST ANOTHER HALF AN HOUR TO YOUR DESCRIPTION OF EACH INDIVIDUAL BITE.

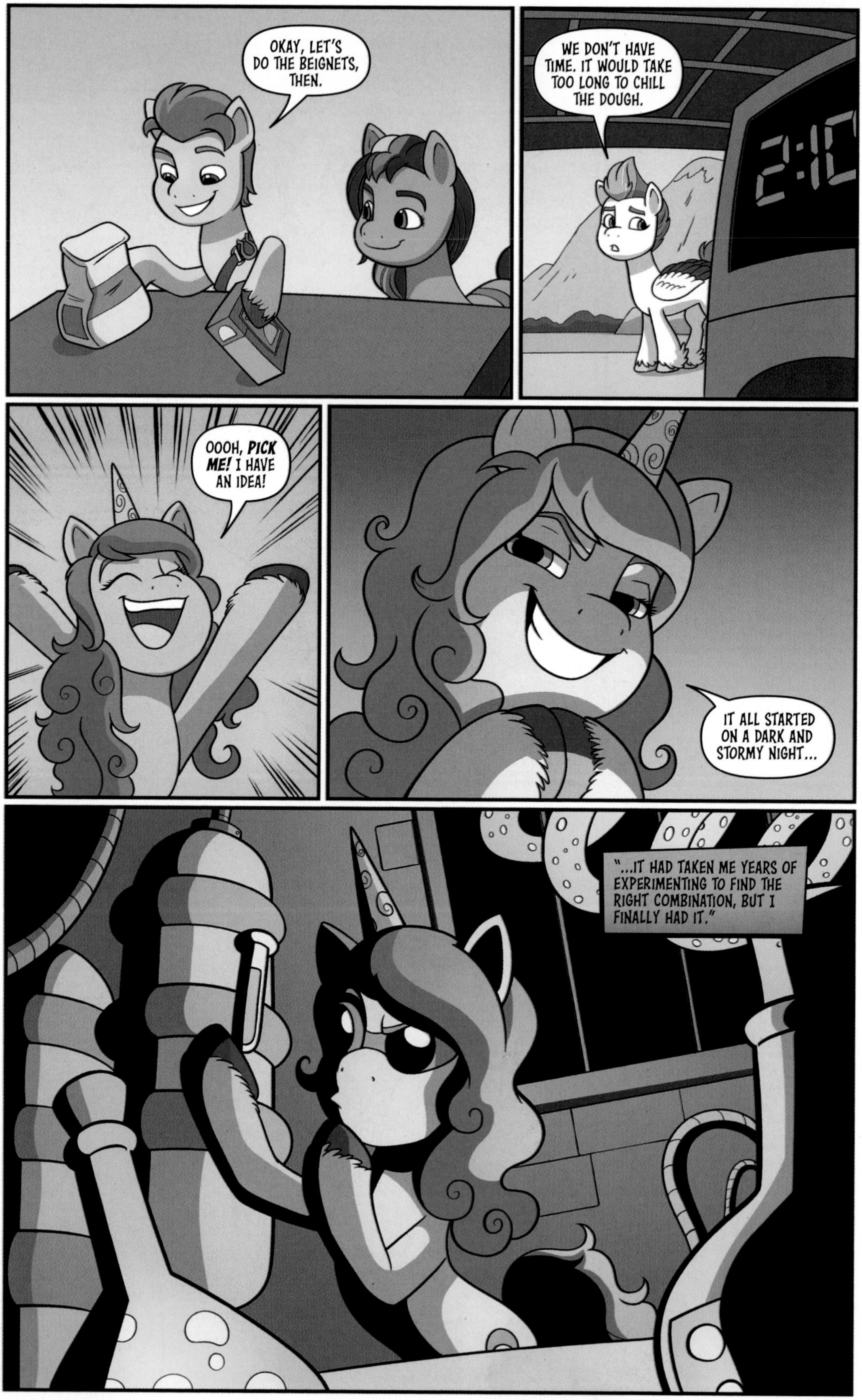
OKAY, LET'S DO THE BEIGNETS, THEN.
WE DON'T HAVE TIME. IT WOULD TAKE TOO LONG TO CHILL THE DOUGH.
2:10
OOOH, PICK ME! I HAVE AN IDEA!
IT ALL STARTED ON A DARK AND STORMY NIGHT...
"...IT HAD TAKEN ME YEARS OF EXPERIMENTING TO FIND THE RIGHT COMBINATION, BUT I FINALLY HAD IT."

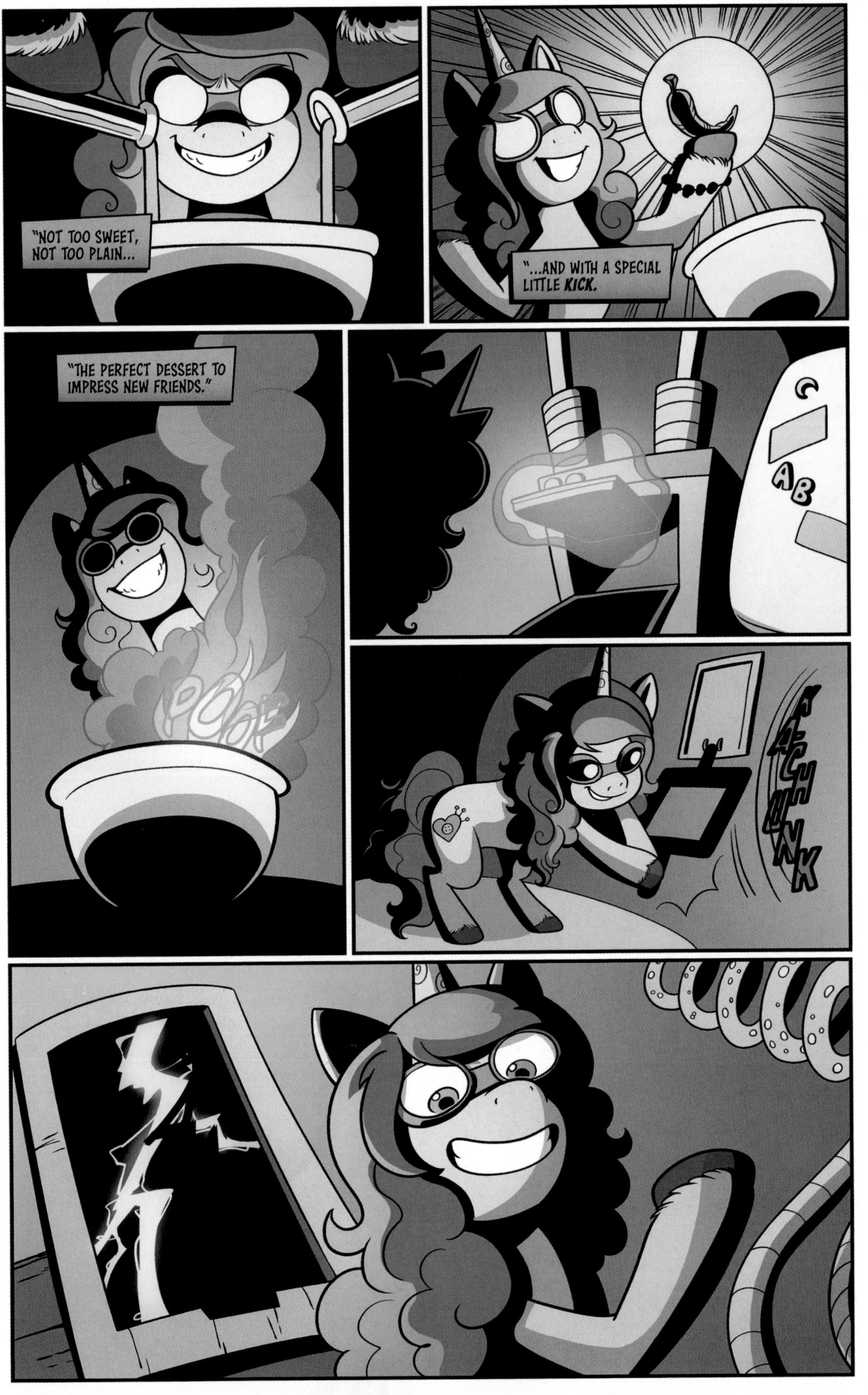
"NOT TOO SWEET, NOT TOO PLAIN...
"...AND WITH A SPECIAL LITTLE **KICK**.
"THE PERFECT DESSERT TO IMPRESS NEW FRIENDS."
POOF
KACHUNK

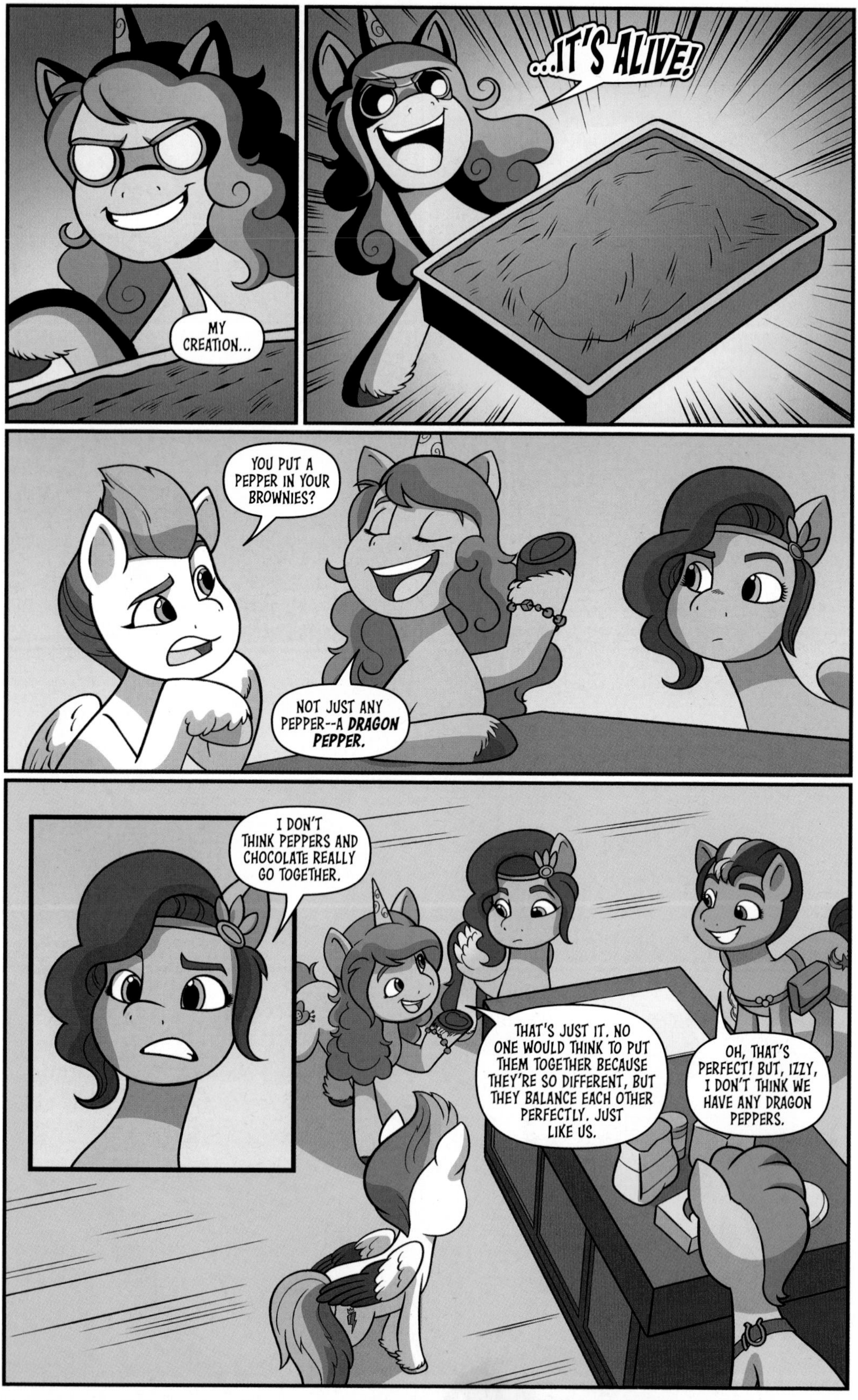
MY CREATION...
...IT'S ALIVE!
YOU PUT A PEPPER IN YOUR BROWNIES?
NOT JUST ANY PEPPER--A **DRAGON PEPPER.**
I DON'T THINK PEPPERS AND CHOCOLATE REALLY GO TOGETHER.
THAT'S JUST IT. NO ONE WOULD THINK TO PUT THEM TOGETHER BECAUSE THEY'RE SO DIFFERENT, BUT THEY BALANCE EACH OTHER PERFECTLY. JUST LIKE US.
OH, THAT'S PERFECT! BUT, IZZY, I DON'T THINK WE HAVE ANY DRAGON PEPPERS.

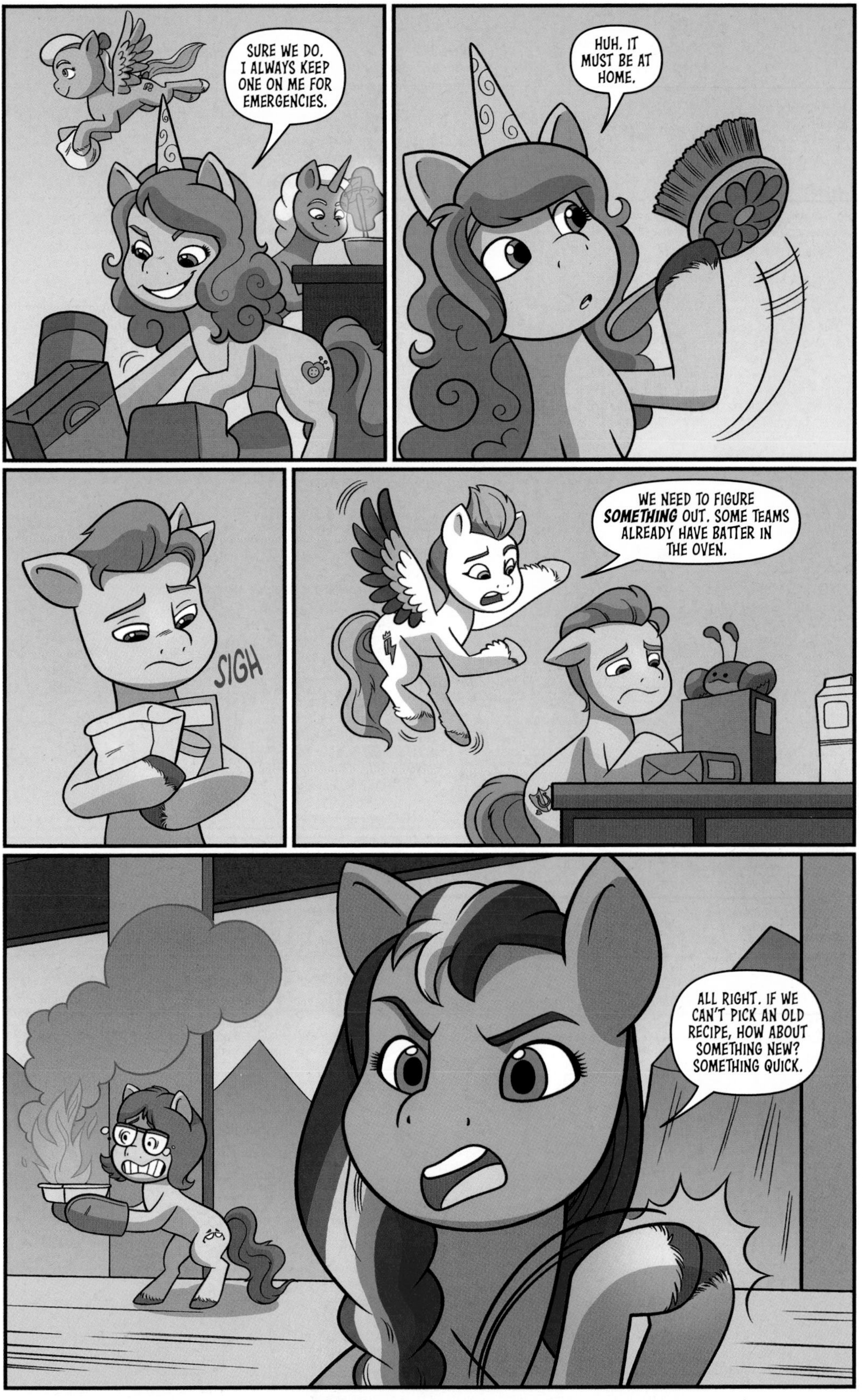
SURE WE DO. I ALWAYS KEEP ONE ON ME FOR EMERGENCIES.
HUH. IT MUST BE AT HOME.
SIGH
WE NEED TO FIGURE **SOMETHING** OUT. SOME TEAMS ALREADY HAVE BATTER IN THE OVEN.
ALL RIGHT. IF WE CAN'T PICK AN OLD RECIPE, HOW ABOUT SOMETHING NEW? SOMETHING QUICK.

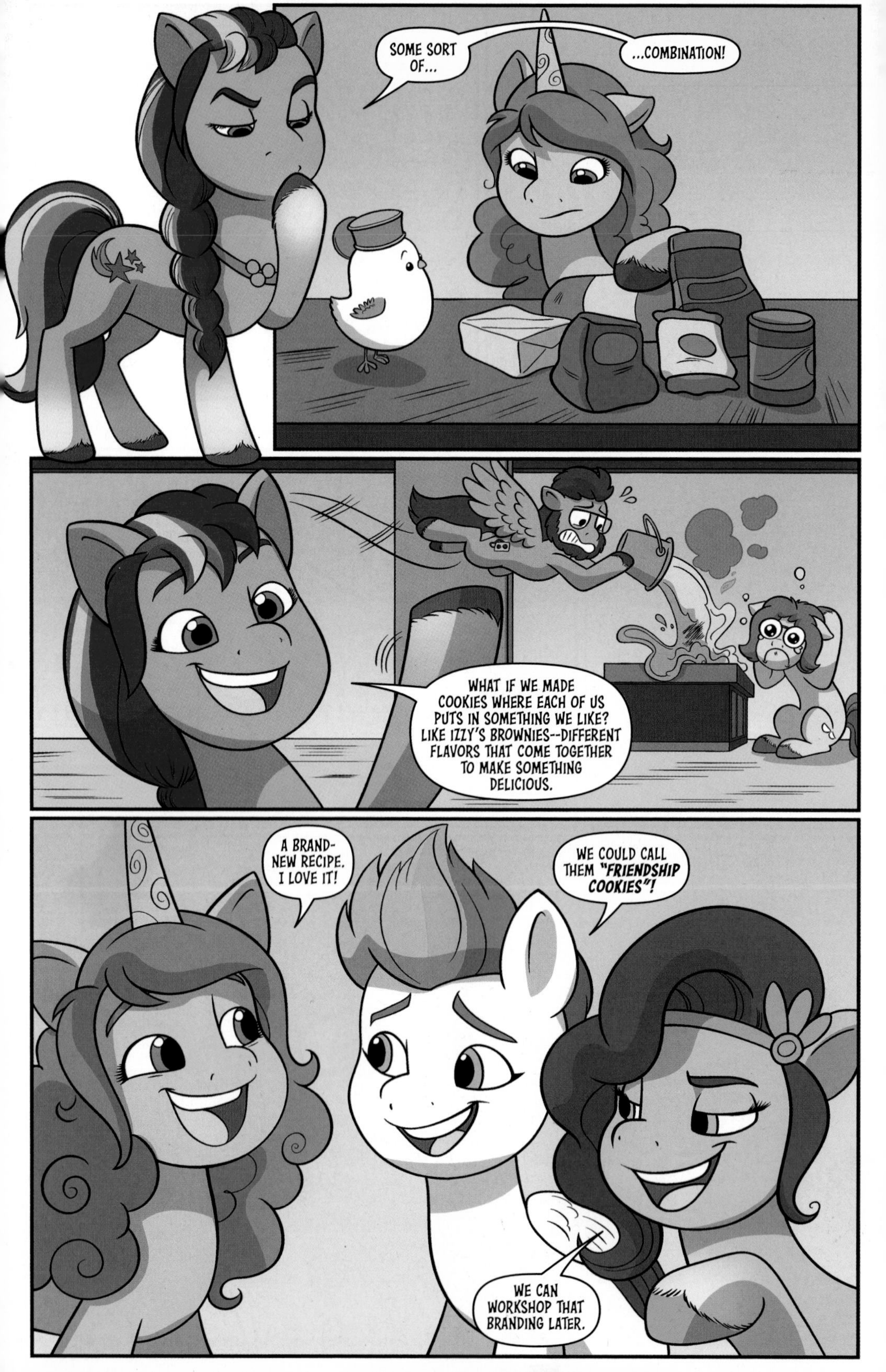
SOME SORT OF...
...COMBINATION!
WHAT IF WE MADE COOKIES WHERE EACH OF US PUTS IN SOMETHING WE LIKE? LIKE IZZY'S BROWNIES--DIFFERENT FLAVORS THAT COME TOGETHER TO MAKE SOMETHING DELICIOUS.
A BRAND-NEW RECIPE. I LOVE IT!
WE COULD CALL THEM "FRIENDSHIP COOKIES"!
WE CAN WORKSHOP THAT BRANDING LATER.

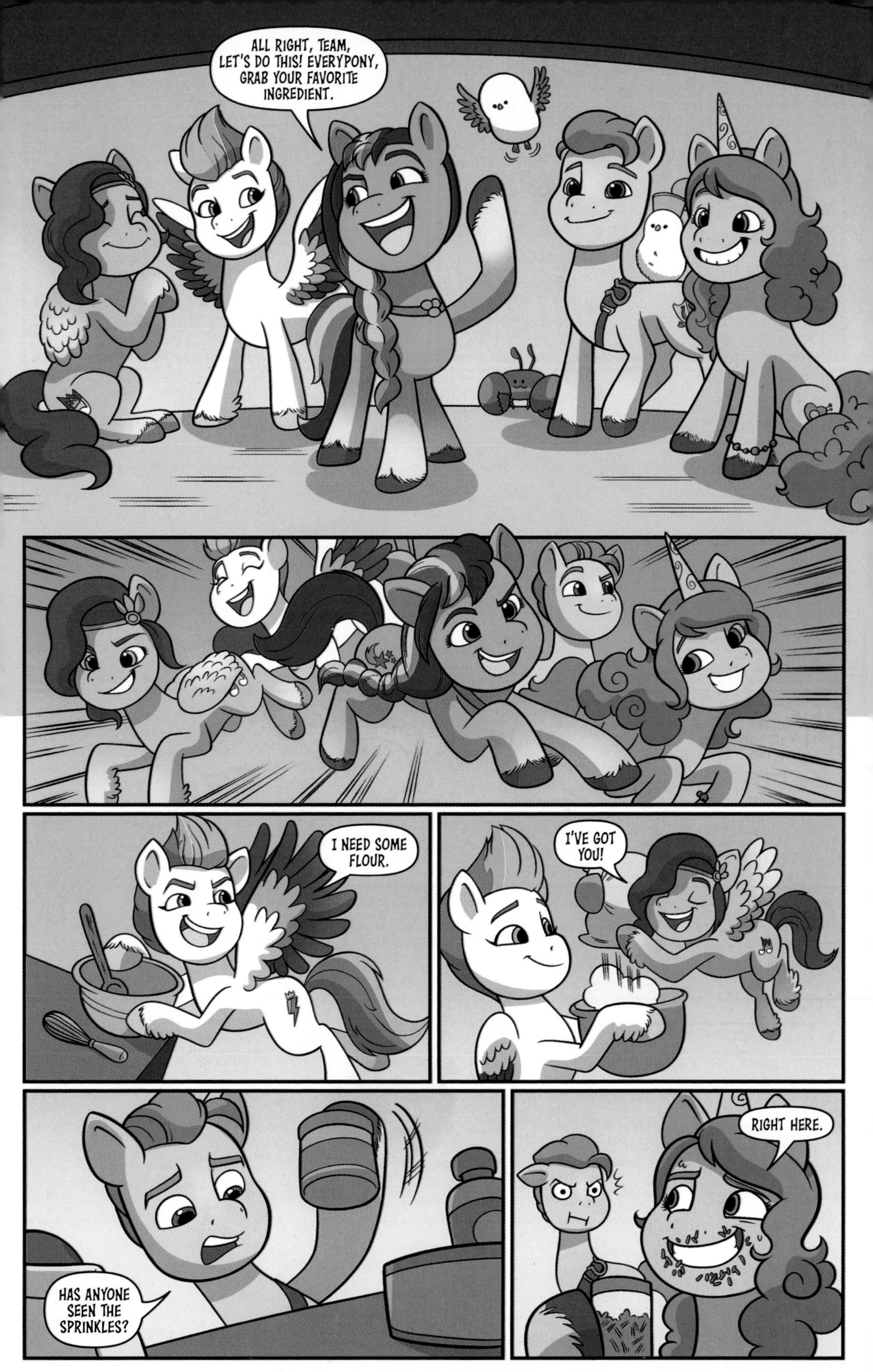
ALL RIGHT, TEAM, LET'S DO THIS! EVERYPONY, GRAB YOUR FAVORITE INGREDIENT.
I NEED SOME FLOUR.
I'VE GOT YOU!
HAS ANYONE SEEN THE SPRINKLES?
RIGHT HERE.

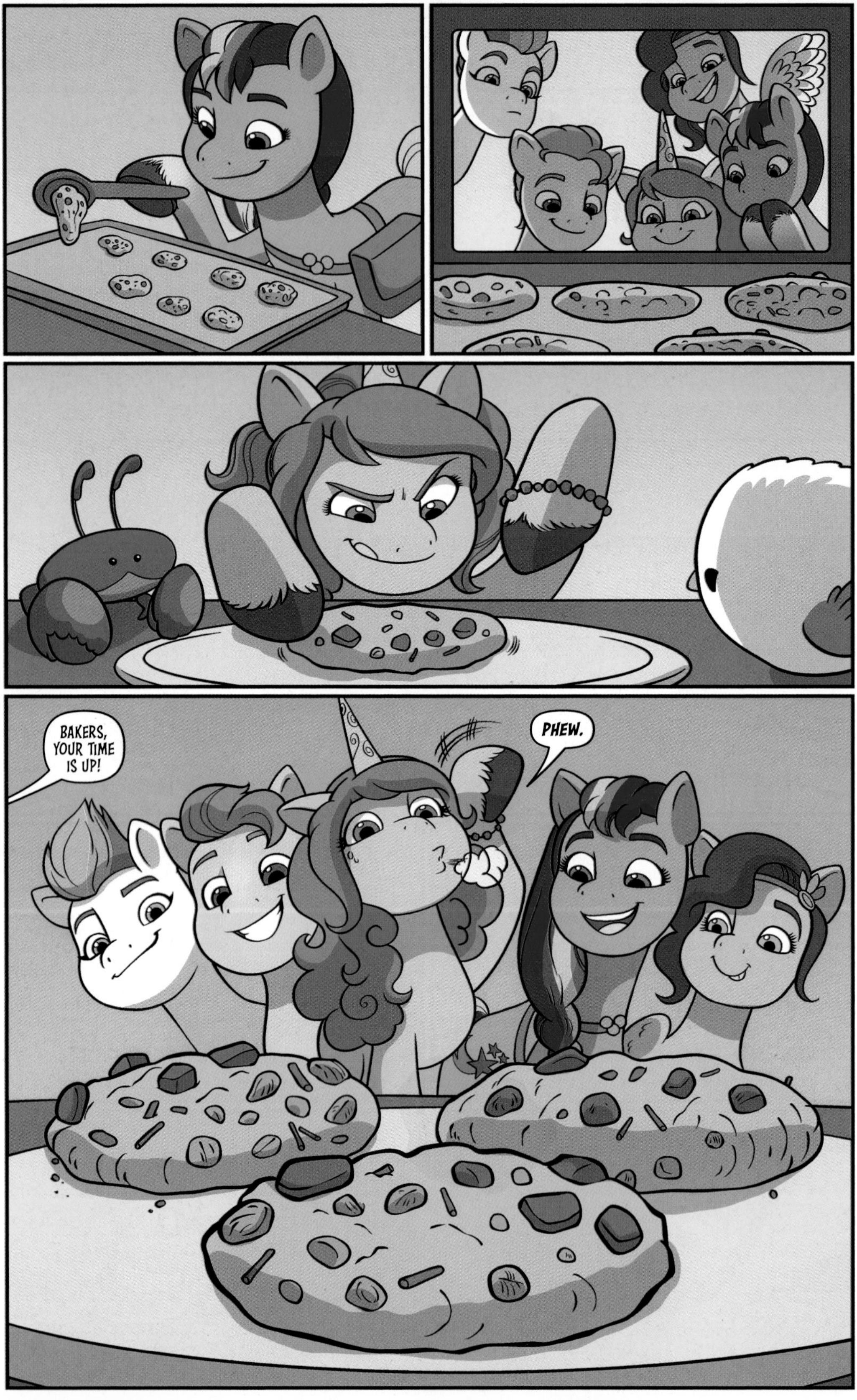
BAKERS, YOUR TIME IS UP!
PHEW.

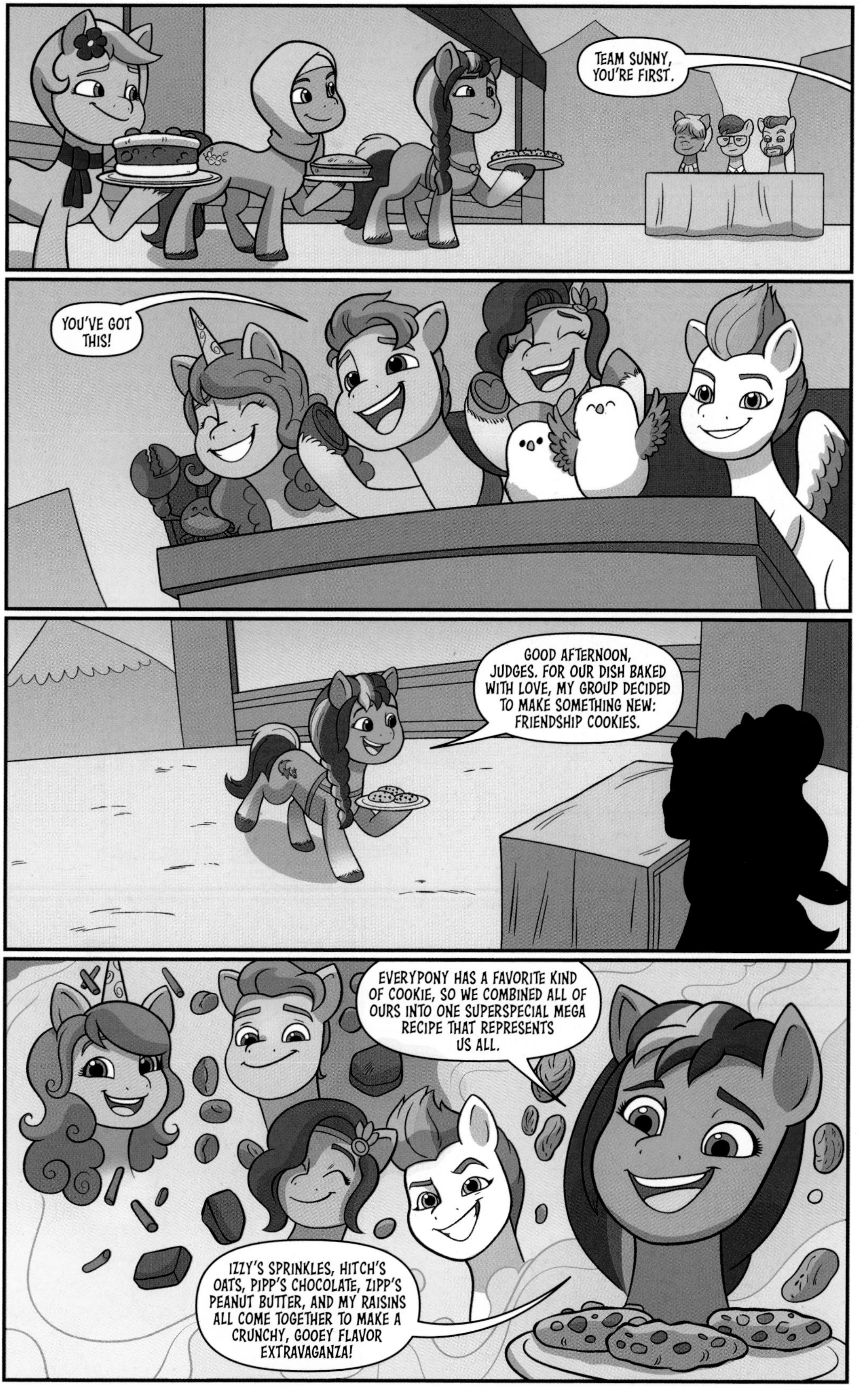
TEAM SUNNY, YOU'RE FIRST.
YOU'VE GOT THIS!
GOOD AFTERNOON, JUDGES. FOR OUR DISH BAKED WITH LOVE, MY GROUP DECIDED TO MAKE SOMETHING NEW: FRIENDSHIP COOKIES.
EVERYPONY HAS A FAVORITE KIND OF COOKIE, SO WE COMBINED ALL OF OURS INTO ONE SUPERSPECIAL MEGA RECIPE THAT REPRESENTS US ALL.
IZZY'S SPRINKLES, HITCH'S OATS, PIPP'S CHOCOLATE, ZIPP'S PEANUT BUTTER, AND MY RAISINS ALL COME TOGETHER TO MAKE A CRUNCHY, GOOEY FLAVOR EXTRAVAGANZA!

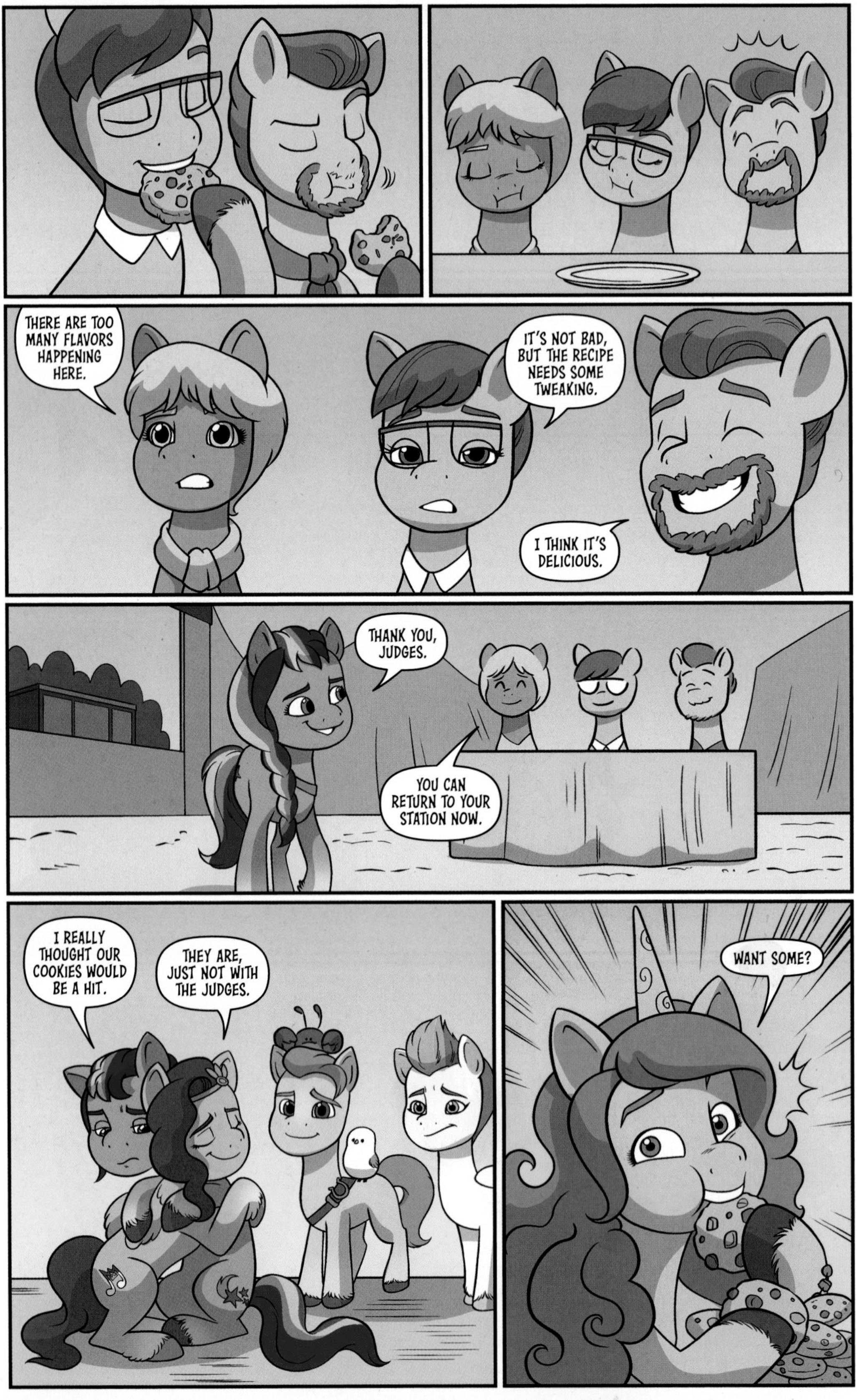
THERE ARE TOO MANY FLAVORS HAPPENING HERE.
IT'S NOT BAD, BUT THE RECIPE NEEDS SOME TWEAKING.
I THINK IT'S DELICIOUS.
THANK YOU, JUDGES.
YOU CAN RETURN TO YOUR STATION NOW.
I REALLY THOUGHT OUR COOKIES WOULD BE A HIT.
THEY ARE, JUST NOT WITH THE JUDGES.
WANT SOME?

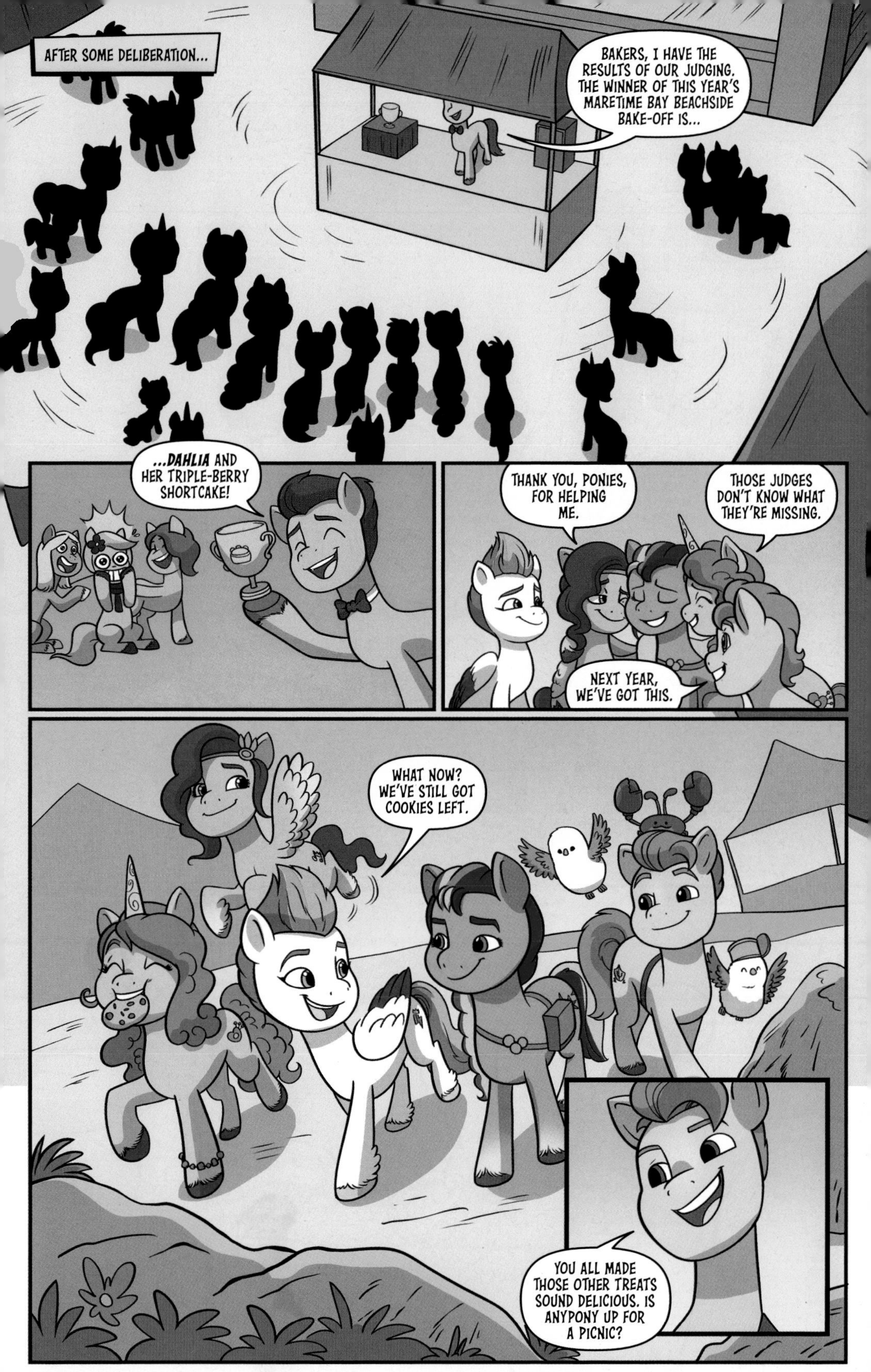
AFTER SOME DELIBERATION...
BAKERS, I HAVE THE RESULTS OF OUR JUDGING. THE WINNER OF THIS YEAR'S MARETIME BAY BEACHSIDE BAKE-OFF IS...
...DAHLIA AND HER TRIPLE-BERRY SHORTCAKE!
THANK YOU, PONIES, FOR HELPING ME.
THOSE JUDGES DON'T KNOW WHAT THEY'RE MISSING.
NEXT YEAR, WE'VE GOT THIS.
WHAT NOW? WE'VE STILL GOT COOKIES LEFT.
YOU ALL MADE THOSE OTHER TREATS SOUND DELICIOUS. IS ANYPONY UP FOR A PICNIC?

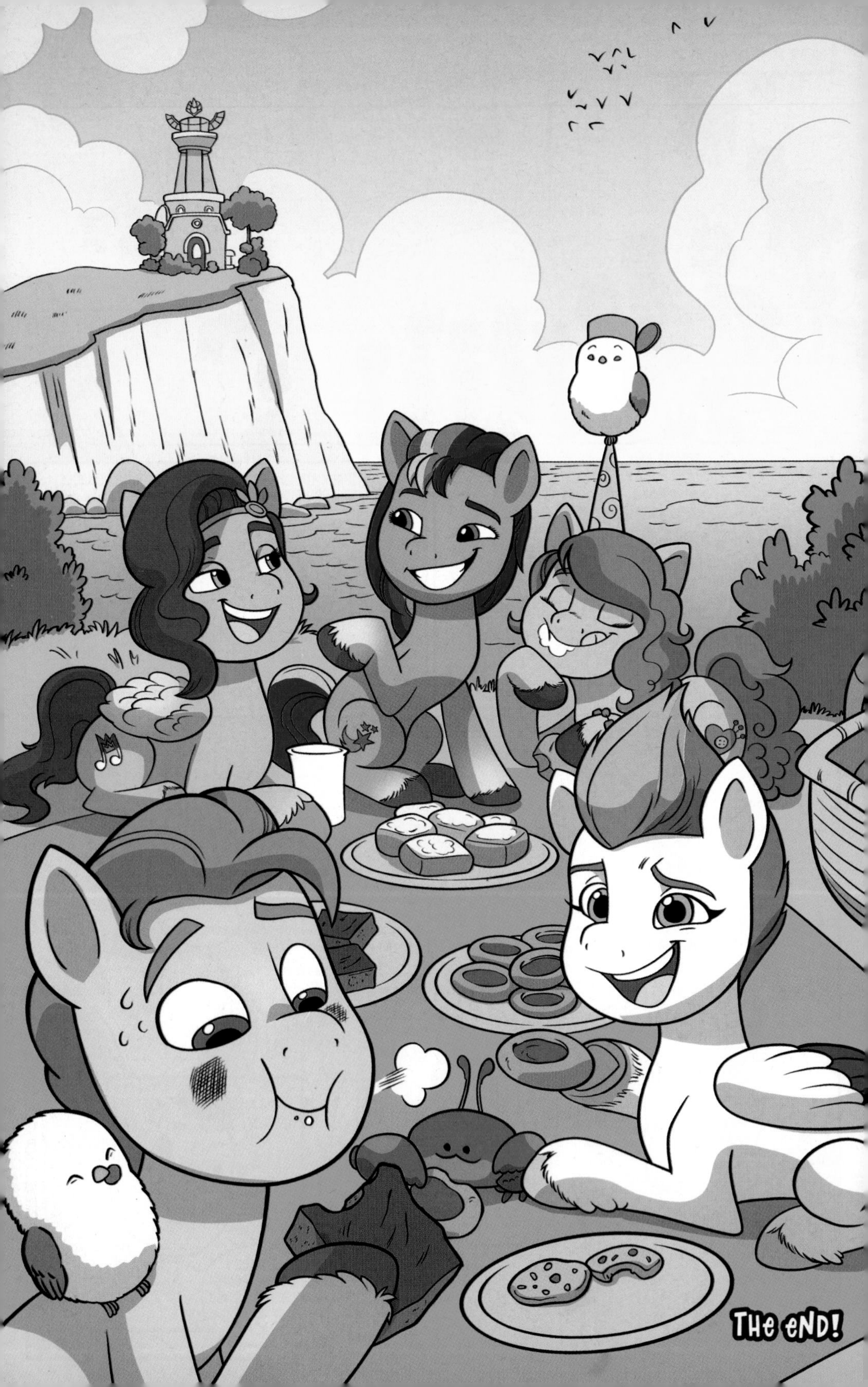
THE END!

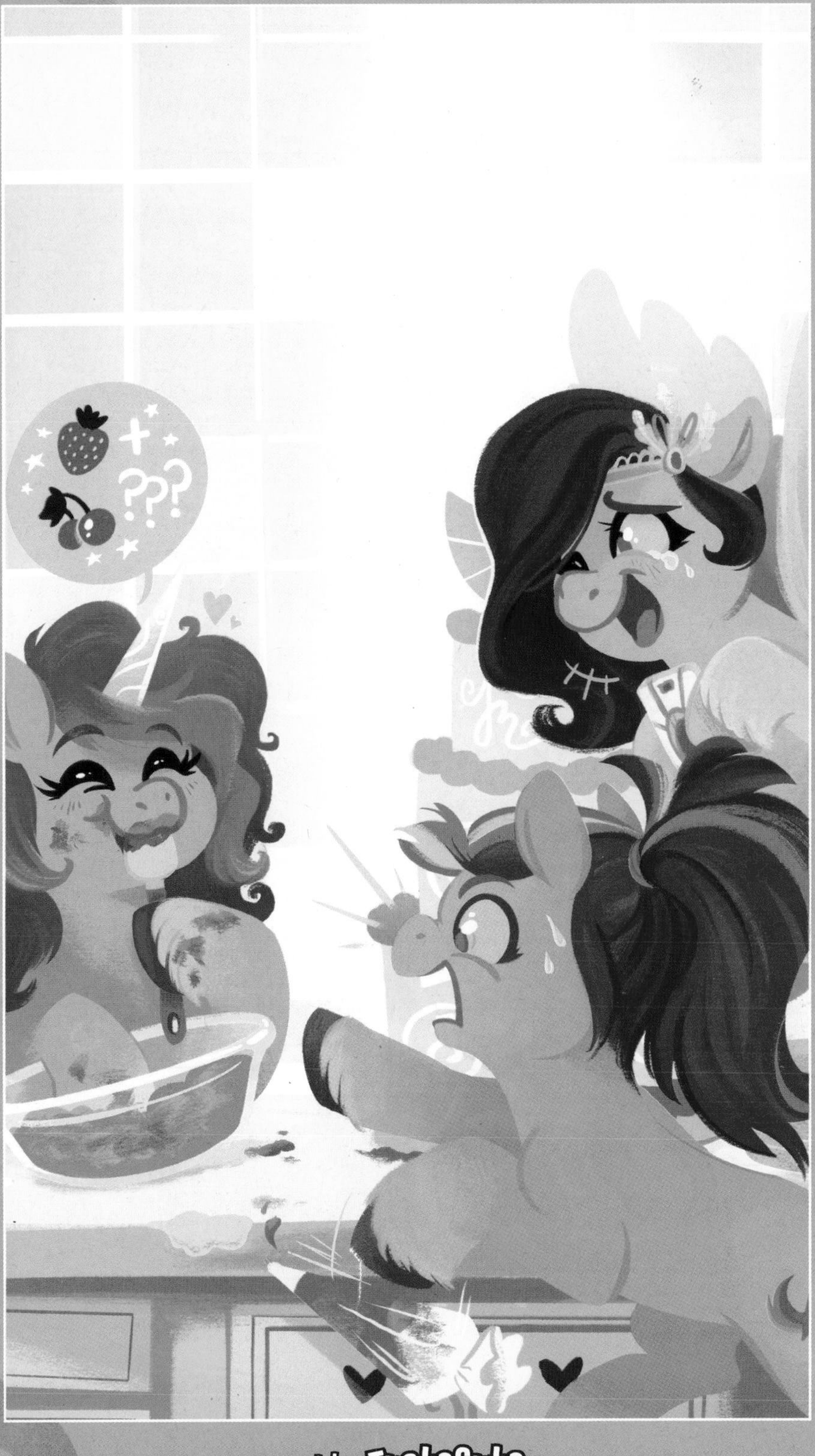
+ ???

art by JustaSuta

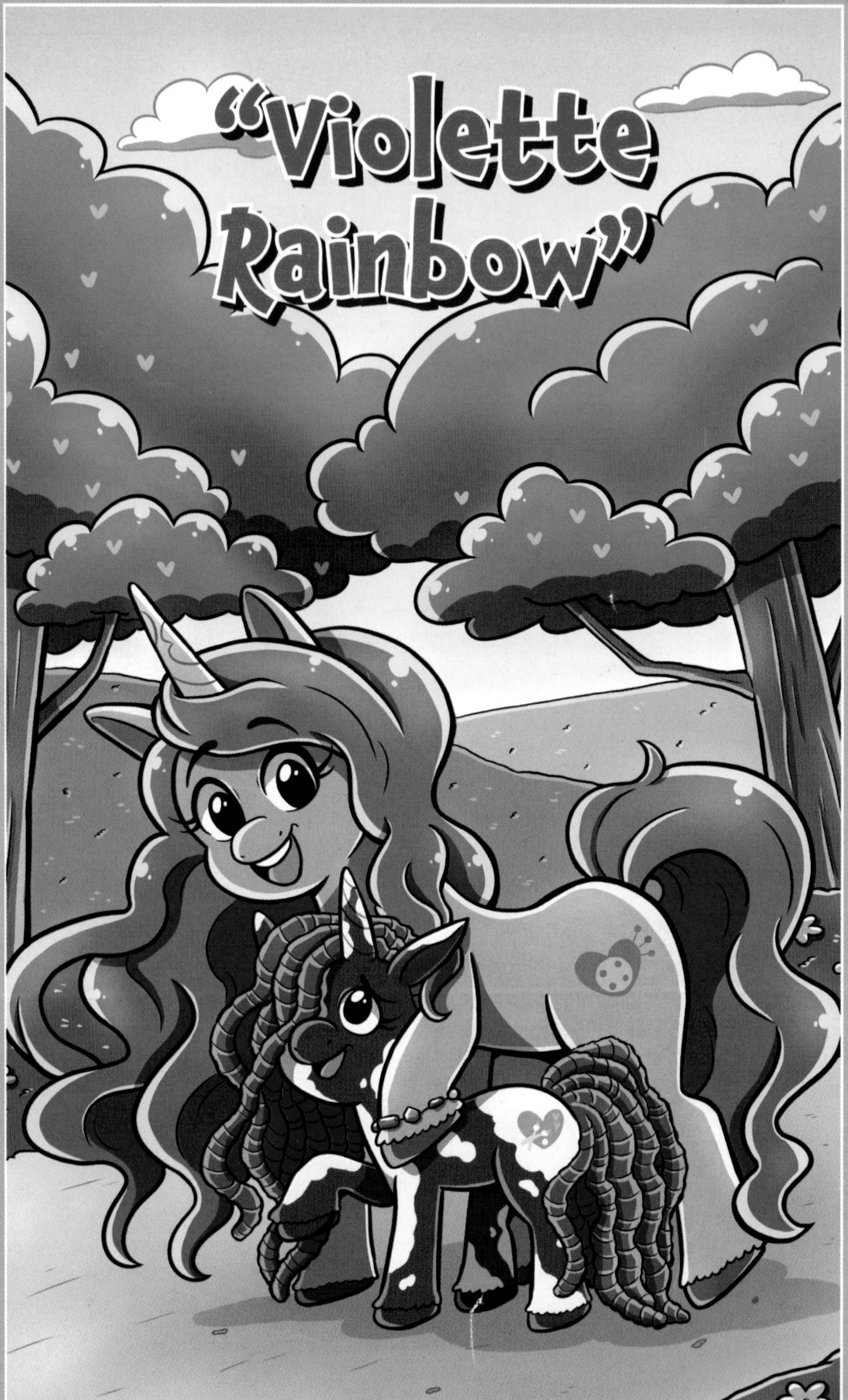
"Violette Rainbow"
Shauna

art by Shauna J. Grant

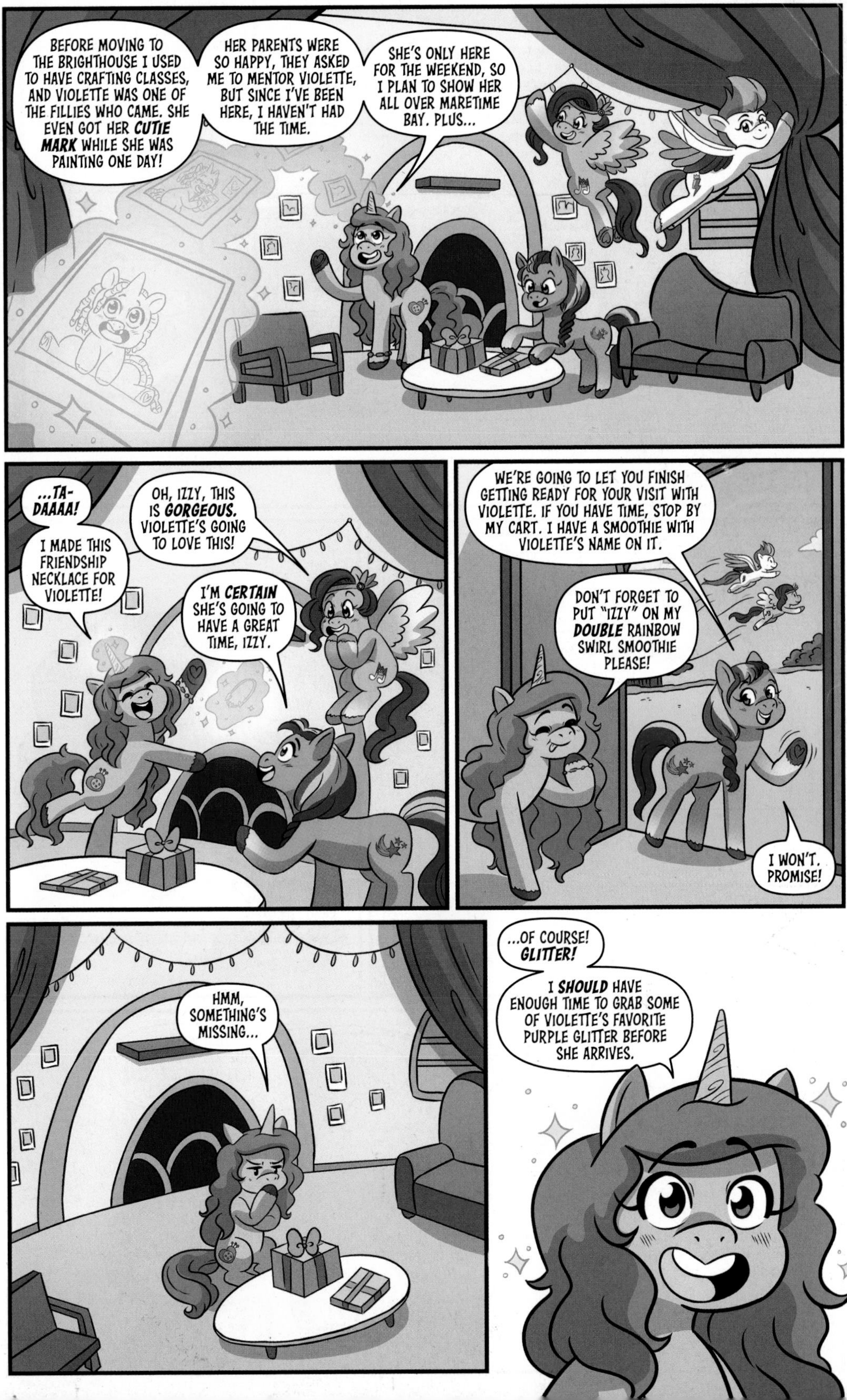
BEFORE MOVING TO THE BRIGHTHOUSE I USED TO HAVE CRAFTING CLASSES, AND VIOLETTE WAS ONE OF THE FILLIES WHO CAME. SHE EVEN GOT HER CUTIE MARK WHILE SHE WAS PAINTING ONE DAY!
HER PARENTS WERE SO HAPPY, THEY ASKED ME TO MENTOR VIOLETTE, BUT SINCE I'VE BEEN HERE, I HAVEN'T HAD THE TIME.
SHE'S ONLY HERE FOR THE WEEKEND, SO I PLAN TO SHOW HER ALL OVER MARETIME BAY. PLUS...
...TA-DAAAA!
I MADE THIS FRIENDSHIP NECKLACE FOR VIOLETTE!
OH, IZZY, THIS IS GORGEOUS. VIOLETTE'S GOING TO LOVE THIS!
I'M CERTAIN SHE'S GOING TO HAVE A GREAT TIME, IZZY.
WE'RE GOING TO LET YOU FINISH GETTING READY FOR YOUR VISIT WITH VIOLETTE. IF YOU HAVE TIME, STOP BY MY CART. I HAVE A SMOOTHIE WITH VIOLETTE'S NAME ON IT.
DON'T FORGET TO PUT "IZZY" ON MY DOUBLE RAINBOW SWIRL SMOOTHIE PLEASE!
I WON'T. PROMISE!
HMM, SOMETHING'S MISSING...
...OF COURSE! GLITTER!
I SHOULD HAVE ENOUGH TIME TO GRAB SOME OF VIOLETTE'S FAVORITE PURPLE GLITTER BEFORE SHE ARRIVES.

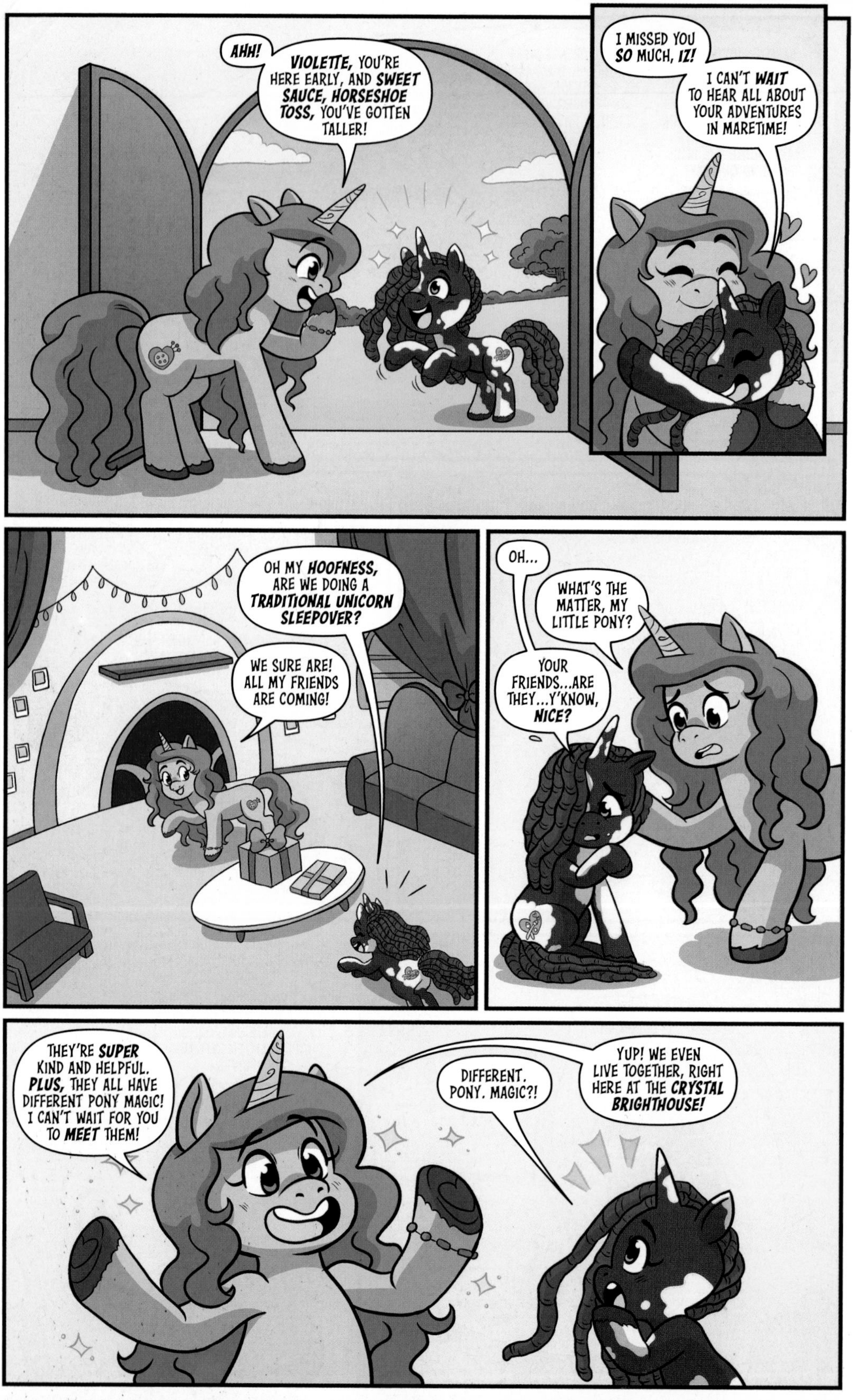
AHH!
VIOLETTE, YOU'RE HERE EARLY, AND SWEET SAUCE, HORSESHOE TOSS, YOU'VE GOTTEN TALLER!
I MISSED YOU SO MUCH, IZ!
I CAN'T WAIT TO HEAR ALL ABOUT YOUR ADVENTURES IN MARETIME!
OH MY HOOFNESS, ARE WE DOING A TRADITIONAL UNICORN SLEEPOVER?
WE SURE ARE! ALL MY FRIENDS ARE COMING!
OH...
WHAT'S THE MATTER, MY LITTLE PONY?
YOUR FRIENDS...ARE THEY...Y'KNOW, NICE?
THEY'RE SUPER KIND AND HELPFUL. PLUS, THEY ALL HAVE DIFFERENT PONY MAGIC! I CAN'T WAIT FOR YOU TO MEET THEM!
DIFFERENT. PONY. MAGIC?!
YUP! WE EVEN LIVE TOGETHER, RIGHT HERE AT THE CRYSTAL BRIGHTHOUSE!

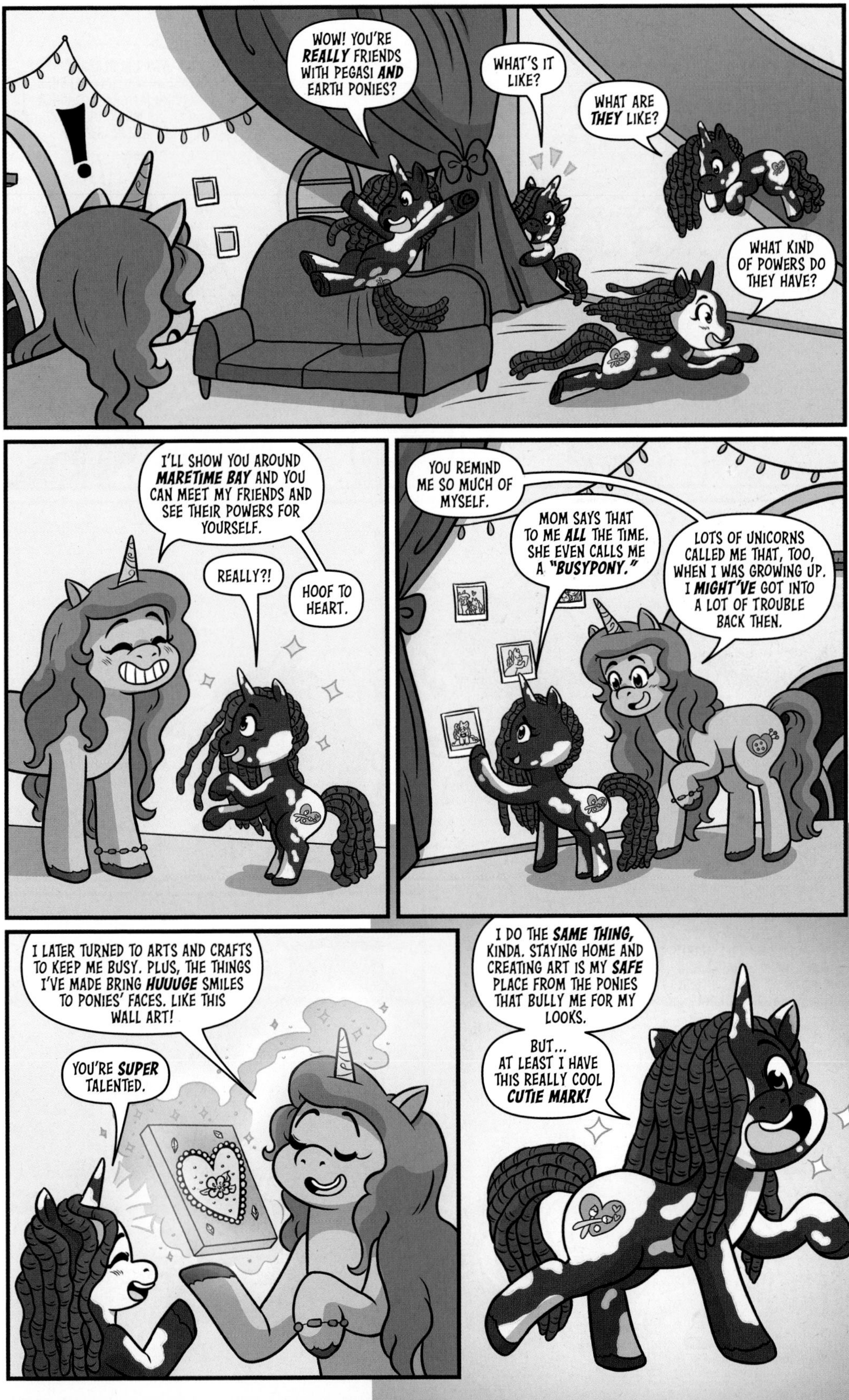
!
WOW! YOU'RE REALLY FRIENDS WITH PEGASI AND EARTH PONIES?
WHAT'S IT LIKE?
WHAT ARE THEY LIKE?
WHAT KIND OF POWERS DO THEY HAVE?
I'LL SHOW YOU AROUND MARETIME BAY AND YOU CAN MEET MY FRIENDS AND SEE THEIR POWERS FOR YOURSELF.
REALLY?!
HOOF TO HEART.
YOU REMIND ME SO MUCH OF MYSELF.
MOM SAYS THAT TO ME ALL THE TIME. SHE EVEN CALLS ME A "BUSYPONY."
LOTS OF UNICORNS CALLED ME THAT, TOO, WHEN I WAS GROWING UP. I MIGHT'VE GOT INTO A LOT OF TROUBLE BACK THEN.
I LATER TURNED TO ARTS AND CRAFTS TO KEEP ME BUSY. PLUS, THE THINGS I'VE MADE BRING HUUUGE SMILES TO PONIES' FACES. LIKE THIS WALL ART!
YOU'RE SUPER TALENTED.
I DO THE SAME THING, KINDA. STAYING HOME AND CREATING ART IS MY SAFE PLACE FROM THE PONIES THAT BULLY ME FOR MY LOOKS.
BUT... AT LEAST I HAVE THIS REALLY COOL CUTIE MARK!

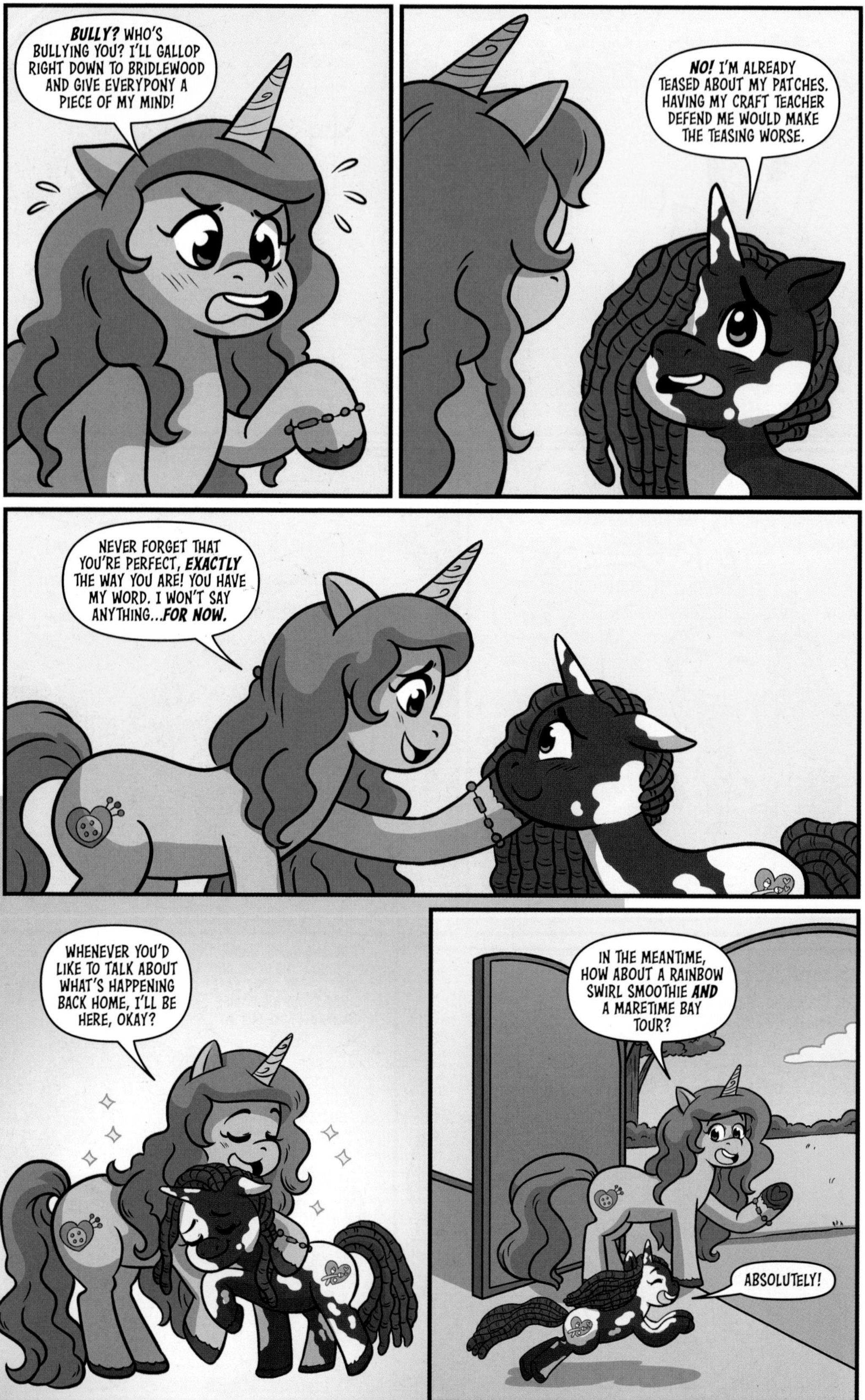
BULLY? WHO'S BULLYING YOU? I'LL GALLOP RIGHT DOWN TO BRIDLEWOOD AND GIVE EVERYPONY A PIECE OF MY MIND!
NO! I'M ALREADY TEASED ABOUT MY PATCHES. HAVING MY CRAFT TEACHER DEFEND ME WOULD MAKE THE TEASING WORSE.
NEVER FORGET THAT YOU'RE PERFECT, EXACTLY THE WAY YOU ARE! YOU HAVE MY WORD. I WON'T SAY ANYTHING...FOR NOW.
WHENEVER YOU'D LIKE TO TALK ABOUT WHAT'S HAPPENING BACK HOME, I'LL BE HERE, OKAY?
IN THE MEANTIME, HOW ABOUT A RAINBOW SWIRL SMOOTHIE AND A MARETIME BAY TOUR?
ABSOLUTELY!

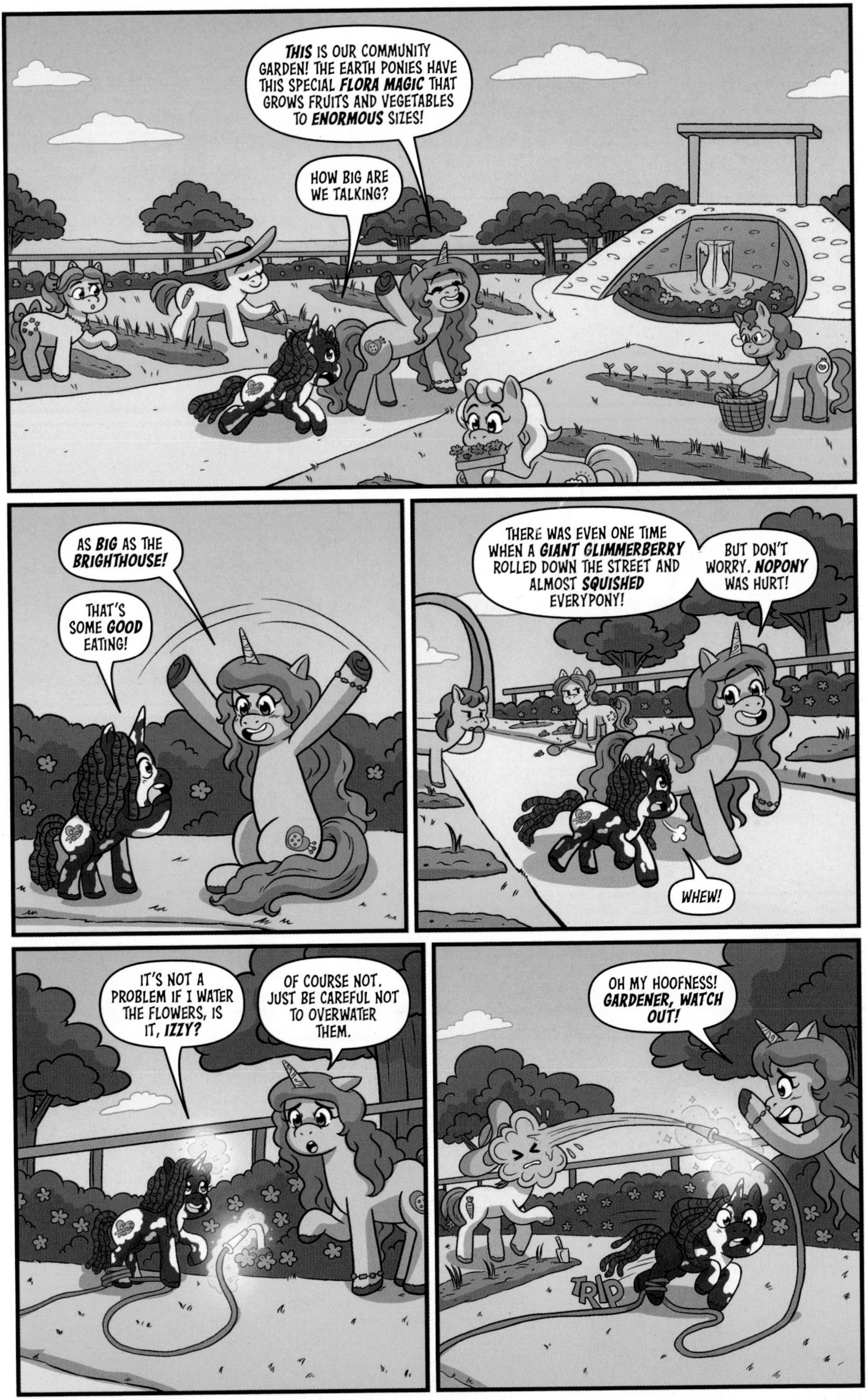

THIS IS OUR COMMUNITY GARDEN! THE EARTH PONIES HAVE THIS SPECIAL FLORA MAGIC THAT GROWS FRUITS AND VEGETABLES TO ENORMOUS SIZES!
HOW BIG ARE WE TALKING?
AS BIG AS THE BRIGHTHOUSE!
THAT'S SOME GOOD EATING!
THERE WAS EVEN ONE TIME WHEN A GIANT GLIMMERBERRY ROLLED DOWN THE STREET AND ALMOST SQUISHED EVERYPONY!
BUT DON'T WORRY. NOPONY WAS HURT!
WHEW!
IT'S NOT A PROBLEM IF I WATER THE FLOWERS, IS IT, IZZY?
OF COURSE NOT. JUST BE CAREFUL NOT TO OVERWATER THEM.
OH MY HOOFNESS! GARDENER, WATCH OUT!
TRIP

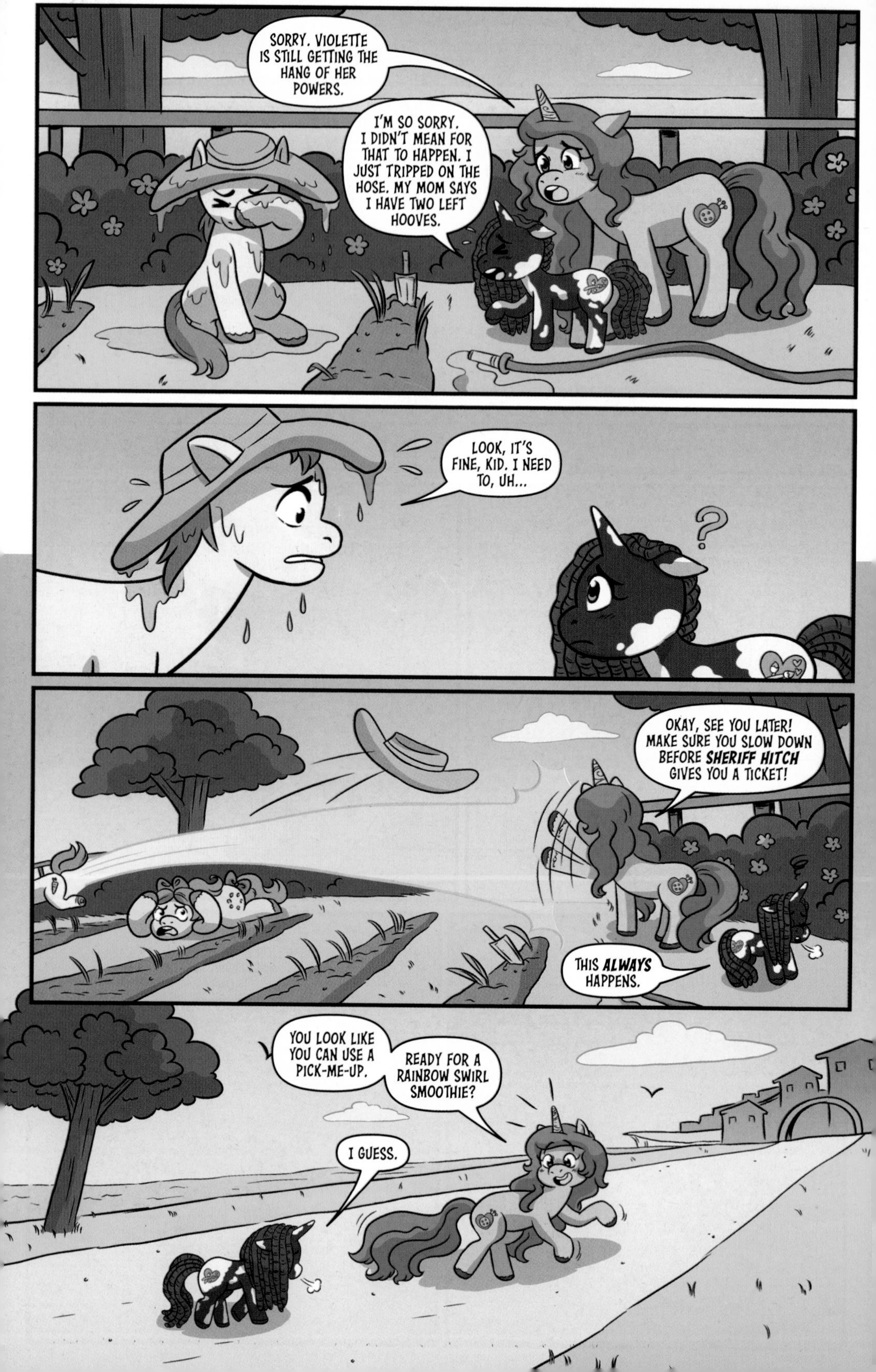
SORRY. VIOLETTE IS STILL GETTING THE HANG OF HER POWERS.
I'M SO SORRY. I DIDN'T MEAN FOR THAT TO HAPPEN. I JUST TRIPPED ON THE HOSE. MY MOM SAYS I HAVE TWO LEFT HOOVES.
LOOK, IT'S FINE, KID. I NEED TO, UH...
?
OKAY, SEE YOU LATER! MAKE SURE YOU SLOW DOWN BEFORE SHERIFF HITCH GIVES YOU A TICKET!
THIS ALWAYS HAPPENS.
YOU LOOK LIKE YOU CAN USE A PICK-ME-UP.
READY FOR A RAINBOW SWIRL SMOOTHIE?
I GUESS.

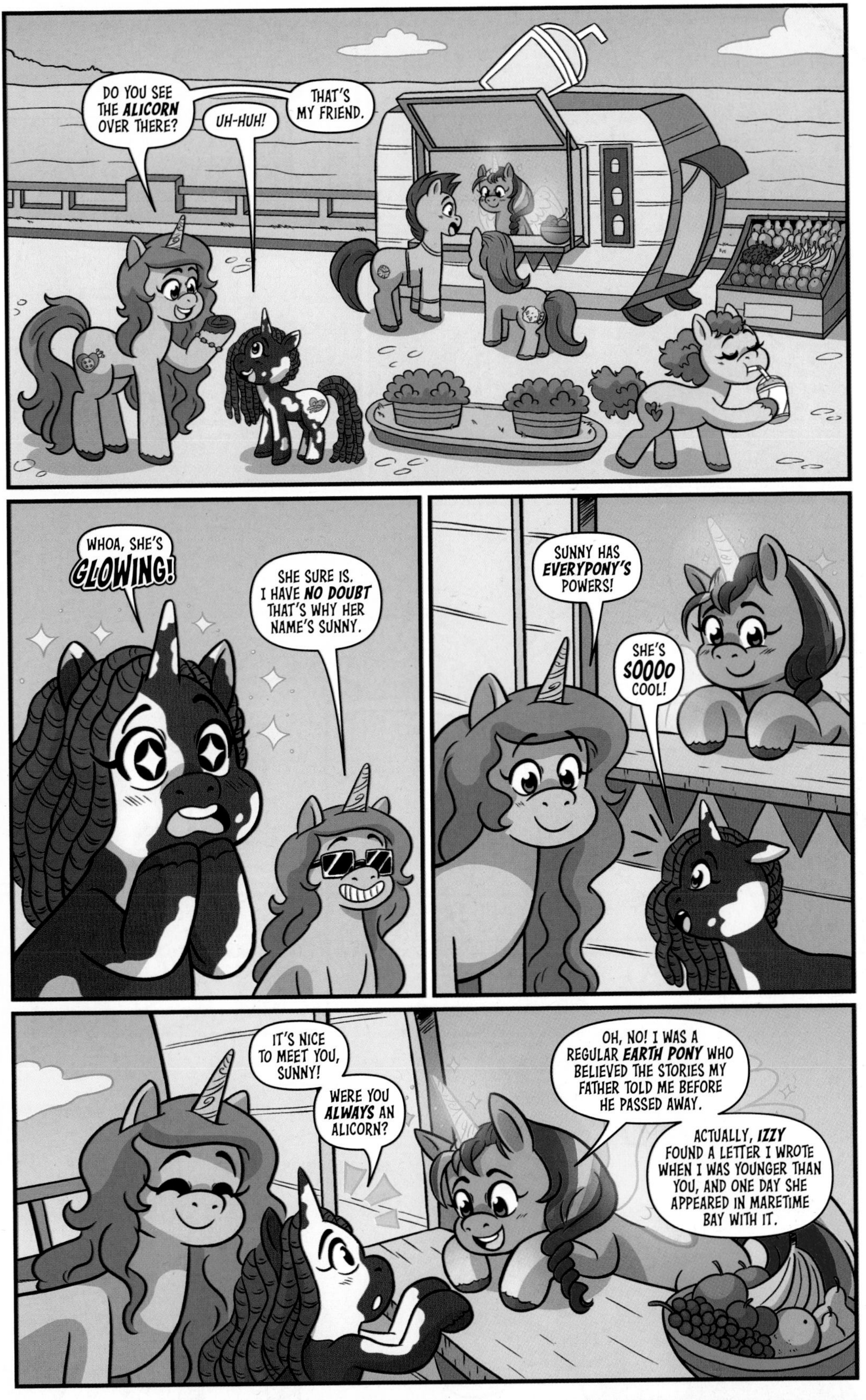

DO YOU SEE THE ALICORN OVER THERE?
UH-HUH!
THAT'S MY FRIEND.
WHOA, SHE'S GLOWING!
SHE SURE IS. I HAVE NO DOUBT THAT'S WHY HER NAME'S SUNNY.
SUNNY HAS EVERYPONY'S POWERS!
SHE'S SOOOO COOL!
IT'S NICE TO MEET YOU, SUNNY!
WERE YOU ALWAYS AN ALICORN?
OH, NO! I WAS A REGULAR EARTH PONY WHO BELIEVED THE STORIES MY FATHER TOLD ME BEFORE HE PASSED AWAY.
ACTUALLY, IZZY FOUND A LETTER I WROTE WHEN I WAS YOUNGER THAN YOU, AND ONE DAY SHE APPEARED IN MARETIME BAY WITH IT.

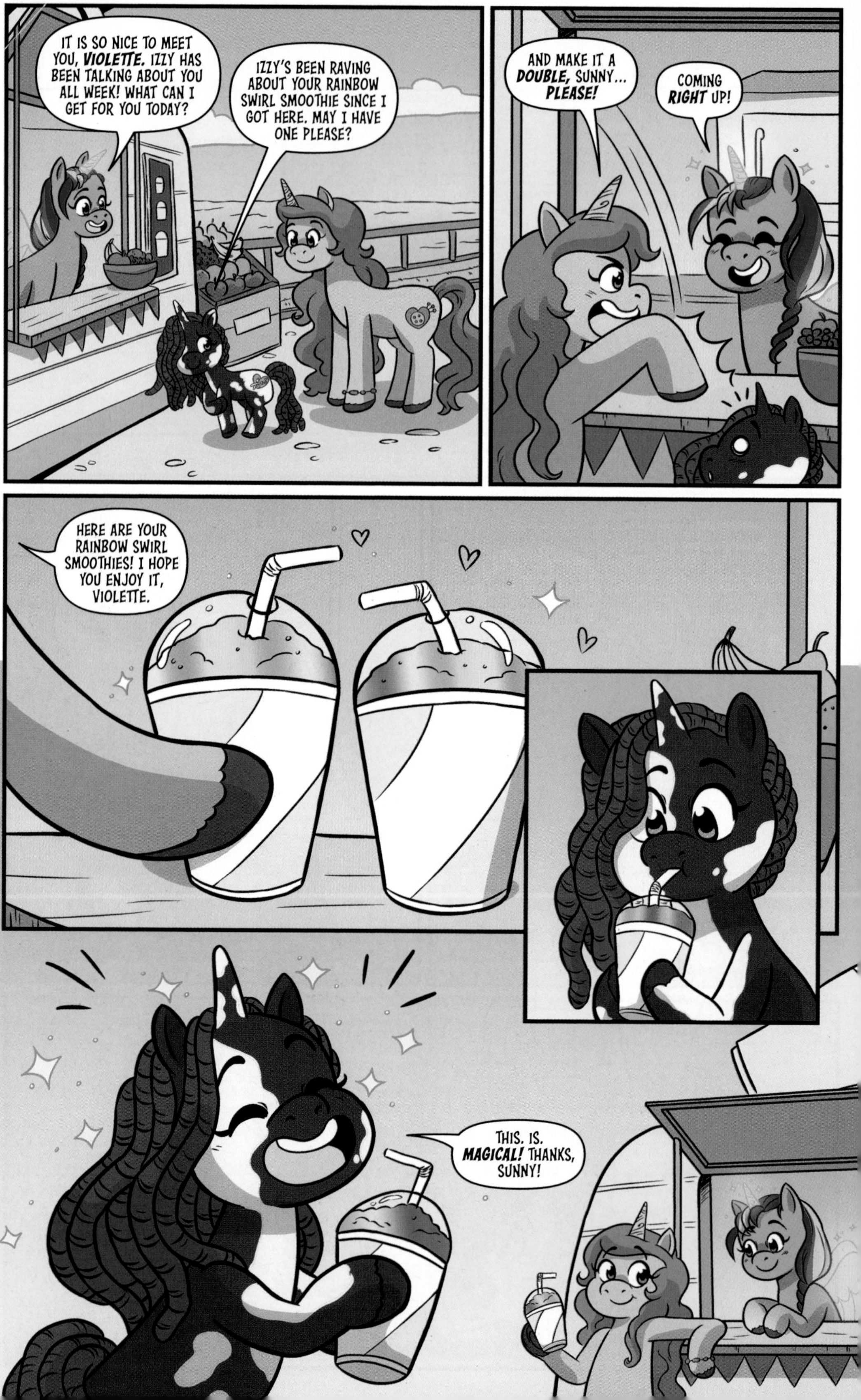
IT IS SO NICE TO MEET YOU, VIOLETTE. IZZY HAS BEEN TALKING ABOUT YOU ALL WEEK! WHAT CAN I GET FOR YOU TODAY?
IZZY'S BEEN RAVING ABOUT YOUR RAINBOW SWIRL SMOOTHIE SINCE I GOT HERE. MAY I HAVE ONE PLEASE?
AND MAKE IT A DOUBLE, SUNNY... PLEASE!
COMING RIGHT UP!
HERE ARE YOUR RAINBOW SWIRL SMOOTHIES! I HOPE YOU ENJOY IT, VIOLETTE.
THIS. IS. MAGICAL! THANKS, SUNNY!

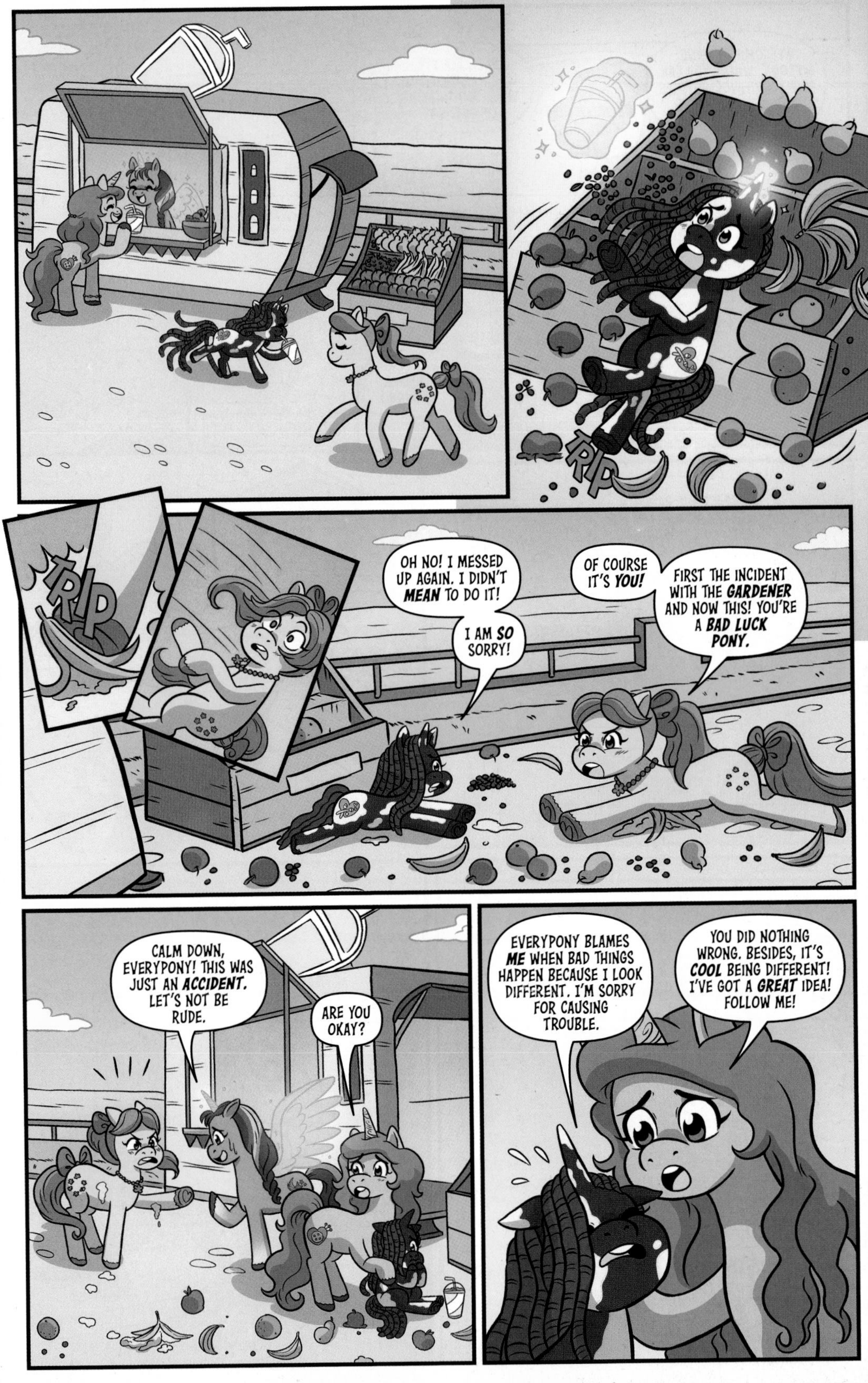
TRIP
TRIP
OH NO! I MESSED UP AGAIN. I DIDN'T MEAN TO DO IT!
I AM SO SORRY!
OF COURSE IT'S YOU!
FIRST THE INCIDENT WITH THE GARDENER AND NOW THIS! YOU'RE A BAD LUCK PONY.
CALM DOWN, EVERYPONY! THIS WAS JUST AN ACCIDENT. LET'S NOT BE RUDE.
ARE YOU OKAY?
EVERYPONY BLAMES ME WHEN BAD THINGS HAPPEN BECAUSE I LOOK DIFFERENT. I'M SORRY FOR CAUSING TROUBLE.
YOU DID NOTHING WRONG. BESIDES, IT'S COOL BEING DIFFERENT! I'VE GOT A GREAT IDEA! FOLLOW ME!

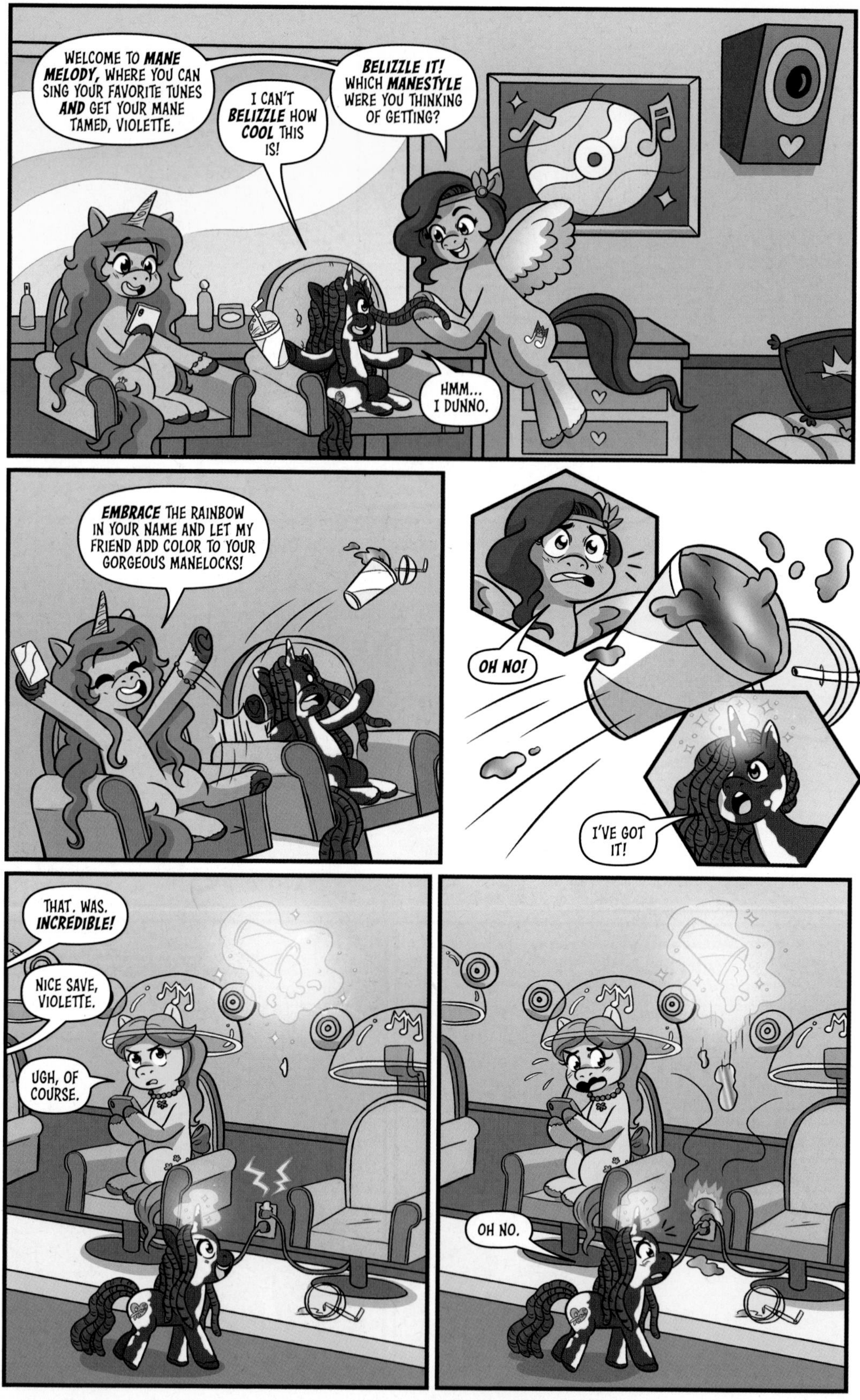
WELCOME TO **MANE MELODY,** WHERE YOU CAN SING YOUR FAVORITE TUNES **AND** GET YOUR MANE TAMED, VIOLETTE.
I CAN'T **BELIZZLE** HOW **COOL** THIS IS!
BELIZZLE IT! WHICH **MANESTYLE** WERE YOU THINKING OF GETTING?
HMM... I DUNNO.
EMBRACE THE RAINBOW IN YOUR NAME AND LET MY FRIEND ADD COLOR TO YOUR GORGEOUS MANELOCKS!
OH NO!
I'VE GOT IT!
THAT. WAS. **INCREDIBLE!**
NICE SAVE, VIOLETTE.
UGH, OF COURSE.
OH NO.

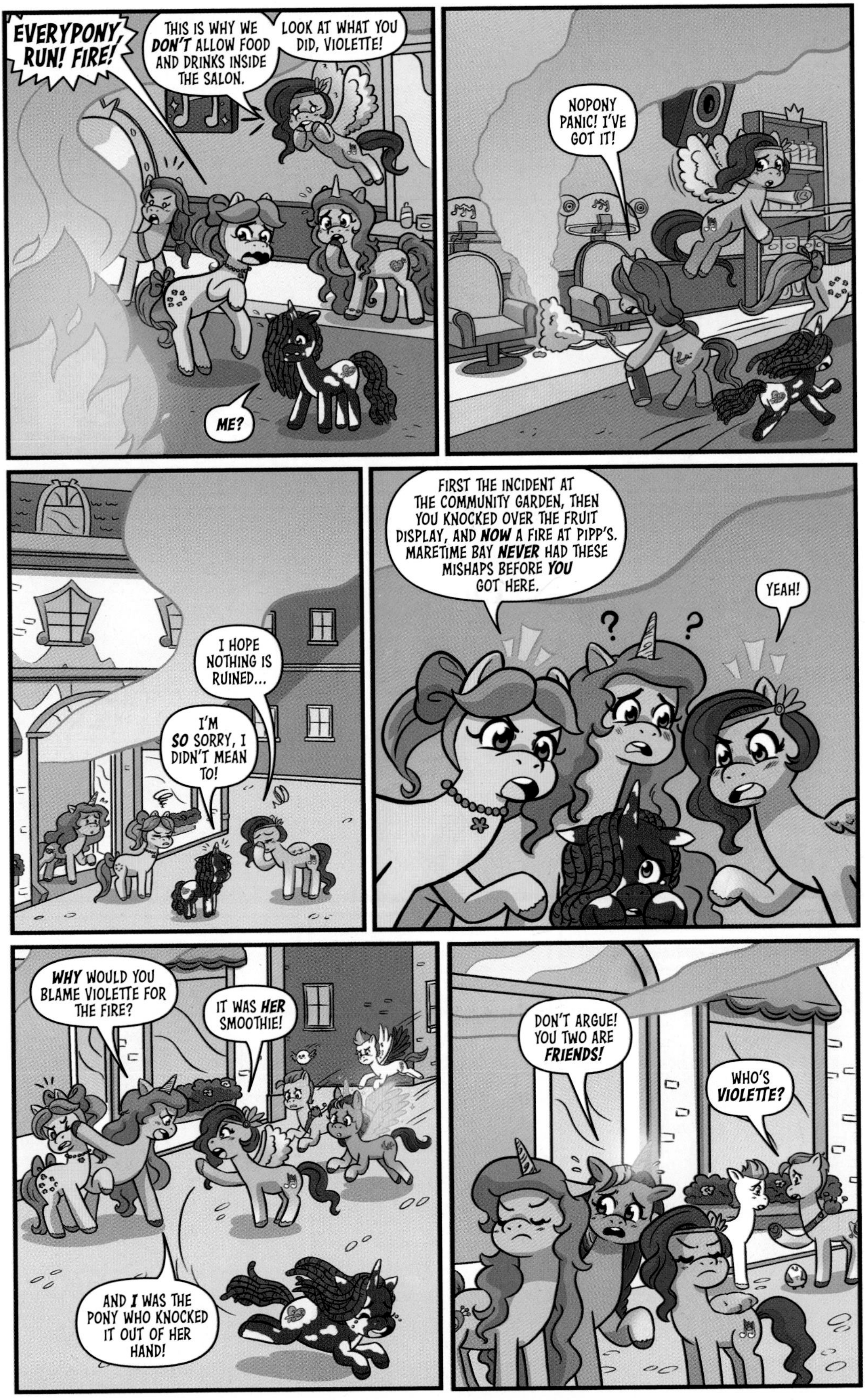
EVERYPONY, RUN! FIRE!
THIS IS WHY WE DON'T ALLOW FOOD AND DRINKS INSIDE THE SALON.
LOOK AT WHAT YOU DID, VIOLETTE!
ME?
NOPONY PANIC! I'VE GOT IT!
I HOPE NOTHING IS RUINED...
I'M SO SORRY, I DIDN'T MEAN TO!
FIRST THE INCIDENT AT THE COMMUNITY GARDEN, THEN YOU KNOCKED OVER THE FRUIT DISPLAY, AND NOW A FIRE AT PIPP'S. MARETIME BAY NEVER HAD THESE MISHAPS BEFORE YOU GOT HERE.
? ?
YEAH!
WHY WOULD YOU BLAME VIOLETTE FOR THE FIRE?
IT WAS HER SMOOTHIE!
AND I WAS THE PONY WHO KNOCKED IT OUT OF HER HAND!
DON'T ARGUE! YOU TWO ARE FRIENDS!
WHO'S VIOLETTE?

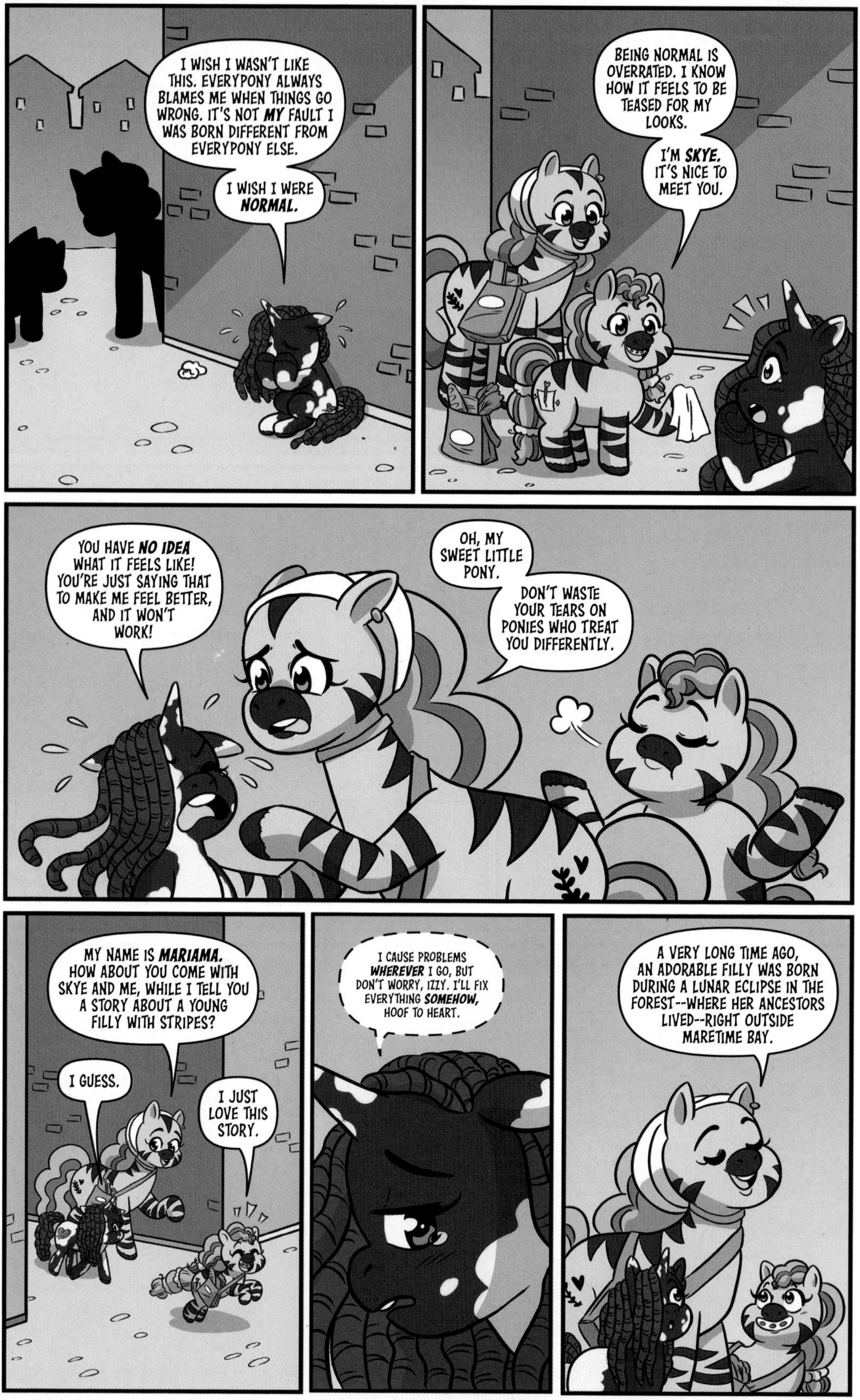
I WISH I WASN'T LIKE THIS. EVERYPONY ALWAYS BLAMES ME WHEN THINGS GO WRONG. IT'S NOT MY FAULT I WAS BORN DIFFERENT FROM EVERYPONY ELSE.
I WISH I WERE NORMAL.
BEING NORMAL IS OVERRATED. I KNOW HOW IT FEELS TO BE TEASED FOR MY LOOKS.
I'M SKYE. IT'S NICE TO MEET YOU.
YOU HAVE NO IDEA WHAT IT FEELS LIKE! YOU'RE JUST SAYING THAT TO MAKE ME FEEL BETTER, AND IT WON'T WORK!
OH, MY SWEET LITTLE PONY.
DON'T WASTE YOUR TEARS ON PONIES WHO TREAT YOU DIFFERENTLY.
MY NAME IS MARIAMA. HOW ABOUT YOU COME WITH SKYE AND ME, WHILE I TELL YOU A STORY ABOUT A YOUNG FILLY WITH STRIPES?
I GUESS.
I JUST LOVE THIS STORY.
I CAUSE PROBLEMS WHEREVER I GO, BUT DON'T WORRY, IZZY. I'LL FIX EVERYTHING SOMEHOW, HOOF TO HEART.
A VERY LONG TIME AGO, AN ADORABLE FILLY WAS BORN DURING A LUNAR ECLIPSE IN THE FOREST--WHERE HER ANCESTORS LIVED--RIGHT OUTSIDE MARETIME BAY.

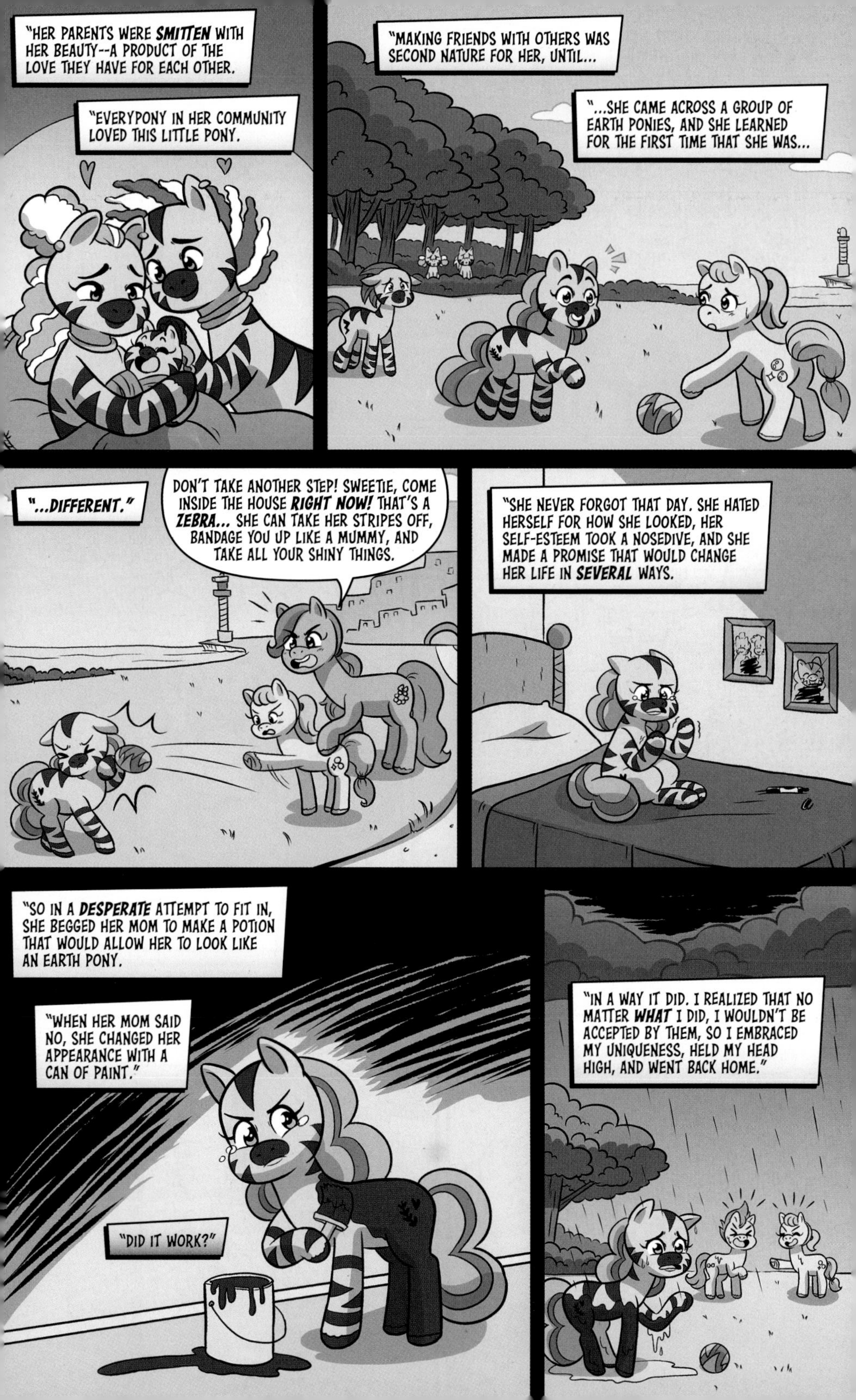
"HER PARENTS WERE SMITTEN WITH HER BEAUTY--A PRODUCT OF THE LOVE THEY HAVE FOR EACH OTHER.
"EVERYPONY IN HER COMMUNITY LOVED THIS LITTLE PONY.
"MAKING FRIENDS WITH OTHERS WAS SECOND NATURE FOR HER, UNTIL...
"...SHE CAME ACROSS A GROUP OF EARTH PONIES, AND SHE LEARNED FOR THE FIRST TIME THAT SHE WAS...
"...DIFFERENT."
DON'T TAKE ANOTHER STEP! SWEETIE, COME INSIDE THE HOUSE RIGHT NOW! THAT'S A ZEBRA... SHE CAN TAKE HER STRIPES OFF, BANDAGE YOU UP LIKE A MUMMY, AND TAKE ALL YOUR SHINY THINGS.
"SHE NEVER FORGOT THAT DAY. SHE HATED HERSELF FOR HOW SHE LOOKED, HER SELF-ESTEEM TOOK A NOSEDIVE, AND SHE MADE A PROMISE THAT WOULD CHANGE HER LIFE IN SEVERAL WAYS.
"SO IN A DESPERATE ATTEMPT TO FIT IN, SHE BEGGED HER MOM TO MAKE A POTION THAT WOULD ALLOW HER TO LOOK LIKE AN EARTH PONY.
"WHEN HER MOM SAID NO, SHE CHANGED HER APPEARANCE WITH A CAN OF PAINT."
"DID IT WORK?"
"IN A WAY IT DID. I REALIZED THAT NO MATTER WHAT I DID, I WOULDN'T BE ACCEPTED BY THEM, SO I EMBRACED MY UNIQUENESS, HELD MY HEAD HIGH, AND WENT BACK HOME."

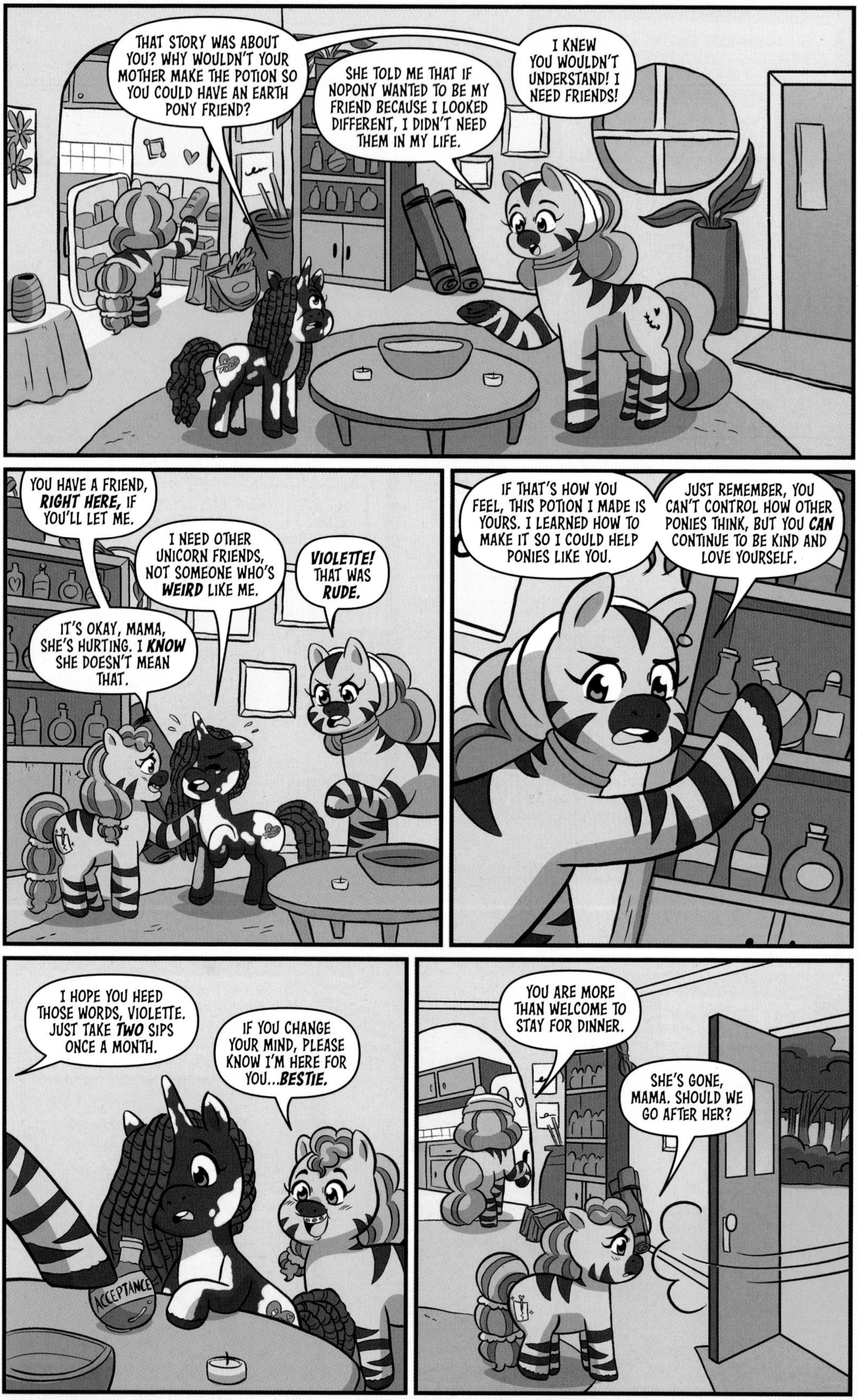
THAT STORY WAS ABOUT YOU? WHY WOULDN'T YOUR MOTHER MAKE THE POTION SO YOU COULD HAVE AN EARTH PONY FRIEND?
SHE TOLD ME THAT IF NOPONY WANTED TO BE MY FRIEND BECAUSE I LOOKED DIFFERENT, I DIDN'T NEED THEM IN MY LIFE.
I KNEW YOU WOULDN'T UNDERSTAND! I NEED FRIENDS!
YOU HAVE A FRIEND, ***RIGHT HERE,*** IF YOU'LL LET ME.
I NEED OTHER UNICORN FRIENDS, NOT SOMEONE WHO'S ***WEIRD*** LIKE ME.
VIOLETTE! THAT WAS ***RUDE.***
IT'S OKAY, MAMA, SHE'S HURTING. I ***KNOW*** SHE DOESN'T MEAN THAT.
IF THAT'S HOW YOU FEEL, THIS POTION I MADE IS YOURS. I LEARNED HOW TO MAKE IT SO I COULD HELP PONIES LIKE YOU.
JUST REMEMBER, YOU CAN'T CONTROL HOW OTHER PONIES THINK, BUT YOU ***CAN*** CONTINUE TO BE KIND AND LOVE YOURSELF.
I HOPE YOU HEED THOSE WORDS, VIOLETTE. JUST TAKE ***TWO*** SIPS ONCE A MONTH.
IF YOU CHANGE YOUR MIND, PLEASE KNOW I'M HERE FOR YOU...***BESTIE.***
ACCEPTANCE
YOU ARE MORE THAN WELCOME TO STAY FOR DINNER.
SHE'S GONE, MAMA. SHOULD WE GO AFTER HER?

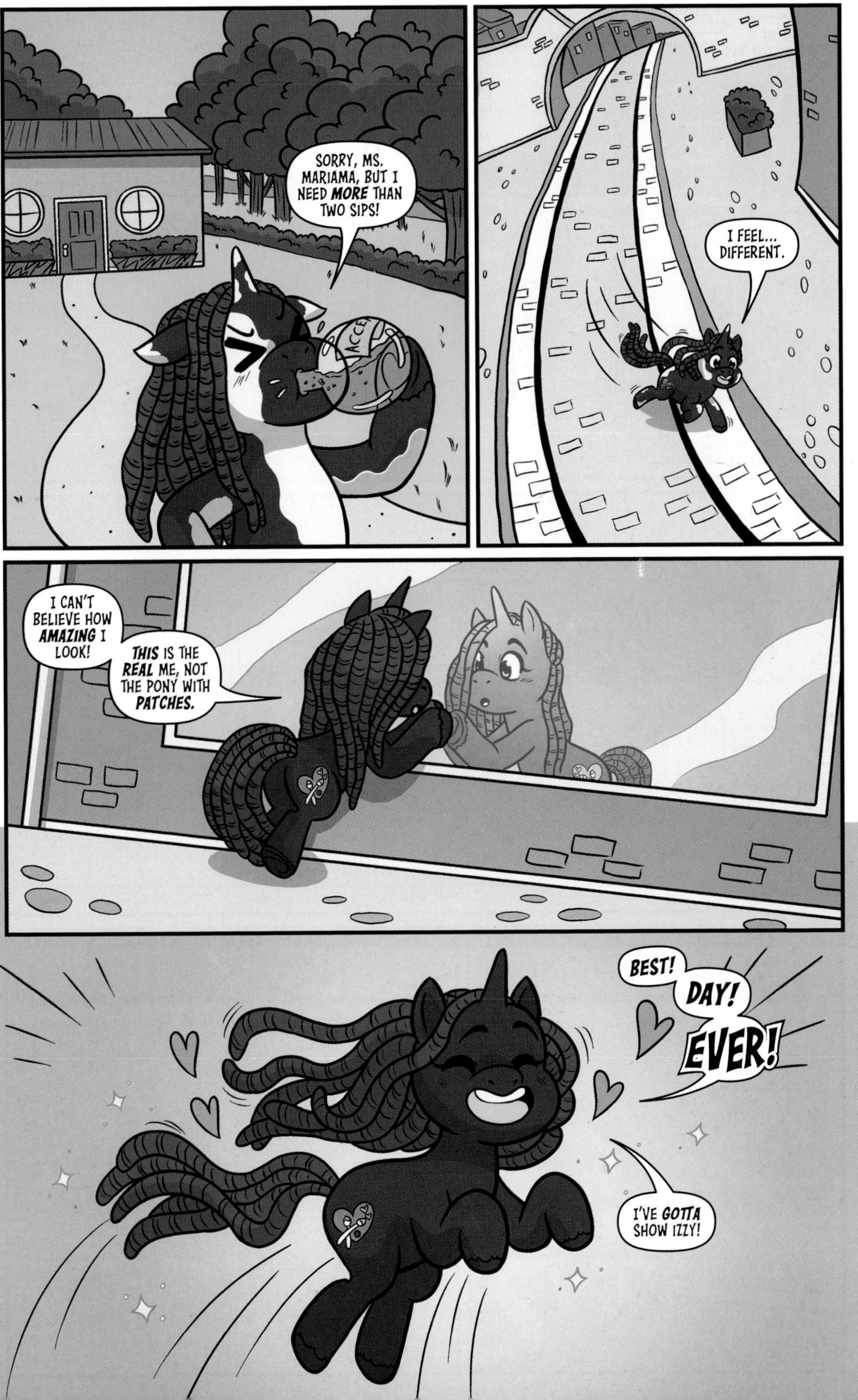
SORRY, MS. MARIAMA, BUT I NEED MORE THAN TWO SIPS!
I FEEL... DIFFERENT.
I CAN'T BELIEVE HOW AMAZING I LOOK!
THIS IS THE REAL ME, NOT THE PONY WITH PATCHES.
BEST!
DAY!
EVER!
I'VE GOTTA SHOW IZZY!

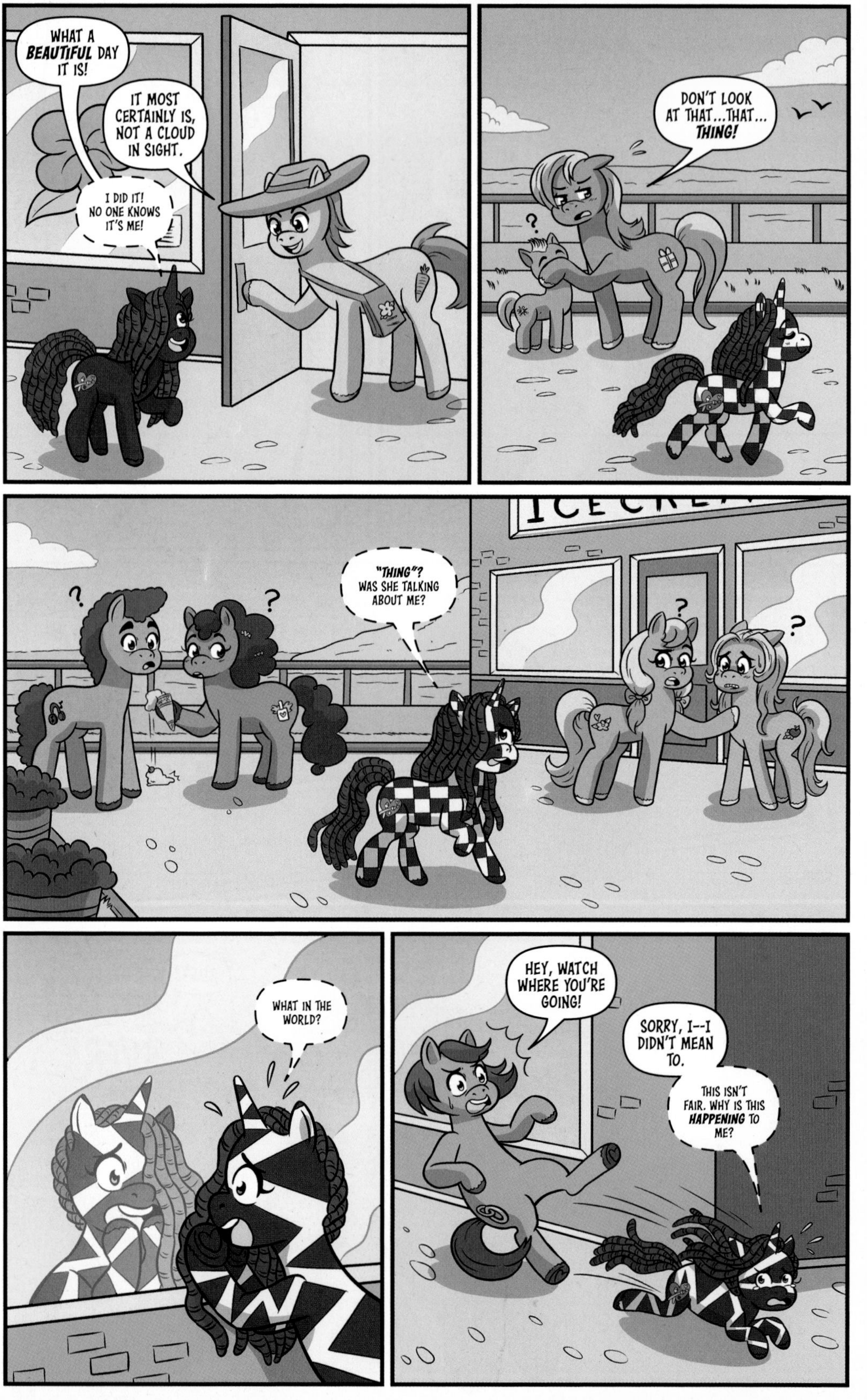
WHAT A BEAUTIFUL DAY IT IS!
IT MOST CERTAINLY IS, NOT A CLOUD IN SIGHT.
I DID IT! NO ONE KNOWS IT'S ME!
DON'T LOOK AT THAT...THAT... THING!
ICE CREA
"THING"? WAS SHE TALKING ABOUT ME?
WHAT IN THE WORLD?
HEY, WATCH WHERE YOU'RE GOING!
SORRY, I--I DIDN'T MEAN TO.
THIS ISN'T FAIR. WHY IS THIS HAPPENING TO ME?

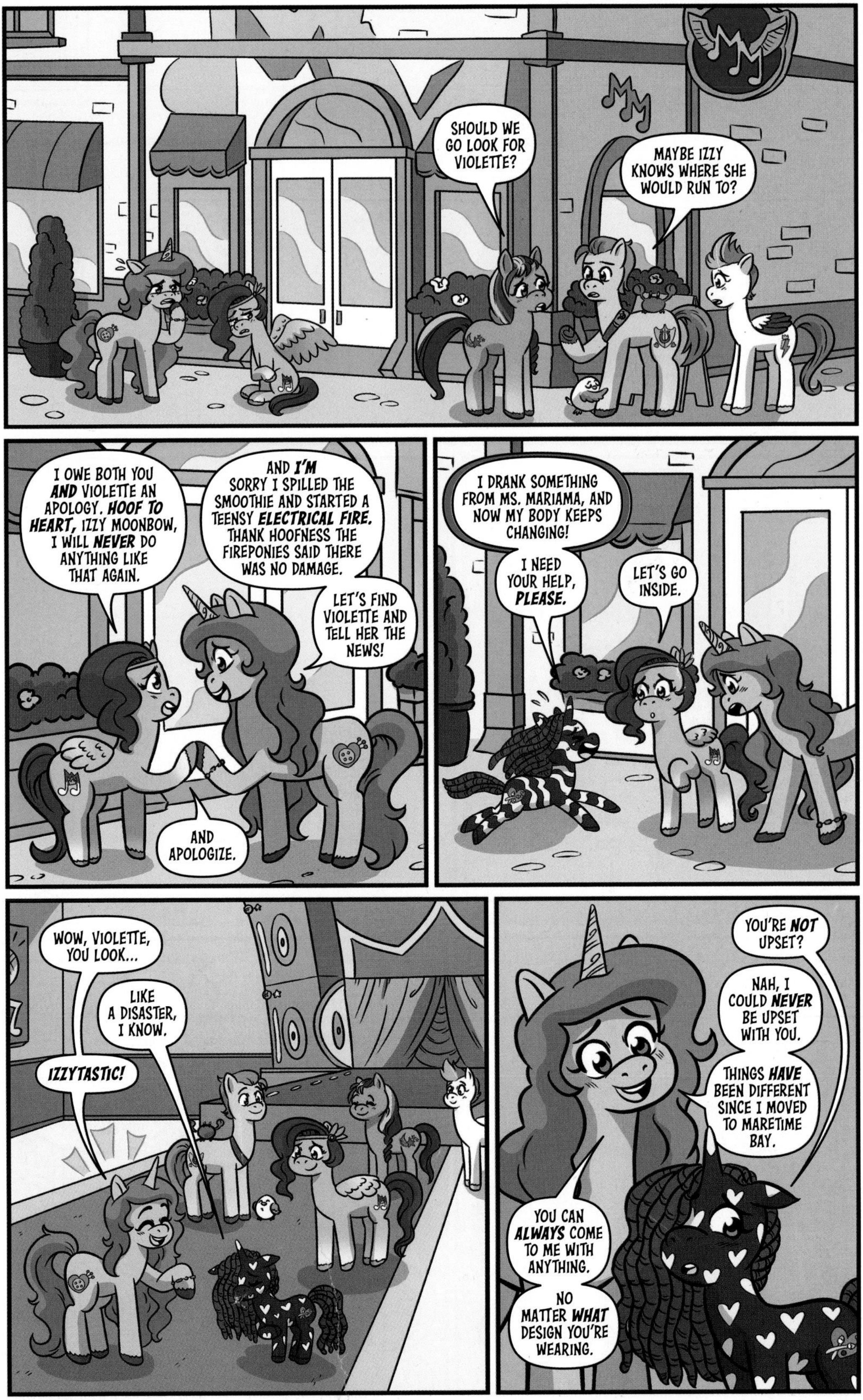
SHOULD WE GO LOOK FOR VIOLETTE?
MAYBE IZZY KNOWS WHERE SHE WOULD RUN TO?
I OWE BOTH YOU AND VIOLETTE AN APOLOGY. HOOF TO HEART, IZZY MOONBOW, I WILL NEVER DO ANYTHING LIKE THAT AGAIN.
AND APOLOGIZE.
AND I'M SORRY I SPILLED THE SMOOTHIE AND STARTED A TEENSY ELECTRICAL FIRE. THANK HOOFNESS THE FIREPONIES SAID THERE WAS NO DAMAGE.
LET'S FIND VIOLETTE AND TELL HER THE NEWS!
I DRANK SOMETHING FROM MS. MARIAMA, AND NOW MY BODY KEEPS CHANGING!
I NEED YOUR HELP, PLEASE.
LET'S GO INSIDE.
WOW, VIOLETTE, YOU LOOK...
LIKE A DISASTER, I KNOW.
IZZYTASTIC!
YOU'RE NOT UPSET?
NAH, I COULD NEVER BE UPSET WITH YOU.
THINGS HAVE BEEN DIFFERENT SINCE I MOVED TO MARETIME BAY.
YOU CAN ALWAYS COME TO ME WITH ANYTHING.
NO MATTER WHAT DESIGN YOU'RE WEARING.

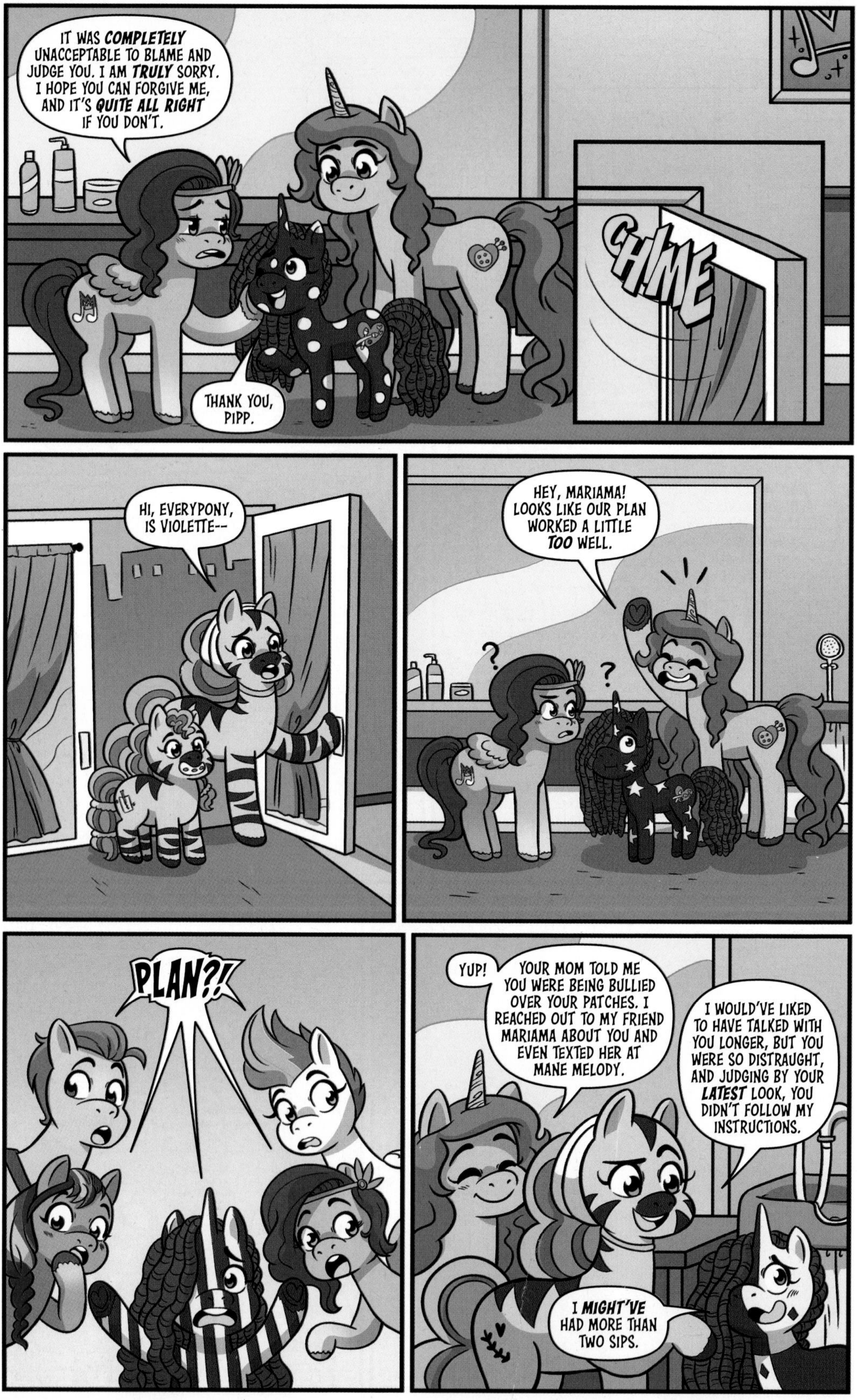
IT WAS COMPLETELY UNACCEPTABLE TO BLAME AND JUDGE YOU. I AM TRULY SORRY. I HOPE YOU CAN FORGIVE ME, AND IT'S QUITE ALL RIGHT IF YOU DON'T.
THANK YOU, PIPP.
CHIME
HI, EVERYPONY, IS VIOLETTE--
HEY, MARIAMA! LOOKS LIKE OUR PLAN WORKED A LITTLE TOO WELL.
PLAN?!
YUP!
YOUR MOM TOLD ME YOU WERE BEING BULLIED OVER YOUR PATCHES. I REACHED OUT TO MY FRIEND MARIAMA ABOUT YOU AND EVEN TEXTED HER AT MANE MELODY.
I WOULD'VE LIKED TO HAVE TALKED WITH YOU LONGER, BUT YOU WERE SO DISTRAUGHT, AND JUDGING BY YOUR LATEST LOOK, YOU DIDN'T FOLLOW MY INSTRUCTIONS.
I MIGHT'VE HAD MORE THAN TWO SIPS.

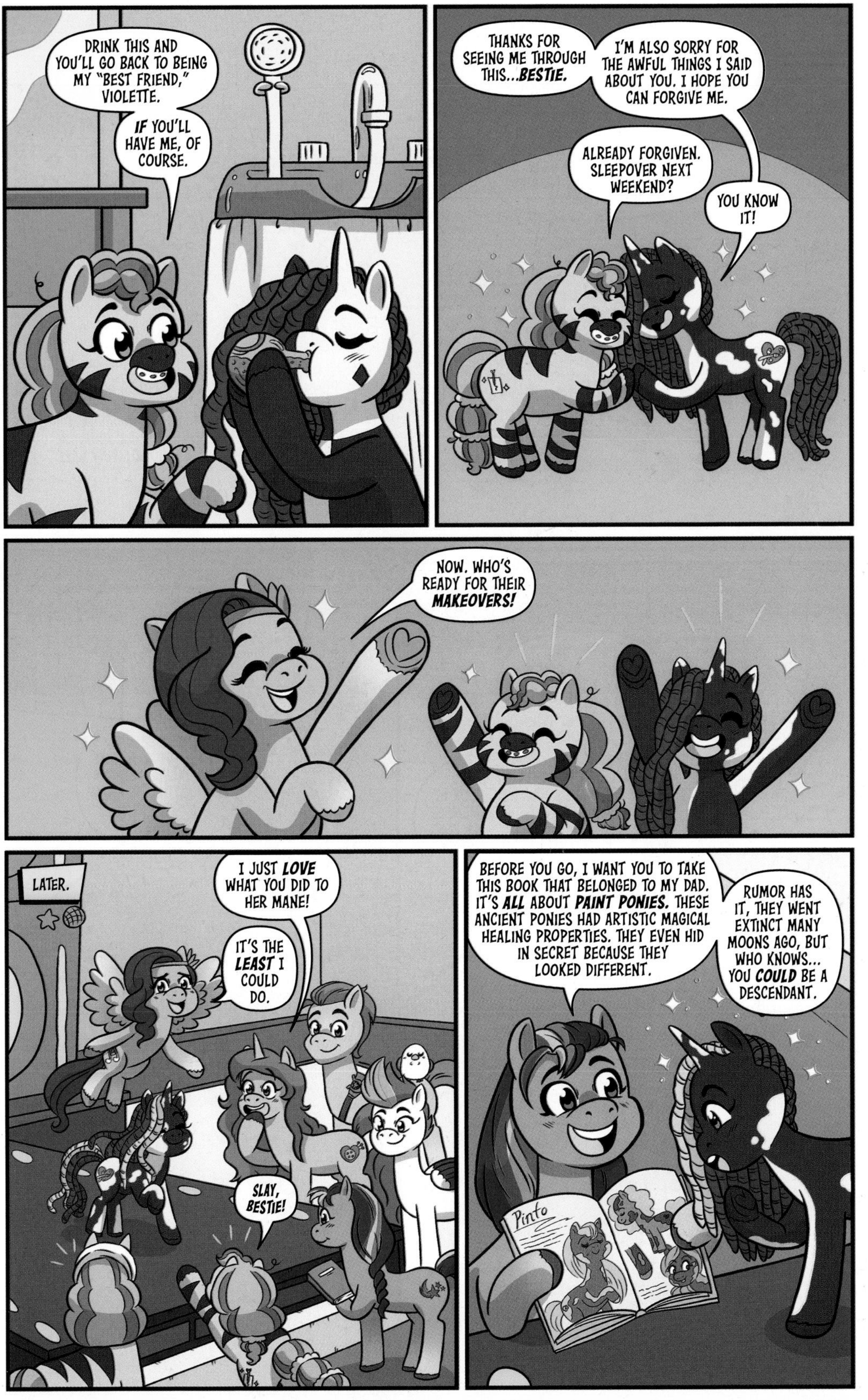
DRINK THIS AND YOU'LL GO BACK TO BEING MY "BEST FRIEND," VIOLETTE.
IF YOU'LL HAVE ME, OF COURSE.
THANKS FOR SEEING ME THROUGH THIS...BESTIE.
I'M ALSO SORRY FOR THE AWFUL THINGS I SAID ABOUT YOU. I HOPE YOU CAN FORGIVE ME.
ALREADY FORGIVEN. SLEEPOVER NEXT WEEKEND?
YOU KNOW IT!
NOW. WHO'S READY FOR THEIR MAKEOVERS!
LATER.
I JUST LOVE WHAT YOU DID TO HER MANE!
IT'S THE LEAST I COULD DO.
SLAY, BESTIE!
BEFORE YOU GO, I WANT YOU TO TAKE THIS BOOK THAT BELONGED TO MY DAD. IT'S ALL ABOUT PAINT PONIES. THESE ANCIENT PONIES HAD ARTISTIC MAGICAL HEALING PROPERTIES. THEY EVEN HID IN SECRET BECAUSE THEY LOOKED DIFFERENT.
RUMOR HAS IT, THEY WENT EXTINCT MANY MOONS AGO, BUT WHO KNOWS... YOU COULD BE A DESCENDANT.
Pinto

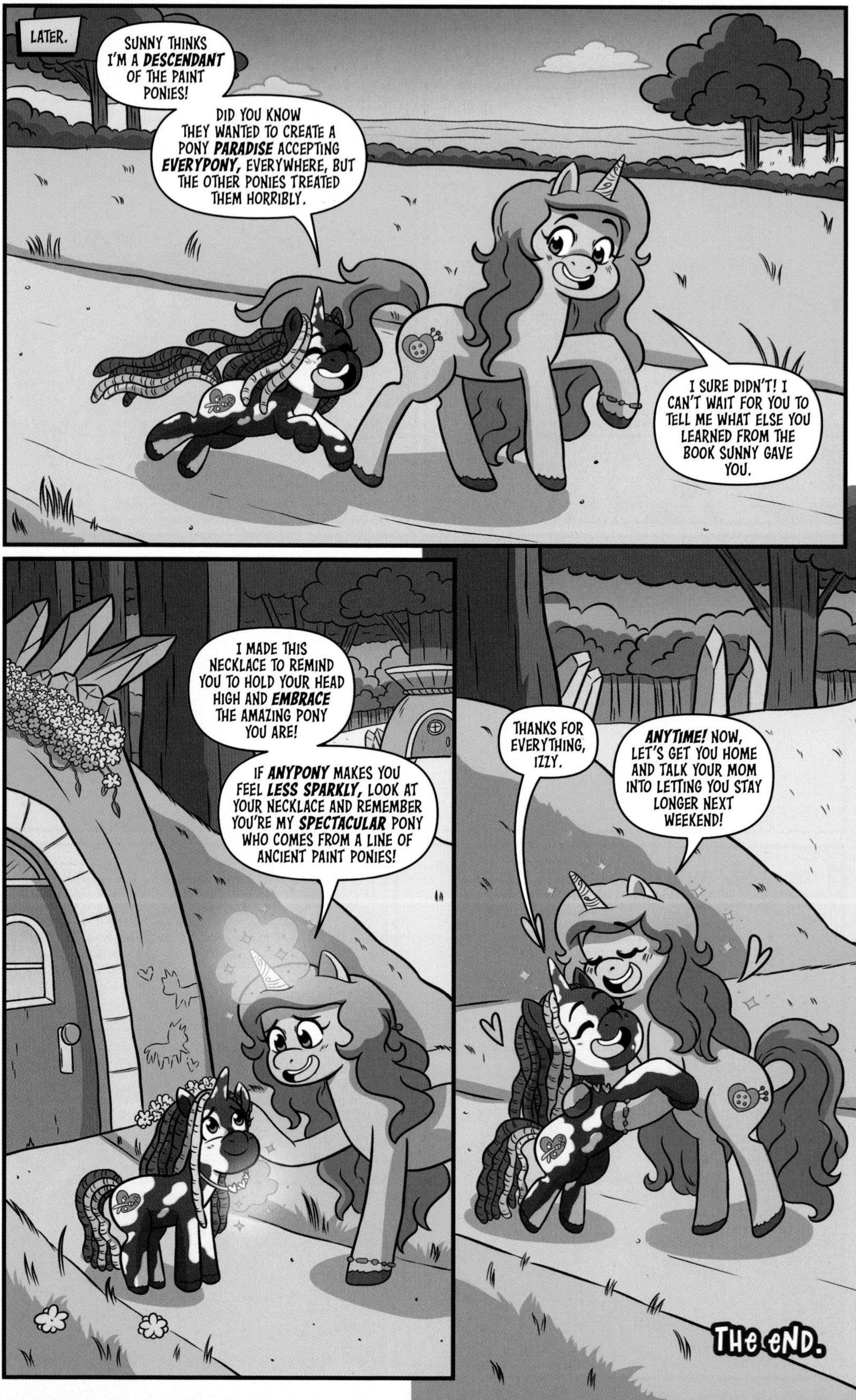

LATER.
SUNNY THINKS I'M A DESCENDANT OF THE PAINT PONIES!
DID YOU KNOW THEY WANTED TO CREATE A PONY PARADISE ACCEPTING EVERYPONY, EVERYWHERE, BUT THE OTHER PONIES TREATED THEM HORRIBLY.
I SURE DIDN'T! I CAN'T WAIT FOR YOU TO TELL ME WHAT ELSE YOU LEARNED FROM THE BOOK SUNNY GAVE YOU.
I MADE THIS NECKLACE TO REMIND YOU TO HOLD YOUR HEAD HIGH AND EMBRACE THE AMAZING PONY YOU ARE!
IF ANYPONY MAKES YOU FEEL LESS SPARKLY, LOOK AT YOUR NECKLACE AND REMEMBER YOU'RE MY SPECTACULAR PONY WHO COMES FROM A LINE OF ANCIENT PAINT PONIES!
THANKS FOR EVERYTHING, IZZY.
ANYTIME! NOW, LET'S GET YOU HOME AND TALK YOUR MOM INTO LETTING YOU STAY LONGER NEXT WEEKEND!
THE END.

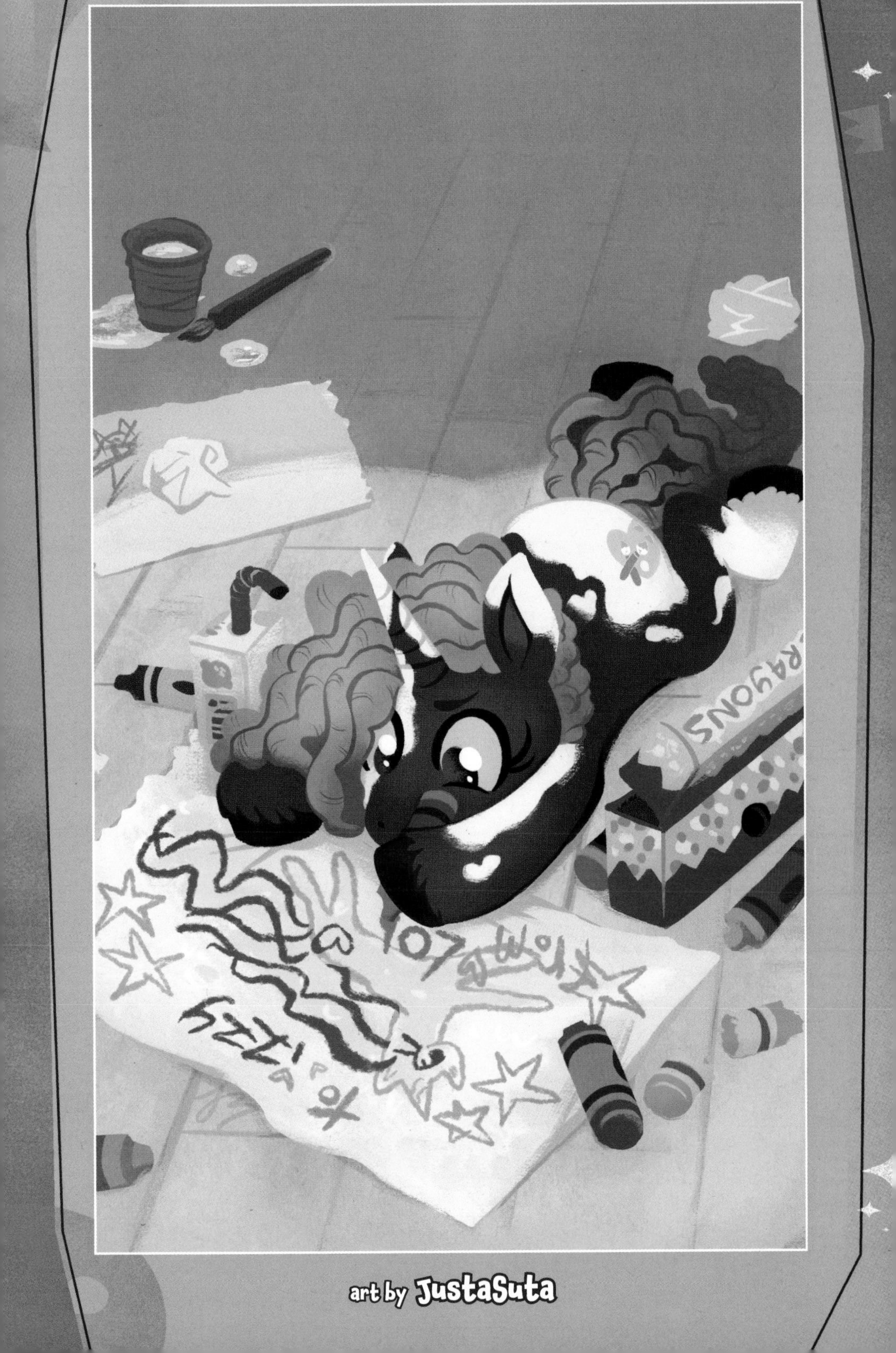
CRAYONS

art by JustaSuta

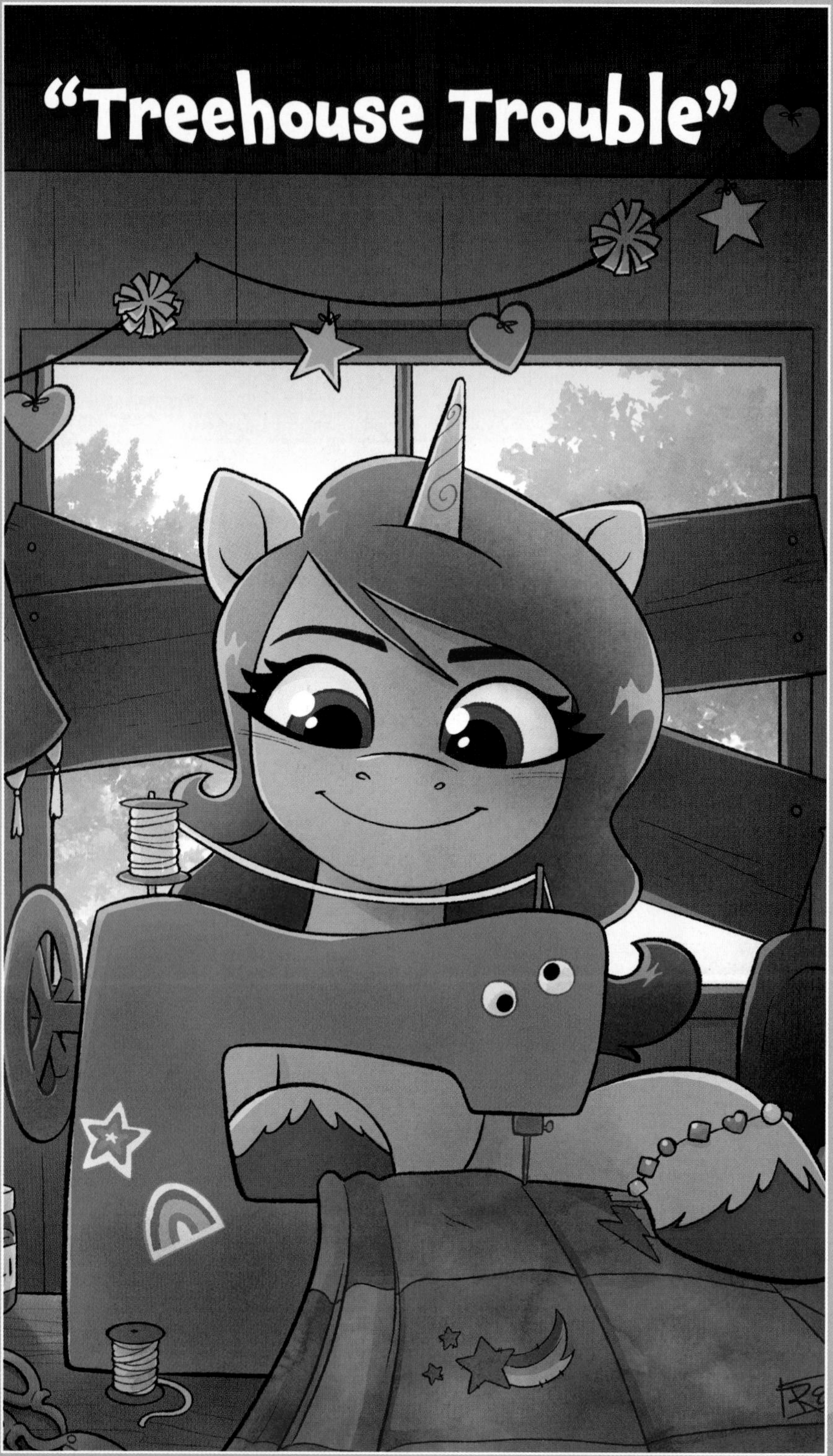
"Treehouse Trouble"

art by Robin Easter

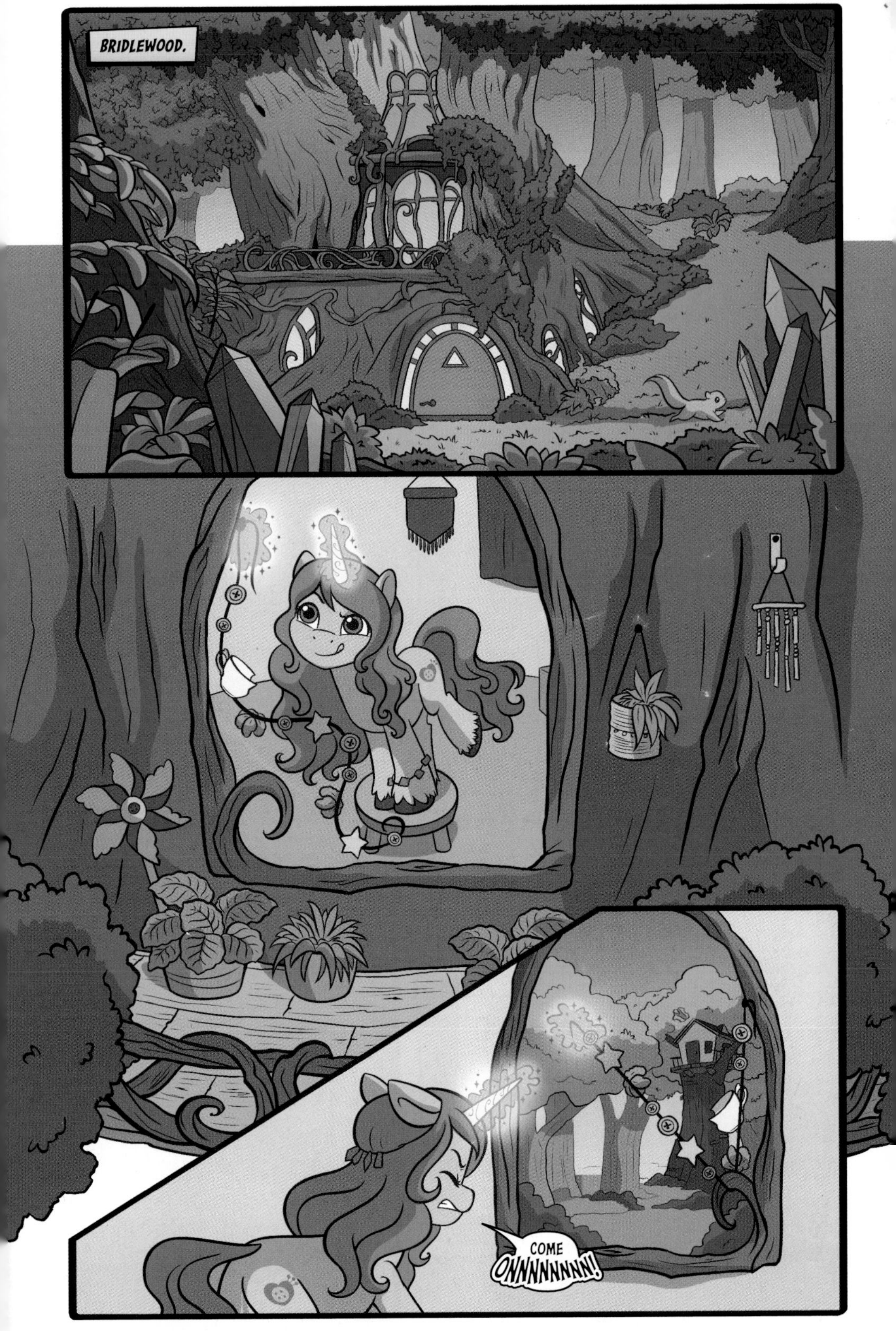
BRIDLEWOOD.
COME ONNNNNNNN!

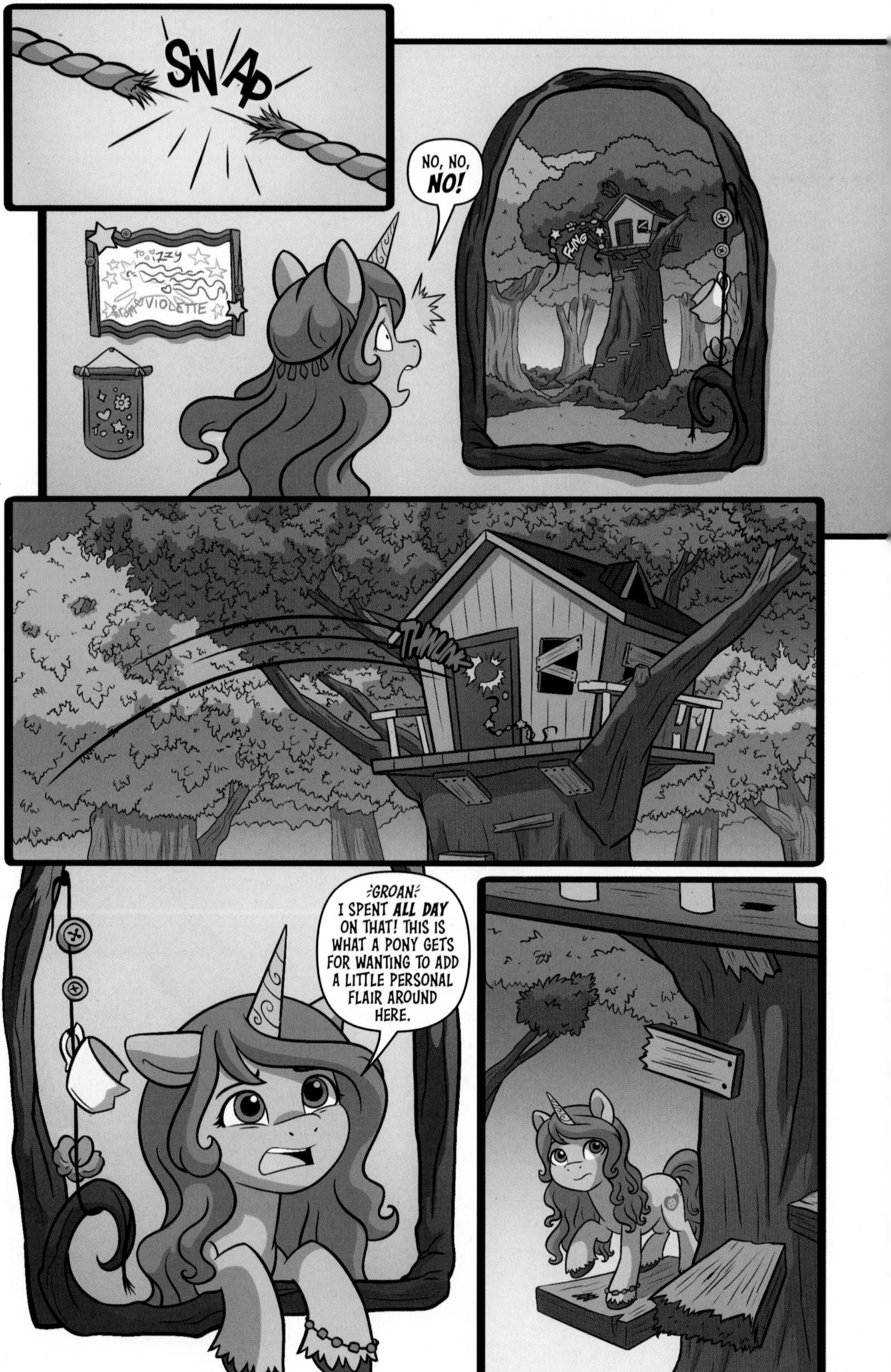
SNAP
NO, NO, NO!
to Izzy from VIOLETTE
FLING
THUNK
GROAN
I SPENT ALL DAY ON THAT! THIS IS WHAT A PONY GETS FOR WANTING TO ADD A LITTLE PERSONAL FLAIR AROUND HERE.

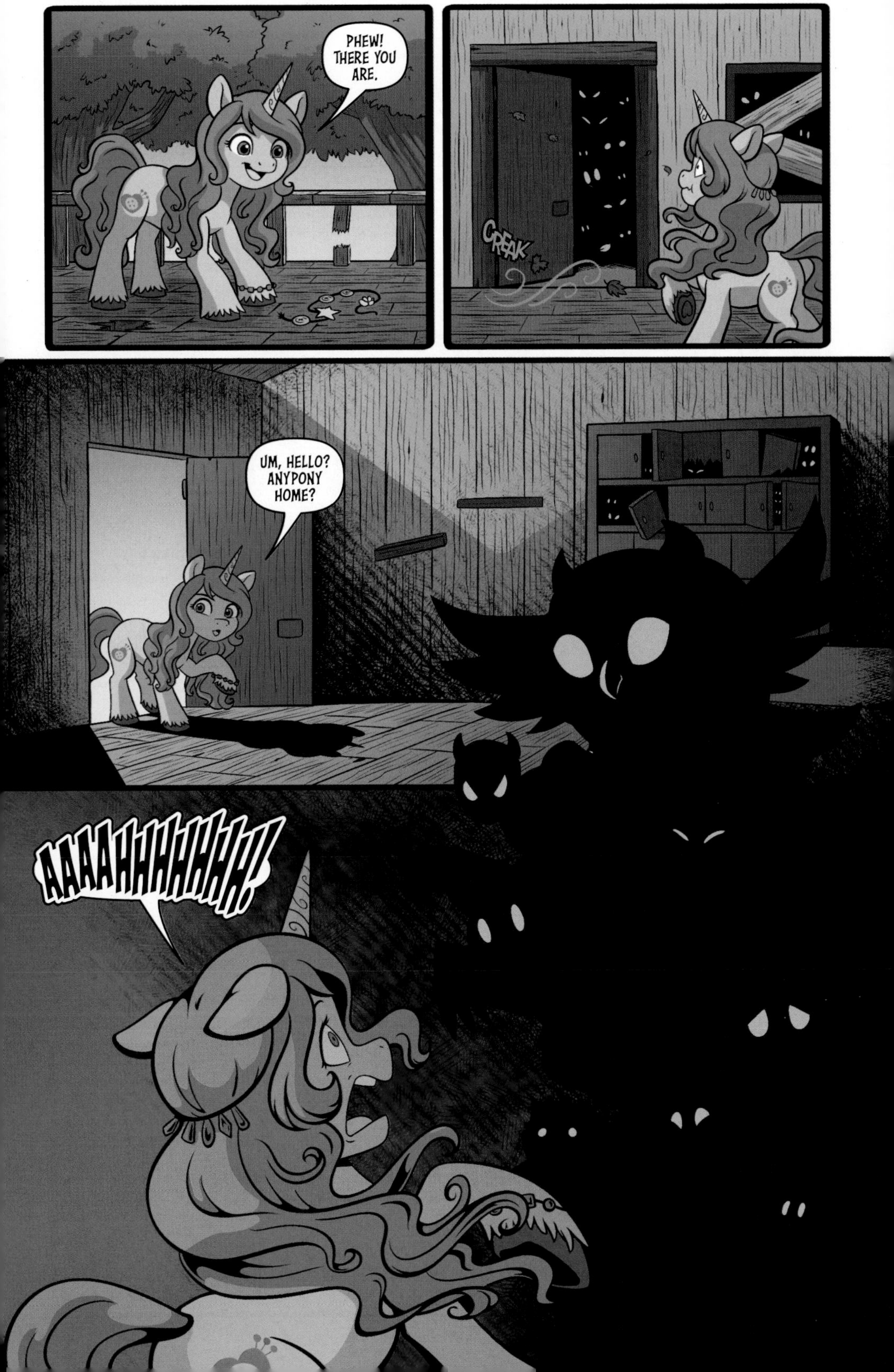
PHEW! THERE YOU ARE.
CREAK
UM, HELLO? ANYPONY HOME?
AAAAHHHHHHH!!

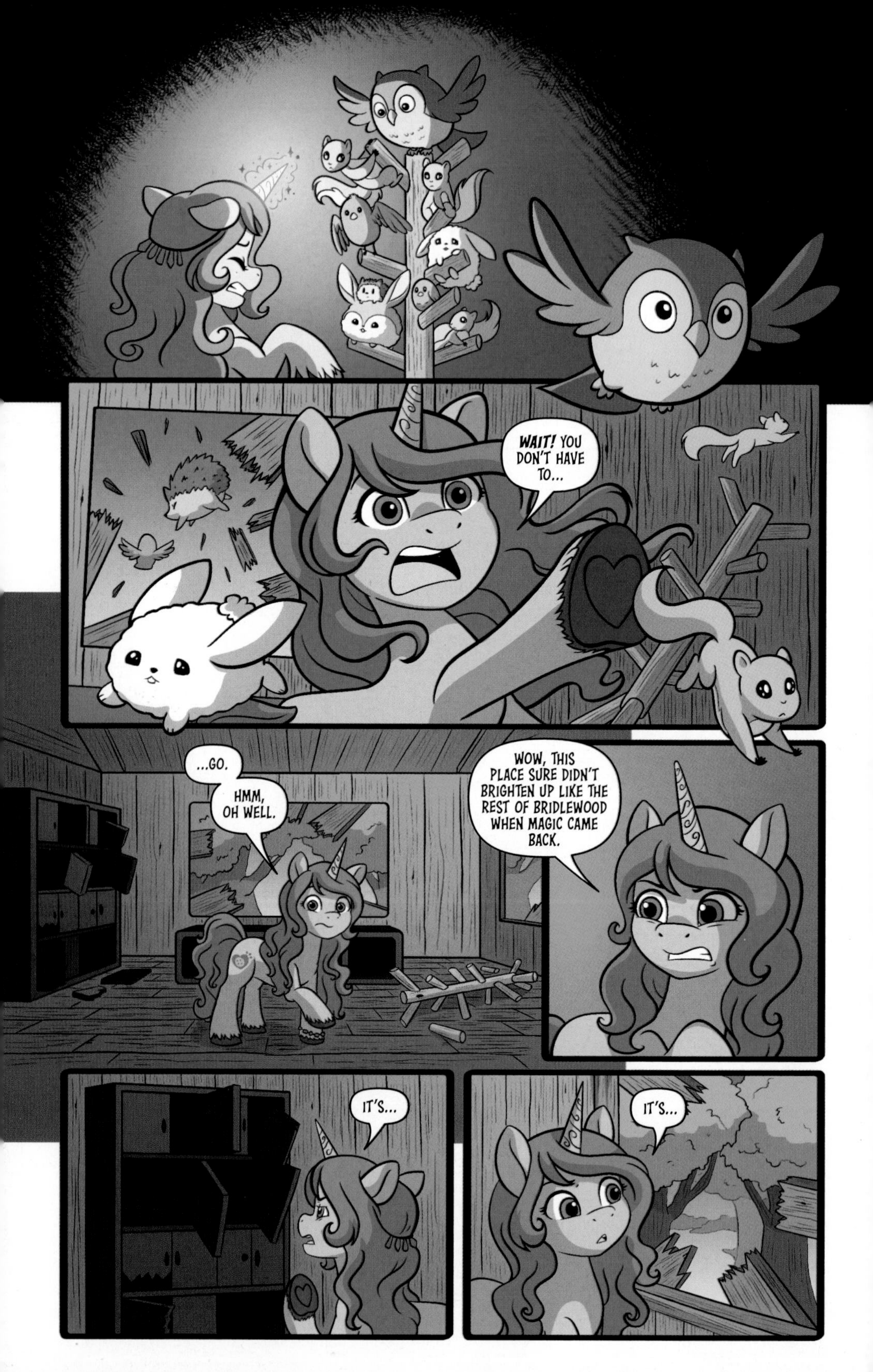
WAIT! YOU DON'T HAVE TO...
...GO.
HMM, OH WELL.
WOW, THIS PLACE SURE DIDN'T BRIGHTEN UP LIKE THE REST OF BRIDLEWOOD WHEN MAGIC CAME BACK.
IT'S...
IT'S...

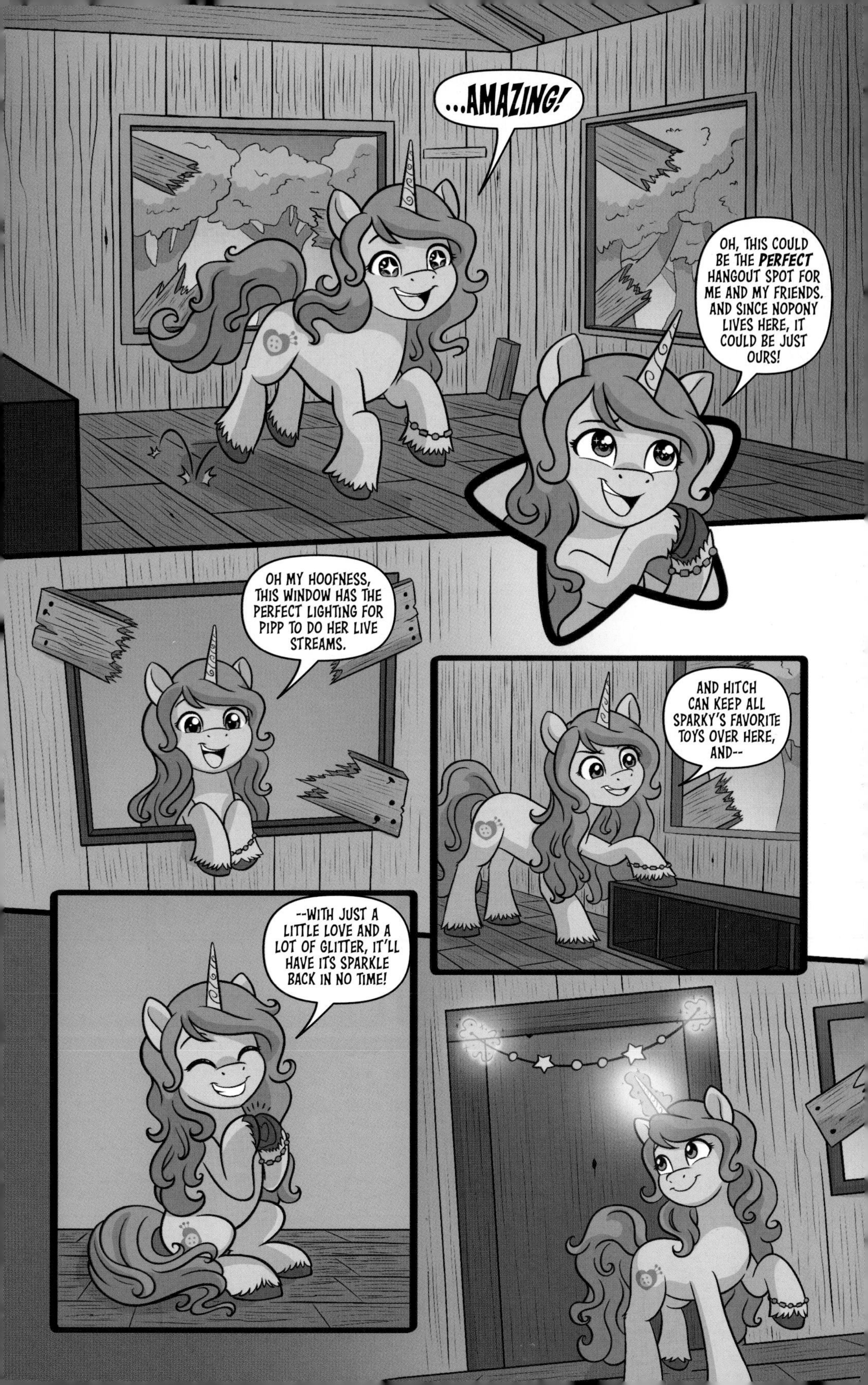
...AMAZING!
OH, THIS COULD BE THE PERFECT HANGOUT SPOT FOR ME AND MY FRIENDS. AND SINCE NOPONY LIVES HERE, IT COULD BE JUST OURS!
OH MY HOOFNESS, THIS WINDOW HAS THE PERFECT LIGHTING FOR PIPP TO DO HER LIVE STREAMS.
AND HITCH CAN KEEP ALL SPARKY'S FAVORITE TOYS OVER HERE, AND--
--WITH JUST A LITTLE LOVE AND A LOT OF GLITTER, IT'LL HAVE ITS SPARKLE BACK IN NO TIME!

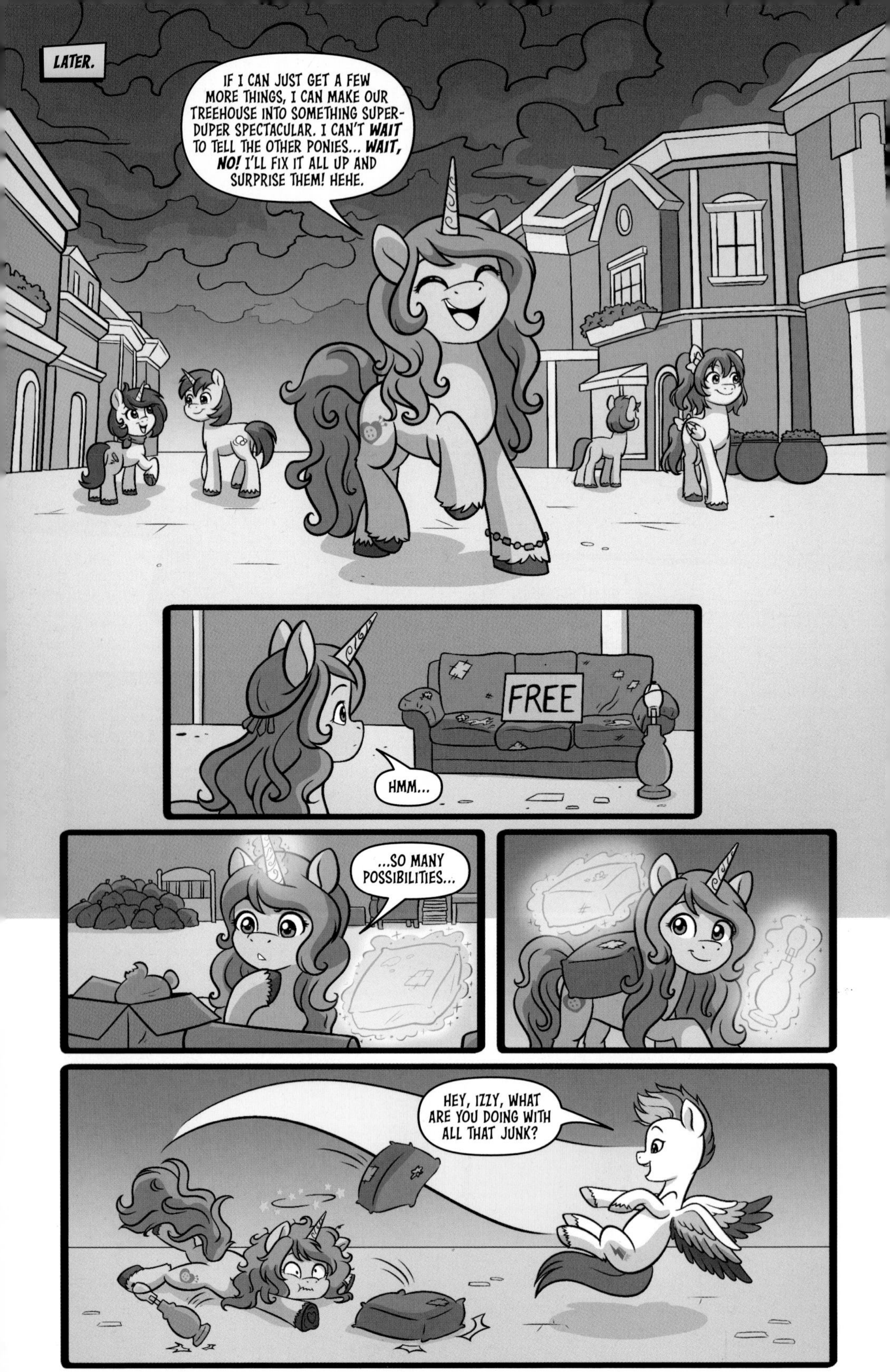
LATER.
IF I CAN JUST GET A FEW MORE THINGS, I CAN MAKE OUR TREEHOUSE INTO SOMETHING SUPER-DUPER SPECTACULAR. I CAN'T WAIT TO TELL THE OTHER PONIES... WAIT, NO! I'LL FIX IT ALL UP AND SURPRISE THEM! HEHE.
FREE
HMM...
...SO MANY POSSIBILITIES...
HEY, IZZY, WHAT ARE YOU DOING WITH ALL THAT JUNK?

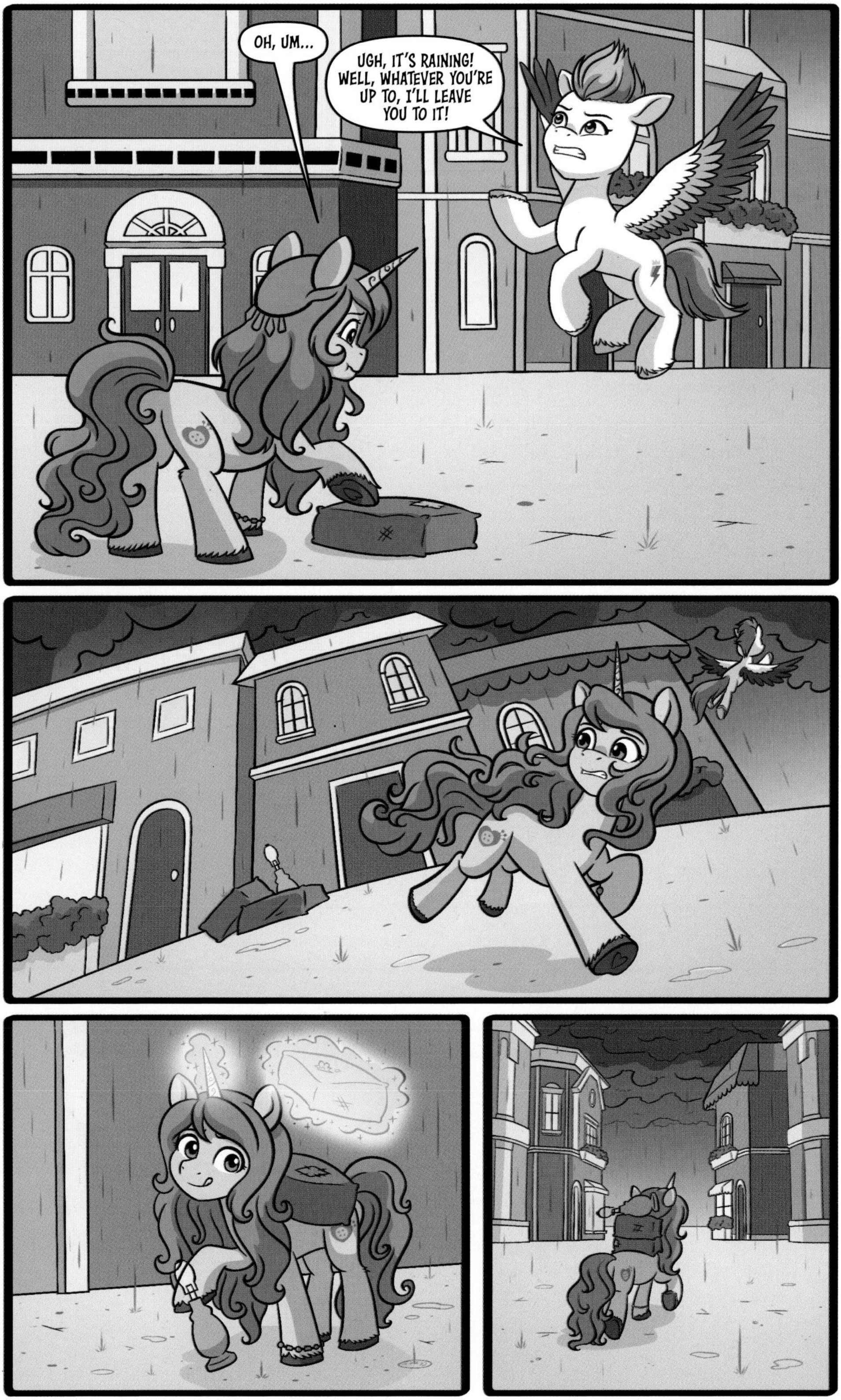
OH, UM...
UGH, IT'S RAINING! WELL, WHATEVER YOU'RE UP TO, I'LL LEAVE YOU TO IT!

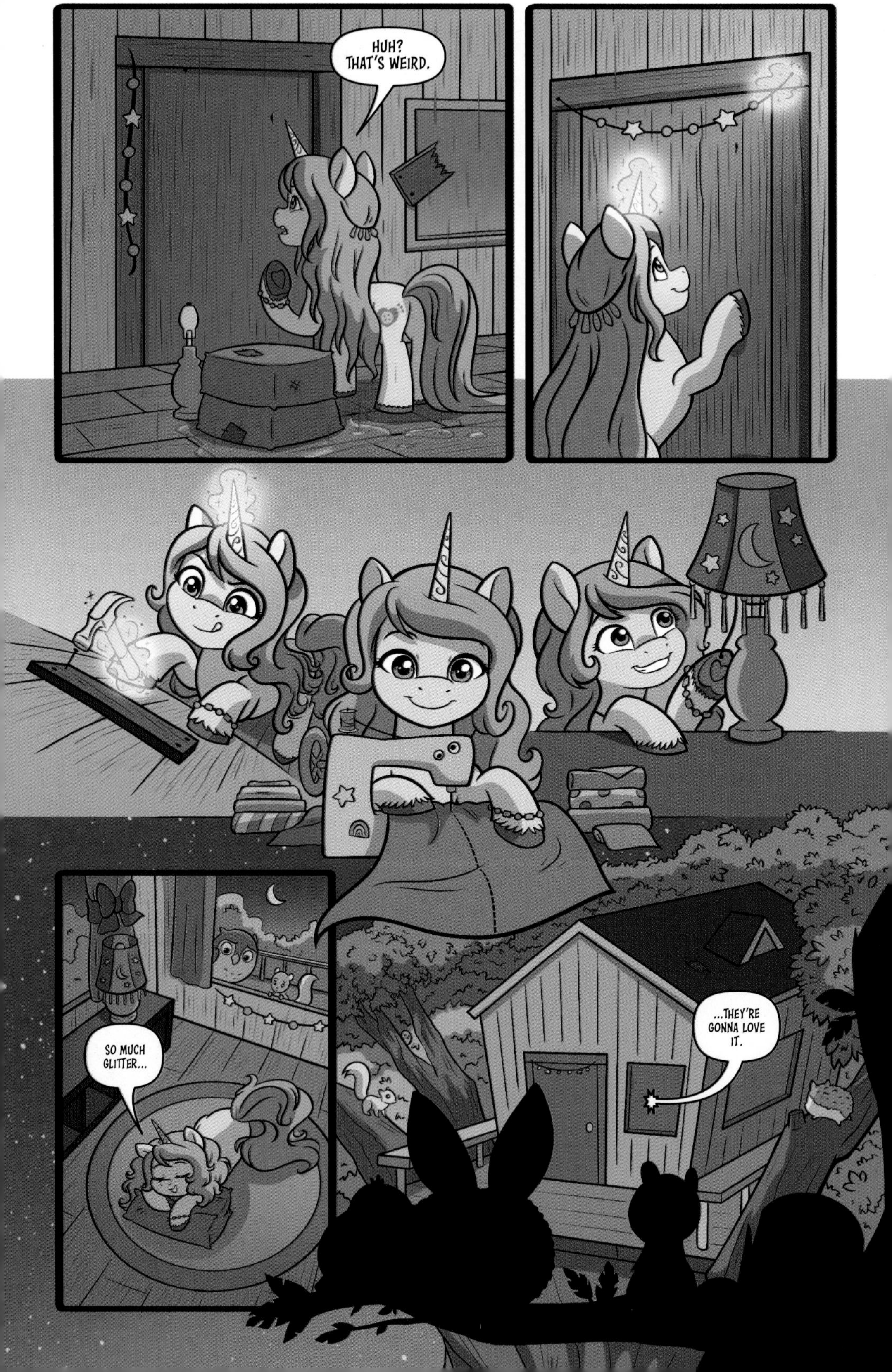
HUH? THAT'S WEIRD.
SO MUCH GLITTER...
...THEY'RE GONNA LOVE IT.

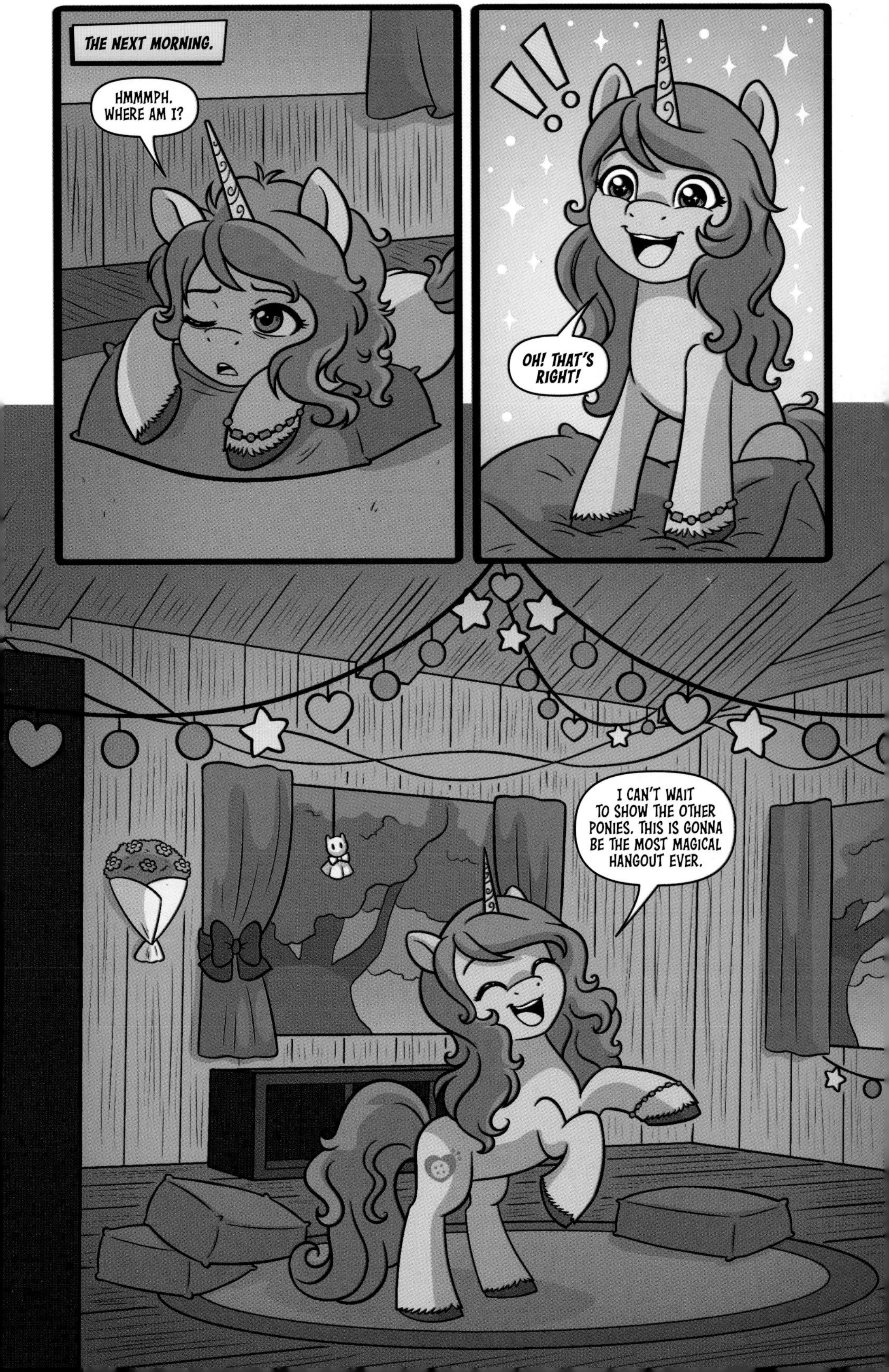
THE NEXT MORNING.
HMMMPH. WHERE AM I?
OH! THAT'S RIGHT!
I CAN'T WAIT TO SHOW THE OTHER PONIES. THIS IS GONNA BE THE MOST MAGICAL HANGOUT EVER.

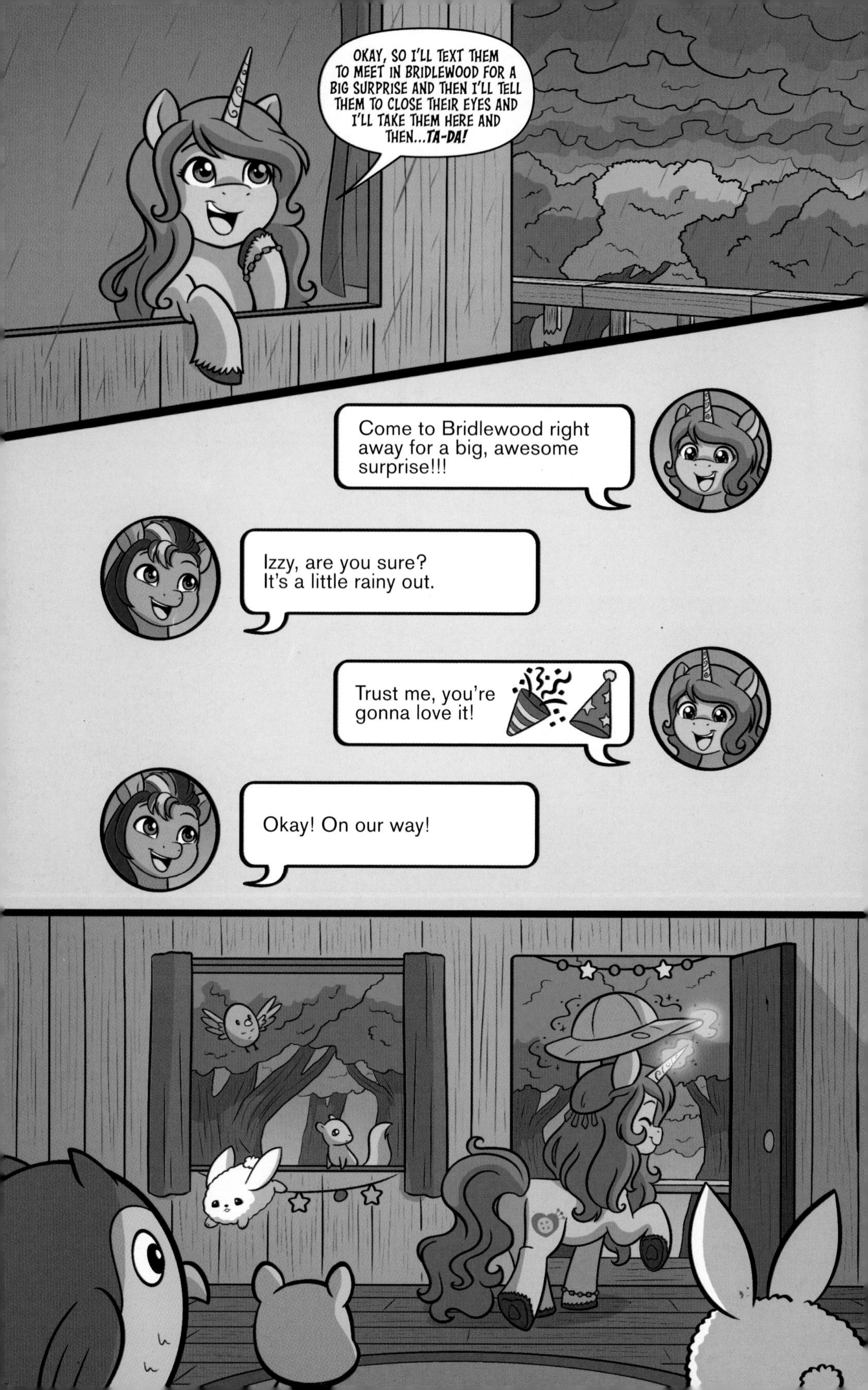
OKAY, SO I'LL TEXT THEM TO MEET IN BRIDLEWOOD FOR A BIG SURPRISE AND THEN I'LL TELL THEM TO CLOSE THEIR EYES AND I'LL TAKE THEM HERE AND THEN...TA-DA!
Come to Bridlewood right away for a big, awesome surprise!!!
Izzy, are you sure? It's a little rainy out.
Trust me, you're gonna love it!
Okay! On our way!

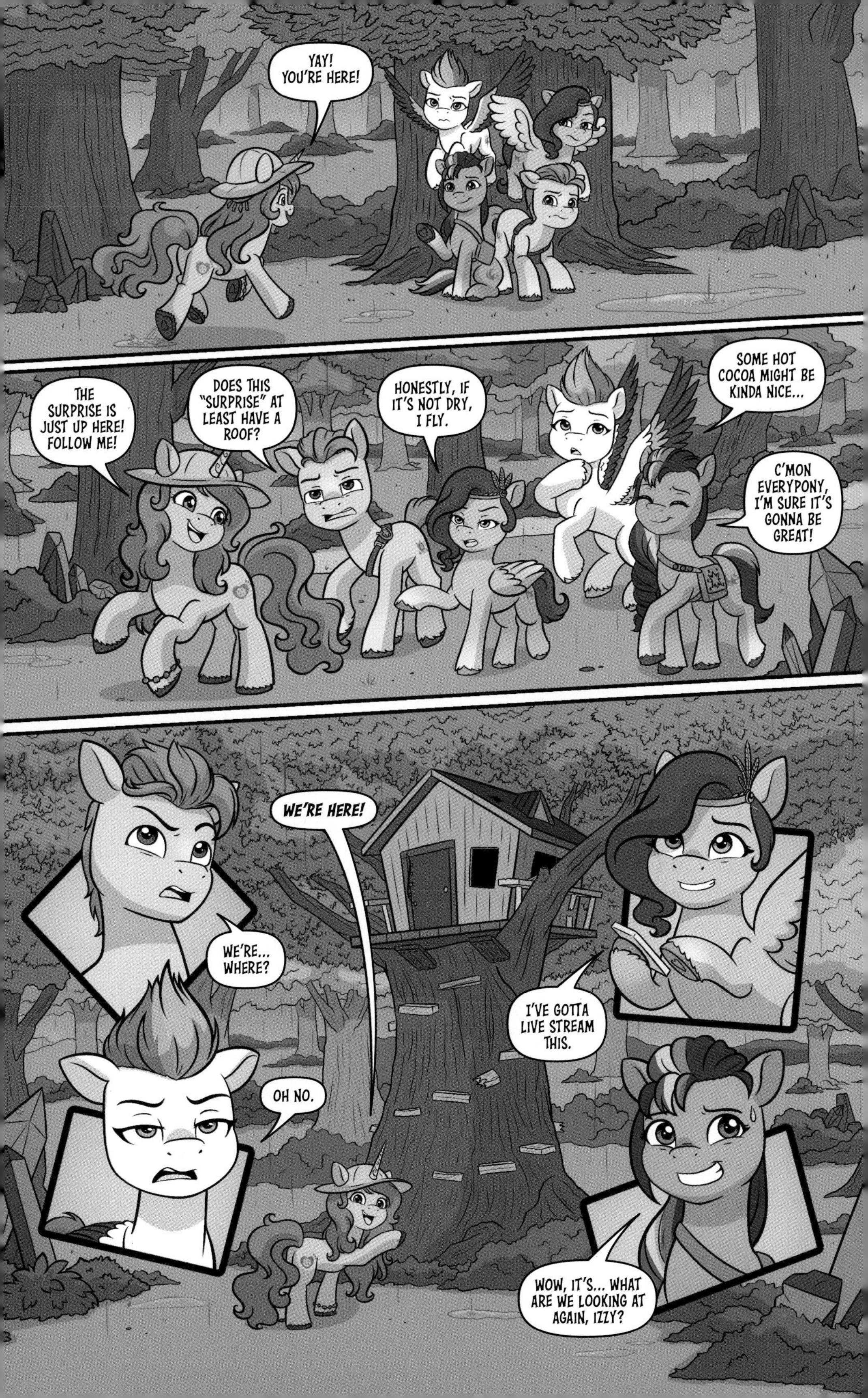
YAY! YOU'RE HERE!
THE SURPRISE IS JUST UP HERE! FOLLOW ME!
DOES THIS "SURPRISE" AT LEAST HAVE A ROOF?
HONESTLY, IF IT'S NOT DRY, I FLY.
SOME HOT COCOA MIGHT BE KINDA NICE...
C'MON EVERYPONY, I'M SURE IT'S GONNA BE GREAT!
WE'RE HERE!
WE'RE... WHERE?
OH NO.
I'VE GOTTA LIVE STREAM THIS.
WOW, IT'S... WHAT ARE WE LOOKING AT AGAIN, IZZY?

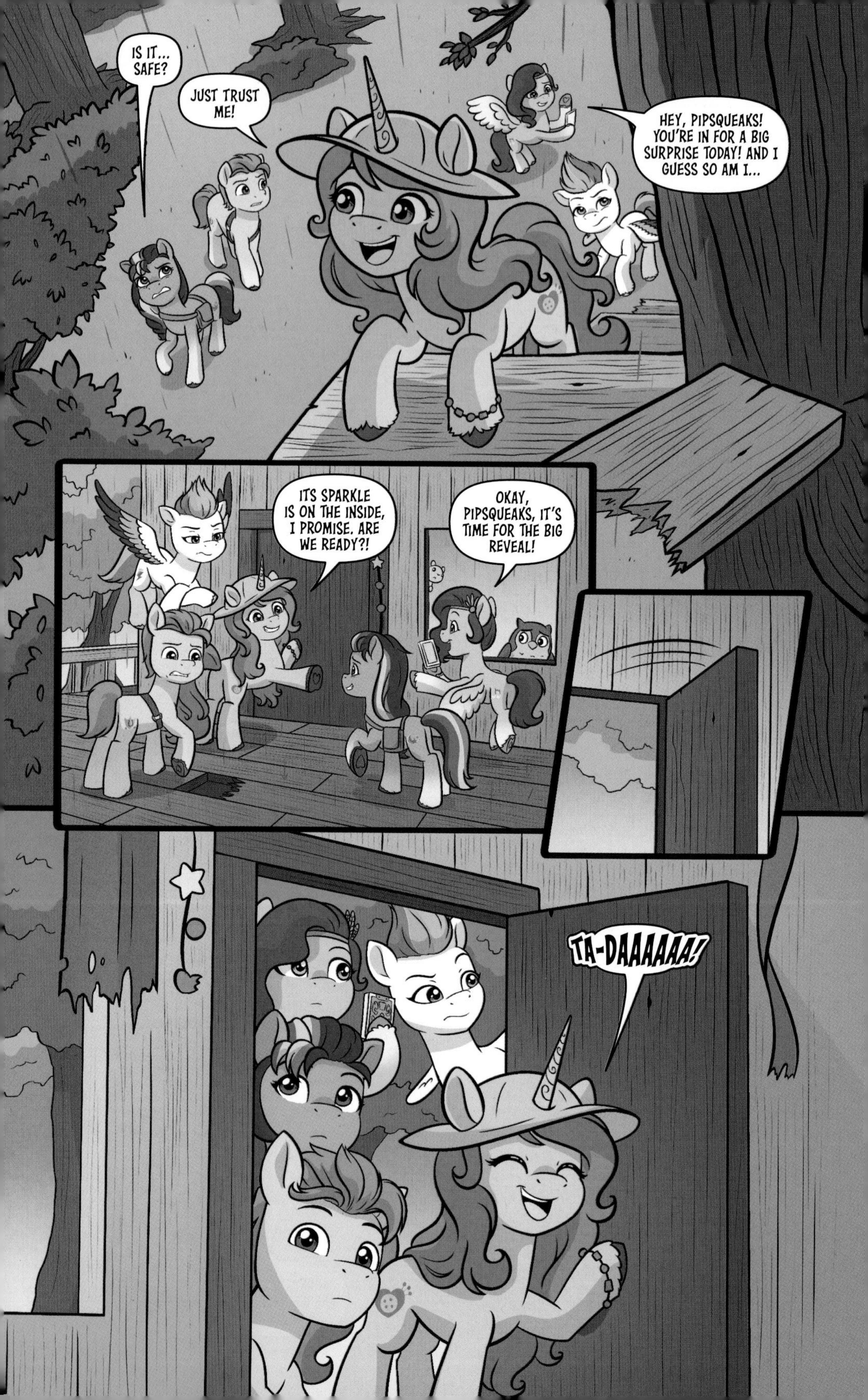
IS IT... SAFE?
JUST TRUST ME!
HEY, PIPSQUEAKS! YOU'RE IN FOR A BIG SURPRISE TODAY! AND I GUESS SO AM I...
ITS SPARKLE IS ON THE INSIDE, I PROMISE. ARE WE READY?!
OKAY, PIPSQUEAKS, IT'S TIME FOR THE BIG REVEAL!
TA-DAAAAAA!

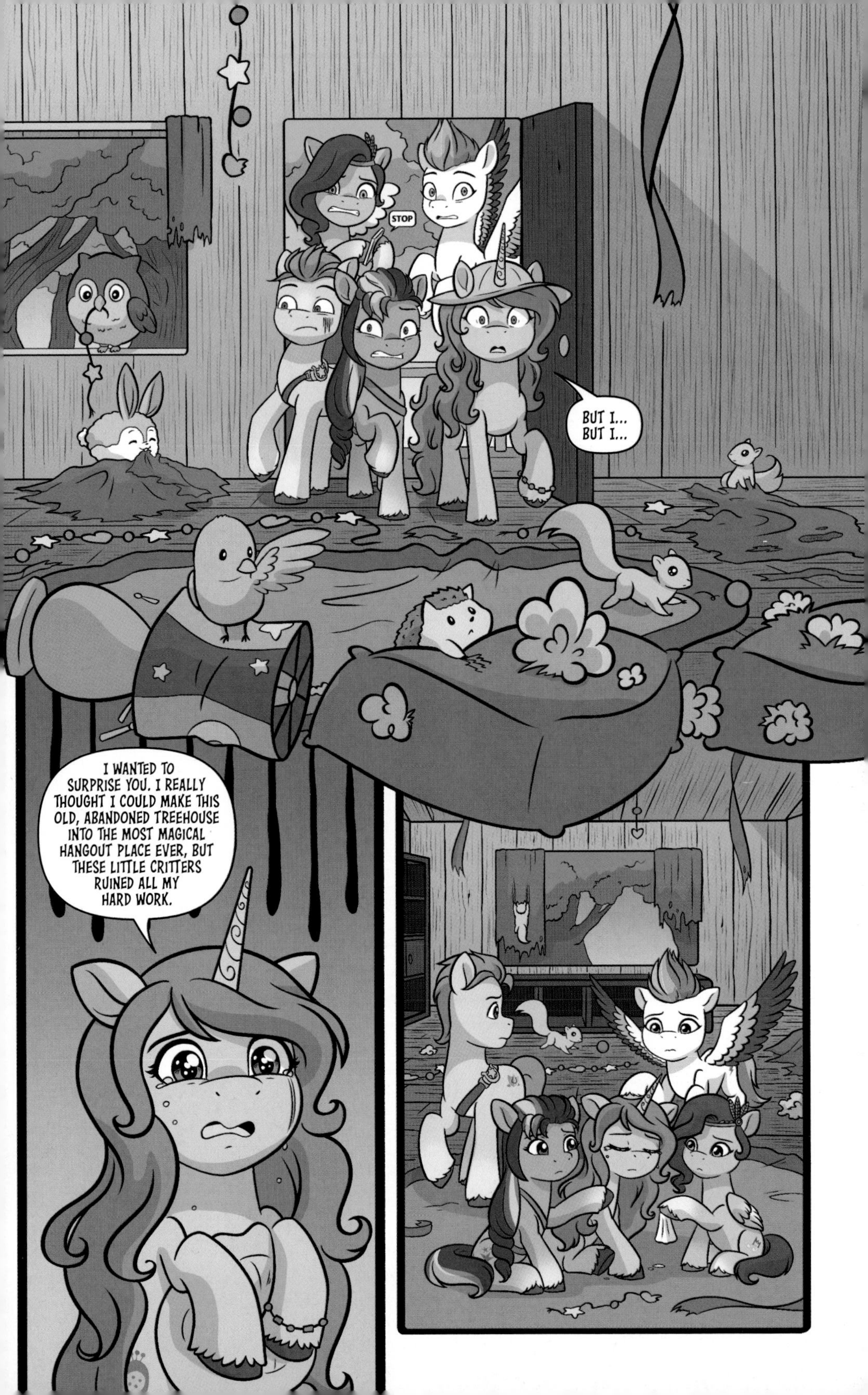
STOP
BUT I... BUT I...
I WANTED TO SURPRISE YOU. I REALLY THOUGHT I COULD MAKE THIS OLD, ABANDONED TREEHOUSE INTO THE MOST MAGICAL HANGOUT PLACE EVER, BUT THESE LITTLE CRITTERS RUINED ALL MY HARD WORK.

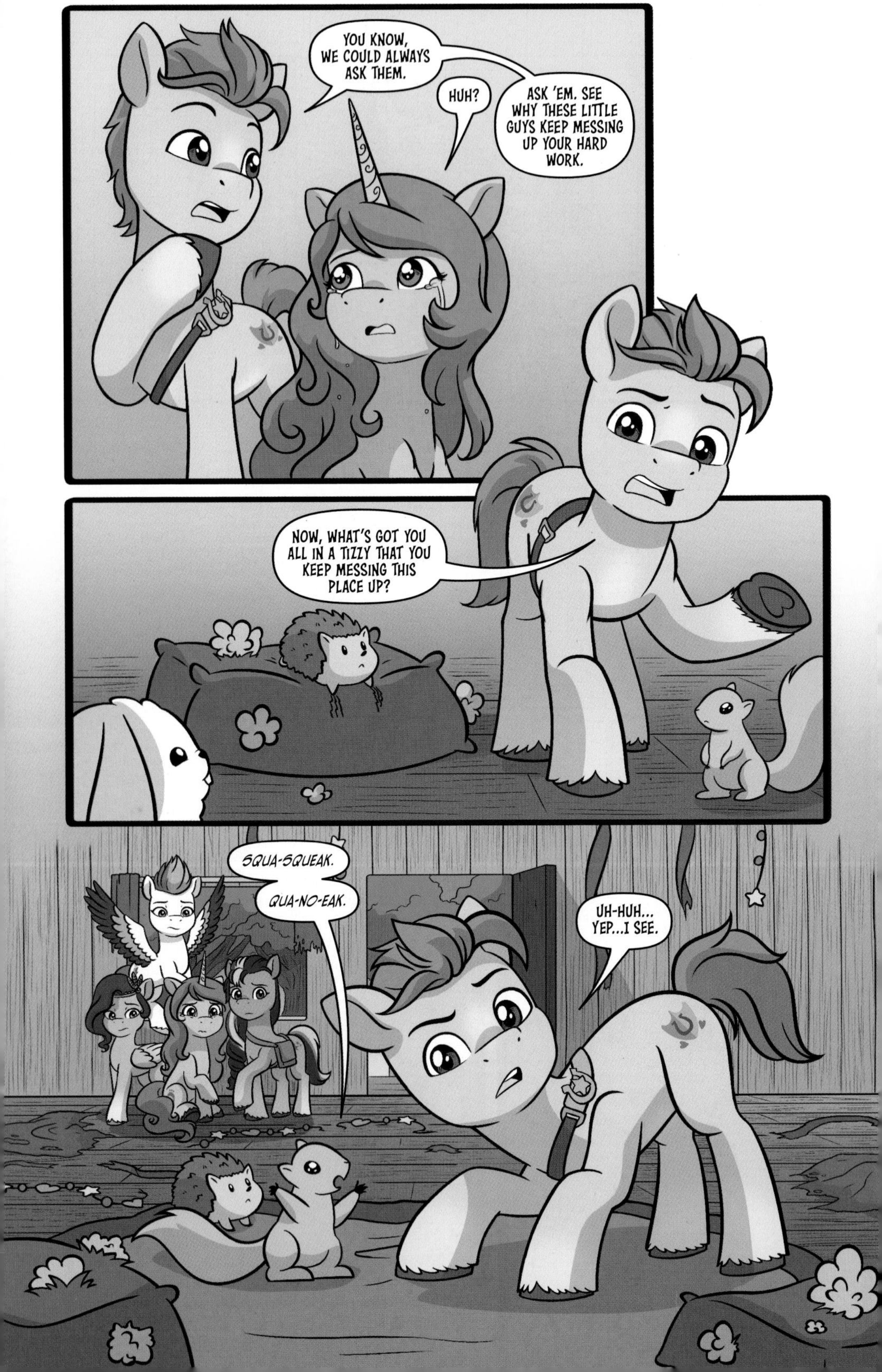
YOU KNOW, WE COULD ALWAYS ASK THEM.
HUH?
ASK 'EM. SEE WHY THESE LITTLE GUYS KEEP MESSING UP YOUR HARD WORK.
NOW, WHAT'S GOT YOU ALL IN A TIZZY THAT YOU KEEP MESSING THIS PLACE UP?
SQUA-SQUEAK.
QUA-NO-EAK.
UH-HUH... YEP...I SEE.

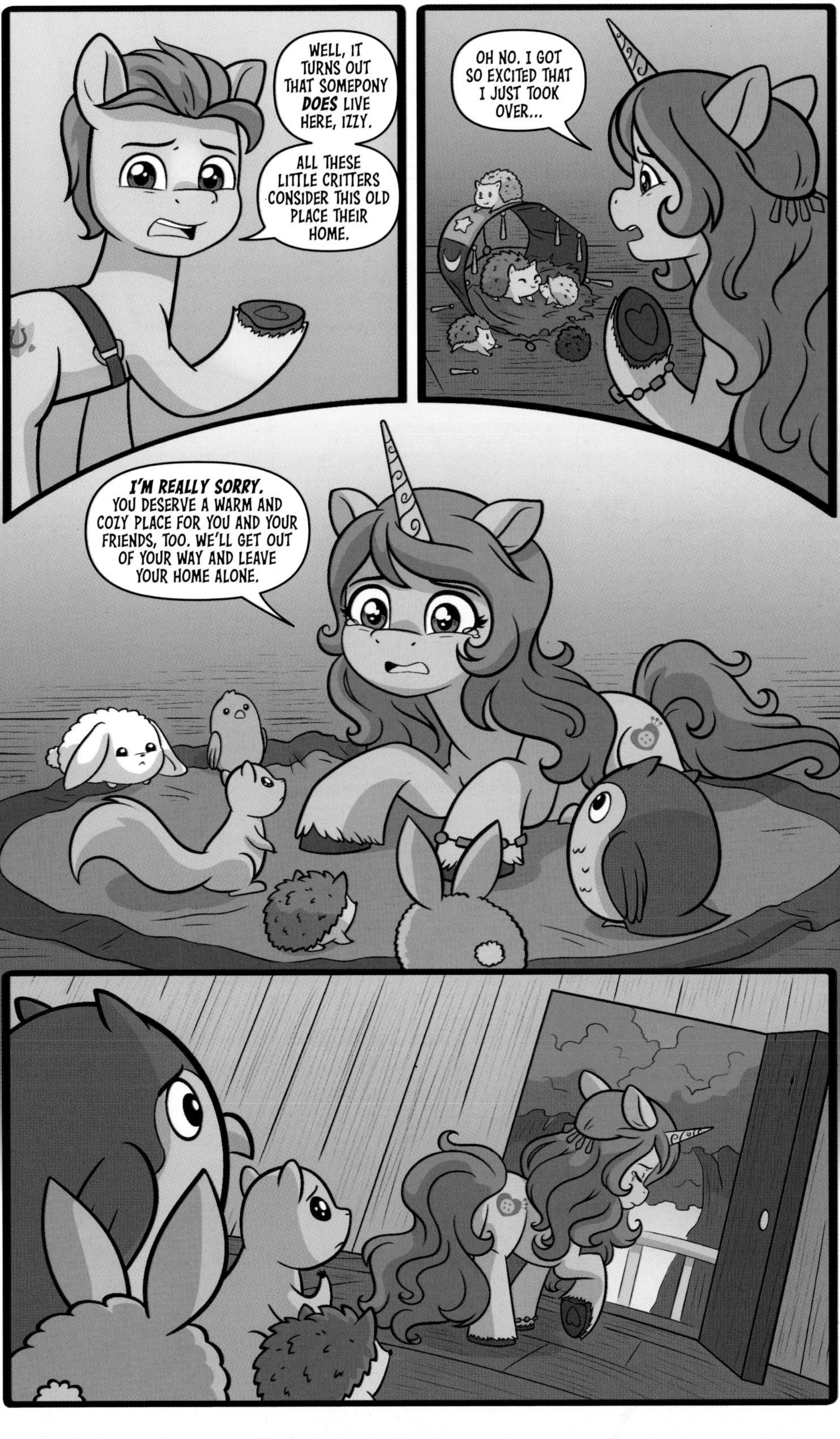
WELL, IT TURNS OUT THAT SOMEPONY **DOES** LIVE HERE, IZZY.
ALL THESE LITTLE CRITTERS CONSIDER THIS OLD PLACE THEIR HOME.
OH NO. I GOT SO EXCITED THAT I JUST TOOK OVER...
I'M REALLY SORRY. YOU DESERVE A WARM AND COZY PLACE FOR YOU AND YOUR FRIENDS, TOO. WE'LL GET OUT OF YOUR WAY AND LEAVE YOUR HOME ALONE.

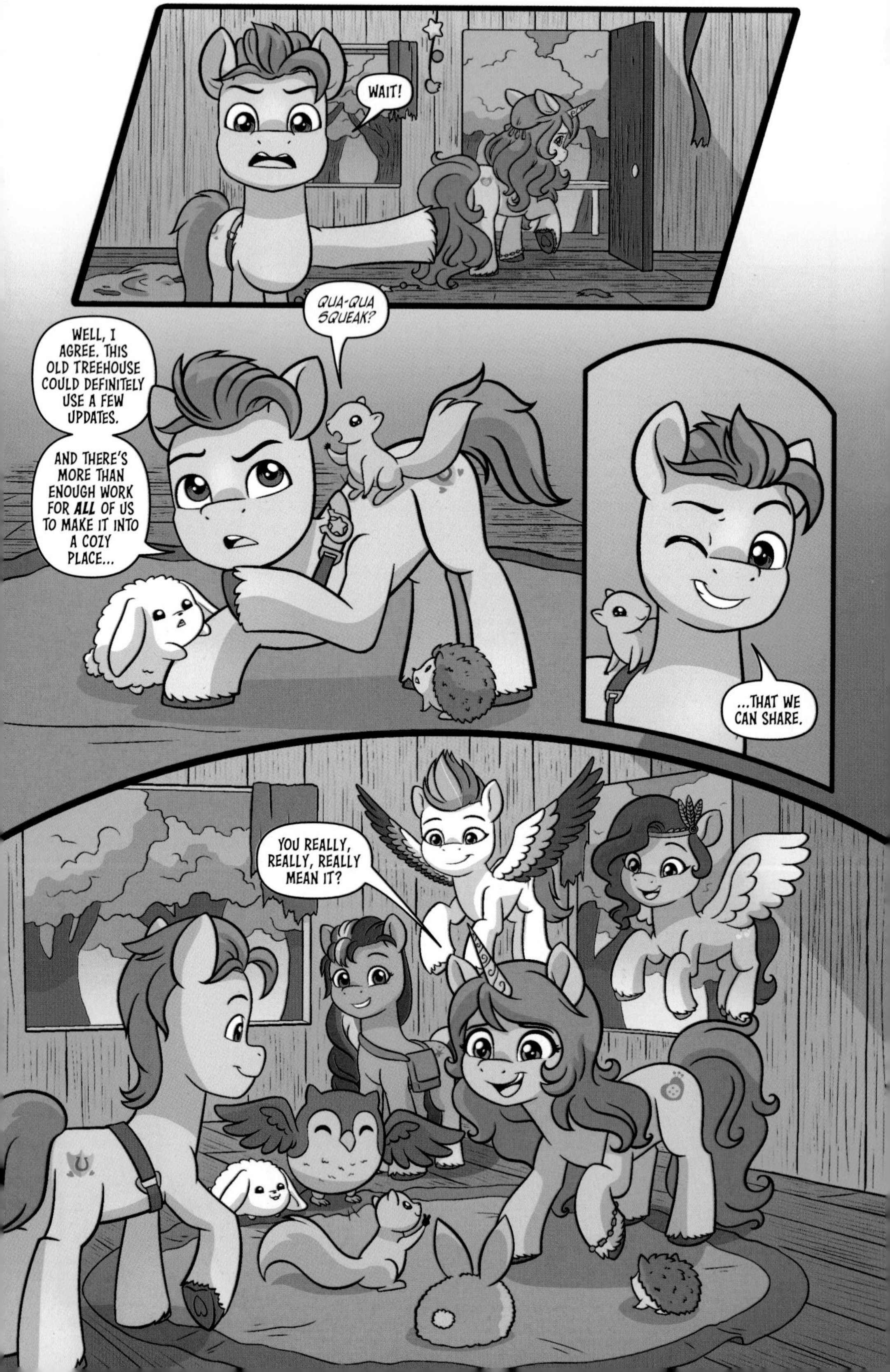
WAIT!
QUA-QUA SQUEAK?
WELL, I AGREE. THIS OLD TREEHOUSE COULD DEFINITELY USE A FEW UPDATES.
AND THERE'S MORE THAN ENOUGH WORK FOR ALL OF US TO MAKE IT INTO A COZY PLACE...
...THAT WE CAN SHARE.
YOU REALLY, REALLY, REALLY MEAN IT?

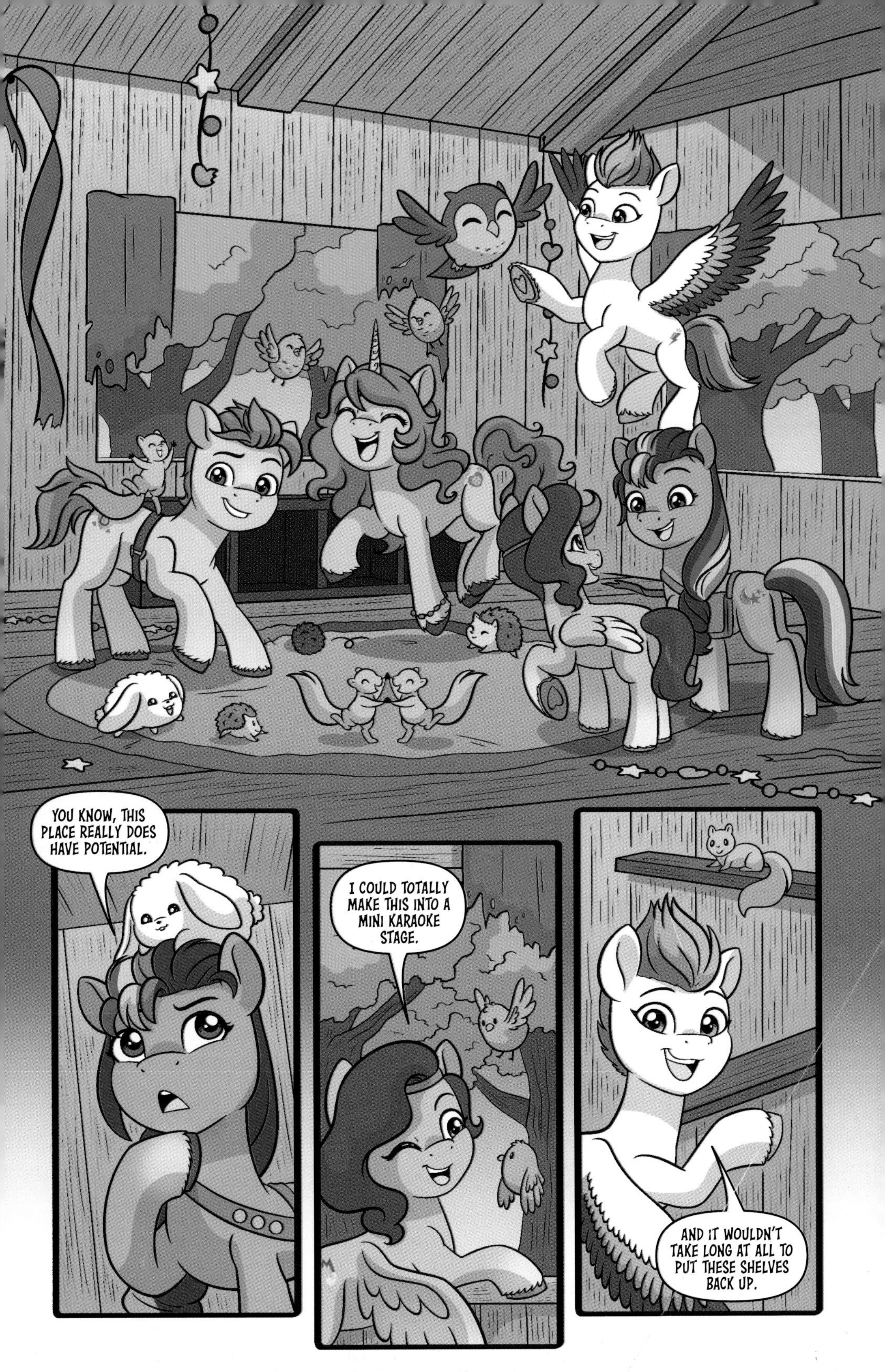
YOU KNOW, THIS PLACE REALLY DOES HAVE POTENTIAL.
I COULD TOTALLY MAKE THIS INTO A MINI KARAOKE STAGE.
AND IT WOULDN'T TAKE LONG AT ALL TO PUT THESE SHELVES BACK UP.

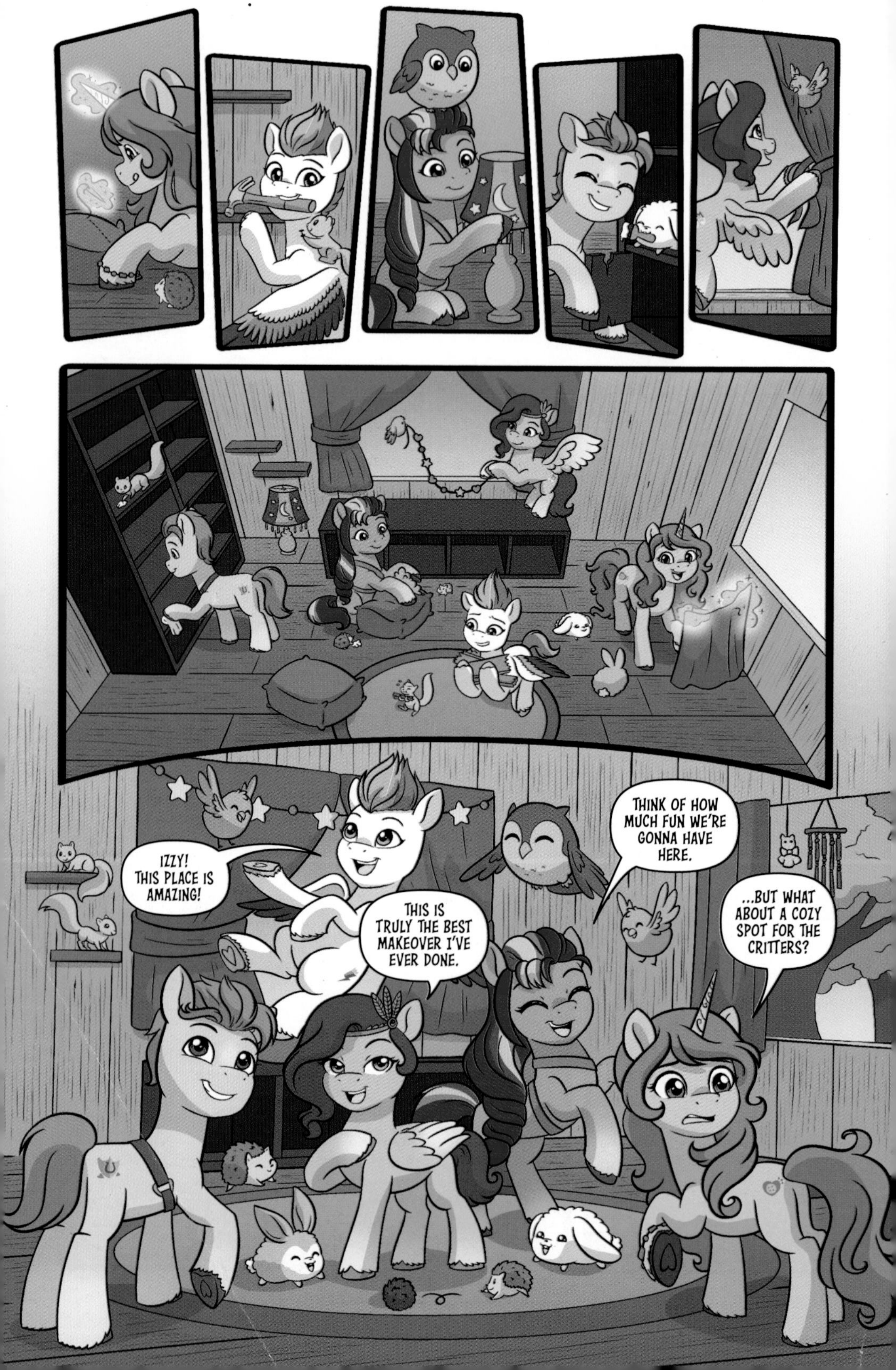
IZZY! THIS PLACE IS AMAZING!
THIS IS TRULY THE BEST MAKEOVER I'VE EVER DONE.
THINK OF HOW MUCH FUN WE'RE GONNA HAVE HERE.
...BUT WHAT ABOUT A COZY SPOT FOR THE CRITTERS?

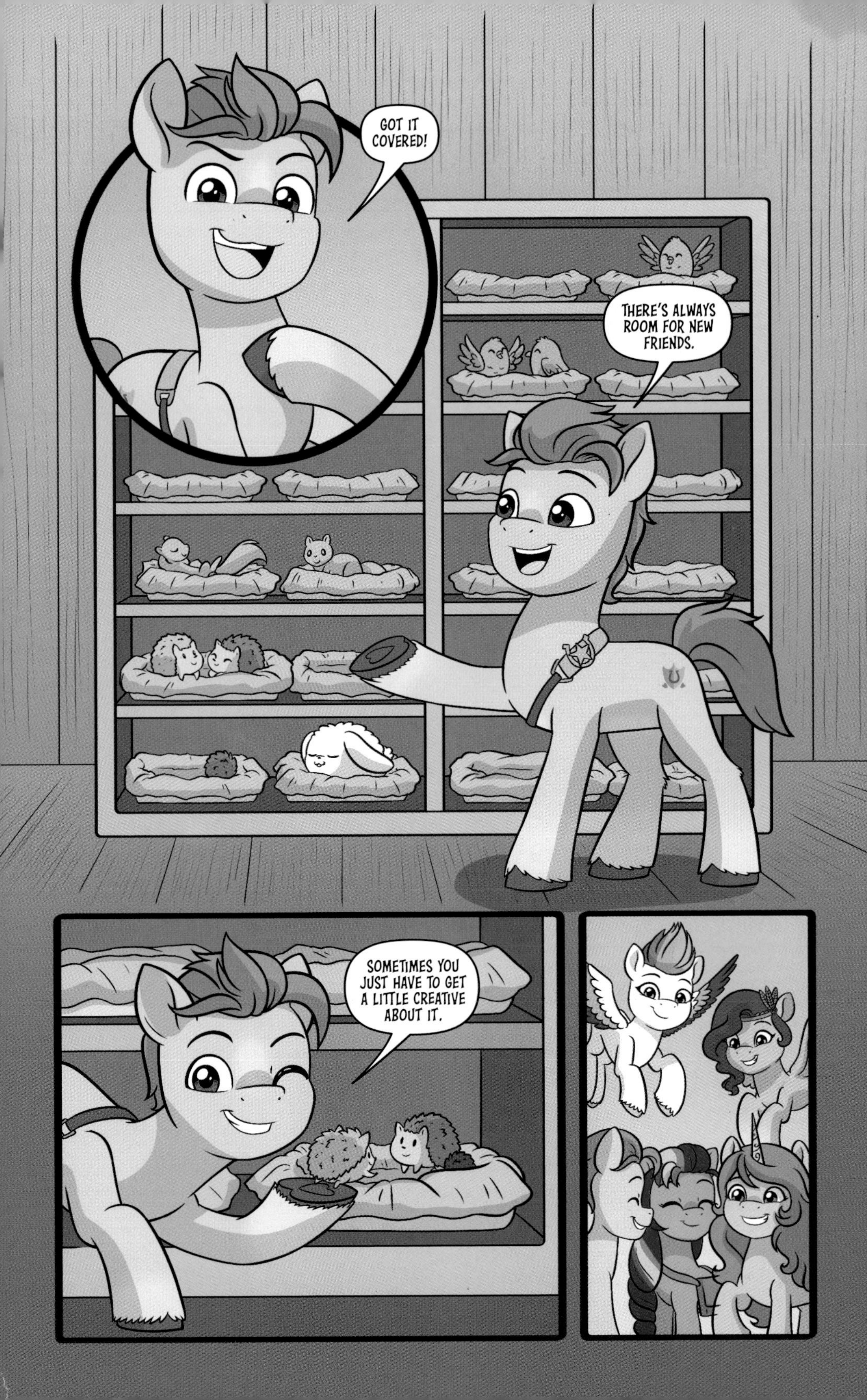
GOT IT COVERED!
THERE'S ALWAYS ROOM FOR NEW FRIENDS.
SOMETIMES YOU JUST HAVE TO GET A LITTLE CREATIVE ABOUT IT.

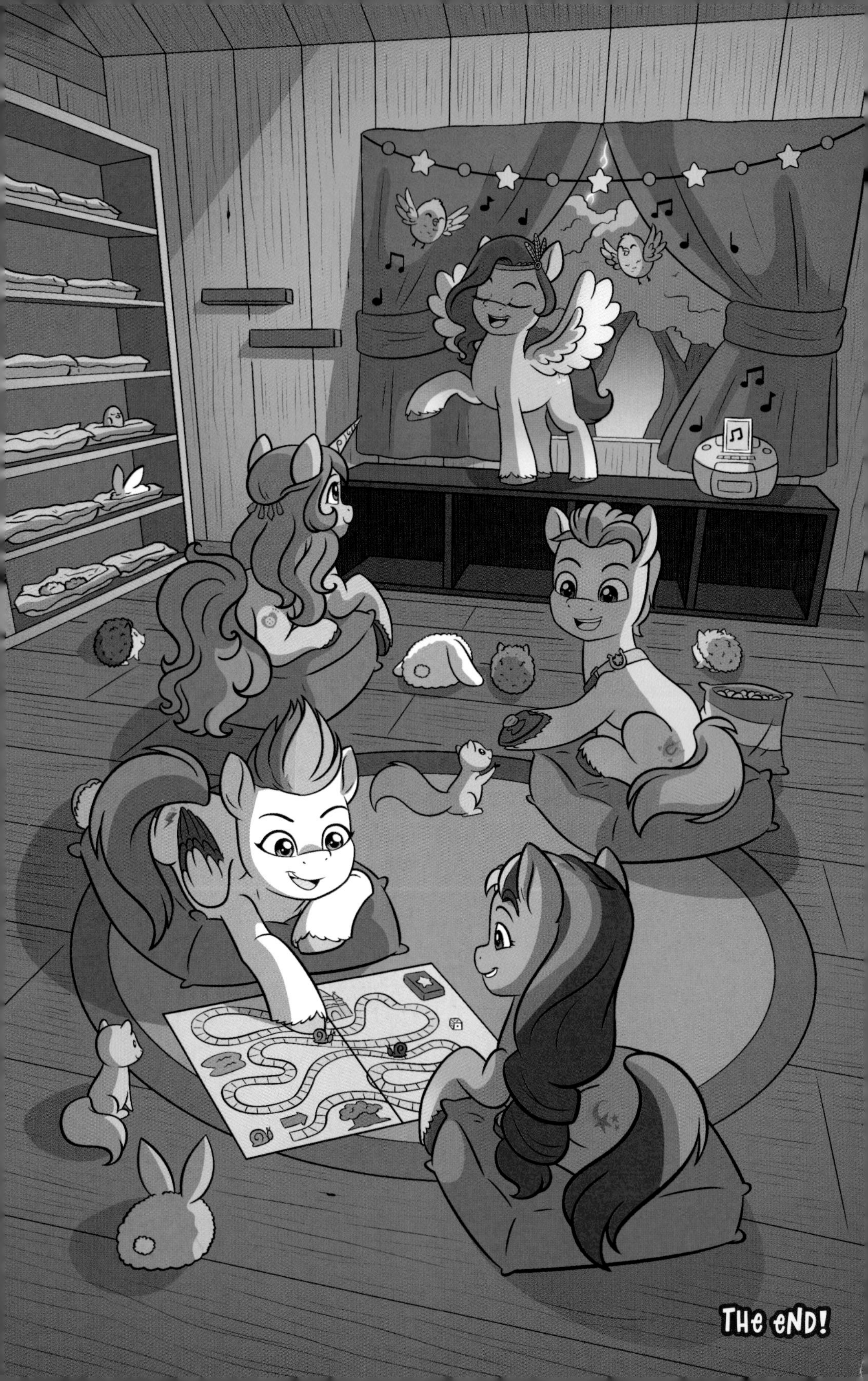
THE END!

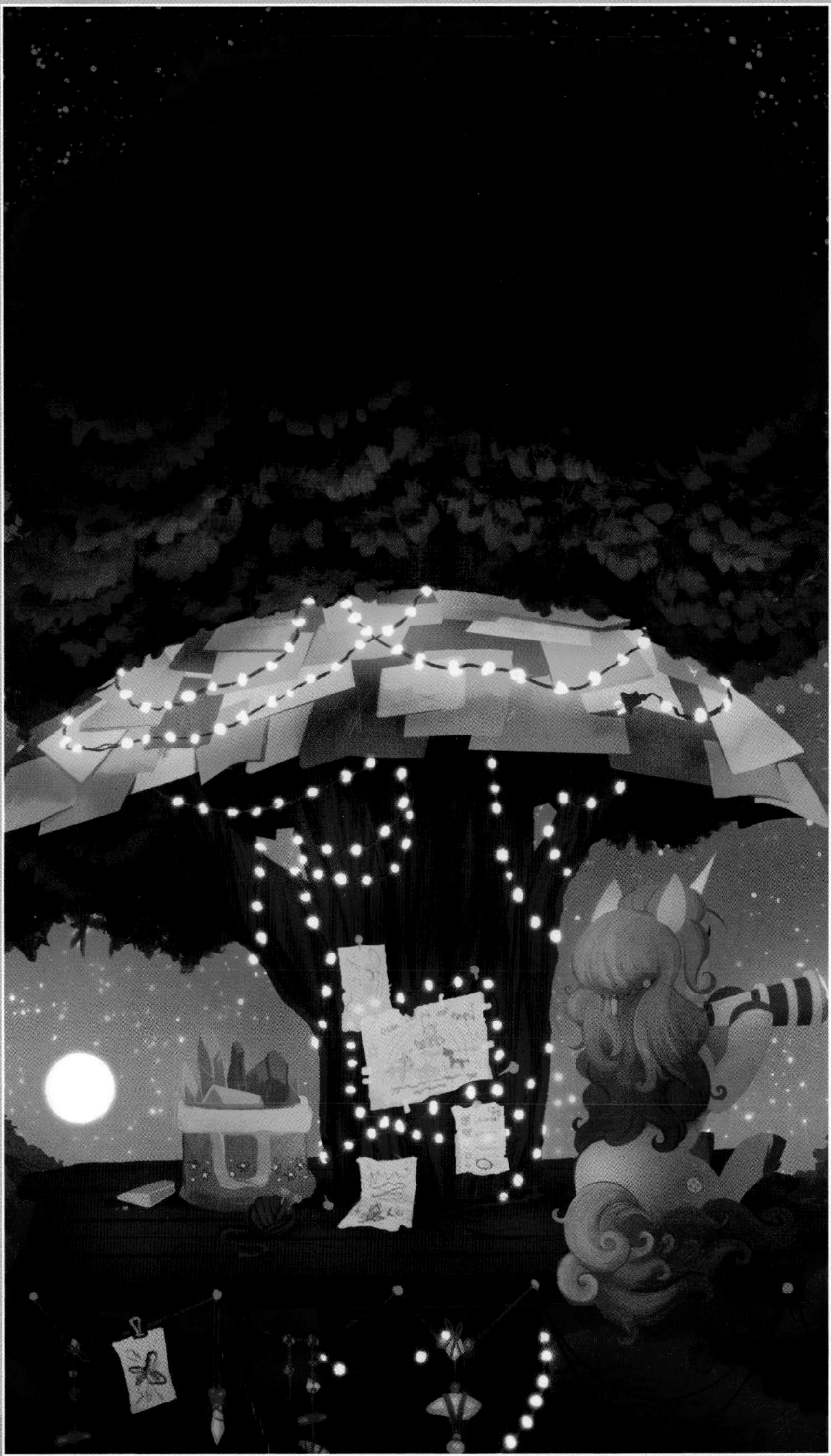

art by JustaSuta

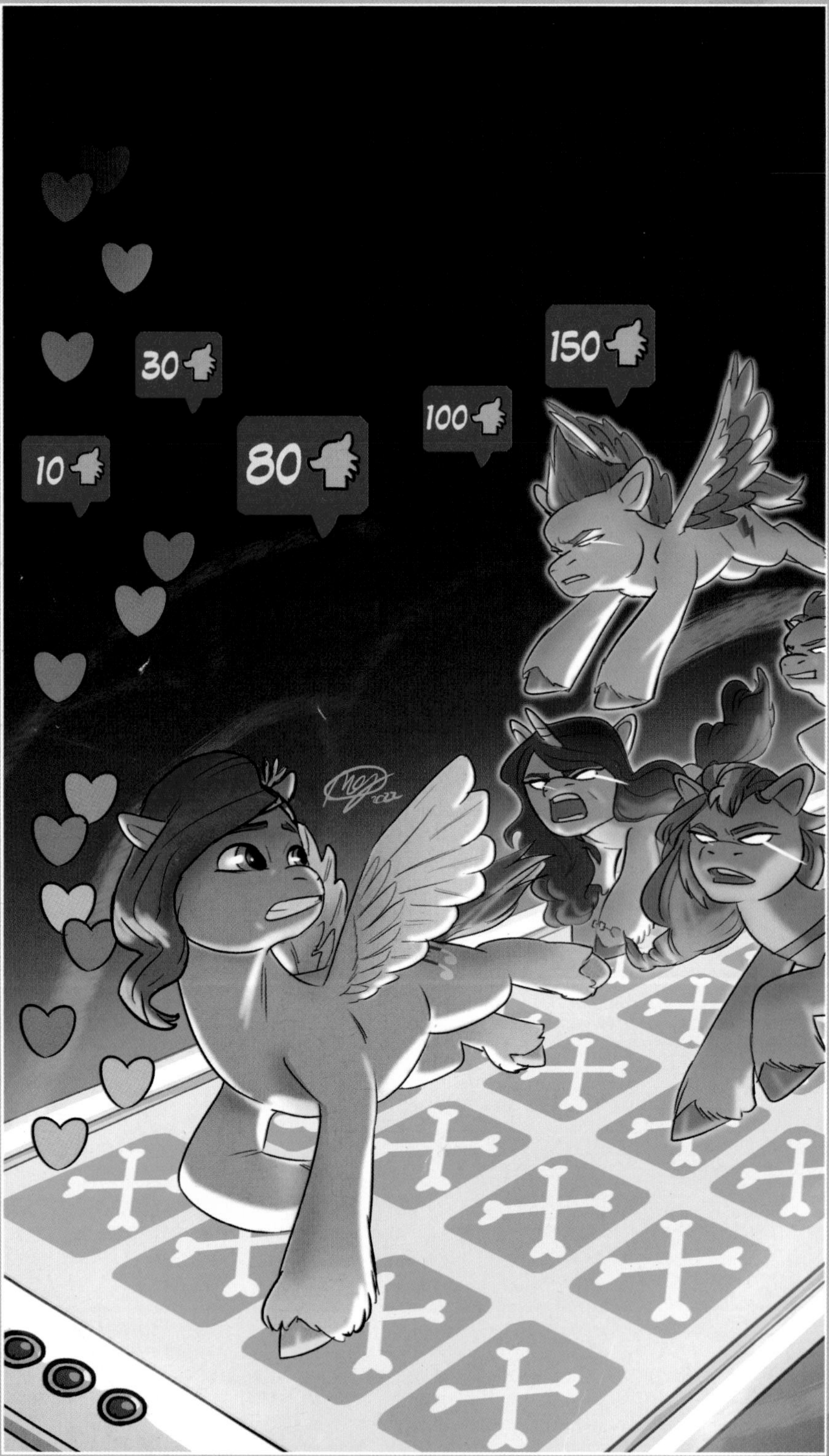
30
10
80
100
150

art by Megan Huang

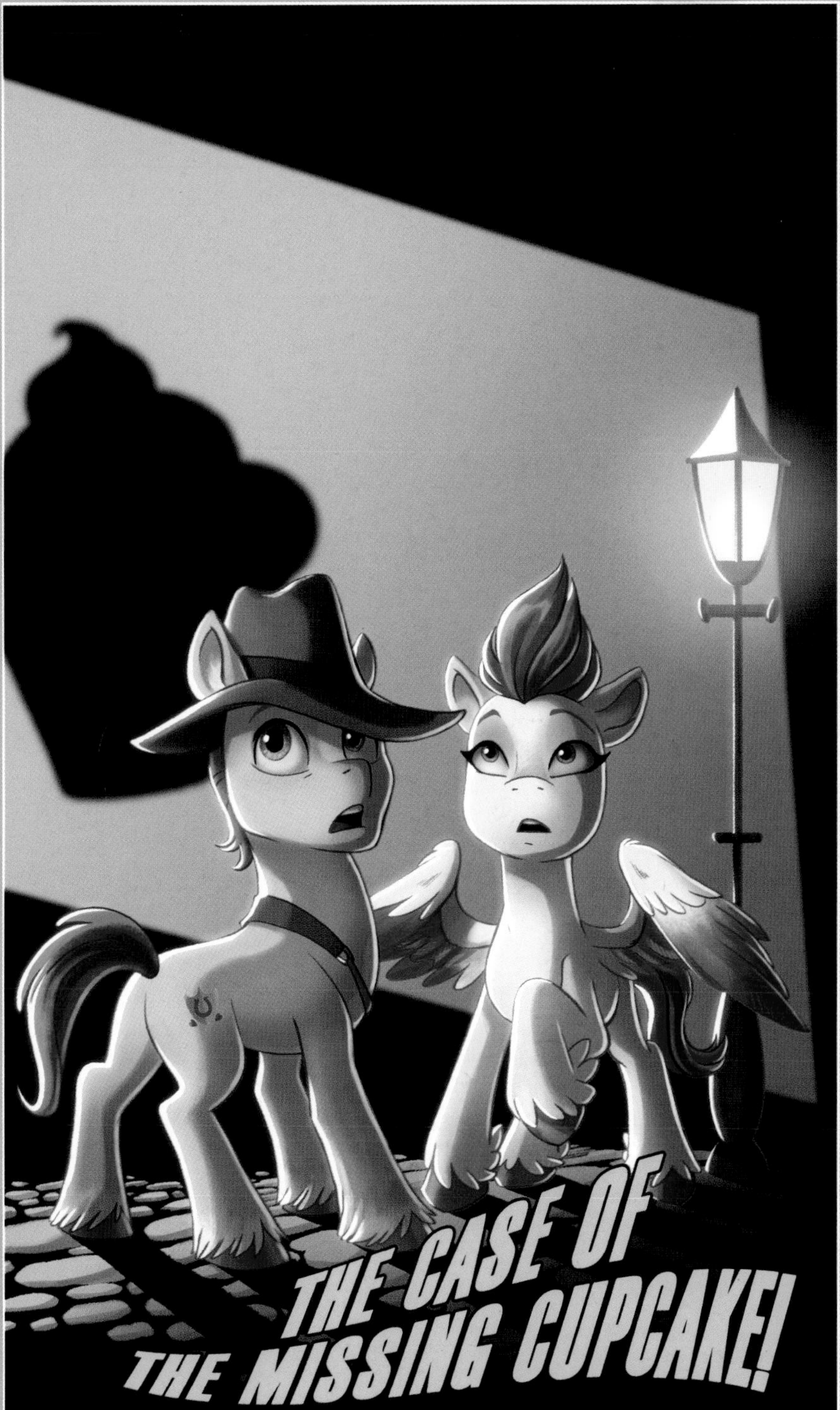
THE CASE OF
THE MISSING CUPCAKE!

art by Brianna Garcia

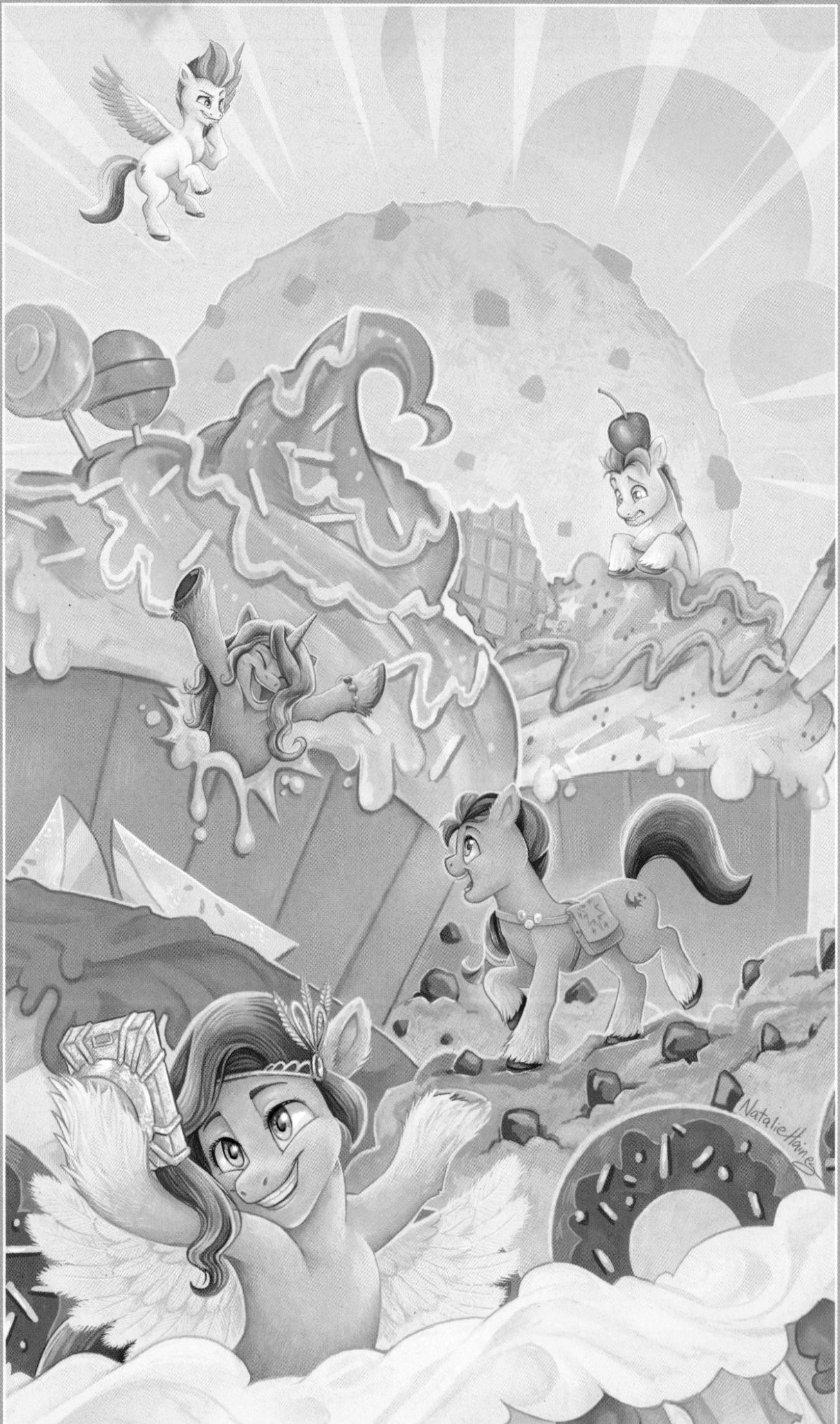
NatalieHaines

art by Natalie Haines

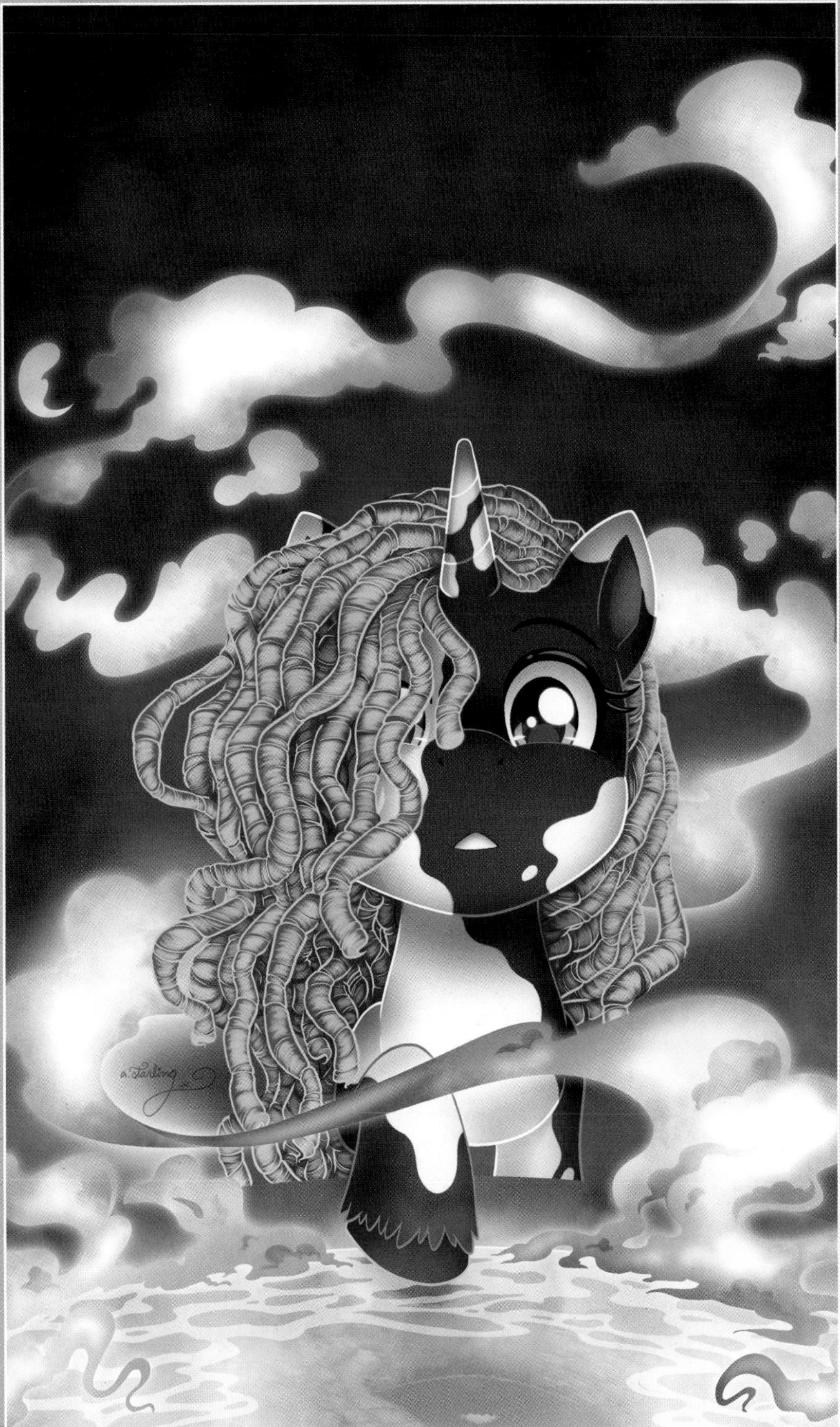

art by Abigail Starling

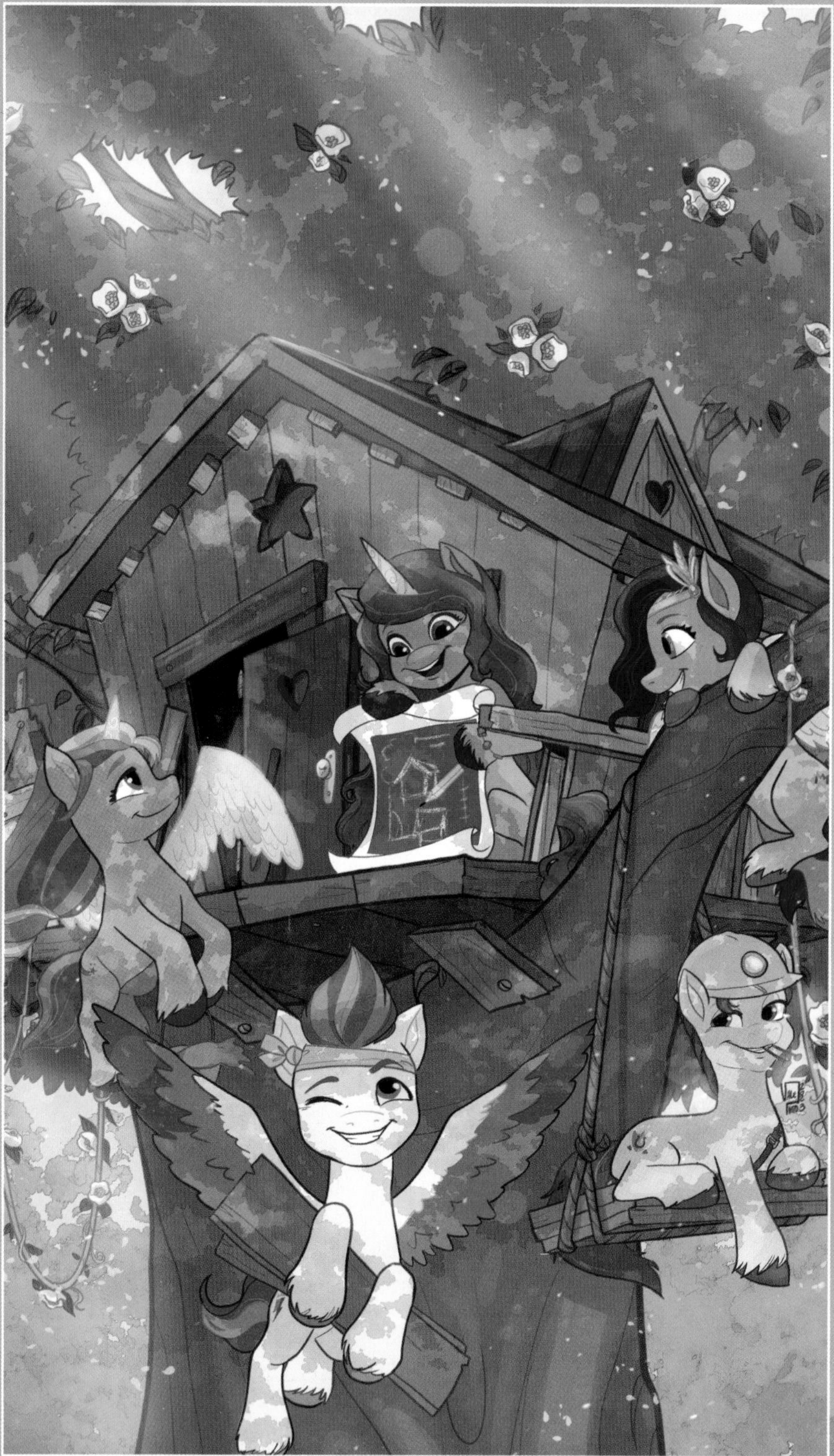

art by Valentina Pinto